A

Harry thought h̲ perfect marriage. At first he refuses to believe it when he learns that his best friend Ron has had an affair with Thelma, and worse, gotten her pregnant. But Thelma is quick to inform everyone that her life with Harry is over, that she and Ron are going to run away to California together, start a new life. However, Ron has gone missing under very mysterious circumstances. Harry won't give up—he knows that Thelma will come back to him if he is just persistent enough. After all, with Ron gone, what can she do? But Thelma has plans of her own, plans that can only lead to tragedy for them all.

Do Evil in Return

When the young girl visits Dr. Charlotte Keating, begging her for an illegal abortion, the doctor insists that she cannot help her. But something about Violet O'Gorman haunts Charlotte, and she goes to her house that evening to see if she can offer her help. Her Uncle Voss tells her that she's out, but the next day Violet's body is found washed up on the beach. The detective on the case, Lt. Easter, takes a sudden interest in Charlotte, casting doubt on the man she's in love with, Lewis Ballard, who is married to Gwen, a nervous woman and Charlotte's devoted patient. Charlotte is soon over her head in suspicions and shady characters as she tries to unravel a mystery that is both elusive and increasingly personal.

MARGARET MILLAR BIBLIOGRAPHY

Mysteries:

The Invisible Worm (1941)*

The Weak-Eyed Bat (1942)*

The Devil Loves Me (1942)*†

Wall of Eyes (1943)†

Fire Will Freeze (1944)

The Iron Gates (1945)
[aka Taste of Fears, UK, 1950]†

Do Evil in Return (1950)

Rose's Last Summer (1952)
[aka The Lively Corpse, 1956]

Vanish in an Instant (1952)

Beast in View (1955)

An Air That Kills (1957)
[aka The Soft Talkers, UK, 1957]

The Listening Walls (1959)

A Stranger in My Grave (1960)

How Like an Angel (1962)

The Fiend (1964)

Beyond This Point are Monsters
(1970)

Ask for Me Tomorrow (1976)**

The Murder of Miranda (1979)**

Mermaid (1982)**

Banshee (1983)

Spider Webs (1986)

Dr. Paul Prye series
**Tom Aragon series*
† Inspector Sands series

Novels:

Experiment in Springtime (1947)

It's All in the Family (1948)

The Cannibal Heart (1949)

Wives and Lovers (1954)

Autobiography:

The Birds and Beasts Were There
(1968)

AN AIR THAT KILLS

DO EVIL IN RETURN

By Margaret Millar

Stark House Press • Eureka California

AN AIR THAT KILLS / DO EVIL IN RETURN

Published by Stark House Press
2200 O Street
Eureka, CA 95501, USA
griffinskye@cox.net
www.starkhousepress.com

AN AIR THAT KILLS
Originally published and copyright © 1957 by Margaret Millar
Copyright © renewed 1985 by The Margaret Millar Charitable Remainder
Unitrust u/a 4/12/82

DO EVIL IN RETURN
Originally published and copyright © 1950 by Margaret Millar
Copyright © renewed 1977 by The Margaret Millar Charitable Remainder
Unitrust u/a 4/12/82

The "Post-Freudian Mysteries" of Margaret Millar copyright © 2006
by Tom Nolan.

ISBN: 1-933586-09-5

Text set in Figural and Dogma.
Cover design and layout by Mark Shepard, shepdesign.home.comcast.net
Proofreading by Joanne Applen

First Stark House Press Edition: August 2006

0 9 8 7 6 5 4 3 2

TABLE OF CONTENTS

7

THE "POST-FREUDIAN MYSTERIES"
OF MARGARET MILLAR
by Tom Nolan

15

AN AIR THAT KILLS

183

DO EVIL IN RETURN

The "Post-Freudian Mysteries" of Margaret Millar

by Tom Nolan

Her characters are palpitatingly human and very much a part of the moral fabric of our time, with its Cadillac worship, pill swallowing, over-drinking, and marital foul-ups. She goes into the deepest recesses of their minds and takes readings of the pressures there as they are thrown together in a common crisis. And, like another fine psychological novel-ist, Georges Simenon, she appears to conceal nothing – until the very last, when you realize that by disguising one little thing... she has fooled you magnificently all along.
                              - Luther Nichols, San Francisco Examiner, 1957

Mrs. Millar, detached but wary, with an ear exquisitely adjusted to the diversities of the human voice, keeps one as absolutely fixed as the Ancient Mariner. The consequence is a narrative that burns itself into one's remembrance and gives us all still another reason to be immensely glad that she is around.
                              - James Sandoe, New York Herald Tribune Book Review, 1957

ॐ

No American mystery novelist in the middle years of the 20th century received better reviews than Margaret Millar: winner of the Edgar Allan Poe Award (for her 1955 novel *Beast in View*), president of the Mystery Writers of America (1957-58) and in 1982 recognized as an MWA Grand Master.

Margaret Millar, born in Ontario, Canada, in 1915, published her first book in 1941. Her work in the early 1940s won immediate praise and attention. In the mid- and late '40s, she developed significantly as an artist. By the 1950s, living in Santa Barbara, California, she'd truly hit her stride, writing books that drew the highest praise from critics and colleagues in both America and England.

Millar crafted intricate and surprising tales of neurotic adults and willful children in a post-World War II society where traditional values and behavior patterns seemed to be in unsettling flux.

One of the traditions under siege in her work was the mystery-novel itself. Reviewers (and publishers) often didn't know quite how to describe this or that Millar book. "A novel of death and deception"? "A psychological thriller"? "A mystery story told with murderous wit"?

Margaret Millar did not write an ordinary sort of mystery. As her entry in *World Authors: 1950-1970* explained: "The majority of Margaret Millar's sardonic and tough-minded psychological suspense novels center on a psychopathic personality and its victims, rather than on an idealized investigator."

Millar created a type of story all her own: what critic John M. Reilly termed "the post-Freudian mystery," one which shifted attention away from any expected detective-figure and onto "the source of the mystery itself" – a source found "in the submerged realm of the irrational." In such tales, Reilly wrote, "the reader enters a reality beyond protective commonsense or diverting puzzles, a reality where reason does not control events"; and where the solving of a given puzzle leaves "a residue of uncertainty rather than optimism."

Characters often disappeared in the novels of Margaret Millar, as they did in other mystery-writers' books. But in Millar's tales, people were just as apt to disappear inside themselves. As Santa Barbara writer Lin Rolens pointed out, in an era when a sizable segment of a science-fiction-conscious public seemed distressed by the idea of conquerors from another planet, Margaret Millar "introduced the notion that the real terror could be the invasion from inner space."

But despite such grim undercurrents, Millar was hardly writing lugubrious case-studies of post-war angst. She had too much of a sense of humor.

And while she bent and twisted the conventions of her genre, she also stayed true to them – using her range as a writer to further surprise the customer. No sooner had you decided that what you were reading was not really a mystery but a novel of domestic manners, say, than the author pulled the rug out from under with a surprise-ending that cast everything previous in a strange new light.

"You look back and down the long vistas of seemingly inconsequential events or remarks; they have all had their meaning and importance, and hardly one is what you thought," observed Lenore Glen Offord, who wrote mysteries as well as reviewing them. "… [T]he brilliance is so understated that you don't realize until days later how superlative a technician she is."

Julian Symons, another novelist-critic, judged admiringly of Margaret Millar: "she has few peers, and no superior, in the art of bamboozlement."

Margaret Millar could seem as hard-boiled as any '50s writer ("running through her pity," she wrote of the female lead in *Do Evil in Return*, "was an iron stripe of bitterness") and as lyrical as a poet. Hers was a unique talent, and it won her a wide and intelligent readership. Among her avowed admirers over the years were such disparate critics as Anthony Boucher and Anatole Broyard, such dissimilar peers as Raymond Chandler and Agatha Christie, and such literary masters as W.H. Auden and Truman Capote.

Do Evil in Return (1950) and *An Air That Kills* (1957) are both representative of Margaret Millar's well-regarded work of the 1950s.

Juxtaposed, the two novels represent an example of the sort of reversals of theme typical of Margaret Millar's fiction: The first book concerns a pregnant woman who desperately wants an abortion (though that word is never uttered, in this Truman-era work). The second book concerns a pregnant woman who desperately wants a baby.

Both books also get their titles from poems.

Do Evil in Return takes its name from some lines by W.H. Auden (whom the author had once had to dinner) – while the book itself is dedicated to Faith Baldwin, a well-known romance-novelist of the time. One might say the conjunction of these two bylines is itself emblematic of Margaret Millar's fiction: stories written for mass-consumption, and informed by a poet's eye.

Margaret Millar turned that eye – "cool, sardonic, not unfriendly," to quote Offord – on a host of her usual-unusual characters, the sort whom critic Anatole Broyard would find "sharply drawn and... outrageously idiosyncratic... without slipping into slapstick."

With that eye, Millar could snap crisp psychological portraits in a sentence or two – as in these, from *Do Evil*:

"He was the kind of man who would immediately construe a smile from a strange woman as an invitation to intimacy; a man as quick to take offense as to take liberties."

"She stopped the car and got out and walked up to the house, rapidly, as if she were trying to keep ahead of her better judgment."

"The boy was a handsome twelve-year-old, small for his age, and timid. His mother was a giant of a woman. When she sailed into the office with Tommy behind her she looked like a three-masted schooner towing a dinghy."

"Throwing words at Gwen was like throwing bubbles; they burst before they got anywhere."

"Eddie was scared to death, and violence was the denial of his fears."

"His smile was uglier than a frown."

"A little girl's room, Charlotte thought, looking at the teddy bear propped on the chifforobe, the smiling French doll sitting at the window. The years were passing, but the little girl was afraid to grow up. Here, in her own room, she was immune to time."

No one of course is immune to time – especially in a Margaret Millar novel. *Do Evil in Return* takes place in a transitional era: after World War II but before the truly "modern" age.

Its protagonist, Dr. Charlotte Keating, herself seems a transitional figure: a self-sufficient professional woman who nonetheless places her emotional fate in the hands of an inappropriate and insensitive male; an up-to-date rationalist ("There's no longer any stigma attached to going to a psychiatrist, you know") who habitually views the world through the eyes of a superstitious animist: "Voss's house was dark, a corrupt monster with one dying eye." "The moon leered through the leaves of the giant oaks, veiled, provocative..." "The cypresses... fought the wind, bent and convulsed in fury like mad boneless dancers."

And *Do Evil* itself – billed on its hardcover jacket as "Margaret Millar's first mystery novel since her memorable *The Iron Gates*," a much-hailed thriller which the author had followed up with three more-or-less mainstream-fiction books – seems for much of its length to be a transitional work: a tale of deaths which may not be murders, a story pitched some-where closer to romance than suspense.

But, as noted, appearances are meant by Millar to be deceiving; she has one of her unexpectedly startling endings in store after all. And, as critic Anthony Boucher said of another Millar fictional infinity-of-mirrors: "be warned that even the word 'deception' is itself deceptive."

The title An Air That Kills, written seven years after Do Evil in Return, is from an A.E. Housman poem. And Shakespeare is alluded to in the text of this contemporary novel of Elizabethan-worthy intrigues – a work (set mostly in Ontario, Canada) that reviewers at the time ranked among Margaret Millar's very best.

James Sandoe (after Anthony Boucher, probably the most-respected mystery critic of the 1950s) thought An Air excelled even Beast in View, Millar's Edgar Award-winner (and Air's immediate predecessor in print). "Only Mrs. Millar, I believe," Sandoe wrote, "could have taken such apparently grubby materials, lent them such compulsion and supplied so shocking a coup de grace."

The long lead-up to that startling finale begins with the disappearance, en route to an all-male fishing vacation, of one Ron Galloway: the sort of seemingly unprepossessing fellow who "drove his Cadillac convertible with the top down even in weather which forced him to turn the heater on full blast to keep from freezing to death"; the type of male who didn't believe "in spoiling women by paying them compliments." But once out of sight, the absent Ron gives off a sense of hidden depths – ones crying out to be explored by his wife Esther, the sort of woman who can't help "picking at the past like a bird at a stale loaf of bread, dislodging a crumb here, a crumb there."

And so we're off on another of Ms. Millar's wild rides – a journey with at least one or two more twists than might be imagined, before the trip ends more or less where it did or did not begin.

An Air That Kills (a more ambitious and accomplished book than Do Evil in Return) enlarges and constantly shifts points of view to accommodate an ever-increasing number of characters, major and minor – with many of the latter appearing in but a single scene. This ongoing caravansary would seem more of an obvious tour de force were it not handled so seamlessly and with such subtlety.

The whole book is written by Millar at the top of her now formidable form. The thumbnail character-sketches come as fast as pictures in a flip-book by Daumier:

Poor "Bill Winslow, who can't hold his liquor but would die trying" and "had reached the point of saturation. The excess fluid was seeping out of his eyes in the form of tears."

The educated, argumentative couple: "Instead of throwing ash trays at each other, the Turees, in the modern manner, threw Oedipus complexes, father fixations and compulsive neuroses."

The shrewd and somewhat shrewish wife, of whom a "friend" observes: "*she's too damned bright for her own good. And too honest to hide it.*"

The fanciful, garrulous woman of whom it's noted: "Mabel's imagination was like her car. Once it started to move, it moved all over, in every joint and with a great deal of noise."

The author, with her canny, omniscient eye (and ear), observes each figure in equal measure, giving all their proper due – for, as the wisest person in the book realizes, it is "simple-minded... to believe that a catastrophe" (as good a word as any for what transpires in this novel) "could be caused by only one person. A lot of people were involved, not just the leading characters, but the bit players, the prop man, the stagehands, waiting in the wings."

And everywhere the odor "of stale drinks and stale dreams," while the prevailing breeze – the air that kills – carries "the scent of wind and water, delusion and betrayal."

Not all who read the innovative *An Air* in 1957 were charmed. "[T]he people are cheap and detestable and absolutely humorless," sniffed a reviewer in Harper's, "and it's very hard to care what happens to them."

But a preponderance of critics felt the opposite. Luther Nichols, of the San Francisco Examiner, thought the "soundness in [Millar's] psychology" and her "sympathetic understanding of human frailty" made for a healing catharsis: "When we finally know the guilty and their motives in her books, our wrath is usually turned to compassion."

Perhaps the most thoughtful review of *An Air That Kills* was written by Robert R. Kirsch, the Los Angeles Times's eclectic-minded daily book-critic, who declared that the book defied definition: "It might be called a mystery, for it deals with violent death and the cause of that death. It might be called a psychological novel, for it is concerned with the deepest insights into men and women. It might be called a social novel, for it is rich in the study of a particular group and setting...

"But it is all of these – and something more. You cannot read this without a mounting sense of excitement... that you are witnessing the work of a brilliant writer."

That brilliant writer kept turning out books – several of them even better than *An Air That Kills* – until her death in 1994. And those books, it seems, continue to find readers – in part because, while reflecting in interesting ways the years in which they were written, they achieved a certain timelessness – through evoking moods and situations that never go out of date.

"Millar's gift is for the ordinary, just where it joins with the sinister," thought a Washington Post Book World writer in 1985, "and her subtle humor informs every situation."

Author-critic Edward D. Hoch put it this way, circa 1980: "Best of all in the novels of Margaret Millar has been her ability to conjure up what Julian Symons rightly describes as 'an atmosphere of uneasiness.' Things are never quite right in the worlds she so vividly portrays, and we keep reading to find out why."

— Tom Nolan
Burbank, California
June 2006

Tom Nolan is the author of *Ross Macdonald: A Biography* and editor of *The Couple Next Door: Collected Short Mysteries* by Margaret Millar.

AN AIR THAT KILLS

By Margaret Millar

To the Grushes, my favorite house haunters,
Paul
Bernis
Diane
Douglas
Dale

Into my heart an air that kills
       From yon far country blows;
What are those blue remembered hills,
       What spires, what farms are those?

That is the land of lost content,
       I see it shining plain,
The happy highways where I went
       And cannot come again.

       —A. E. Houseman

ONE

The last time his wife saw Ron Galloway was on a Saturday evening in the middle of April.

"He seemed in good spirits," Esther Galloway said later. "Almost as if he was up to something, planning something. More than just a fishing trip to the lodge, I mean. He's never really enjoyed fishing, he has a morbid fear of water."

This was true enough, though Galloway wouldn't have admitted it. He tried desperately hard to be a sport. He fished, played golf and cricket in the summers, curled at the Granite Club in the winters, wore a crew cut, and drove his Cadillac convertible with the top down even in weather which forced him to turn the heater on full blast to keep from freezing to death. Now in his late thirties, he still appeared somewhat lacking in coordination in spite of all the exercise he took, and his round face showed residual traces of teen-age acne and adolescent uncertainty.

He was packing a duffel bag when his wife, Esther, came into his bedroom. She was going out for dinner and she had on a new pink taffeta dress trimmed with seed pearls and topped by a white mink stole. Galloway noticed the dress and approved of it, but he made no remark about it. There was no point in spoiling women by paying them compliments.

"So here you are, Ron," his wife said, as if it were a surprising and interesting coincidence that a man should be found in his own bedroom.

Galloway did not respond.

"Ron?"

"Esther, angel, I'm right here, as you just pointed out, so if you have anything to say, go ahead."

"Where are you going?" Esther knew where he was going, but she was the kind of woman who liked to ask questions to which she already knew the answers. It gave her a sense of security.

"I told you last week. I'm going over to Weston to pick up Harry Bream and we're driving up to the lodge to do some fishing with a couple of the fellows."

"I don't like Harry Bream's wife."

"Harry Bream's wife is not coming along."

"I know that. I was merely making a remark. I think she's queer. She called me last week and asked if there was anybody dead I wanted to get in touch with. I couldn't think of anyone offhand except Uncle John and I'm not sure he'd want to be gotten in touch with. Don't you think that's queer, her call, I mean?"

"Harry's away a lot. Thelma has to do something to keep herself from getting bored."

"Why doesn't she have children?"

"I don't know why she doesn't have children," Galloway said impatiently. "I haven't asked her."

"You and Harry are such cronies, you could broach the subject to him casually some time."

"Perhaps I could, but I don't intend to."

"If Thelma had children she wouldn't have time to go around being psychic and making other people nervous. *I* haven't got time to be psychic."

"Thank God for small mercies."

Galloway fastened the straps of the duffel bag and set it near the door. The act was a definite invitation for Esther to say good-bye and be on her way, but she declined it. Instead, she moved across the room with an elegant swish of taffeta and stood in front of the mirror smoothing her dark hair. Over her shoulder she could see Galloway watching her with a prodigious frown of annoyance. He looked quite comical.

"I'm sick of my hair like this," she said. "I think I'll become a blonde. An interesting and psychic blonde like Thelma."

"You're psychic enough. And I don't like phony blondes."

"What about natural ones, like Thelma?"

"I like Thelma all right," he said obstinately. "She's my best friend's wife. I have to."

"Just all right?"

"For Pete's sake, Esther, she's a fattish little hausfrau with some of her marbles missing. Even your imagination can't build her up into a femme fatale."

"I guess not."

"When are you going to get over these crazy suspicions?"

"Dorothy..." She swallowed as she spoke the name, so that he wasn't sure what it was until she repeated it. "Dorothy had no suspicions."

"Why bring her up?"

"She didn't suspect a thing. And all the time behind her back you and I were..."

"Be quiet." His face was white with anger and distaste. "If your conscience is bothering you at this late date, that's too bad. But leave mine alone. And for God's sake let's not have a scene."

Esther had been going in for scenes lately, picking at the past like a bird at a stale loaf of bread, dislodging a crumb here, a crumb there. He hoped it was merely a passing phase and would soon be over. The past didn't often worry or interest Galloway. When he thought of his first wife, Dorothy, it was without pity or regret. Even his vindictiveness against her on account of the divorce had faded with the years. Divorces in Canada are not common or easy to obtain, and the Galloway scandal had been an ugly one, widely publicized throughout the country and the border states.

Esther let her hands drop to her sides and turned from the mirror. "I heard she's dying."

"She's been dying for years," Galloway said brusquely. "Who told you that, anyway?"

"Harry."

"Harry's a pill salesman. He likes to think everybody's dying."

"Ron."

"I don't want to be rude, but if I don't start moving, the fellows will be kept waiting at the lodge."

"The caretaker can let them in."

"Even so, as the host I should be there first."

"They'll be too boozed up to care."

"Are you deliberately trying to start another argument?"

"No. Really, I'm not. I guess I just wish I were going with you."

"You don't like fishing. All you do is sit around moaning about how sorry you feel for the poor little fish and what did they ever do to deserve a hook in the throat."

"All right, Ron, all right." She approached him rather shyly and put her hands on his shoulders and kissed him on the cheek. "Have a good time. Don't forget to say good-bye to the children. Next time perhaps we can all go."

"Perhaps."

But she looked a little sad when she went out the door, as if she had borrowed some of Thelma's psychic powers and sensed that there wouldn't be a next time or even a this time.

Galloway stood in the doorway for a moment listening to the rustle of her dress and the tapping of her heels muted by the stair carpet.

Suddenly, without knowing why, he called out in a loud urgent voice, "Esther! Esther!"

But the front door had already closed behind her and Galloway felt a little relieved that she hadn't heard him because he hadn't planned anything to say to her. The call had come from a part of his mind which was inaccessible to him and he didn't know what it meant or why it happened.

He leaned against the door frame, dizzy, breathing very hard, as if he had just awakened from a dream of suffocation, and while the dream was forgotten, the physical symptoms of panic remained.

I'm ill, he thought. She shouldn't have walked out on me like that. I'm ill. Perhaps I ought to stay home and call a doctor.

But as his breathing returned to normal and the dizziness abated, it occurred to him that a doctor wasn't really necessary as long as Harry was around. Harry worked for a drug company and his pockets were always bulging with pills, his brief case full of pamphlets describing the newest medical discoveries which some of the doctors didn't even know about until Harry told them, or gave them the pamphlets to read. Harry was extremely liberal with free pills, diagnoses and advice. On occasion, he was more effective than a regular doctor since he was unhampered by training, medical ethics or caution, and some of his cures were miraculously quick. These were the ones his friends remembered.

"I will get some pills from Harry," Galloway said, and the very thought was soothing. Harry had a pill for everything, even sudden and inexplicable calls to one's departing wife: *It's your nerves, old boy. Now, my company has just come out with a dandy little item....*

Galloway flung his trench coat over his arm, picked up his duffel bag, and went down the hall to say good-bye to the two boys. They were ostensibly in bed; that is, the bedroom door was open and the night light was turned on. But they were not asleep. Their low, furious voices bounced across the room and back again.

"Mama said the dog could sleep on my bed tonight. Let go of him."

"Won't, won't, won't."

"I'll scream for Annie."

"I'll tell her you pinched me. I'll tell Annie and Mrs. Browning and old Rudolph and Mama and my Sunday School teacher..."

"Why not tell me?" Galloway said, and pressed the light switch.

The two boys stared at him, silenced by amazement. They saw little of Galloway, and when they noticed the duffel bag he was carrying, they weren't sure whether he was coming or going.

Gregory, who at seven was already an opportunist, made a quick decision. "Daddy's home," he shouted. "Goody, goody, Daddy's home! Did you bring me something, Daddy? What did you bring me?"

Galloway stepped back as if he had been shoved in the chest. "I—haven't been away."

"Well, then, you're going away."

"Yes."

"So if you're going away you've got to come back."

"Yes, I guess I do."

"So when you come back will you bring me something?"

Galloway's face was flushed and a nervous tic nagged at one corner of his mouth. That's all I mean to them, he thought.

Or to Esther. I'm the guy who brings them something.

"You could bring everybody something," said Marvin, who was five and a half. "Annie and Mrs. Browning and old Rudolph and my Sunday School teacher."

"I suppose I could. What do you think they'd like?"

"Dogs. Everybody would like dogs."

"Everybody? You're sure?"

"I asked them," Marvin lied emphatically. "I asked them what did they want brung in a suitcase, and they all said dogs." To prove his point he ran over to his brother's bed and flung both arms around the little dachshund. The dog was quite used to these outbursts of affection and went on placidly chewing a corner of the blanket. "Everybody could have a dog like Petey on their beds every single night, even old Rudolph."

"Rudolph says dogs dig holes in the flower beds."

"Petey never digs holes. *I* dig holes. I dig about a million holes a week."

Galloway smiled sadly. "That's a lot of work for a little man like you. You must be pretty strong."

"Feel my muscle."

"Feel mine too," Greg said. "I can dig a million holes too if I want."

Muscles were being duly tested when Annie, the maid who looked after the boys, appeared in the doorway. During the daytime when she wore her blue and white uniform, Annie was prim and self-contained and respectable. Tonight, dressed and groomed for an evening out, she was barely recognizable, with her mouth swollen by lipstick, and her eyebrows coyly arched in black, and her eyes cavernous behind a coating of mascara.

"Oh, it's you, Mr. Galloway. I thought the boys were alone arguing about that dog again."

"They won't have to argue about Petey much longer. I have orders to bring them another dog when I come back."

"Indeed."

"Surely you want me to bring you something too, Annie? Everyone else does."

She looked a little startled and disapproving. "I have my wages, thank you, sir."

"I'm certain you could think of something if you tried, Annie. Perhaps a necklace? Or a bottle of perfume to stun the senses of the local boys?"

"Bring Annie a dog," Marvin shouted. "Annie wants a dog!"

"I do *not* want a dog," the girl said sharply. "Nor anything else. Now you two settle down and go to sleep without any more nonsense. My boy friend's waiting for me, but I'm not going to set one foot outside this house until you two are quiet." To Galloway she added in a whisper, "They get overexcited sometimes."

"You want me to leave, is that right?"

"I really think it would be better, sir. They were tucked in an hour ago."

He looked over Annie's head at the two boys. For a minute, before Annie came on the scene, he had felt quite close to them, he had thought what handsome and precocious children they were. Now, once again, they were strangers to him, a couple of little barbarians who wanted nothing from him but presents, who liked to see him go away because he would come back with something in his luggage.

The dizziness returned, and with it a sharp sour taste in his mouth. He said quickly, "Good night, boys," and stepped out into the hall and moved unsteadily toward the stairs. The duffel bag was like lead in his hand. He walked like an old man.

I must get some pills from Harry. Harry has all kinds of pills.

Esther's pink and cream De Soto was missing from the garage, but Galloway's Cadillac convertible was in its place with the top down, freshly washed and waxed, the way old Rudolph liked to keep it, as if it were an irreplaceable heirloom instead of something that would be traded in within a year.

It was cold, even for April. But Galloway left the top down and climbed, shivering, into the front seat.

Upstairs, the two boys continued their argument but its content had changed.

"What if he forgets to bring the dogs?"

"He can't forget."

"Or maybe he will never come back, like old Rudolph's wife."

"Oh shut up," Gregory said fiercely. "When you go away, you *got* to come back. There's no place else to go, you got to come back."

For Gregory it was that simple.

TWO

When Galloway referred to his friends as a group he usually called them "the fellows." Two of the fellows, Bill Winslow and Joe Hepburn, drove up together from Toronto and arrived at the lodge, which was located on Georgian Bay a few miles beyond Wiarton, at about ten o'clock. A third, Ralph Turee, came alone a few minutes later.

They were admitted by the caretaker, and each of them launched immediately into his special task. Turee took the luggage upstairs, Hepburn started a fire in the huge stone fireplace, Winslow pried the lock off the liquor cabinet, and, as Esther had predicted, the fellows began the process of getting themselves boozed up.

These were Galloway's special friends, of approximately the same age, and with a mutual aim, having as good a time as possible when they were away from the pressures of business and family: Bill Winslow, an executive in his father's milling company; Joe Hepburn, manager of a firm which manufactured plastic toys and novelties; and Ralph Turee, who taught economics at the University of Toronto. Except for Turee, they were men of average intelligence and above average income. Turee never let them forget this. Chronically broke, he made fun of their money and borrowed it; possessing a superior education, he jeered at their ignorance and used it to his own advantage. But the group was, on the whole, a congenial one, especially after small differences had been dissolved in alcohol.

It was Turee who first remarked on the passage of time and the absence of Harry Bream and Galloway. "Peculiar thing Galloway hasn't come yet. He makes such a point of being punctual."

"I hate punctuality," Winslow stated. "It is the hobgoblin of small minds. Right, fellows?"

Hepburn said it was chastity that was the hobgoblin of small minds and Turee corrected them both, as usual, and said it was consistency, and eventually they got back to Galloway.

"Galloway called me last night," Turee said, "and told me he was going to pick Harry up in Weston and drive on up here and arrive about nine-thirty."

"There," Winslow said. "There you have it."

"Have what?"

"The crux of the situation. Harry. Harry's always late for everything."

It was a logical as well as an agreeable theory, and they were all having another drink to toast Harry, the crux of the situation, when, about eleven-thirty, Harry unintentionally ruined the whole thing by walking in the front door. He was wearing a mackintosh, a deer-hunter's cap with the flaps up, and carrying his fishing gear.

"Sorry I'm late," he said cheerfully. "Something went wrong with the fuel pump the other side of Owen Sound."

They all stared at him in such a peculiar and disgruntled way that even Harry, who was not given to subtleties, sensed something was wrong.

"What's the matter with you guys anyway? Have I broken out in spots or something?"

"Where's Galloway?" Turee asked.

"I thought he was here."

"Wasn't he supposed to come with you?"

"That was the original plan, but I had an emergency call to make at a clinic down in Mimico, so I left word with Thelma to tell Galloway to go ahead without me. I know how he hates to be late. You don't suppose Thelma got her signals switched?"

It was generally agreed among the fellows that Thelma had been born with her signals switched, but none of them wanted to state this outright because it might hurt Harry's feelings. Harry adored his wife. Her little eccentricities seemed endlessly fascinating to him and he was always entertaining his friends with detailed reports of her opinions and experiences.

Because he'd been the sole support of his parents, Harry had not married until they were both dead and then he wasted no time. His marriage, at the age of thirty-five, to a woman who worked as a receptionist in a doctor's office, came as a shock to his friends, especially to Galloway who had become used to having Harry at his beck and call, and ready for anything. The carefree bachelor Harry had been suddenly replaced by the hopelessly married Harry, subject to rules and restrictions and at the mercy of whims and worries. Though Thelma and Esther did not get along well, the two men remained the best of friends, partly because Thelma seemed to like Galloway and encouraged Harry to see him, and partly because the two men had been friends ever since their prep school years together. As a senior, Harry had been president of the class. He still possessed the yearbook with his graduation picture in it, and the caption: *Henry Ellsworth Bream. A great future is predicted for our Harry, who holds a warm place in all our hearts.*

He still held a warm place in a good many hearts but the future remained elusive. He had missed a number of boats, by inches or minutes, by oddities of fate like a flat tire, a delay in traffic, a wrong turning, a misplaced key, a sudden blizzard, a mistake in a telephone number.

"Poor Harry," people said. "Always running into bad luck."

It was generally expected that when his parents died fate would step in and make up to Harry for all his misfortunes by handing him a real stroke of luck. By Harry's standards, fate had. The luck was Thelma.

"She probably didn't give him the message," Turee said. "Perhaps she suddenly decided to go to a movie or something and Galloway's still sitting there waiting for you to turn up."

Harry shook his head. "Thelma wouldn't do a thing like that."

"Not on purpose, of course."

"Not accidentally, either. Thelma's got a wonderful memory."

"Oh?"

"That girl's never forgotten a thing in her life."

"Well, all right, all right. It just seemed the logical explanation, that's all."

It was midnight by this time, and Bill Winslow, who couldn't hold his liquor but would die trying, had reached the point of saturation. The excess fluid was seeping out of his eyes in the form of tears.

"Poor old Galloway, sitting down there on his can, sitting on his poor old lonely can, while we're up here lapping up his liquor and having a swell time. It's not cricket. Fellows, I ask you, is that *cricket?*"

Turee scowled at him across the room. "For God's sake, stop blubbering, will you? I'm trying to think."

"Poor old Galloway. Not cricket. Here we are having a swell time and there he sits on his poor old..."

"Hepburn, see if you can haul him off to bed."

Hepburn put his hands under Winslow's armpits and pulled him to his feet. "Come on, Billy-boy. Let's go beddy-bye."

"I don't want to go to bed. I want to stay down here and have a swell time with you fellows."

"Look, Billy-boy, we're not having a swell time."

"Y'aren't?"

"No. So let's get moving. Where'd you leave your suitcase?"

"I don't know."

"I put it upstairs with mine, in the room next to Galloway's," Turee said.

"I don't want to go to bed. I'm sad."

"So I see."

Winslow tried to brush the moisture off his cheeks with his forearm. "I keep thinking about poor old Galloway and poor little Princess Margaret."

"How did Princess Margaret get into this?"

"Ought to marry somebody, have kids, be happy. Everybody should be happy."

"Certainly."

"*I'm* happy."

"Sure you are."

"I'm having a swell time with you fellows, aren't I?"

"Not for long, Billy-boy. Come on."

With the tears still spouting from his eyes, Winslow shuffled across the room and began to ascend the staircase on all fours like a trained dog going up a ladder. Halfway up he collapsed and Hepburn had to drag him the rest of the way.

Turee got up and put another log on the fire and kicked it impatiently with his foot. "Well, what do we do now?"

"I don't know," Harry said gloomily. "This isn't like Ron, to keep people waiting."

"He might have had an accident."

"He's a good driver. He's got a real bug on safety, seat belts and everything."

"Even good drivers occasionally have accidents. The point is, since there's no phone here, if something happened we'd have no way of finding out unless Esther sent a telegram to Wiarton and it was delivered out here."

"Esther would be too upset to think of doing that."

"All right, here's another theory: Galloway never left home. He suffered an attack of indigestion, perhaps, and decided not to come."

"Now that's more like," Harry said with enthusiasm. "Last time I saw him he was complaining about his stomach. I gave him a couple of those new ulcer capsules my firm's putting out."

"Galloway hasn't got an ulcer."

"He may have. The capsules worked like a charm."

Turee turned away with an expression of distaste. He was the only one of the group who refused to have anything personal to do with either Harry's diagnoses or Harry's pills.

"All right, all right. Galloway's ulcer started kicking up and he went to the hospital. How does that sound?"

"Splendid," Harry said, beaming.

When Hepburn returned, a conference was held and it was decided that Turee, the brainiest, and Harry, the soberest, should drive back to Wiarton and call Galloway's house to test the ulcer theory.

The road wound along the cliffs above the bay and Turee had to concentrate on his driving while Harry, in case the ulcer theory might be incorrect, kept his eye peeled for signs of a Cadillac in distress. They met only two cars, neither one a Cadillac.

By the time they reached the town of Wiarton, nearly all the lights were out, but they finally located a pay phone in the lobby of a small tourist hotel which was just opening for the season. Since both the men were wearing fishing clothes, the manager of the hotel assumed they were customers and treated them very cordially until he learned they merely wanted to use the telephone. When, in addition to suffering a disappointment, he had to make change for five dollars, he became quite bitter about the whole thing and sat behind the desk glowering as Turee stepped into the phone booth.

It required ten minutes or more to put the call through to Galloway's house in Toronto, and then the connection was bad and the conversation was punctuated by what sounded like static.

"Esther?"

"Ron?"

"No, this is not Ron. Is that you, Esther?"

"Just who is this, please?"

"Ralph. Ralph Turee. Is that you, Esther?"

"Yes," Esther replied, rather coldly, since she'd been awakened from a sound sleep and even under the best of circumstances didn't care much for Turee, Turee's wife, or any of the little Turees. "Isn't it rather *late?*"

"I can't hear you. Would you speak up?"

"I'm practically screaming already."

"Listen, Esther—what in hell is that noise? Operator, operator, do something about that noise—Esther? Are you there? Well, listen a minute. Is Ron all right?"

"Of course he's all right."

"No attack of indigestion or anything?"

"Are you drunk, by any chance?" This was one of Esther's favorite questions and after long practice she read the line with spirited contempt, rolling the *r* in drunk and broadening the *a* in chance.

"I am not drunk," Turee shouted. "Why should I be?"

"I'm sure you have reasons. Now what's all this about Ron?"

"Well, it's like this. Harry's up here at the lodge with the rest of us."

"So?"

"Ron hasn't arrived. Harry drove up alone in his own car. He had a business appointment to keep in Mimico and he told Thelma to tell Ron not to wait for him but to come up to the lodge by himself and Harry would get here when he could. Well, Harry got here all right, but Ron hasn't. The fellows were beginning to get worried so we thought we'd better call you."

Esther suffered from a chronic case of jealousy, and the first image that flashed through her mind was not of Galloway lying dead somewhere in a car wreck, but of Galloway lying cosily beside Thelma in a bed. She said, "Maybe Ron was delayed."

"Where?"

"In Weston."

"How?"

"How? Ask Harry. He's married to the woman."

"Now that," Turee said irritably, "is the silliest remark in history. What's got into you, Esther?"

"Just an idea."

"Honest to God, I gave you credit for better sense. I can't say more than that right now because I'm shouting as it is and Harry's not ten feet away. Do you understand?"

"Naturally."

"Listen, Esther..."

At this point the operator's voice cut in and demanded another ninety cents. Turee deposited the money, cursing audibly. "Are you still there, Esther?"

"Naturally."

"I think you should call the police."

"Why? It might embarrass poor Ron. He's rather sensitive about being caught by the cops in bed with another man's wife."

"For Pete's sake, Esther, get off that kick, will you? This might be serious. Ron could be lying in some hospital or even a morgue."

"He carries all kinds of identification in his wallet. If there'd been an accident I would have been notified."

"Then you're not worried?"

"Worried? Yes, I'm *worried*, but it's not the kind of worry I want to share with the police department."

"I'm amazed at your attitude, Esther, genuinely amazed."

"You go right on being amazed, I can't stop you."

"But what about Ron?"

"Ron," she said dryly, "will be home in due course with a perfectly believable story which I may even believe, for a time. You needn't concern yourself about Ron. Wherever he is and whatever he's doing, I assure you he's not concerning himself about you, or me, or Harry, or anyone else."

"That could mean he's dead."

"The trouble with you and the fellows is that you all get maudlin when you've been drinking."

The statement contained such a large element of truth that Turee didn't attempt to refute it. "I must say that's not a very friendly remark."

"I'm not feeling too friendly at the moment. Now look. You and the fellows went up to the lodge for a week end of fishing. Or whatever. If Ron shows up here I'll tell him you're worried and ask him to wire you. If he shows up there, you might do the same for me. Right?"

"Right," Turee agreed, though he didn't feel it was right at all. The whole thing was wrong, Galloway's absence, Esther's attitude, Winslow's wild, drunken sobbing. *What a week end this is shaping up to be*, he thought. *I ought to turn right around and drive home.*

The air in the telephone booth had become hot and stale and when Turee opened the door and stepped out into the lobby he was sweating, red-eyed and ill-tempered.

Harry was standing beside the window looking intently out over the bay, as if there were many interesting things to be seen. But the bay was dark, nothing could be seen, and Turee knew that Harry had been listening—listening and perhaps hearing.

"Well, well," Turee said with an attempt at heartiness. "It seems as though we were getting all discombobulated for nothing."

"Ron's at home, then?"

"Not exactly. But I assure you Esther's not in the least worried about his well-being."

"That sounds as if she's worried about something else."

"Oh, you know Esther. She's hatched the idea that Ron went off on a bat. Who can tell, maybe she's right."

"Maybe." Harry turned back to the window, his jaw clenched so tight that his voice seemed to be coming from some other place, like a ventriloquist's. "I thought I heard you say something about me."

"You? Oh, certainly. I explained about the mix-up in Weston, how you had to keep your business appointment and..."

"I don't mean that."

"All right," Turee said quietly. "What else did you hear?"

"You told Esther you couldn't talk any more about something because I was only ten feet away."

"That's right."

"What were you referring to?"

"Well, it's like this." Turee was an inexperienced liar, and the circumstances—the wearing off of the drinks he'd had, the lateness of the hour, and the presence of the hotel manager behind the desk, wide-eyed with curiosity—contributed to his awkwardness. "The fact is, Esther had a suspicion that you and Ron went off on a bat together."

"Esther should know me better than that. In the old days, well, perhaps, she might have had a point, but I'm a married man now."

"Yes."

"Esther *does* know me better than that."

"What Esther knows and what she feels are often miles apart."

"Are you telling me the truth?"

"About what?"

"Come off it, Ralph. We're friends."

"Well, as one friend to another, I suggest we go back to the lodge and get some sleep." Turee took a couple of tentative steps toward the door, but when he saw that Harry didn't intend to follow, he turned around and came back. "We can't stay here all night, old boy."

"Can't we?"

"Look, Esther's crazy suspicions shouldn't make the least difference to anyone. Now come on, let's go back to the lodge. There's nothing more we can do here."

"Yes, there is," Harry said. "I'm going to phone Thelma."

"Why?"

"You don't have to have a reason for phoning your own wife. Besides, I want to find out if Ron ever showed up at the house."

"But it's late, Thelma will be asleep. She may not even hear the phone."

"It's right beside our bed."

"Go ahead and call her then. Just don't say I didn't warn you."

"Warn me?"

"What I mean is, if I phoned my wife at this hour of the morning she'd think I was drunk, and the next time I was invited to come up here with the fellows she'd raise a hell of a smell."

"Thelma's not like that. She wants me to have a good time. She's a remarkably unselfish woman."

Turee didn't argue. It was one of Harry's most ingratiating qualities, to attribute to other people the virtues he himself possessed.

As Harry slid into the phone booth and closed the door, Turee watched anxiously, thinking, *God, suppose Esther's right for once and Ron's there with Thelma... No, that's impossible. Thelma's just as crazy about Harry as he is about her.*

He began to whistle, almost inaudibly, *I'm just wild about Harry.*

THREE

Thelma was not asleep, as Turee had predicted. She answered the phone on the second ring and her voice sounded alert, as if she'd been expecting the call. Or one like it.

"This is the Bream residence."

Harry laughed. "I know that, sweetheart."

"Oh, it's you, Harry."

"None other. I hope I didn't wake you up."

"No."

"Are you glad to hear from me?"

"Of course."

"Cross your heart and hope to die?"

"Cross my heart," she said flatly, "and hope to die. How you enjoy playing games, Harry. You're like a child. But isn't it too late for games? Oughtn't children to be in bed? I think so. Tomorrow," she added, "tomorrow you can play all the games you like."

In their three years of marriage she had never addressed him in such a wearily patronizing manner. Harry colored, as if his face had been slapped. "Thelma, what's the matter?"

"Nothing."

"That's not true. I know it's not true. What's happened, Thelma? Tell me. Tell Harry."

Her only response was a sigh. He could hear it quite plainly; it was long and deep and sad.

"Thelma. Listen to me. If you want me to come home, I will. I'll start out right this minute."

"No! I *don't* want you to come home!"

"What's the matter, Thelma? Are you feeling all right?"

Again she made no reply. Harry felt smothered by her silence. He pulled open the door of the phone booth a few inches and breathed in the new air deeply and rhythmically. With the door open Turee could overhear, but Harry didn't care. He was not timid or embarrassed about sharing his troubles with his friends since he had so frequently shared theirs.

"I'm ill," Thelma said finally. "I've been ill all evening."

"Get a doctor. Get a doctor right away."

"I don't need a doctor. I know what's the matter."

"What is it, sweetheart?"

"I can't tell you. This isn't—the time or place."

"Look, Thel, take it easy. Lie down and relax. I'm coming home right away."

"If you do, I won't be here."

"For God's sake..."

"I mean it, Harry. I'll run away. I've got to be alone for a while to think. Don't come home, Harry. Promise me."

"But I. . ."

"Promise me."

"All right, I promise. I won't come home, not tonight, anyway."

She seemed relieved by his promise and when she spoke again her tone was quite friendly. "Where are you calling from?"

"A hotel in Wiarton."

"Haven't you been to the lodge yet?"

"Yes, but Turee and I drove back to find a phone so we could call Ron's house."

"Why on earth should you call Ron's house at this hour?"

"To find out why he hasn't arrived here."

"He hasn't arrived," she repeated dully. "Is that what you said? Ron's not there?"

"Not yet."

"But he left here hours ago. He came before eight and I gave him your message and we had a drink together. And then..."

She stopped, and Harry had to urge her to continue. "And then what, Thelma?"

"I—I asked him—I begged him not to go up to the lodge."

"Why?"

"Because I had this feeling when he came in—it was so strong I nearly fainted—I had this *feeling.*" She began to weep and the rest of her words were distorted by great choking sobs. "Oh, my God—warned—my fault— Ron's dead—Ron—Ron..."

"What are you saying, Thelma?"

"Ron..." She repeated the name half a dozen times while Harry listened, his heart on fire, his face like stone.

Turee came over to the phone booth and opened the door. "Is anything the matter?"

"Yes. But I don't know what."

"Perhaps I can help."

"I don't think so."

"Let me try, anyway. Go and sit down, Harry, you look terrible."

The two men exchanged places at the telephone and Turee spoke briskly into the mouthpiece: "Hello, Thelma. This is Ralph."

"Go away."

"Listen, Thelma, I don't know what the situation is, but calm down for a minute, will you?"

"I can't."

"Why don't you have a drink? I'll hang on for a minute while you go and pour yourself..."

"I don't want a drink."

"All right, all right. just a suggestion."

"It wouldn't stay down anyway. I'm ill. I've been vomiting."

"Maybe you have a touch of flu."

"I haven't got the flu." She hesitated for a moment. "Is Harry standing anywhere near you?"

"No, he went outside."

"You're sure?"

"I can see him walking up and down on the veranda."

"I'm pregnant."

"What? What did you say?"

"I'm going to have a baby."

"Well, for—well, I'll be double-damned. That's great Thelma, that's wonderful!"

"Is it?"

"Have you told Harry?"

"Not yet."

"God, he'll be thrilled to pieces when he finds out."

"Maybe he will. At first."

"What do you mean, at first?"

"When he starts thinking about it he won't be so thrilled."

"I don't get the point."

"Harry and I haven't taken any chances along that line for over a year," she said slowly. "Harry didn't want me to have a baby, he was afraid complications might develop because I'm nearly thirty-five."

"No method is foolproof. You could have had an accident."

"It wasn't an accident. It was quite deliberate, on my part anyway. I wanted a baby. I'm getting old, pretty soon it would have been too late. I talked to Harry, I told him how I felt, many times. But be was terrified that something might happen to me. That's what he said, anyway. Maybe his real reasons were deeper, subtler, I don't know. Maybe he was jealous at the idea of my dividing my affections. But whatever Harry's reasons were, at least now you know mine. I want this child. I love him already."

"Him?"

"I have a feeling it's a boy. I call him Ron."

"For the love of God," Turee said. "Ron. Ron *Galloway?*"

"Yes."

"You're sure?"

"Now that's rather insulting, isn't it? It sounds as though I've been promiscuous."

"I only meant, in a thing like this you've got to be absolutely positive."

"I am."

"For the love of God," Turee repeated. "What a mess this is going to be. Think of Harry. And Esther."

"I can't afford to. I have my child to think about. Esther never loved Ron anyway. She married him for his money, he told me so. As for Harry, I feel sorry for him, of course. He's a good man, I hate to hurt him, but..."

"But you will?"

"I will. I must. I have my child to consider."

"That's just it, Thelma. Think a minute. For the child's sake, wouldn't it be better to keep this whole business a secret? Harry would make a wonderful father, and the child could be brought up without any fuss or scandal."

"That's impossible. I don't want to keep this whole business, as you call it, a secret."

"I strongly urge you to think about it."

"I've thought of nothing else for three weeks, ever since I found out I was pregnant. And one thing I'm sure of—I can't go on living with Harry. He doesn't even seem *real* to me any more. How can I explain it? The only thing that's real to me is this baby inside me. Ron's baby. They are my life now, Ron and his baby."

The simple statement, spoken with such conviction, appalled Turee more than the actual circumstances behind it. For a moment he could hardly speak, and when he did, his voice was cold with disapproval. "I don't imagine Ron will feel quite so single-minded about it. After all, he's sired one child by his first wife and two by his second, so this is hardly a unique occasion for him."

"If you're trying to make me jealous or angry, don't bother. Ron's had other women, other children, yes, but this is special. The baby's special. I'm special."

There was no answer to this. Turee could only sit and stare silently and helplessly into the mouthpiece of the telephone, wishing with all his heart that he had stayed home and painted the garage, as his wife wanted him to.

"Ralph? Are you there?"

"Yes?"

"Ralph, I don't want you to get the idea that I'm—that I thought this all out ahead of time, that I planned it. I really didn't. It just happened, but once it happened, I realized how right it was for me."

"*Right.* Are you out of your mind, woman? What you're doing, what you've done, is completely and unjustifiably immoral."

"Don't preach at me. Words aren't going to change anything."

"Well, for God's sake, consider Harry. This will kill him."

"I don't think so. Oh, he'll be upset for a while, but eventually he'll meet some nice clinging-vine sort of woman who'll let him fuss over her and pour pills down her throat."

Turee was shocked. "You sound as if you actually hate him."

"No. Just the pills. He was making an invalid out of me. I'm really quite strong. The doctor says I should have a fine, healthy baby. It's what I've wanted all my life. I was an only child living with a maiden aunt, and terribly lonely. I used to dream of growing up and getting married and having a dozen children so I'd never be lonely again."

"You may," he said heavily, "be lonelier than ever. People around here take a dim view of..."

"Oh, people. I don't care about them. All I need is Ron and the baby."

"You're pretty sure of yourself, Thelma."

"Yes."

"Are you equally sure of Ron?"

"Yes. I told him about the baby tonight when he came over to pick up Harry. It seemed the right time to tell him."

Turee wasn't certain he agreed with her. "How did he take the news?"

She said defensively, "Naturally I didn't expect him to be deliriously happy about it right at first. He needs time to think, to adjust to the situation. Any man would."

"I'm glad you realize that," Turee said dryly.

"He loves me, that's the important factor."

"Is it?"

"Don't worry, everything will work out fine. I have a feeling."

Thelma's was a contradictory nature. This new feeling, that everything would work out fine, immediately eclipsed the old feeling that something had happened to Ron. Thelma could, in fact, superimpose one feeling on another feeling, like bricks, and it was always the latest, the top one, that was valid.

She added, "Oh, I know it's going to be messy in some ways, the divorce, for instance."

"Ron can't get a divorce from Esther. He has no grounds."

"I meant, Ron will pay her off and she can get the divorce."

"Suppose she refuses?"

"Oh nonsense. Esther loves money. Besides, why should she refuse?"

"Some women," Turee said with heavy irony, "aren't exactly thrilled at the prospect of breaking up their home and family."

"Don't sentimentalize Esther. I haven't done anything more to her than she did to Ron's first wife. Except that my motives are cleaner."

"How does Ron like the idea of going through the courts and the newspapers again as an adulterer?"

"Oh, for heaven's sake, can't you say something *cheerful?*"

"I can't think of anything cheerful," Turee said truthfully. "This isn't the type of situation that appeals to my sense of humor. Maybe Harry will be able to think of something cheerful. He's still outside on the veranda. Shall I call him?"

"No!"

"How are you going to tell him, Thelma?"

"I don't know. I've tried, I've led up to it, but—oh, it's all so difficult."

"You should have thought of that when you and Ron were hopping into bed together."

"What a terribly coarse remark!"

"The situation isn't exactly genteel either."

"Listen, Ralph. About telling Harry. I was wondering, you're such a good friend of his..."

"Kindly leave me out of it."

"I only thought, you can be so tactful when you choose..."

"On this occasion, I don't choose."

"Very well. But I won't tell him. I can't. I don't even want to see him again."

"For God's sake, woman, you owe him that much, an apology, an explanation."

"Why should I apologize? I'm not sorry. As for an explanation, how can I explain something I don't understand myself? I didn't know it was going to happen to Ron and me. If I had, maybe I would have asked Harry for a pill or something, a love-preventative pill." She laughed briefly and bitterly. "He's got every other kind."

"When did it all begin?"

"A couple of weeks before Christmas. I went into town to buy Harry's gift and I met Ron in Eaton's by accident. We had lunch together at the Park Plaza and afterwards we went out on the terrace in the snow and looked down at the city. It was so pretty. I'd never cared much for Toronto before, I was brought up in the West, Vancouver. Well, that's all, we just stood there. There was no flirtation, no hand-holding, we didn't even talk personally or look at each other much. But when I got home I didn't tell Harry. I had no reason not to. But I didn't. I even made up a lie for him, told him I had lunch with a nurse I used to work with at the Murray Clinic in Hamilton. The next day I took a bus into Toronto again because I'd forgotten to buy Harry's Christmas present. At least that was the excuse I gave myself. I went back to the same store, at the same time, and hung around the Yonge Street entrance for nearly an hour. I had this terribly strong feeling that Ron would show up. He didn't, but later he told me that he'd wanted to very much, that he'd thought of me all morning but he couldn't get away because Esther was giving a luncheon party at the club."

A couple of dimwits, Turee thought contemptuously, dramatizing themselves, out of boredom, into a situation that neither of them was equipped to handle. He said, "And Harry hasn't suspected a thing?"

"No."

"For your information, Esther has and does."

"I thought as much. She was very cold when I called her last week and invited her to go to a séance a friend of mine was giving. I was only trying to be affable."

"Why?"

"For Ron's sake. I don't want him cut off from Esther's children the way he was cut off from his first wife's. It's not fair."

"The courts seem to think so."

"The courts in this country, yes. Oh, this place is so stodgy and provincial. I wish we could live in the States, Ron and I and the baby."

The front door opened and Harry came back into the hotel lobby walking unsteadily and with his feet wide apart like a newly debarked sailor bracing himself against the pitch and roll of a ship that was no longer under him. Although the night air was still balmy, his lips were blue with cold and his eyes had a glassy stare as if unshed tears had been trapped there and frozen.

"...some place where they don't have these long terrible winters," Thelma was saying. "Oh, how I hate them! I've reached the point where I can't even enjoy the spring any more because I know how short it will be and how soon fall is coming when everything is sad again, everything dying."

"Let's go into that some other time," Turee said brusquely. "Now tell me, was Ron driving the Cadillac when he came to your house tonight?"

"I think so."

"Did it have the top down or up?"

"Down, I think. Yes, definitely down. I remember waving out the window to him and wondering if he might catch cold with all that draft on the back of his neck. He complained of feeling ill anyway."

"I can believe it."

"No, I mean he complained about it *before* I told him anything about the baby. Really, Ralph, you're in a nasty mood tonight."

"I wonder why."

"After all, it's not *your* funeral."

Harry walked slowly but directly toward the telephone booth and in spite of Turee's restraining hand he forced open the door. "Let me talk to her."

Turee said, "Thelma, here's Harry. He wants to talk to you."

"I don't want to talk to him. I have nothing to say."

"But..."

"Tell him the truth or give him a story, I don't care. I'm going to hang up now, Ralph. And if you call back I won't answer."

"Thelma, wait."

The click of the receiver was unmistakably final. "She hung up," Turee said.

"Why?"

"Didn't feel like conversation, I guess. Don't let it worry you, old boy. Women can get pretty flighty at..."

"I want to call her back."

"She said if you did, she wouldn't answer."

"I know Thelma," Harry said with a wan smile. "She can't resist the ringing of a telephone."

Once again the two men exchanged places and Harry put in a collect call to Mrs. Harry Bream in Weston.

The operator let the telephone ring a dozen times before she cut back to Harry. "I'm sorry, sir, there's no answer at that number. Shall I try again in twenty minutes?"

"No. No, thanks." Harry came out of the booth wiping his forehead with the sleeve of his fishing jacket. "Sonuvabitch, I don't get it. What's the matter? What did I do?"

"Nothing. Let's go back to the lodge and have a drink."

"What were you and Thelma talking about all that time?"

"Life," Turee said. Which was true enough.

"Life, at three o'clock in the morning, long distance?"

"Thelma wanted to talk. You know women, sometimes they have to get things off their chest by talking to somebody objective, not a member of their family. Thelma was in an emotional state."

"She can always count on me to understand."

"I hope so," Turee said softly. "I hope to God so."

"It's this uncertainty that gets me down. Why won't she talk to me? Why did she keep saying Ron's name over and over again?"

"She's—fond of Ron and worried about him. We all are, aren't we?"

"My God, yes. He's my best friend. I saved him from drowning once when we were in school together, did I ever tell you that?"

"Yes," Turee said, not because it was true but because he'd had enough irony for one day, he couldn't swallow any more; his throat felt tight and raw and scraped. "Come on, Harry, you look as if you need a drink."

"Maybe I should stay in town for the night, take a room here and get a couple of hours' sleep and then try to reach Thelma again."

"Leave the woman alone for a while. Give her a chance to collect herself."

"You may be right. I hope she remembers to take the orange pills I left for her. They're very good for relieving tension. I'm told they're the ones that cured the Pope of hiccoughs when he had that bad spell."

Turee felt, simultaneously, a certain sympathy for Thelma and a twinge of impatience with Harry. He would have liked to point out that Thelma's ailment was quite remote from hiccoughs and that it would require more than orange pills, or blue, or pink, to cure her. "There's nothing more we can do here," he said, "unless we inform the police that Ron is missing."

"He may not be missing any more. By the time we drive back to the lodge, he'll very likely be there. Don't you agree?"

"It's possible." But not, Turee added to himself, very probable. If I were in Ron's shoes, the last thing in the world I'd want to do would be to come up here and face Harry. Ron may have taken a room at a hotel for the night. Or gone down to his cottage near Kingsville. Or maybe he's just driving around alone the way he does sometimes when he and Esther are on the verge of a quarrel. Ron can't stand scenes, trouble of any kind makes him sick. The time Bill Winslow and I had the big argument about politics Ron simply disappeared, and Esther found him later, retching behind the boxwood hedge.

Harry looked at his watch and the very sight of it made him yawn and brought water to his eyes. "My God, it's nearly four o'clock."

"I'm well aware of it."

"In another hour or two the fellows will be up and raring to go. We'd better start back, don't you agree?"

"I agreed some time ago."

"By Jove, you know something, Ralph? I feel better, I feel much, much better. I don't know what you said or did exactly, but you've given me a little perspective on things."

Turee forced a feeble smile. "Good."

"Yes sir, you've given me a new slant. Why should we worry over two perfectly mature adults like Ron and Thelma? After all, neither of them would ever do anything foolish."

"That's the spirit."

"Let's go back to the lodge and have a drink to celebrate."

"Celebrate what?"

"I don't know, I felt so bad before and now everything's fine again and I feel like celebrating."

He went ahead to open the door. He was smiling and his step was jaunty.

"By Jove, it's a glorious night," Harry said. "Smell that air, will you?"

Turee had little choice. He smelled the air. It carried the scent of wind and water, delusion and betrayal.

FOUR

The ride back to the lodge began quietly enough. After a brief spurt of conversation Harry climbed over into the back seat, folded himself up and went to sleep.

Turee drove slowly, his mind oppressed by the problem of telling Harry the truth in a way that would cause him a minimum of shock. Pain was inevitable—there was no way of sparing him that—but it might be possible to break his fall and lessen the concussion.

Until tonight Turee had always considered Thelma as something of a birdbrain. He now began to realize how cleverly Thelma had maneuvered him into the role of custodian of the secret. It was like finding himself custodian of a fissionable mass of uranium; if he didn't get rid of some of it, the whole thing might blow up in his face. The problem, then, was to unload it a little at a time, with due respect for its explosive powers.

"Tell him the truth or give him a story," Thelma had said, but it was clear that she intended him to tell Harry the truth, not because she felt he could do it in a more kindly and tactful way, but because she wanted to save herself the trouble. Thelma could no longer be bothered with Harry, she had no compunctions about hurting him, no apologies to offer him, no explanation to give him, no intention of ever seeing him again. This final fact seemed somehow more incredible to Turee than any of the others. For three years the Breams had been regarded as a model couple. They did not argue or correct each other in public, take verbal potshots at parties or confide their mates' failings to friends. Turee had always envied them a little, since he and his wife Nancy engaged in frequent and spirited arguments which usually culminated in a series of glib psychological terms: *Your Uncle Charles has that same paranoid streak—you're a cyclic depressive, that's all—it's no wonder the kids are going through a manic phase...* Instead of throwing ash trays at each other, the Turees, in the modern manner, threw Oedipus complexes, father fixations and compulsive neuroses.

In the back seat Harry began to snore, rather gently and apologetically, as if he expected to be told to turn over and shut up. For some reason the sound exasperated Turee. It was like a sick puppy whimpering in its sleep.

"Harry," he said sharply.

"Umph," Harry said, as if he'd been prodded in the stomach by an elbow. "Aaaah. What? What?"

"Wake up."

"Must have dozed off. Sorry."

"Don't apologize all the time. It gets on my nerves."

"Nearly everything does," Harry said with a patient sigh. "I don't intend that as a criticism, old boy. Far from it. You're too high-strung, that's all. You ought to learn to relax. Say, you remember those orange pills I told you about, the ones that cured the Pope of hiccoughs?"

"They're quite difficult to forget."

"I happen to have a few in my pocket. You could take one now and let me drive for a while."

Turee had as little faith in Harry's driving as he had in Harry's ministrations. "Thank you, no. I prefer to remain tense."

Harry climbed back into the front seat and then, out of a habit that was becoming almost a compulsion, he began to talk of Thelma again, of her rare and various virtues. Harry didn't claim that all other women were clods, he merely let it be implied.

"...so Thelma took the old man in the house and made him a cup of tea. Thel's like that, opens her heart to everyone..."

"Harry."

"...even a total stranger. Then she got in touch with the old man's daughter-in-law..."

"Harry, I have something to tell you."

"All right, old boy, I'd practically finished anyway. Go ahead."

"Don't expect Ron to be at the lodge when we get there."

"Why not?"

"I don't think he's going to show up at all, either at the lodge or any other place he's likely to run into you."

"What have I got to do with it?"

"I believe Ron may be trying to avoid you."

"Avoid me? Why?"

"Because he's become quite fond of your wife."

"Why, he's always been fond of Thelma. They hit it off fine, right from the start."

"Now they're hitting it off finer." Turee took his eyes from the road for an instant to glance at Harry's face in the dim light from the dashboard. Harry was smiling. "Did you hear me, Harry? Ron's in love with your wife."

"That's Thelma's story, of course?"

"Yes."

"Don't let it worry you, there's nothing to it," Harry said firmly.

"You seem pretty confident."

"Listen, Ralph, I wouldn't tell this to anyone else in the world, but you're my friend, I can trust you with a secret."

Turee opened the car window. He had a sensation that he and Harry were stationary and the night was moving past them swiftly, turbulent with secrets. To the right the bay was visible in the reflection of a half moon. The waves nudged each other and winked slyly and whispered new secrets.

"The fact is," Harry said, "Thelma daydreams. Nothing serious, of course, but once in a while she gets the notion that so-and-so is in love with her. There's never anything to it. A week later she's forgotten the whole thing."

"I see."

"This time it's Ron. Once, it was you."

"Me. Why, for God's sake, I never even..."

"I know. Thelma imagines things. She can't help it. She's got a romantic streak in her nature. It gives her satisfaction to believe that someone is hopelessly in love with her, makes her feel glamorous, I guess." Harry sighed. "So she thinks Ron is in love with her, that's what she was upset about? That's what she told you?"

"She told me that among..."

"Poor Thelma. This daydreaming—well, it's like the séances she goes to. Thelma doesn't really believe in them and she hasn't anybody dead she'd like to communicate with. It's just she wants to be different, exciting, ah, you know, don't you, Ralph?"

"I suppose so."

"I've never talked about my wife like this before," Harry said solemnly. "I hope you won't think I'm being disloyal."

"Of course not."

"The séances, they're new, a neighbor of ours got her interested. But the daydreaming started when she was a girl and she's never managed to get over it. It makes up for some of the things that are missing from her life, romance and excitement. I try to provide them but I'm afraid I'm not the type who—put it this way: I sell pills. That's not very glamorous, I guess. Thelma makes up for it by daydreaming a little."

Or a lot, Turee added silently. "You don't think daydreaming can be dangerous?"

"Not to Thelma and me. How could it?"

"A prolonged dream can become mixed up with reality."

"Now, look here, Ralph, you have this tendency to be critical. I know you mean well, but it's not always wise. Thelma and I are perfectly happy as we are. If daydreams make up for certain inadequacies in her life..."

"You're contradicting yourself."

"All *right*," Harry said, with the first sign of irritability he'd shown all evening. "That's my business. I can contradict myself to hell and gone if I feel like it."

"Certainly. Do that."

Harry lit a cigarette before he spoke again, in a softer tone. "You're smart, Ralph, you're deep, you know a lot of things me and the other fellows don't on account of your advanced education and so on. Only..."

"Only what?"

"Just don't start analyzing Thelma. I love her the way she is. Let her have her dreams."

"She's welcome to them, as far as I'm concerned."

"My marriage is the most wonderful thing that ever happened to me. I wouldn't do anything in the world to undermine the relationship between Thelma and me."

"You won't have to," Turee said, but the noise of the engine and the sound of the water below the cliffs submerged his words. He didn't try to dredge them up. Well, that's that, he thought. Harry wants to stay on cloud seven. Let him.

They covered the remaining miles, not in silence, since Harry had begun to whistle very cheerfully, but at least without conversation. Turee shut his ears to the whistling and busied himself sorting out the various images of Thelma that had flashed across his mind throughout the night.

First there was, of course, the Harry's-wife Thelma, a short, placid, pleasant-looking woman in her early thirties. An excellent cook and skillful housekeeper, she seemed to have few interests outside the small red-brick house she and Harry had bought in Weston. Turee had always found her a little on the dull side since she seldom made any observations or remarks of her own, but instead, chimed in her agreement with Harry, in a kind of wifely echolalia: *Harry's perfectly right—as Harry was saying only yesterday—Harry told me and I agree that* ... She appeared, on the surface, to be a woman unwilling to make any decisions by herself, and incapable of originating any plans or ideas. Even her recent addiction to seances, and the ensuing psychic feelings, had been instigated by a neighbor.

But Turee's mind was getting ahead of itself, because the seances belonged more properly in the second picture of Thelma, Thelma the daydreamer, who fed her mediocrity with meaty chunks of dreams until it was fat beyond her own recognition. Under this system of mental dietetics Thelma became a woman equipped with great psychic powers, as well as femme fatale with whom men fell hopelessly in love. It was girl stuff, this daydreaming, and Thelma was no girl. Perhaps she was no daydreamer either; the possibility occurred to Turee that Harry might have invented the whole thing to protect himself from the truth, that Ron Galloway actually was in love with Thelma.

This led to the third picture, blurred and more distorted yet somehow more real than either of the others, of Thelma, the woman who wanted a child, and with single-minded determination and not a trace of moral misgiving, had gone ahead and found the means to conceive one.

Harry had stopped whistling and was peering out of the window for the turnoff to the lodge.

"Why do you feel," Turee said suddenly, "that if I start to 'analyze' Thelma, as you call it, something will happen to your marriage?"

"I don't feel that."

"It was implied."

"Oh, Ralph," Harry said with sadness, "don't. Don't go on. Some things are better left alone. Analyze your students, if you like, or your family, anyone else but Thelma. Perhaps she isn't entirely happy, but I'm doing my best to change that. There are certain factors involved that I won't go into."

"She wants a child."

Harry looked surprised. "How did you know?"

"She told me."

"Just tonight? On the phone?"

"Yes."

"Oh, then that's what upset her. She must have gone to sleep and been awakened by another of her nightmares. She's had quite a few of them this spring. She dreams she's borne a baby, only something happens to it, it's deformed, or it gets sick and dies; once it was kidnapped by a Chinaman. She'd been to the laundry to pick up my shirts that day, that's how the Chinaman got into it, I guess.... I haven't told Thelma yet, I want it to be a surprise, but I've visited two adoption agencies this week, making inquiries.... The turnoff should be along here some place."

The turnoff was months ago, Turee thought. *You missed it, Harry.*

The lodge had been built by Galloway partly as a wedding present to Esther and partly as a place to hide out in until the scandal of his divorce from his first wife had blown over. It turned out not as a hideaway but as a showplace the natives around the bay, all the way from Penetanguishene to Tobermory, came to admire and criticize. The structure was, in fact, too elaborate for its setting and its function. The lower story had been built of native stone and the second story was in English half-timbered style, with a shake roof angled sharply to shed the heavy snow that fell during the long winters.

The caretaker's quarters over the garage, which was an exact miniature of the house proper, were inhabited from spring to fall by an elderly, morose ex-mechanic named MacGregor. Theoretically, MacGregor's job was to keep the house and ground tidy, the woodboxes filled and the plumbing in order. In actuality, he spent most of his time down in the boathouse fussing over Galloway's Estron, a diesel-powered launch.

MacGregor and only MacGregor operated the boat. He did not insist on this prerogative, he merely let it be understood that the Estron was high-spirited and temperamental, and, like any such woman, needed a strong and knowing hand if she were to avoid the disastrous impulses of her nature.

No one, not even his wife, knew why Galloway had bought the boat. Galloway hated and feared the water, the slightest swell made him seasick, and he had no talent for or interest in the Estron's mechanical aspects. When MacGregor was at the wheel, Galloway sat up front beside him, his fists clenched, his eyes moving uneasily in their sockets so that they seemed to be separately afloat, responding to every wave. When the trip was over and he was back on dry land, he always looked pale but exhilarated, as if he had proved himself by conquering an ancient enemy.

MacGregor's quarters were dark. When there was a weekend party going on he kept aloof, disdaining what he called the shenanigans, and appearing only when Galloway and his guests wanted to use the boat.

Turee parked his car between two jack pines and the two men began walking toward the lodge, single file and in step, like a pair of convicts chained together by invisible irons. Only one light was burning, in the main room downstairs, and the fire in the grate was barely alive.

Hepburn had gone to sleep in the red leather lounging chair, a book on his lap. He woke up at the sound of the front door opening, squinted across the room and said crossly, "About time somebody showed up. I feel as if I've been conducting a one-man wake."

Turee raised a sardonic eyebrow. "Maybe you have."

"No luck finding Ron?"

"He's not at home. We called Esther and she hasn't seen him or heard from him and doesn't seem to care one way or another. Then we talked to Thelma." He shot a glance at Harry to see if he would react to the name, but Harry was standing in front of the dying fire, his back to the room. "Thelma says Ron came by to pick up Harry, they had a drink together and some talk and then Ron left, presumably to come up here."

It was merely the skeleton of the truth. Only an expert could add the flesh and blood and muscle and all the vital organs that would make it a whole, borrowing a little here, a little there, from Thelma, from Harry, from Ron, from Esther, from all the other people who had affected all these people. A truth is as complicated as a man. Constructing and articulating a skeleton is not enough. It must be made to live.

So now what, Turee thought. What do I do now?

Hepburn provided a temporary answer. "You fellows want a drink?"

Harry had turned from the fire and picked up a magazine from the drum table. The magazine was an old *Maclean's* left over from the last time the lodge had been occupied, October of the previous year. The sight of the date sent a spasm of pain across Harry's eyes. *Last year*, he thought. *Last year at this time I was happy. I owned the world. Only last year. . .*

On a sudden impulse he folded the magazine and threw it with vicious accuracy into the center of the fire. It began to smolder.

"Now what the hell did you do that for?" Hepburn said.

"I don't know."

"There was an article in it I wanted to read."

"Sorry." The magazine had caught fire. Harry watched it burn with a kind of bitter satisfaction. Last year was over. "It's late. I'm tired. I'd better be going to bed."

"I've just made you a drink."

"I don't want it."

"You need it, Harry-boy."

"No thanks. It's been a long day. Good night."

"Take it easy, Harry-boy."

"Oh yes. Sure."

He dragged himself upstairs, leaning heavily on the banister as if his legs had withered. A minute later Turee heard the dropping of shoes, the squeak of springs, a long sigh.

Hepburn handed Turee his drink. "What's the matter with him, anyway?"

"What he said. A long day."

"Baloney. I've never seen Harry tired in my life."

"Now you have."

"There must be a reason. Something's up with Thelma, maybe?"

"Maybe."

"Thelma's a funny girl, if you ask me."

"I don't have to ask you," Turee said, staring gloomily into the fire, trying to imagine what Thelma was doing right now. Planning? Weeping? Having second and third thoughts, or sleeping peacefully in the conviction that she'd been absolutely right the first time? It was impossible to tell.

"But I guess all women are."

"Not all. Nancy's different." Turee believed this, and would continue to believe it until the next time he and his wife had a misunderstanding.

"You're prejudiced." Hepburn finished his drink and laid his empty glass decisively on the stone mantel. "Well, anyway, thank God I'm not married. On which cheerful note I shall depart."

"Go ahead. I'll turn out the lights."

"Perhaps you'd better leave a couple of them on in case Ron. . ."

"Oh. All right."

"Good night, Ralph."

"Good night."

Hepburn hesitated, stroking his chin. He was already beginning to need a shave, his eyes were red from too little sleeping and too much drinking, and his flannel shirt was dirty and lacking a button.

Why, he looks like a bum, Turee thought. Maybe he is. Maybe they all are, and this is no place for me. I should be home with my family, not up here pretending to be like the rest of them.

"Go to bed and get some sleep," he said roughly, irritated by his own thoughts. "God, what a night this has been."

"It's not finished."

"Well, finish it."

"O.K., but don't go into one of your famous grouches. That's not going to help. We're all in this together."

FIVE

The following morning, a few minutes after eight o'clock, Turee was awakened by the heavy pounding of the lion's-head knocker on the front door and the simultaneous ringing of the old cowbell that served as a mess call. Making little noises of distress, he reached for his shoes and put them on. This was all the dressing he had to do because he had, like the others, slept in his clothes. It was part of the tradition of these week ends at the lodge, originated many years before by Harry Bream. ("Makes me feel sporty," Harry had said. "Roughing it and all that.")

Feeling somewhat less than sporty, Turee stepped out into the hall where he met Winslow, wild-eyed and trembling, his back pressed against the wall.

"My God," Winslow croaked. "I'm dying. Dying."

"There's some bromo in the bathroom."

"My God. That bell. Tell it to stop. My ears..."

"Pull yourself together."

"I'm dying," Winslow said again and slid down the wall like a puppet whose strings had broken.

Turee stepped fastidiously around him and went on down the staircase. The encounter had done nothing to dispel the feeling he'd had the previous evening, that he didn't belong in this place, with these people. Though they were old friends, they seemed, under stress, to have become strangers, and their ways of living—or, in Winslow's case, dying—were alien to him. As he walked down the stairs the air from the room below rose up and struck his nostrils, and it seemed to him subtly poisonous, smelling of stale drinks and stale dreams.

He drew back the heavy wooden bolt on the front door and opened it, half expecting to see Ron.

During the early morning hours the wind had died down and the temperature had dropped. The ground was covered with hoarfrost glittering so whitely in the sun that, by contrast, Esther Galloway's skin looked very dark, as if she had quite suddenly and unseasonably acquired a tan.

She appeared to have dressed in a hurry and not for a trip. She was hatless, the shoes she wore were summer shoes without toes, and the Black Watch plaid coat she had clutched around her was one Turee remembered from a long way back. Esther always made such a point of elegance that it was a shock to see her looking quite ordinary, if not actually dowdy.

"Why, Esther."

"Hello, Ralph," she said crisply. "Surprise, surprise, eh?"

"Come in."

"I intend to."

He held the door open for her and she came inside, peeling off her gloves and agitating her head as if to shake the frost out of her hair.

"My ears ache. I drove with the windows open to help keep me awake. Silly, I guess." She laid her gloves on the mantel between two empty glasses left over from the night before. Then she picked up one of the glasses and sniffed with distaste. "Gin. When will Billy Winslow ever learn?"

"That's a difficult question."

"Did you have a nice party?"

"Not very."

"Ron—he's not here, of course?"

"No."

"No word at all?"

"None."

"Damn his eyes."

Some time during the early morning the fire had gone out, and the room was so cold that Esther's breath came out in little clouds of mist like smoke from a dragon's mouth.

Turee thought it suited her mood admirably.

"Damn his beady little eyes," she said. "All right, start making excuses for him, as usual, why don't you?"

Turee didn't answer because he was afraid of saying the wrong thing and there seemed no possible right thing.

"The way you fellows stick together, it's a scream really."

"Sit down, Esther, and I'll go and put on some coffee."

"Don't bother."

"It's no bo—"

"MacGregor's coming over in a minute to set the fires and make some breakfast." She turned and looked carefully around the room, one nostril curled very slightly. "The place needs an airing. It smells."

"I hadn't noticed." He had, though.

"I didn't expect him to be here, of course. I don't even know why I came except that I couldn't go back to sleep after you called last night, and I hate waiting, waiting and doing nothing. So I drove up here. I don't know why," she repeated. "It just seemed a good idea at the time. Now that I'm here I realize there's nothing I can do, is there? Except possibly help nurse a few hangovers. How's yours?"

"I don't have one," he said coldly.

"It couldn't have been a very good party, then."

"I said it wasn't."

"You could have another one today. Perhaps I'll even be invited to join in for once?"

"It's your house."

"All right, I'll invite myself. We'll all sit around and be jolly until His Nibs decides to reappear."

"You think it's that simple?"

She turned and addressed him very slowly and distinctly, as if she were talking to someone quite deaf or stupid. "Ron has complete identification papers in his wallet and his car registration fastened to the steering wheel. If there had been any accident I would have been notified. Isn't that correct?"

"I suppose it is."

"There's no supposing about it, surely. When an accident happens, it's reported immediately. That's the law."

It hadn't seemed to occur to her, and Turee didn't mention it, that laws could be broken.

Sounds of rattling and crashing from the kitchen indicated that Mac-Gregor was at work making breakfast. This was not part of his regular duties, and Turee knew from past experience that MacGregor would make himself as objectionable as possible; the coffee would be like bitter mud, the bacon burned and the eggs unrecognizable except for bits of broken eggshell that would crunch between the teeth like ground glass.

"MacGregor's in a sour mood," Turee said lightly. "We'll probably all be poisoned."

"At this particular moment I wouldn't care."

"Esther, for Pete's sake..."

"Oh, I know—you think I'm a drag and a droop. You think I always go around with a long face, spoiling for a fight."

"I don't..."

"You're Ron's friend, naturally you're on his side. I have to admit, I guess, that Ron makes a pretty good friend. But he's a lousy husband."

"Spare me the details."

"I wasn't going into details," she said flatly. "I was just about to make a generalization."

"Go ahead."

"Oh, I know you loathe generalizations, Ralph. You prefer intimate statistics like how many tons of mackerel were shipped last month from Newfoundland."

Turee's smile was wan. "Let's have the generalization."

"All right. Some men just shouldn't get married, they have nothing to give to a woman, not even the time of day. Oh, they can bring her an expensive diamond watch so she can tell the time of day for herself, but that's not *sharing* anything."

She sat down on the leather hassock in front of the unlit fire as if the sudden release of emotions had exhausted her, like a blood-letting. "I wanted very much to come up here with Ron this week end. Not that I'm particularly keen on fishing or even outdoor life, but I thought it would be fun to do the cooking and eat in front of the fireplace and take walks in the woods with Ron and the two boys. I asked him if I could come along and he didn't even take me seriously, the whole idea was so incredible to him."

She paused to take a long breath. "Why, the boys hardly know this place. They've only been here three times. Ron keeps making excuses—the boys might fall over the cliff, they might get bitten by a snake, they might drown, etcetera. But the real excuse he never mentions—the boys might interfere with him, they might want something from him that can't be bought with money, they might demand two or three ounces of Ron's very own self. They might even take a bite of his precious hide, not knowing, as I do, that it's quite unpalatable and indigestible."

"Esther..."

"That's all. I've finished."

"I don't mean to shut you up."

"You do, of course. But it's nice of you, anyway, to say you don't. I blab, don't I? But not to everybody. I wouldn't dream of saying any of these things to Billy Winslow or Joe Hepbum or even to Harry. They're a pretty stupid lot."

Turee was inclined to agree but he didn't care to encourage her in a new subject. He said, "You need some hot food and coffee, Esther. I'll go and see how MacGregor is getting along."

MacGregor was getting along exactly as Turee had anticipated. The bacon was already burned, the eggs were having convulsions in the skillet, and the odor of coffee was sharp as acid. MacGregor, wearing a chef's apron over his grease-stained overalls, was trying to sedate the eggs with liberal doses of salt and pepper.

"I'll take over," Turee said.

"What say, sir?"

"I'll carry on from here. You go and set the fire in the main room."

"Things got a mite burned," MacGregor said with satisfaction, as he removed the apron and handed it to Turee. "It's the will of the Lord."

"It's a funny thing that whenever the Lord picks something to be burned He chooses you as His instrument."

"Aye, sir, it's peculiar." He headed for the main room, whistling cheerfully through the gap between his two remaining front teeth. He had scored a victory, not just a personal victory, but one on behalf of all employees over all employers, and while Turee was not exactly an employer, still he was lined up on the same side. That was good enough. Let the bastard eat burned bacon. It was the will of the Lord.

After breakfast they sat in front of the pine-wood fire MacGregor had built and drank the bitter coffee out of heavy stone-ware mugs. Food and warmth had improved the situation. The pinched look around Esther's mouth and nostrils disappeared, and the uneasy little animals that Turee had felt moving around in his stomach were temporarily placated.

There was no sound at all from the upper rooms. Either Billy Winslow had gone back to sleep, or else his own prediction had been accurate and he had died. In either case, Turee didn't much care at the moment. The heat and color and movement of the flames held him in a kind of pleasant stupor. He listened to Esther talking the way one listens to background music, recognizing the songs but without paying any real attention. Esther's songs were about her two boys, Marv and Greg, and their latest pranks, and such was Turee's state of mind that he was able to listen without even wanting to cap her stories with stories about his own children.

"...are you paying attention, Ralph?"

"Eh? Oh, certainly, certainly."

"Well, don't you think I'm right?"

"Absolutely." This was safe enough. Every woman wanted to be told she was absolutely right, especially if she had some doubt of it.

"Well, she got quite unpleasant about it. She said I shouldn't spank either of them, no matter what they did. She said I shouldn't even *threaten* to spank them, that it would destroy their confidence in me, and that I was simply indulging my own anger. Now I ask you, how can you bring up two normal, lively boys without a spanking now and then?"

"I wouldn't know. I have four girls."

"That's a different matter. Girls are more—well, you can *reason* with them."

Turee was extremely surprised to learn this. "You can, eh?"

"Besides, she's got her nerve telling me how to bring up my children when she doesn't even have any of her own." Esther paused long enough to take a sip of coffee. "It's funny about that."

"About what?"

"She's so crazy about children," Esther said, "why doesn't she have some of her own?"

"Who?"

"The *who* we've been talking about."

"I must have missed the name."

"Thelma. She's so crazy about children, it's funny she doesn't have any of her own."

Turee rose and went over to the fire and kicked one of the logs with his foot. The pleasant stupor had vanished; the background music had turned into a loud cacophonous modern symphony, and he was compelled to listen to it carefully, to make sense out of it, distinguish the parts and players—Harry moaning on the trombone, Esther nagging at the drums, Thelma crowing through the clarinet, Ron off-stage with a silver whistle waiting for his cue. And the conductor out to lunch.

"After all, she's still young and healthy," Esther said. "Harry makes a decent salary, and he's just as fond of children as she is, I think. Don't you agree?"

"I haven't given it much thought."

"Neither have I, really. But it's not the kind of thing that needs much. I mean, the way he horses around with our two boys, you can tell he loves children. I think a baby would do them both a world of good."

A baby, yes, Turee thought. But not this baby. He remembered what Harry had said while they were driving back to the lodge from Wiarton: *"I haven't told Thelma yet, I want it to be a surprise, but I've visited two adoption agencies this week, making inquiries."*

"Well, don't you agree, Ralph? That's what they need, a baby?"

"Yes. For heaven's sake, *yes.*"

Esther looked at him in surprise. "What's gotten into you all of a sudden? Did I say something wrong?"

"No. I just consider it a subject that's none of my business."

"And none of mine either, is that what you're implying?"

Her face had hardened. "Very well, let's drop it. I don't like Thelma much anyway, if you want the truth."

"I've gathered that."

"Am I so obvious?"

"Obvious enough."

"Well, do you?"

"Do I what?"

"Like Thelma."

"I don't like anybody this morning," Turee said with an attempt at lightness. "Not even myself."

Esther smiled without humor. "We're in the same boat then... Listen, do you hear a car?"

"No."

"I'm sure I heard a car." She hurried to the front door pulling her plaid coat around her in anticipation of the cold air. "Maybe it's Ron. I'm *sure* it's Ron."

In spite of all the things she'd said about him she sounded excited and eager at the prospect of seeing him. Turee followed her outside. He could hear the car now quite plainly, and a moment later it came into sight, winding up the driveway between the spruce trees, leaving parallel black tracks in the frost.

It was a black and white car bearing the insignia of the Ontario Provincial Police on the front door. Esther turned, without a word, and went back into the lodge.

Turee waited while two uniformed policemen climbed ponderously out of the car and began walking toward him. *Well, this is it. Ron's been hurt. Or killed. They've come to tell us. This is it.*

The two policemen moved slowly, looking around at the property with the careful scrutiny of a pair of assessors. The older man was heavy-set and red-faced with a scar along the crease of his right cheek that gave him a false one-sided smile.

He spoke first. "Hello there. Is this where Mr. Ronald Galloway lives?"

"Yes," Turee said. The single word came out with difficulty. His contact with policemen had been limited to minor traffic tickets and he felt tongue-tied and uneasy, as if they had come to accuse him of a crime he had committed unawares.

"You're not Mr. Galloway, by any chance?"

"No. A guest."

"Mr. Galloway is here, then?"

"No. We—the other guests and myself—have been waiting for him since last night. I thought—that is, when I first saw you, I presumed you had some news of him."

"A missing report, if that's news. I'm Lieutenant Cavell and this is my colleague, Sergeant Newbridge. May I ask your name, sir?"

"Ralph Turee. I'm an associate professor at the University of Toronto." The words and the tone sounded snobbish and pretentious, as if he were deliberately attempting to lay a cloak of respectability over himself, like a child covering himself with a blanket and thinking he was well hidden. Yet the image irritated him. It seemed unfair to himself. He had committed no crime, he had nothing to hide, no reason to feel guilt.

Lieutenant Cavell's eyes narrowed, and the scar along his cheek deepened into a smile, as if he was quietly amused by such boyish antics as hiding under blankets. "Is that a fact, sir. Now suppose we go inside and talk a little about Mr. Galloway. Newbridge, you can look around out here."

"Yes sir," Newbridge said, but he appeared puzzled as if he hadn't any idea what to look for or what to do if he found it.

Turee and Cavell went into the lodge. Esther had taken her place in front of the fire and was sitting with her legs crossed and her hands in her lap, looking poised and casual. Too casual. Turee suspected that she'd been hiding behind the door listening to the conversation.

She acknowledged the introduction to Cavell politely enough, but she didn't rise or offer her hand or even appear anxious to hear what he had to say.

It turned out to be very little. "I have only the barest facts. Less than an hour ago I received a radio message from the Toronto division that Mr. Galloway had been reported missing by his wife. I have the time and place he was last seen, the make, model of his car, and that's about it. I am not in charge of the case or anything like that. I was merely asked to check up at this end, see if he had arrived or anything had been heard from him."

"Nothing," Esther said brusquely, "Not a word."

"Well now it seems to me that if he's still on the road it will be an easy matter to spot him. Late model Cadillac convertibles aren't common in this neck of the woods, and if he had the top down in this weather, as I've been informed, he should stick out like a fire engine. If, on the other hand, he got tired and pulled into some motel for the night, we shouldn't have too much trouble there either. Motels aren't common in this area."

"Suppose he isn't in the area."

"Why should we suppose that, Mrs. Galloway? He intended to come up here, didn't he?"

"Intentions can change."

"Is he the unpredictable kind who might take a notion to go off on a trip somewhere?"

Esther shook her head. "No. At least, not in the past."

"Is he a heavy drinker?"

"He gets drunk sometimes, but it's a quiet thing with Ron. He simply goes to sleep."

"I hesitate to ask this, Mrs. Galloway, but it's my duty. Have you any reason to believe he was interested in another woman?"

Esther glanced briefly at Turee before she answered. "Absolutely none."

Her tone was so positive that it seemed to fluster Cavell. As if to cover his confusion with some activity, he removed from an inner pocket of his jacket a small brown notebook. "According to my information, Mr. Galloway was last seen by a Mrs. Bream who lives in Weston. Is she a friend of yours, Mrs. Galloway?"

"Her husband and mine have been friends since Upper Canada College. Ron went to Weston to pick up Harry, that's Mr. Bream, and bring him along to the lodge. Only Harry had an emergency call to make first, so he came on alone. He's upstairs now, still asleep. I can wake him up, if you like."

Turee made a grimace of protest, but if Esther noticed it she paid no attention.

"I don't think Harry can tell you any more than you already know," Turee said. "I suggest we let him sleep. He had a rough night."

Cavell raised his eyebrows. "Rough in what sense, Mr. Turee?"

I've got to learn to curb my tongue, Turee thought, *and not to volunteer any information. Eventually they'll find out everything, about Thelma and the baby and Ron, but it's not my business to bring it out.* He said cautiously, "We were up nearly all night attempting to track Ron down."

"We?"

"Harry Bream and I, and the other two guests, Bill Winslow and Joe Hepburn."

"And just what form did these attempts take?"

"Harry and I drove back to Wiarton and called Esther—Mrs. Galloway—on the chance that Ron hadn't left the house for some reason or other. She told us he had left so then we called Harry's wife. She said that Ron had turned up on schedule, stayed long enough for a drink and then set out again."

"Is that all?"

"Well, Thelma—Mrs. Bream—said Ron had complained of feeling ill. There's a possibility there, don't you think?"

"Such as?"

"Well, Ron takes his symptoms pretty seriously. He may have stopped off to see a doctor, he may even be in a hospital somewhere."

"He's as healthy as a horse," Esther said.

"Yes, but *he* doesn't think so."

"Besides, he's scared to death of hospitals. He had to be practically dragged to come and see me when the boys were born."

Cavell stared at her thoughtfully. "It seems to me you're not very willing to accept any theory, Mrs. Galloway."

"Willing, yes. Able, no. I know my husband quite thoroughly and none of the possibilities suggested so far has seemed plausible."

"Have you any theory of your own, Mrs. Galloway?"

"I might have."

"If you had," Cavell said dryly, "what would it be?"

"I think Ron may be trying to avoid me, for some reason."

It was so close to what Turee himself was thinking that he made a little sound of surprise, like a man who's just had his mind read.

Cavell said, "Why should your husband be trying to avoid you, Mrs. Galloway?"

"I don't—know." She flashed another sharp look at Turee as if she half suspected that he could supply the answer if he chose to.

Turee thought, *she's too damned bright for her own good. And too honest to hide it. No wonder she and Ron have some bad times.*

"You might," Esther added, to Cavell, "talk to Harry Bream."

"Why?"

"He and my husband are what you might call buddies." She put a sneer in the word. "If Ron has any secrets, Harry is his most likely confidant."

Turee made one more attempt to spare Harry the ordeal. "No more likely than I, surely, Esther?"

"Much more and you know it."

"All right then. I'll go and wake him up."

SIX

Harry was still asleep, lying on his stomach and without a pillow, like a baby; and, as a baby will suck at things for comfort and security, so Harry had seized a corner of the blanket and had it pressed tightly against his mouth.

The night table beside the bed held an unlabeled bottle of red capsules and a nearly empty water glass.

"Harry? Hey. Harry."

He did not respond either to his name or the touch of Turee's hand on his shoulder. Turee leaned down and with great effort rolled him over on his back. Then he put his hand firmly under Harry's chin and moved his head from side to side several times until Harry's eyes opened.

"Don't do that," Harry said.

"Come on, wake up."

"It's cold."

"It's warmer downstairs. Get your shoes on. We have a visitor."

"Don't care." He closed his eyes again. "Don't care a damn."

"How many of those red capsules did you take?"

"Don't remember. Doesn't matter."

"It matters now." Turee put his hands under Harry's shoulders and forced him to a sitting position. Harry's head lolled back and forth as if his neck was broken.

"Why?" Harry said. "Why it matters?"

"There's a policeman downstairs, he wants to talk to you."

"Why?"

"About Ron. They're still trying to find Ron. Esther reported his absence to the police and then she drove on up here."

"Esther? Here?" He shook off Turee's hand and sat up by himself. His tone was more alert and his eyes had begun to focus properly. "Esther shouldn't have come here."

"Why not?"

"The place is a mess."

"So?"

"We'll have to clean it up a bit. Esther hates a mess."

Like the other fellows, Harry stood in considerable awe of Esther. It was not that she was unpleasant to them, but she had a subtle way of always being right that reduced them to a state of self-doubt and confusion. She could, without saying a word, walk through a room and indicate, merely by her posture and a faintly lifted eyebrow, that there were cobwebs on the rafters and dust under the rugs. And sure enough, if anyone took the trouble to look, the cobwebs would be there, and so would the dust.

Harry peered down at his wrist watch. "It's not even nine o'clock."

"I know."

"Esther—she must have stayed up all night."

"Practically."

"Why did she decide to come here?"

"To check up on Ron, for herself."

"She doesn't trust us, I guess."

"Not very much."

"What does she think we're doing, covering up for him?"

"Maybe."

"Covering up what, I'd like to know. Does she think we bring *women* up here, or something?"

"Could be."

"My God, that's a laugh."

"Not to her, it isn't."

"Esther's a funny girl. When I compare her with Thelma, for instance—why that's the last thing in the world Thelma would suspect. Thelma *likes* me to go away and have a good time. There isn't a selfish bone in her body."

Turee felt like gagging but he managed to say quite calmly, "Hurry up and get ready."

"All right." Harry swung his legs over the side of the bed and began putting on his shoes. "A policeman, eh?"

"Yes.

"What kind?"

"One of the Provincial Police on duty in this area. He got the report from Toronto by radio and was asked to check up."

"And you say Esther reported it?"

"Yes."

"Funny, when you talked to her last night she wasn't worried at all, wouldn't hear of bringing in the police."

Turee, too, had noticed the discrepancy but had ascribed it merely to the unpredictability of women.

Harry stood up, ran a comb through his hair, and buttoned the collar of his flannel shirt. "I ought to shave, Esther being here and all that."

"There isn't time."

"Thelma wouldn't like it if she..."

"Thelma's not here."

"Well, all right."

"And Harry, listen, this inspector, he seems pretty cagey. Watch yourself."

"How do you mean?" Harry asked.

"Don't talk too much."

"About what?"

"About anything you and I discussed last night."

"We discussed a lot of things last night."

"You know what I'm referring to."

"But I don't. So help me, I don't."

"About Thelma—Ron's having a crush on her, I mean. Don't mention it."

Harry blinked. "Why should I? It's not true. I told you that last night. Thelma likes to daydream, to pretend things. I told you that last..."

"I know you told me."

"Well, don't you believe it?"

"Certainly, certainly," Turee said, trying to keep the irritation out of his voice. "But the Inspector might not. He doesn't know Thelma the way we do. So keep quiet about it, eh?"

"You never give me any damn credit for any damn sense. You'd think I was a moron."

"Everybody's a moron about something."

"Meaning?"

"No meaning, no meaning at all," Turee said and walked out of the room with Harry following along behind taking short angry little steps.

Downstairs, Esther and the Inspector had apparently reached the end of their conversation. Cavell, an unlit pipe in his hand, was studying the rows of books in the bookshelves, while Esther stood with her back to the fire, watching him with silent intensity. She was smoking a cigarette, rapidly and furiously, as if she had a great many things that she wanted to say and couldn't, and was using the cigarette as a cork to bottle them up.

Turee introduced Harry and Cavell, and then he turned and said pointedly to Esther, "You and I can wait in the game room. The Inspector might want to talk to Harry alone."

Esther gave him a sharp look, but she made no verbal objection as he put his hand on her elbow and guided her out into the hall.

The game room, which was across the hall from the kitchen, contained ample proof that the fellows were not as enthusiastic about fishing as they were about certain other sports: a well-used poker table with ivory chips, a pinball machine, an elaborately carved billiard table with a dozen cues racked up on the knotty pine wall.

Esther perched on the side of the billiard table, her right leg swinging aggressively as if it wanted to kick at something or someone.

She said, "All right, let's have it."

"Have what?"

"The reason you spirited me away from Harry and the Inspector."

Turee smiled. "My dear Esther, no one spirited you away. You're too big a girl to be spirited away, for one thing."

"Don't go off on verbal maneuvers. Why were you so anxious to get rid of me?"

"I wasn't anxious. I simply thought it would be polite if you and I let the Inspector talk to Harry in private."

"Politeness. That was one reason?"

"Certainly."

"Now what are some others?"

"Others?"

"You always have an ulterior motive, Ralph, sometimes several of them. You remind me of a set of boxes the boys used to play with when they were younger—when you open the largest one, you find a smaller one, and inside that, still a smaller one, and so on."

"I'm not sure I follow you."

"Every time you give me a motive for doing something, I know there's another reason inside it, and yet another inside that one. Inside every box there's a motive."

"It can't go on ad infinitum. What's in the smallest box?"

"Your fat little ego."

Turee's laugh had a brittle note. "You make me sound extremely complicated."

"Or devious."

"I'll make you a promise, Esther. If I ever open that last box, I'll invite you over. Will you come?"

"With bells on," Esther said primly. "I wouldn't miss it for the world."

"Of course, I don't guarantee there'll be much of a surprise inside. Just one fat little ego." Turee could see that she was enjoying the game; he was even beginning to enjoy it himself. "What do you suppose it'll look like?"

"A kewpie doll. One of those tiny celluloid kewpie dolls you can buy in the dime store."

"That's not very flattering."

"Oh it is, really. Compared to what I think mine would look like. Or Ron's."

"What about Ron's?"

"Ron would never get to the last box. Or if he did, he'd never invite me over to see it, or anyone else. It would be strictly a private showing."

"I wish you could think more kindly of Ron."

"I wish I could, too," Esther said slowly. "I happen to love him."

MacGregor had laid a fire in the fireplace and the room by this time was so warm that the windows had steamed up. Turee had a childish impulse to go over and write his name in the steam, or print a message or draw a picture—a heart with an arrow piercing it, and underneath, ESTHER LOVES RON.

"I'm not very sensible," Esther said, in a detached manner. "I appear to be sometimes—very sensible and efficient and practical. Actually it's all a front. I'm a fool, and the worst kind, too, the kind that knows it, that sees ahead of time all the wrong things to do and does them anyway. I fell in love with Ron the first time I met him. I knew he had a wife and child. I knew he was spoiled by too much money and a terribly foolish set of parents, I knew our backgrounds and our tastes were completely different. I went after him anyway, tooth and nail. It was easy. Ron was a perfect setup. He still is."

"How do you mean that?"

"If I could do it, any woman could. Or can."

"Now, Esther, don't go..."

"Ron is a patsy. The perfect patsy."

"Your circumstances aren't quite the same as Dorothy's."

"Oh, they're different, all right. But are they any better?"

It was, perhaps, the opportune time to tell her everything he knew about Thelma and Ron, but Turee had neither the courage nor the desire, nor even all the facts. It seemed to him a fateful piece of irony that Esther should now find herself in the same position into which she had forced another woman a long time ago. Somebody would have to tell her. Who, he wondered, had told Dorothy?

Turee had not seen Ron's first wife, Dorothy, for a number of years. Dorothy was a wispy blonde, the daughter of a furniture manufacturer, and as badly spoiled in her own way as Ron was in his. A confirmed hypochondriac before she was out of her teens, by the time she married, at twenty-one, she had become the prey of every quack in the city. Her infrequent outings with her husband, to concerts or plays or dinner parties, were always interrupted between acts, during intermission or before dessert, by sharp and mysterious pains that sent her home, usually alone. Her one pregnancy, spent largely in bed, had resulted, to everyone's surprise, especially Dorothy's, in a perfectly normal girl child. The girl was raised from the beginning by a governess, so that Dorothy was left free to concentrate on her multitude of symptoms. If Ron had been, as Esther claimed, the perfect setup, it was, without doubt, largely due to Dorothy.

The last news Turee had had of Dorothy was from Harry who went to see her once or twice a year for old times' sake. Harry reported that she was living in her mother's town house on the north side, with two special nurses in attendance, a recluse before she was forty. She had confided to Harry, whom she had always liked, perhaps because of his interest in drugs and medicines, that she was suffering from an obscure malady of the bloodstream and would not last the year. She invited Harry to attend her funeral and Harry, ever one to oblige, had accepted the invitation.

Dorothy and Esther—they were poles apart, and Turee wondered how Ron could have married them both. Perhaps Dorothy's frailty had made him feel more masculine, but after a liberal dose of that, he married Esther as an antidote, someone he could lean on.

Esther said suddenly, "Would you like to play a game of billiards?"

"Not much."

"Nor I, really. I just thought it would help pass the time. I guess I should-n't have come up here. There's nothing I can do, is there?"

"Now that the police are in charge we'd better let them handle every-thing. A bunch of amateurs milling around won't help."

"Ah, yes, the jolly old police."

"Come here a minute." Turee took his handkerchief and rubbed some of the steam off one of the windows. Outside, the younger policeman, New-bridge, was examining the tire tracks on the driveway. "Look out there."

Esther looked. "Well?"

"The police know what they're doing."

"Do they?" She turned from the window. "They can examine all the tire tracks to hell and back, but they're not going to find Ron that way."

"All right, be cynical," Turee said. "At least you had sense enough to call them in."

"That was sense?"

"Yes."

"Maybe you're right. But it wasn't mine."

"What do you mean?"

"I didn't call the police," Esther said. "I didn't call anyone."

SEVEN

The instant she put down the phone she knew she'd done something foolish. Not the call itself, that was necessary, but claiming to be Mrs. Galloway—that was the mistake. And yet, while she was talking, it had seemed so natural to pretend to be Ron's wife. "This is Mrs. Ronald Galloway"—the sound of it was exactly right.

After the phone call she went back upstairs to bed and to sleep, but in less than an hour she was awakened again by a bad dream. She could not remember the details of the dream, only that they had all been caught in a great flood, she and Ron and the baby and Harry, and they were being swept, screaming, out to sea. She awoke with the scream on her lips.

Her first thought was not of Ron or of Harry, but of the baby growing inside her. She pressed one hand gently to her stomach to calm the child in case it had been disturbed by the dream. Staring wide-eyed up at the ceiling she tried to imagine through her fingertips the child's contours, the tiny head, the curved neck, the curled-up little body. Thelma had worked in a doctor's office before she married Harry, and she knew quite well that the fetus at this early stage was quite hideous and bore almost no resemblance to a human baby. But when she pictured her own baby in her mind, it was beautiful, and perfectly formed and proportioned, like a tiny doll.

She kept her hand pressed to her stomach until she was satisfied that she'd felt a very faint movement, then she swung her feet over the side of the bed and stood up. Almost immediately a wave of nausea flooded over her. She opened her mouth and breathed deeply, watching herself in the bureau mirror and thinking how funny she looked and how glad she was that Harry wasn't there to see her, or to ask questions or give advice.

Throughout most of her life Thelma had suffered from a nagging self-consciousness about her appearance. She knew she was not pretty, and now that she was beginning to gain weight she looked almost dumpy. But Harry's unlimited devotion had given her both self-confidence and a sense of herself as a woman, so that the over-all impression she presented was one of graciousness and femininity. Her friends spoke of her as "attractive," a term intended to obscure some of nature's mistakes. What justified the term in Thelma's case was the quality of her expression, which was warm and friendly and humorous. Children passing on the street smiled at her spontaneously, clerks in stores usually gave her special attention, and strangers she met at bus stops confided in her the most intimate details of their lives, mainly because Thelma looked at them as if she were really interested. Occasionally she was. But most of the time her expression was automatic and had nothing to do with how or what she was feeling. Turee called it "Thelma's wan smile," Harry called it her "sweet look," Ron had never noticed it.

When the nausea had passed, Thelma put on her Sunday housecoat and combed her long hair carefully and tied it back with a ribbon to match the housecoat. Her eyes were still swollen from last night's weeping, and the lids were transparent and tinged with purple like the skin of an onion. She bathed them in cold water and applied witch-hazel pads before going out to the back veranda to pick up the milk and the Sunday paper.

It was a beautiful spring day, alive with promises. Her neighbor, a widow named Mrs. Malverson, was already out in the garden cultivating her daffodils which had just come into bloom.

"Hi there, Thelma."

"Good morning, Mrs. Malverson."

"This is a day, isn't it? Isn't this a day, though?"

"It's lovely, yes."

"You don't look so good, dear."

"I'm fine." A minute ago it had been true, but now the stab of the sharp sunlight hurt her eyes and its warmth made her feel feverish. She hugged the cold milk bottle to her breast.

"I bet you're tired this morning. I saw your lights on till all hours last night."

That snoop, Thelma thought, that nasty old snoop. But she couldn't have seen Ron here—she always goes to the movies on Saturday night. "I couldn't sleep."

"Couldn't sleep, my land, you should have asked your husband for some pills. The ones he gave me last month for my neuralgia, they were a real blessing."

"My husband went up north, fishing."

"Did he now. Well, he couldn't have picked nicer weather. I suppose you've noticed my early daffodils?"

"You showed them to me yesterday."

"Mulching, that's the secret. You and your husband should start a compost heap. How long's he going to be away?"

"I'm not sure."

Mrs. Malverson pushed back her straw gardening hat and wiped the perspiration off her forehead with her canvas glove. The gesture left a streak of dirt. "I'll tell you what. Let's go to church."

"No, thank you just the same. I don't feel..."

"You should come and get better acquainted at our little church. Today we're having a very special service. Our leader is going to read the flowers."

"Read the *flowers?*"

Mrs. Malverson threw back her head and laughed. "Spoken like a true unbeliever, curl of the lip and all. Well, I don't mind. I was an unbeliever once myself. I said those very words exactly the way you just said them. Reads the *flowers*, I said, just like that. Nevertheless, that's what our leader does. He reads the flowers that we bring, and in every flower there is a message from someone dear to us who is far away."

Thelma stood nervous and indecisive, still clutching the Sunday paper and the milk bottle, which was beginning to weigh a ton. Yet she could not seem to drag herself away. Mrs. Malverson's tongue and eye held her as securely as a lepidopterist's pin holds a moth.

"Thelma," Mrs. Malverson said softly, "you've changed. What's happened to you?"

"Nothing."

"I see such sorrow in you lately. Have you lost touch with someone dear to you?"

Thelma stared at her, pale and silent.

"Ah, that's it. You've lost touch with someone dear to you and now you want a message, don't you? Yes, I can see you badly want a message. Well, that's easy. Come to church with me and bring a flower to be read."

"No, I really..."

"Fresh, the flower must be fresh, and if you bring its root too, smelling of God's earth, so much the better. Often the messages are stronger when the root is attached. This person you want a message from, is it a woman?"

"No."

"A man, then. A man you have lost touch with. No, Thelma, I'm not prying. I only need to find out one other detail, for the color of the flower you bring will depend on it."

"Color?"

"The color's important. If he is alive, you will take a red flower, bright as blood. If he is what you call dead—we hate to use that term, it's so misleading—but if he is dead, you will take a white flower."

Thelma closed her eyes and began to sway. She could feel the milk bottle slipping out of her hands, she could hear the crash of glass and Mrs. Malverson's cry of dismay, but she was powerless to respond. *If he is what you call dead—we hate to use that term—dead ...*

"My goodness, I hope I didn't say anything to upset you." Mrs. Malverson lifted her skirt, stepped over the tiny boxwood hedge that divided the two properties, crossed the the driveway, and started up the steps of Thelma's back veranda, "Here, let me help you clean up that mess."

"No!"

"Well, it's the least I can do, seeing I..."

"Go away. Just go away."

"Well, my goodness, you fly off the handle at anything these days. A body might think you were pregnant."

"Shut up and leave me alone!"

"Well. Well," Mrs. Malverson said and retreated to her own yard, her straw hat bouncing angrily as she moved. This was the thanks you got for trying to bring a little joy into someone's life.

Ignoring the mess on the veranda, Thelma went back into the house and sat down at the kitchen table. A pair of curious houseflies chased each other in and out of the open window and Thelma watched them, thinking, Harry must put on the screens this week...

She had been doing this quite often lately, considering the future as if it were going to be a repetition of the present, thinking of little things that should be done around the house or yard, making tentative plans for the Decoration Day week end. She knew better. She knew that Harry and she weren't going to live in this house any longer; whoever put the screens on for the summer, it would not be Harry. She knew, too, that there were other, greater changes waiting for her around the next corner of time. She could not avoid this corner, every tick of the clock brought her inexorably closer to it, no matter how tenaciously a part of her mind tried to stay on a secure day-to-day basis.

Harry will...

No, Harry will not, she thought. I must get used to the idea the we won't be here. Some stranger will be putting on the screens, at the request of his wife, also a stranger. They will live in our house, these two strangers, and pretty soon it will be theirs entirely. Well, I mustn't get sentimental about it. I've never liked the place much. It's the same as thousands of other houses in Ontario, a square red-brick box. I want to live in a house without stairs, a climate without winter.

The telephone began to ring in the dining room. She was sure it was Harry calling but she was not sure enough to keep from answering it.

"Hello?"

"Thelma, is that you, honey?"

"Yes."

"Are you feeling all right again?"

"Yes."

"Listen, dear, I'm phoning from Wiarton. Ron hasn't shown up yet. I don't suppose you've had any news at that end?"

"No."

"Well, don't worry, everything will turn out right."

"Will it," Thelma said, and hung up.

A minute later the phone began ringing again. Thelma turned her back on it. As she walked toward the kitchen she counted each ring deliberately, like a defiant child counting the number of times she is called to supper: "Thelma. Thelma? Thelma! Thelma..."

Long after the final ring, the sharp shrill sound kept echoing in her ears, stirring up memories.

"*Thelma? You hear me, Thelma?*"

Oh yes, Aunt May, I hear you. Everyone in the city can hear you.

"*You come in this house right away and finish up these dishes.*"

No, Aunt May.

"*Hiding again, aren't you, pretending you don't hear me, well, you don't fool me. Thelma!*"

I can fool you any time.

"*Sneaky, that's what you are, a born sneak. If you don't march right in this house, I'm gonna write your ma and tell her I can't look after you. The Lord knows you're eating me out of house and home, and not a penny does she send for your keep. We'll all end up in the poorhouse, how would you like that, Miss Royalty too good to do dishes?*"

If you end up in the poorhouse I'll come and visit you dressed in mink and diamonds.

"*Thelma Schaefer, where you are you hiding?*"

Under the porch. You could reach out and touch me. Do. I'll bite.

"*That no-good sister of mine, what else would you expect from her but a no-good child. You answer me, you hear?*"

Aunt May had been dead for years, but every shrill sound reminded Thelma of her, an alarm clock, a telephone, a doorbell. Each was the voice of authority, the call to duty: Come in and do the dishes. Get up and go to work. Answer the phone and talk to Harry.

The child hiding under the porch was imprisoned forever within Thelma. Aunt May's voice still soured the sweetest melody, and the bile green of her nature had colored the universe.

Thelma began to make breakfast, moving around the kitchen with a kind of grim efficiency, as if she had in some way been challenged to prove her worth.

Aunt May was wrong, she thought. I won't end up in the poorhouse. There's Ron's money, a lot of money. My baby will have security and love. There'll be no Aunt May for him, no poverty, no fear. He'll have a house without stairs, a climate without winter, no running nose for him from fall to spring like the kids around here. He'll have the best care, the best clothes, the best schools...

She ate her breakfast as if in a dream, not enjoying it, not even tasting it, eating for the sake of the baby which needed nourishment. After she had finished, she took her coffee into the parlor at the front of the house.

The room was cool and dark, the shades still drawn from the previous night when she had waited there listening for the sound of Ron's car on the driveway. It was spring now, but the parlor still smelled of winter, of the long weeks of unopened windows and artificial heat, a close dusty smell which, even into autumn, never quite disappeared.

Thelma pulled up the shades and opened two of the windows. Summer sounds drifted in, the children from down the street fighting over a bicycle, the whirr of roller skates, the pounding of a hammer. The young married man who lived across the road was busy removing his storm windows while his wife watched him with great pride as if he were performing some unusual feat. The sun had drawn everyone out of doors like a magnet, but because the spring was new and people were still a little self-conscious about being outside, idle, and bare-armed and bareheaded, they had to find excuses to stay out. Cars were being washed, screens painted, babies walked, lawns rolled, gossip exchanged.

And Thelma, watching, thought, I wonder how much each of them knows about me. When it all comes out in the papers—and it will, I must face that fact—when they find out, will they be surprised, or will they claim they suspected it all along because they'd often seen Ron's car here?

The telephone in the dining room began to ring again. She was positive this time that it was Harry, and she would have let the call go unanswered, except for the fact that the front windows were now open and the people across street could hear the phone ringing quite plainly. They knew she was at home, they'd seen her at the window, and they would wonder why she didn't answer. It was the kind of neighborhood, the kind of country, where little things like that didn't go unnoticed.

She hurried into the dining room and picked up the receiver, annoyed by Harry's persistence. "Hello."

"Is this the Bream residence?"

"Yes."

The woman's voice was low and soft, and self-consciously cultured. "Is Mr. Bream at home?"

"No. I'm his wife, Thelma Bream."

"This is Joyce Reynold calling, Mrs. Bream. You may recall we met two or three years ago, and of course I've known Harry for a long time. He's been very kind to my poor daughter, Dorothy. Do you expect him home soon?"

"I'm afraid not. But if there's anything I can do..."

"Sweet of you, my dear, but I'm not sure, I'm simply not sure. A very perplexing thing has happened. It happened last night, actually, but it seemed too late to call Harry and besides I wasn't sure what I was expected to do. I'm still not. You didn't receive a rather peculiar call from Ron Galloway last night?"

"No." Thelma took a deep breath. "How do you mean, peculiar?"

"Confused. Rambling. Those are Dorothy's words. You see, the call wasn't to me but to Dorothy. I was tucking her in bed for the night when the telephone rang and it was Ron wanting to talk to Dorothy. We haven't heard from him in years, and I assumed it must be important so I allowed Dorothy to talk to him. She'd had a good day and was feeling stronger than usual, and I like to let her have a bit of excitement when I'm certain no harm will come of it. I was wrong, of course. I should have realized the man was drunk or out of his mind. Dorothy's been in a frightful state ever since."

"How does Harry come into it, Mrs. Reynold?"

"He mentioned Harry several times, something about making amends and regretting what he'd done to Harry. Now obviously that doesn't make sense, does it? Ron would never do anything to Harry, the two have been thick as thieves ever since they were children. And why, after all these years, should Ron suddenly call Dorothy and get maudlin about his treatment of her?"

"I don't—know."

"The poor child has suffered enough. I thought perhaps if Harry were there and could come and talk to her it might calm her down a bit. She's always been fond of Harry, and she seems to think, from Ron's conversation, that Ron wanted her to see Harry."

"Why?"

"He seemed to believe he'd done something terrible. Has he?"

"No." The word was sharp and final.

"Have you seen him recently?"

"Yes."

"Did he seem quite normal to you?"

"Yes. Quite normal."

"How very puzzling. Surely a normal man doesn't suddenly call up a former wife he hasn't seen in years and tell her he wants to apologize before he leaves."

"*Leaves?*"

"He said he was going away. And when Dorothy asked him where, he said he couldn't tell her, it was an undiscovered country. According to Dorothy, it sounded as if he was quoting a line of poetry."

Thelma leaned back and closed her eyes. *The undiscover'd country, from whose bourn no traveller returns.*

"Mrs. Bream? Are you still there?"

"Yes." A reluctant whisper. When Aunt May called, Thelma could hide and pretend she hadn't heard. But this time there was no place to hide. "Yes, Mrs. Reynold, I'm here."

"Did Ron say anything to you or Harry about taking a trip?"

"No."

"I'm perplexed, I truly am. How inconsiderate of Ron to annoy people like this, and I shall tell him so the first chance I get. As a matter of fact, I tried to call his house a little while ago but no one answered. Do you suppose he's already left?"

"I don't know."

"Undiscovered country," Mrs. Reynold said. "Undiscovered country, *indeed.*"

"I must—I must go now, Mrs. Reynold."

"Of course. I'm sorry to have taken up so much of your time. And I do hope I haven't upset you in any way."

I'll—I'll give Harry your message when he comes home."

"Thank you, child. I'm sure Harry will know what to do."

"Good-bye."

When she'd put down the telephone, she wiped her right hand carefully with a handkerchief, as if she had touched something dirty and had been contaminated. Then she rose and groped her way to the stairs. The child in her womb felt as heavy as stone.

She reached her room, exhausted, and fell across the bed on her stomach with her arms outstretched. *High school. The smell of books and dust, and oiled wood floors. Memory work today, class. It's your turn, Thelma. We had the first part of the soliloquy last week. No need to repeat. Start with "For who would bear..." Quiet, class, while Thelma recites.*

> *"For who would bear the whips and scorns of time,*
> *Th' oppressor's wrong, the proud man's contumely,*
> *The pangs of despis'd love, the law's delay,*
> *The insolence of office, and the spurns*
> *That patient merit of th' unworthy takes,*
> *When he himself might his quietus make*
> *With a bare bodkin? Who would these fardels bear,*
> *To grunt and sweat under a weary life..."*

Go on, Thelma.
No, I can't. I don't remember!
Go on, Thelma.

> *"...But that the dread of something after death*
> *The undiscover'd country, from whose bourn*
> *No traveller returns..."*

Such beautiful language, the teacher said. Lovely, lovely. But do put a little more feeling into it, Thelma.

EIGHT

It was ten o'clock, Sunday morning, and a woman unknown to any of the principals in the case was getting ready to go to church. Her name was Celia Roy, she lived alone on the outskirts of the small town of Thornbury on Georgian Bay, she was a widow with a pension and two married daughters and no hope of much more in this life.

She was the kind of woman to whom nothing extraordinary had ever happened. True, she'd seen people die, babies born, mistakes committed, tragedies enacted, sacrifices made, but this was all run-of-the-mill stuff to Celia. What she dreamed of, in her declining years, was winning a new car on a radio quiz program, or an all-expense trip to Hollywood in a slogan contest, or a thousand dollars for submitting the best recipe. She would have settled for a really good night at the church bingo on Thursday, but even that hadn't happened.

She put on her hat in front of the sideboard mirror. She'd worn the hat for three years and could have put it on properly in pitch darkness, but she stood in front of the mirror out of habit, not really seeing either the hat or herself under it. Her hands were trembling with excitement and fear. It was the Sabbath, she was on her way to church, and she'd done something wrong, perhaps quite wrong. What was more, she had no intention of telling anyone about it. The dog was dead. She'd buried him herself in the dark of night, and no one knew a thing about it.

She heard her daughter Mabel's old Ford wheeze up in front of the house and cough to a stop. Each time Celia heard this noise she expected it to be the car's last—it sounded exactly like old Mr. Thurston's death rattle—but each time, under Mabel's expert pumping and pounding and shouting, the car would miraculously come to life in every joint and pulsate vigorously as if to deny all charges of age and infirmity.

Mabel bounded in the front door. She was a lively young woman with a hearty laugh and a quick temper and little or no patience with people who slunk, as she called it, through life.

"Hi. Ready, Mom?"

"Just about," Celia said. "I look a fright. It's this hat. It's getting out of shape."

"Who isn't," Mabel said cheerfully. "I told you to get a new one for Easter."

"And what to use for money?"

"Speaking of money, I don't have a cent for the collection plate. John didn't get his check, this is the third time in a row it's been late." She saw her mother's purse lying on the wicker jardiniere and picked it up. "Mind if I borrow a quarter?"

Celia had turned quite white. "Stop. Wait."

"What's the matter with you?"

"I—I don't like other people opening my purse."

"You never objected before."

"Well, I am now. Give it here."

"Honestly, honestly, you'd think I was trying to steal from you or something."

"I want none of your lip. Give me that purse."

"I just don't like your attitude, like I was a thief or something. What's wrong with you anyway? You're shaking like a leaf."

"You show some respect, girl. Now give me..."

"All right. Here's your old purse. Catch."

Celia's reflexes were no longer quick enough to respond to the unexpected, and the purse landed at her feet, the clasp open, the contents strewn on the hooked rug: a lace handkerchief, a pencil, a tarnished silver compact, a creased snapshot of Mabel's two children, a worn calfskin change purse, a prayer book, a post card, an alligator wallet.

"Gee, I'm sorry," Mabel said. "Honestly, I thought you'd catch it. Here, I'll pick everything up for you."

But Celia was already on her knees, scooping up her things and stuffing them back into her purse with fierce determination.

"Mom."

"Fresh. That's what you are. Fresh."

"I didn't know you had a wallet, Mom."

"There's lots you don't know, including how to behave to your elders."

"Where did you get it?"

"Someone gave it to me. As a gift."

"It looks like genuine alligator."

"So?"

"Mom. It don't make sense. Who would give you a genuine alligator wallet?"

"A man, a very rich man." Celia rose, clutching her purse to her chest. "Now that's all I can tell you. The rest is my business, and my business alone."

"You don't know any very rich man."

"I do, too."

"Where did you meet him?"

"On the road, just outside."

"Mom."

"It's the truth, so help me. I met him on the road."

"And he just came up and tipped his hat and said, madam, I'm a very rich man, here is my genuine alligator wallet. Mom."

"Stop saying *mom* like that."

"Well, it don't make sense."

"What's more," Celia said loftily, "you use bad grammar. That's what comes of marrying beneath you. Well, I warned you. I said, he's a common laborer, he'll drag you down with him and you with a high school education..."

"Don't change the subject, Mom. I want to hear more about the very rich man. He intrigues me."

"And don't get ironical-sounding either. It so happens I'm telling the truth and I don't expect my own child to be ironical-sounding to me."

"What are you going to do when other people notice the wallet? Tell them the same story you told me?"

"Nobody else is going to notice it."

"How come?"

"I'm going to get rid of it, that's how come."

"Get *rid* of it! Mom, are you losing your mind? Someone gives you a genuine alligator wallet and now you say you're going to get rid of it. It's worth, well, ten dollars at least. And now you say you're going..."

"Stop it. Stop pestering me."

"But it just don't make sense, Mom. A real genuine alligator wallet and you want to get rid of it, I never heard anything so crazy."

They stared at each other across the room, Celia pale and grim, and her daughter red-faced and bewildered.

"I'll keep the money," Celia said finally.

"What money?"

"There's money in it."

"How much?"

"Nearly a hundred *dollars.*"

"A hundred dollars?"

"Not quite. Nearly." Celia clung to the word as if it somehow provided a saving grace.

"Mom. Where did you get it?"

"I told you. The man gave it to me."

"When?"

"Last night."

"Why?"

"For Laddie. To pay for Laddie."

"What's Laddie got to do with it?"

"Don't you shout at me! I haven't done anything wrong!"

"Something happened to Laddie?"

"Yes."

"He's dead?"

"Yes."

"And you don't even sound sorry," Mabel said coldly. "You don't even sound sorry. Your own dog."

"I *am* sorry! Only it wasn't my fault, he ran out in the road. He couldn't see very well anyway any more, and the car was speeding."

"What car?"

"One of those sporty kinds without a roof."

"A convertible."

"I guess so. There was a man driving. He had on one of those fancy plaid caps people wear sometimes in the movies. He knew right away he'd hit Laddie, I guess he must have heard me scream too. He slowed up and yelled a word back at me, it sounded like 'sorry.' Then he threw something out of the car. At first I didn't know what it was."

"But you found out quick enough, eh?"

"I don't like your tone. It's not respectful."

"Stop bothering about tones and get back to facts. What happened then?"

"The car went on. Laddie was lying by the side of the road. I picked him up and I could tell right away he was dead. So I buried him myself, in the back yard."

"And kept the wallet."

"Why shouldn't I?"

Mabel shook her head. "It just don't sound right to me. It sounds sneaky, if you want the truth."

"The money's mine. It was given me fair and square, in just payment for my dog. Laddie was a very valuable dog."

"He was a half-blind, ten-year-old mongrel and you know it."

"Even so."

"Mom, last night when it happened, why didn't you call me?"

"Why didn't I? *This* is why, all this questioning."

"I'm only trying to get things straightened out so we can decide what to do."

"I've already decided. I'll get rid of the wallet so nosy people won't see it and ask nosy questions. And I'll keep the money because it's mine, given me fair and square."

"How do you know?"

Celia pursed her lips. "How do I know what?"

"The man driving the car, he might have thrown the money out on purpose to keep you quiet, so you wouldn't tell anyone you saw him."

"Why should he do that?"

"Maybe he was a criminal escaping from the scene of a crime."

Celia was shaken but refused to admit it. "Oh, nonsense."

"He hit Laddie and didn't stop to leave his name or to see if he could help. That's hit-and-run driving, right there. That's a crime in itself." Mabel's imagination was like her car. Once it started to move, it moved all over, in every joint and with a great deal of noise. "How do you know he wasn't a bank robber escaping with his loot?"

"The banks," Celia pointed out, "are closed on Saturdays."

"Or a murderer. How do you know he won't come back?"

"Why would he come back?"

"To make sure your lips are sealed."

"Oh, my goodness." Celia sat down abruptly in a wicker chair and began fanning herself with a handkerchief. "I'm not well. I feel—I feel faint."

"I'll fetch you a glass of water, wait there."

The water was administered, and with it, since nothing else was readily available, a chunk of Mabel's horehound. Mabel sang soprano in the choir and used horehound as a ladder to some of the higher notes.

"Are you feeling better, Mom?"

"No thanks to you I'm not dead," Celia said bitterly. "Giving me a fright like that, at my age."

"I was only trying to make you see reason."

"Reason, is it, to throw away nearly a hundred dollars? If that's reason, I want to be crazy, thank you."

"All I'm asking you to do is to tell someone about what happened."

"Such as who?"

"The Reverend Wilton might know what to do."

"Over my dead body," Celia said. "He and I don't see eye to eye on too many things as it is."

"The constable, then, Mr. Leachman."

"Mr. Leachman has fits."

"Now what has that got..."

"His own sister told me. He has fits. He even," Celia added with an air of triumph, "foams at the mouth."

Mabel's face was so red it seemed ready to burst its skin like an overripe tomato. "Will you stop changing the subject?"

"I didn't change the subject. You brought up Mr. Leachman and I merely pointed out that he has fits. Bad ones."

"That's simple gossip."

"Gossip, is it? How is it that when you find out something interesting about a person you get information, I merely get gossip."

"Put your coat on, Mom. We'll be late for church."

"I don't feel like going to church."

"Maybe you don't feel like it but you need it. I think maybe I do too. And after church we'll go see Mr. Leachman. And I don't care if he's foaming like bubble bath, you're going to tell him what happened and show him the wallet and describe the man in the car."

"I didn't see him very well, only by the street light."

"The wallet had a name in it?"

"Yes. Galloway. Ronald Gerard Galloway."

"Sounds phony to me," Mabel said. "Come on, let's get going."

NINE

The news that Ron Galloway had been seen alive at Thornbury at approximately ten o'clock Saturday night was relayed to Esther late on Sunday afternoon.

She had just returned home from the lodge and was having early tea with the two boys in their playroom on the second floor. The boys were on their worst behavior. Sensing Esther's remoteness and preoccupation, they were using every trick in the book to draw her back into immediacy and refocus her attention on them. Food was thrown, epithets exchanged, tears shed. Through it all Esther tried to remain firm and kindly, but the cumulative strain of the past twenty-four hours proved too much for her and she herself had almost reached the point of tears when Annie came in to announce that Mr. Bream was waiting for her in the library.

"I told you I wasn't at home," Esther said sharply, in a transfer of anger. "To anyone."

"I couldn't help it, Mrs. Galloway. He said he had some very important news. And anyway, it's Mr. *Bream*." She inflected the name to give it special importance, partly to excuse her disobedience of orders and partly because she liked Harry. He treated her with respect.

"All right. Take over these hellions. I can't do a thing with them."

Annie gave her a superior you-never-could glance which Esther pretended not to notice. Esther was well aware that Annie had more power over her than she had over Annie. The balance of power lay in the boys, and Annie handled them with the ease and poise of a skilled animal trainer who realizes the exact limitations of her beasts and expects no more from them than what they can give.

"They're really quite good boys," Annie said firmly.

"Yes, of course they are."

Harry was waiting for her in the library. Even before she entered the room she could hear him pacing up and down as if he were angry.

Esther said, "Annie tells me you have news."

"Of a kind."

"Is it about Ron?"

"Some of it is."

"Don't talk in riddles, Harry. This isn't the time or place."

"I can't help that. It is a riddle. Everything is." His hair and clothing were disheveled and his face feverish-red as if he'd just been battling a high wind. He was rather a short man but he usually held himself straight and tall so that people seldom thought of him as short. Yet during the afternoon he seemed to have shrunk by inches, his shoulders sagged, his neck was bent, and he looked small and wizened and old.

Perhaps I've changed just as much as Harry has, Esther thought, and she was grateful that there was no mirror in the room to tell her so.

"It's bad news, of course," she said sounding very detached.

"No. No, it's not. Not about Ron, anyway."

"Tell me."

"Some woman saw him last night in a little town called Thornbury, about ten o'clock. He ran over her dog."

"He what?"

"Ran over her dog and killed it. He slowed down, saw what he'd done and threw some money out of the car to pay for the dog. The woman described the car, and Ron, the cap he was wearing and so on. It was Ron, all right."

"How can you be sure?"

"There was all kinds of identification in his wallet. I guess he didn't have time to take the money from his wallet so he just threw out money, wallet and everything. It was one of those impulsive things Ron does without thinking."

"Without thinking? Oh no. He thought, all right. He thought, as usual, that money will pay for anything."

"Now look, Es, I might have done the same thing myself if I'd been in a terrible hurry."

"Why should he be in a terrible hurry?"

"I don't know. I just say maybe he was."

"And that's why he didn't stop the car, because he was in this terrible hurry?"

Harry hesitated. "He could have been scared, too."

"That's better. That sounds much more like Ron. He makes a mistake and runs away, throws money out of cars instead of stopping. Oh, it must have been Ron, all right. Even if there hadn't been any identification in the wallet, I'd know it was Ron. Will he ever grow up? Will he ever just once stand and face things?"

"Now Es, don't start..."

"Where's Thornbury?"

"Well, it's about halfway between Collingwood and Owen Sound. You pass through it on the way to the lodge. You must have seen it today."

"I didn't notice." She let out a long deep sigh, as if she'd been holding her breath, waiting for an attack. "And that's all the news?"

"Yes."

"It's worse than none."

"I don't see how you figure that."

She turned away so that when she spoke again she seemed to be addressing the window. "All this time, right up until now, I've been thinking that Ron went away deliberately to avoid me. Perhaps he drove to Detroit, I thought, and after wrestling with his conscience for a while, he will call me and tell me where he is and everything will be all right again. Or as close to all right as it ever has been. That's what I've been thinking, that he did something wrong and couldn't bear to face me and ran away."

"That's quite possible."

"No, it isn't. Not now. If he wanted to run away he wouldn't run to the one place in the world where I'd look for him first. If he was seen in Thornbury, that means he was on his way to the lodge, or had been there and was coming back. In which direction was he going when he went through Thornbury?"

"I never thought to ask. There actually wasn't time. The Inspector returned to the lodge right after you left for home and told me about the Thornbury business. I thought you'd want to know right away so I drove down here."

"You could have phoned."

"I wanted an excuse to leave anyway."

"Why?"

"I'd been trying to get in touch with Thelma. I got through to her once but she hung up on me. I tried again several times after that. The phone kept ringing all right, but no one answered. I know the reason, now."

His tone was so peculiar that she turned to stare at him. "What's the matter, Harry?"

"She's left me," Harry said, and began suddenly and silently to cry. He covered his face with his hands in an effort to hide his tears but they dribbled out between his fingers and down his wrists into his cuffs.

Esther had never seen a grown man cry before, and the shock of it temporarily immobilized her. She couldn't speak, and her only thought at first was that Harry needed a handkerchief, somebody should give poor Harry a handkerchief, he was getting his shirt wet.

When she finally found her voice it fitted her strangely, it was so tight and small. "Harry? I'll make you a drink, eh, Harry?"

"No. I'll be—all right. Give me—a minute."

She turned back to the window. She had looked out of this window a thousand times and she still had the same impression, that somewhere, beyond the circling driveway, the high hedges and the iron gates, life was going on without her and she hadn't been invited to the party. Sometimes, over the high hedge, she fancied she could hear the strains of distant music and between the iron rails could catch a glimpse of couples dancing.

"I went home," Harry said. "She wasn't there. Just a letter on the kitchen table saying—saying she'd left me."

"Did she give a reason?"

"Not anything I could understand. She wanted a chance to think things over, she said. I can't believe it. We were so *happy.*" He stumbled over the word and picked himself up again. "Everybody knows how happy we were. I can't understand. What's she got to think over?"

"Perhaps quite a bit."

"But what?"

"It's an interesting coincidence, don't you think? Now they're both gone, Ron and Thelma."

"You're not implying they went off together?"

"Maybe you and I have been pretty stupid about the whole thing."

"They're not together," Harry said sharply. "I *know* where Thelma is. She said in her letter she was going to stay for a while with a cousin of hers over on Eglington Avenue. She asked me not to try and get in touch with her. I did, though. I called Marian, that's her cousin, and Marian said she was there all right but didn't want to talk to me just yet."

"Cousins," Esther said dryly, "have been known to lie."

"Not Marian. She and Thelma aren't that close, for one thing."

"I never heard Thelma mention a cousin in town."

"I just told you, they're not very close. Lunch together downtown twice a year, that sort of thing. Marian's never even been to visit us at the house."

"Then why should Thelma go to stay with her now?"

"She had no place else to go, I guess." He sounded as if he were going to start crying again, but he didn't. Instead, he swallowed hard several times before he resumed speaking. "She must have been desperate, to decide to go to Marian's. She doesn't even like her. She must have been desperate. Poor Thelma."

Esther turned abruptly from the window, her fists clenched tight against her sides. "Poor Thelma. I'm getting bloody sick of the poor Ron, poor Thelma routine. I'd like to hear a little more about poor Harry and poor Esther!"

"No, Es. Don't. Don't be harsh."

"It's time I was harsh."

"It's never time, if you love somebody. I don't know what Thelma's problem is. All I know is that she's in trouble and I want to help her."

"Suppose you can't."

"I've got to," Harry said with quiet firmness. "She's my wife. She needs me. I would do anything in the world to help her."

Esther knew it was true. She stood, pale and motionless, thinking that if Ron ever said that about her she would be the happiest woman in the country. She would feel that at last she'd been invited to the party and the music was no longer distant but in the same room, and the couple dancing to its strains was herself and Ron.

"I wish I had your faith, Harry," she said finally.

"I wasn't born with it. I built it up brick by brick, until now it's so high I can't see over it."

"You don't want to see over it anyway."

"Thelma has done nothing shameful," Harry said. "Whatever your suspicions are about her and Ron, they're wrong, believe me."

"I'd like to."

"Read her letter."

He took the letter out of his coat pocket and handed it to her, but she drew away. "No, I don't want to. It's private."

"Thelma wouldn't object."

"I don't want to," she repeated, but even while she was speaking her eyes were seeking out the words on the paper, written in green ink in a highly stylized backhand. The effect of style was ruined by some misspellings, several clumsy erasures, and one place where the ink was blurred as if by a teardrop.

Dear Harry:

I have gone to stay with Marian for a time. It is so hard to explain to you, I feel so teribbly mixed up, and I thought if I went away by myself to think things over it would be better for all of us, including you. It is hard for me to figure out the right answers when I am so emotionaly upset like this. I can't talk to you just yet, so please don't call me or try to get in touch with me. *Please,* I mean it, Harry. If Mrs. Malverson or any of the neighbours wonder why I'm not there, just tell them I've gone to visit with a cousin, which is the truth anyway.

I know you are wondering what's the matter with me, have I lost my mind or something. Well, I don't think so but right now I'm not sure of anything except that I must go away and figure things out without having to think of other people or feel sorry for anyone. The past is all very well but it's the future I've got to live in. I must find the right course and stick to it.

Please try to be patient with me, Harry. I'll get in touch with you as soon as I feel that I can talk sensibaly and without breaking down. By the way, Marian knows nothing, so please don't try and pump her. I told her you and I had had a little spat.

Thelma

P.S. Mrs. Reynold called this morning and said Dorothy Galloway wants to see you as soon as possible about Ron.

Esther almost dropped the letter in her amazement. "Mrs. *Reynold.* Why on earth should she call *you?*"

"I've no idea. I hardly know the woman. As for Dorothy, well, I go to see her now and then, but God knows we never talk about Ron. If his name were mentioned she'd stage a heart attack."

"Do you think it's possible she's heard something about Ron that we haven't?"

"How?"

"By mistake, perhaps. She's still Mrs. Galloway, a message could have been sent to her by mistake, instead of to me." The idea excited her, splashed color into her cheeks. "Isn't that reasonable?"

"I guess it is."

"You must go and find out, Harry."

Harry sagged against the desk, his head bowed. "Not now."

"You've got to."

"I can't face anyone right now."

"You're facing me."

"That's because we're both in the same spot."

"Not quite," she replied sharply. "You know where your wife is, you know she's alive and well. So we're not *quite* in the same spot, are we?"

He raised his head, slowly and with effort, as if it had turned to stone. Their eyes met, but he didn't speak.

"Harry. I need your help. You'll go and see Dorothy?"

"All right."

"Now?"

"Now," he said wearily.

TEN

He reached out and switched on the radio in his car. The six o'clock news broadcast was just beginning. Trouble in Israel. A train wreck in California. Stock market still going up. A warehouse on fire near the waterfront. A plane crash outside Denver. No mention of Ron's disappearance. Probably because it's Sunday, Harry thought. This whole damn city goes dead on Sundays. Maybe Thelma's right and we ought to move to the States. I'll call her and tell her—no, she said to wait. I must be patient.

He turned north on Avenue Road and west on Grant, and about two miles from the intersection he came to what Dorothy's mother called her town house.

The neighborhood was beginning to crumble around it but the house itself remained intact, as impervious as a stone fortress with its three-storied turrets and barred windows. *A medieval castle,* Harry thought as he parked his car in the driveway. *And inside the castle awaits the princess in her tower of ivory. Not the sleeping beauty, however. Poor Dorothy has insomnia.*

He could laugh at the house, make fun of Dorothy, and even feel pity and contempt for her, but at the same time he was a little awed and uneasy and resentful in the presence of wealth, like a dwarf who has been denied some secret hormone that stimulated growth, suddenly finding himself among giants.

He pressed the door chime and waited, bracing himself as if for attack the instant the huge mahogany door opened. When the door finally opened he almost laughed out loud at the sight of a little old woman in a black uniform, no bigger or braver than Harry's dwarf-image of himself. She stared up at him, roundeyed, as if male visitors to the household were scarce, and objects of suspicion.

"Mrs. Galloway wanted to see me," he said. "I'm Harry Bream."

She didn't speak, and only the slightest nod of her head indicated that she had heard him. But she opened the door wider and Harry took it as an invitation to enter. Then she closed the door, gave a little curtsy in Harry's general direction and darted off down the hall and up the stairs with several backward glances as if she perhaps feared pursuit.

The hall was like a museum, with a domed ceiling and marble floors and massive pieces of statuary. Harry would have liked a cigarette but there were no ash trays in sight and the walls seemed to be posted with invisible No Smoking signs. The only evidence of life in the room was a pair of battered roller skates abandoned at the bottom of the staircase. The skates struck a note of sad surprise in Harry: he was always forgetting that

Dorothy had borne a child and that the child still lived here in this house. Harry hadn't seen her for years. She was kept, or chose to remain, out of sight.

He put his hands in his pockets and waited, and in a few minutes the little old woman came darting back down the steps, her white cap bobbing up and down on her head like a captive bird.

"Mrs. Galloway will see you in her room." She spoke very slowly and not too clearly, as if at some time in the past, through illness or injury, she had lost the ability to speak and had had to learn the use of words all over again.

Harry followed her upstairs. The pace she set was so brisk that Harry was breathing hard by the time he reached the first landing, and openly puffing when he came to the top.

Dorothy's suite was in the south turret and the door was open.

Dorothy was stretched out on a chaise longue in a tangle of satin pillows, wearing a white lace negligee like a bride still dressed and waiting for a bridegroom long overdue. She was almost forty now, but she resembled a frail and fretful child. Extreme emaciation and years of discontent had ruined her good looks without aging her. It was as if she had been kept inaccessible to the weather in the streets. Neither sun nor wind nor rain had ever penetrated her high window.

Her mother sat in a slipper chair at Dorothy's right, and between the two women was a long low table holding a scrabble board with a half-finished game laid out on it.

"Harry, dear, how nice of you to come." Dorothy extended her hand and Harry took it and pressed it for a moment, disliking the feel of the long fleshless fingers that were like claws. He noticed what an unusually high color Dorothy had and the extreme brightness of her eyes and he thought at first that she was in the throes of a fever. But her hand felt cool and her voice was alert and Harry was forced to change his opinion. Dorothy was suffering not from fever but from fury. She was, in fact, as sore as a boil.

"Harry, you remember Mother, of course?"

"Certainly. Good evening, Mrs. Reynold."

"Good evening, Harry. So good of you to come."

"Not at all," Harry said politely. "I hope I'm not interrupting your game?"

"Game," Dorothy repeated with a twist of her mouth. "It's not much of a *game*. I'm miles behind as usual."

Mrs. Reynold flushed with embarrassment. "Now, Dorothy dear, that's not true and you know..."

"It is true. Besides, I *loathe* scrabble. It gives me a headache."

"I can't help winning once in a while if I happen to get the right letters."

"It's not that I mind losing, not in the least. I've always been a good sport, I've made it a *point* to be a good sport, in spite of everything. Losing means nothing at all to me. It's just that you have *all* the luck."

"Now, dear, remember last night, you got the q and the z right at the beginning and made *quartz*."

Dorothy couldn't decide between signalizing last night's triumph and losing the argument about luck, so she turned away deliberately and said to Harry, "You must forgive us. Mother takes her scrabble very seriously."

"I've never played it," Harry said.

"Don't. It's a tiresome thing. It always gives me a headache, especially when other people have all the luck. Sit down, won't you? I'll ring for tea."

"Don't bother."

"It's time for my medicine anyway and I can't take it without tea. It's the foulest stuff."

"I'll get the tea," Mrs. Reynold said, rising. "I hate to bother Miss Parks when I can just as easily do it myself."

"It's her job to be bothered."

"Even so, dear. I'd rather do it myself. Sometimes she forgets to scald the pot."

Mrs. Reynold seemed both grateful for an excuse to leave and guilty about using it. As she passed Harry she gave him an anxious little look. It seemed to ask him to be kind to Dorothy, or at least tolerant.

When she had gone Dorothy said, "Mother's bored with all this hospital routine. I am, too, only I have to stand it. I wouldn't last a week without expert care."

"You're looking better, Dorothy."

Harry knew right away that this remark was a mistake. Dorothy frowned with displeasure and her fingers plucked at one of the satin pillows. "I don't see how I can be. I was *so* upset this morning Miss Parks had to call the doctor. I've got a new doctor, the last one was hopelessly out of date. Nothing but psychology, psychology. What good is psychology when your heart is beating like a triphammer, and the least excitement makes you feel faint?"

"What was the cause of the excitement?"

"Ron's call. I thought your wife might have told you."

"She didn't."

"I'm much calmer tonight, my pulse is just a shade under ninety—the doctor gave me an injection. Honestly, the way I've been prodded and poked with needles!"

"What about Ron?"

"He called here last night and told Mother he wanted to talk to me, and Mother, for some obscure reason, put him on to me. Mother means to do the right thing." Dorothy paused and let the implication go on without her, like a riderless horse: *but she never does, of course.* "I wasn't feeling very well anyway and it was after nine o'clock, past my bedtime, and I'd had a nagging pain in my left kidney all day."

"How long after nine o'clock?"

"A few minutes. I remember taking my pulse after the call. It was," she added with an air of satisfaction, "nearly a hundred and twenty."

"Why did the call upset you to such an extent?"

"It was so unexpected, for one thing. Ron hadn't called me, hadn't communicated with me in any way, for years. He had no reason to. At the time of the divorce I asked for nothing from him but Barbara, and of course I was given sole custody of her, in view of his behavior with that terrible woman—what was she, a stenographer or something? Common, anyway."

"She was a copywriter for an advertising agency."

Dorothy raised her brows. "That's common enough, surely? At any rate, I was totally unprepared for any call from Ron. I'd almost forgotten he existed. He never had a very strong personality, he's not the kind of person one remembers. My father, for instance, died when I was barely ten and yet I can recall him so much more distinctly than I can Ron."

"What was the call about?"

"I'd like to know, really. His words were distorted, confused."

"What was the matter with him?"

"Plain and simple intoxication, that's what I've since decided. He was roaring drunk, maudlin drunk. You know Ron—he never could hold his liquor like a gentleman."

It seemed to Harry that this was the dozenth time in the past twenty-four hours that someone had said to him, "You know Ron." Yes, he knew Ron, better than anyone did, and one of the things he knew very well was that when Ron was drinking, before he reached the point of confusion he always got sick and sobered up. If he had a weak head he also had a weak stomach, and the latter canceled out the former.

"He seemed terribly *contrite*," Dorothy went on. "He apologized for the harm he'd done to me and said he was going to straighten everything out, pay all his debts, I think that was the way he put it. He asked about Barbara. I told him he had no right even to ask. I told him Barbara was being brought up to believe that her father was dead."

"That was pretty—cruel, wasn't it, Dorothy?"

She smiled. "Wasn't it, though? But I thought while he was paying his debts, I'd pay one of mine. I owed him a little cruelty. All those times when I was so ill I could scarcely move and he went off partying—that was the year I had my liver trouble. The doctors says I'm not over it to this day. Just last week I had to have a bromsulfalein—that's the dye test for liver functioning. *More* needles. I tell you I'm getting heartily sick of needles. I'm little better than a pincushion. And what good does it all do anyway. I haven't much longer. They all know it, they simply refuse to admit..."

"Dorothy."

Her name, spoken sharply, almost contemptuously, shocked her into a brief silence. She looked at him with her mouth half open, as if he had ordered her to be quiet. But she could not be quiet for long; an order was what she gave, not took, and a minute later she was off again.

"I know you think I'm feeling sorry for myself, that I oughtn't go on like this about my illness. But what else have I to talk about? What ever happens to me—shut up in this hideous house with an old woman and a pair of incompetent nurses who can't even take a temperature properly? It's always normal—that's what they tell me—it's *normal,* they say, when I know perfectly well that I'm running a fever, when my head feels as if it's burning up. And they're careful, oh, they're very careful, not to leave the thermometer around so I can take my own temperature. They hide it."

Harry was disturbed by what was to him this new development in Dorothy. In the past her egocentricity and her symptoms had been just as extreme, but now they were underlined by delusions of persecution. No longer did the princess dwell at ease in her ivory tower: she was imprisoned in a hideous house at the mercy of an old woman and bumbling nurses who lied and hid thermometers.

She continued to talk, her words coming faster and faster, and it seemed to Harry that she was incapable of stopping voluntarily and must be helped. He wondered how he could draw her attention away from herself without antagonizing her to the point where she would faint or go into hysterics or use any of the other tricks which by this time came as naturally to her as breathing.

He said, "Ron disappeared last night."

She stopped in the middle of a sentence, and her right hand, on the point of making a gesture, dropped quietly into her lap. "Why didn't you tell me before?"

"I tried.",

"Disappeared, that could mean anything."

"In this case it means that he failed to keep an appointment, one that he was looking forward to, and that he hasn't communicated with anyone since."

"Not even his—that woman?"

"Her name is Esther," Harry said with a trace of irritability.

"You needn't bite my head off. I have quite enough trouble as it..."

"Esther has not heard from him."

The words seemed to please her. "Well, well. That's very interesting. Have you a cigarette, Harry?"

"I thought you didn't..."

"I can smoke if I want to. I want to."

He gave her a cigarette and lit it for her. The smoke curled up from her mouth in a quiet smile.

"Very interesting," she repeated. "Doesn't it suggest anything to you?"

"No."

"He told me on the telephone that he was going away on a long trip. Well, he did. Without taking her along."

"What do you mean?"

"He's walked out on her, exactly the way he did on me."

For the first time since he'd known her Dorothy looked contented. Her eyes were serene, her mouth had lost its bitter lines, and when she spoke again her voice was almost dreamy. "I wonder how she feels now. How funny life is sometimes, a mammoth hoax. I was the butt once, now it's her turn."

"Dorothy, it's not..."

"Who is the other woman, this time?"

"There *is* no other woman," Harry said brusquely.

"How can you be so sure?"

"I'm as sure of that as I am of anything. In this life nobody gets a written guarantee of anything, but you do get eyes and ears and the ability to form conclusions. I've formed mine."

"Tell me just one thing, Harry."

"I'll try."

"When Ron first became interested in this woman, this Esther, did he tell you? Did he confide in you?"

"No." It was a lie, but Harry knew the truth would have destroyed whatever relationship he had with her.

The truth was that Harry had been the first to hear about Esther. To this day he remembered Ron's initial reference to her: *"I met a girl at the Temples' last night. She's very attractive, and smart as a whip. I know I sound like a heel but I'd like to see her again. What do you think I should do?"* And Harry had said in reply all the things dictated by his conscience and common sense: Go easy, forget her, you've got a wife and child, and so on. Ron sincerely agreed with everything Harry said. Equally sincerely, he called Esther the next day, took her to lunch and fell in love.

"Well, you see?" Dorothy said with satisfaction. "If Ron didn't tell you about Esther, why should he have told you about this new one?"

"There is no new one."

"Wait and see."

"There isn't much else I can do."

"I know what *I'd* do. Want to hear?"

"All right."

"I'd get the police after him, and when they caught him, I'd make him pay and pay and pay."

I'll bet you would, Harry thought. He felt suddenly too weary to continue talking.

In contrast, Dorothy appeared more and more lively and cheerful, as if she drew some secret nourishment from the woes and afflictions of other people. This was a real banquet: Ron disappeared, Esther deserted, Harry grieving.

She eyed Harry greedily as if he were holding back some fancy tidbit she wanted for dessert. "Poor Esther. I suppose she's taking it *very* badly. Well, that's life. Ye shall reap what ye sow. You'll stay for tea, of course, Harry?"

"No, I really can't, thanks just the same."

"What a pity. I've so enjoyed talking to you. You're a veritable tonic for me, Harry. I feel better than I have for weeks and weeks. I *do* wish you'd stay a bit longer."

"Sorry, I have to get home."

"Home. Of course. I keep forgetting you're married now. I keep forgetting my manners too, I'm afraid. How is your wife?"

"Thelma's fine, thank you."

"Thelma. What a pretty name, it just suits her. Oh, by the way, I forgot to tell you one other thing Ron said on the telephone. I couldn't quite understand it myself. Perhaps you can."

"I'll try."

"He seemed to be under the impression that he had harmed you in some way. I'll see if I can give you his exact words. 'I've done something terrible to Harry and I'm sorry, I want him to know I'm sorry.' Do you know what he meant?"

"No."

"You must have some idea."

"None. None at all." Harry rose. His face felt stiff, like cardboard, as if it would crack if he tried to move it. "I don't know what he was talking about."

"How very odd, don't you think?"

"I—yes. Yes, it is."

"But you mustn't let me keep you with my chattering."

She extended her hand and Harry took it just as he had when he greeted her, but this time he wanted to squeeze it hard, as hard as possible, until he could hear the bones squeak.

"Is something wrong, Harry? You're so pale."

"Nothing is wrong."

"Well, give my best to Thelma. You're a lucky man, she's such an *attractive* young woman."

"Yes. Please say good-bye to your mother for me."

"Of course. It was sweet of you to come, Harry. We must get together more often."

They exchanged brief farewells and Harry went out into the hall, leaving the door of Dorothy's room open as he'd found it.

He should have closed it. All the way down the steps he fancied he heard noises coming from the tower, little chuckling sounds. Dorothy was laughing. The princess was burping after her banquet. Harry wished she would choke.

ELEVEN

Marian Robinson, a spinster at thirty by choice, was now in her middle forties and the choice had long since been taken out of her hands. Marian's reaction to this fact was characteristic: she had begun to hate men, all men, with an almost religious intensity. She saved clippings, and collected stories, of men who had murdered, embezzled, kidnapped, beaten their wives, been unkind to cats, or committed any of fifty other acts which she found distasteful. She was, therefore, in the correct frame of mind when her cousin Thelma phoned and asked if she could share Marian's apartment for a time.

To Marian this could mean only one thing, that Thelma had finally discovered she was married to a brute, a lecher, or at the very least an alcoholic, and the poor girl needed sanctuary. Marian's apartment was small, closet space minimal and bed linen insufficient, but Marian was quite prepared to make sacrifices for a good cause, such as the dissolution of a marriage. When Thelma, upon arriving, made it clear that Harry was not a brute or even an alcoholic, Marian swallowed her disappointment along with two aspirin tablets and a cup of strong hot tea.

Thelma did not confide in Marian either the fact of her condition or the rather circuitous route by which she'd reached it. She told her merely that she and Harry had had a slight argument.

The two women had a light supper in the kitchen and Marian was washing the dishes and Thelma drying, when the front doorbell rang.

"I'm not expecting anyone," Marian said. "Are you?"

Thelma shook her head listlessly.

"You don't suppose it's that husband of yours, do you? I told him quite distinctly on the phone that as far as he was concerned you were incommunicado." She wiped her hands on her apron. "Well, I'll just go and give him a piece of my..."

"No. No, Marian. I'll answer it. You sit down and have another cup of tea, it will do you good."

"I don't need any good done to me," Marian said crisply. "It's you I'm worried about, you look like a ghost."

"I can face—handle things. You just wait here and stop worrying."

Marian would never have admitted it aloud but she found it rather pleasant to be told what to do for a change. At the insurance office where she'd worked for twenty-three years she gave the orders. It wasn't always easy but it had to be done. She had some dozen girls under her. She knew none of them liked her, some of the younger ones made fun of her behind her back and called her Old Corsets, and others sat around hoping she'd fall down and break a leg. Marian knew the whole office would go to pot without her, so she was careful about falling and kept right on giving orders whether or not they made her popular. In the past Marian had never actually paid much attention to Thelma, but now she thought how different Thelma was from the girls in the office, not silly, and not timid by any means, just sort of sweet, in a womanly way.

Marian poured herself a third cup of tea and sat down at the kitchen table to enjoy it. She did not intend to eavesdrop, heaven forbid, but it was surprising the way sounds carried in a small apartment.

When Thelma opened the door Harry did not wait to be asked to enter. He thrust his way inside like an overzealous salesman, then closed the door and stood with his back against it in a kind of childish defiance, as if he were daring her to evict him.

He looked so silly that Thelma wanted to laugh, but she knew if she laughed she might also cry. The two, laughter and tears, seemed inextricably knotted inside her so that she couldn't move one without disturbing the other. She said quietly, "You shouldn't have come here."

"I had to."

"I asked you to wait. I can't—I don't feel *qualified* to discuss anything with you reasonably."

"O.K. Be unreasonable."

"Don't play games, Harry."

"I think it's you playing games," he said, with a little smile to soften the criticism. "Mysterious notes, hints, forebodings. I'm just an ordinary man. I don't understand mysterious notes, I've never had a foreboding in my life, and I guess I can't take hints very well either. What's it all about, Thelma?"

Instead of replying, she moved to the opposite side of the room as if she feared intimacy or anger and wanted to get as much distance between Harry and herself as possible. It seemed safer and easier to face him across Marian's mohair sofa and rose and brown Axminster rug.

Harry raised his voice to bridge the distance. "We're not a couple of kids any more, Thelma. We're married. We've shared a great many things. Whatever's bothering you, we've got to share that too."

"We can't."

"Why not?"

"I have to share it with—with somebody else."

"Marian?"

"Marian." She began to laugh, and almost instantly she could feel the sting of tears inside her eyelids.

He looked away, giving her time to compose herself. "All right, not Marian. Who, then?"

"I begged you not to come here, not to force me to talk before I was ready, before I *knew*."

"Knew what?"

"What's happened to Ron. I can't—I *can't* talk to you until I know where Ron is."

"Ron, he's part of your trouble?"

Her face disintegrated like paper crushed in a fist. "Oh God, I begged you, I asked you not to... Why did you come? Why can't you let me *alone*? Why didn't Ralph tell you?"

"Tell me what?" Harry said, but she just kept moaning, "My God, my God," and swaying back and forth with her hands covering her face.

He waited, watching her quietly, noticing for the first time the slight thickening of her abdomen, and thinking, *this is it. She doesn't have to tell me. I know.*

The things Ralph had said and Esther had suspected and Dorothy had subtly implied—they all added up to the little bulge at Thelma's waistline.

"There's a child," he said finally. "Ron's?"

"Yes."

"How—how far along are you?"

"Three and a half months."

"And Ron knows?"

"I told him. Last night."

He leaned heavily against the door frame, staring down at the roses of Marian's rug. They had pink, fretful faces like babies. "What does Ron intend to do about it?"

"The right thing, of course."

"After having done quite a number of wrong things, do you think it's going to be easy for him to do the right one?"

"There's no use getting sarcastic. It won't accomplish anything. I've thought the whole thing out. It's not going to be easy, but Ron and I, each of us will have to get a divorce and then we'll be married."

"By that time your child will be born a bastard."

The name staggered her like a blow and she might have fallen except that there wasn't room to fall. She was jammed between the wall and the mohair sofa.

"Thelma!"

He started across the room to help her but she waved him away. "No. I'm—all right."

"Let me..."

"No." She clung to the back of the sofa for a moment and then she straightened up, looking strangely dignified. "Don't use that word. Don't use that word about my son."

And Harry, watching her, thought, she's got it all planned, two divorces, a marriage, even the child's sex. "A lot of words are going to be used which you won't like, Thelma. You'd better start thinking of them now so you won't be surprised when they come up."

"I don't care what anyone says about *me*."

"Yes, you do. Try and face reality."

"I am. *This* is reality." She pressed her hand to her abdomen. "This child, this is my reality. I've wanted a baby ever since I can remember, and now I have one right here growing inside me."

"Reality isn't a single fact like that. It's a combination of thousands, millions..."

"You denied me a baby, Harry. You made excuses, you said I was too old to have a first child now, you were afraid something would happen to me and you'd lose me. Well, you have lost me."

He shook his head helplessly, unable to speak.

"It's your fault, Harry. That's why I'm not even apologizing to you, because I think it's your fault, not mine. I wanted this one thing more than anything in the world, and I could see the years slipping by and I was getting older, with nothing to show for it. I felt dead inside, dead and useless. Don't talk to me about reality, Harry. No matter what happens, I'm not sorry. I *won't* be sorry. I have my son to keep me alive."

It sounded almost like a speech she had prepared and practiced in front of a mirror, day after day, so that she would be ready for this moment.

"You had the whole thing planned," Harry said, "in advance?"

"That's not true."

"To put it coarsely, you hooked him."

She looked at him with a kind of contempt. "Believe whatever you want. It's too late to change anything."

"But why? Why Ron? Why my best friend with a wife and family of his own? For God's sake, couldn't you have stopped to think? Couldn't you at least have talked it over with me, told me how you felt?"

"I tried. You never listened. You only heard what you wanted to hear. To you everything was idyllic, you had a house and a wife to look after it, your meals were on time, your clothes laundered..."

"I was satisfied just having you," Harry said. "I didn't require anything or anyone else because I loved you. I still do. Oh God, Thelma, couldn't we forget this nightmare and go back?"

"I don't want to go back. Even if I could. I may be in trouble but at least I feel alive, I've got a future and a child to share it with. And Ron." Her voice shook a little over the name in noticeable contrast to the confident way she spoke of the child. "Ron, too, of course."

"Of course."

"Oh, I know what you're thinking about—that silly notion I had that he was dead. It's not true. Mrs. Malverson got me all upset with her talk about spiritual messages. What nonsense. I know he's not dead. I know where he is."

"Where?"

"Oh, not specifically. I just know he's hiding somewhere for a while because he's frightened. Of Esther, probably. Of course she'll be impossible about the whole thing but he'll simply have to face up to her. She'll make trouble, I expect that, she's the type."

"Name a type who wouldn't, under the circumstances."

"Esther's special, she's so determined. Well, I'm determined too. Let her make trouble. Ron and I won't be living here anyway. When everything is over we'll move to the States, California perhaps. I've never been there, but they say that children brought up in California are bigger and healthier than any other children in the world.

The change in her tone indicated that she was off on another dream, an express train whizzing across the border and through the states toward California. Nothing stood in the way of this train. If it did, it was demolished. Harry knew this from experience. He had stood on the tracks once too often.

"...and because they play outdoors all the time even in winter. They eat outdoors, too. Everyone cooks over a barbecue pit or they go down to the beach and build a bonfire."

Harry stepped in front of the train with the fearlessness of one who had nothing to lose. "Stop. Stop it, Thelma."

"Why should I?"

"Don't start living a year from now when you have to get through tonight, tomorrow, next week."

"I'll get through. Don't worry about me. Harry. Get angry, call me names, anything, but don't *worry* about me."

"I can't afford to get angry. I might—hurt you."

From the kitchen came a sudden sharp crash like a plate breaking.

"Marian," Thelma said. "Dear heaven, I forgot about Marian."

As if she'd been waiting for her cue, Marian thrust herself through the swinging door, head down, like a charging ram.

She didn't look at Harry or give any indication of his presence. She shouted at Thelma, "You slut. You nasty little slut. Pack up your things and get out of here."

Thelma appeared pale but composed, as if her dream of California had blunted the sharp corners of the present. "Do you always eavesdrop on your guests, Marian?"

"Eavesdropping is one thing, cuckolding is another. And I want none of your insolence, do you hear me?"

"I hear you. You sound just like Aunt May."

"You leave her name out of it. We're a respectable family and you've disgraced us all. I want no part of you. You can go on the streets for all I care."

"I might do that. And if business gets too heavy I'll send some customers on to you. The experience might improve you."

"Why, you dirty—you cheap..."

"Shut up!" Harry ordered. "Shut up, both of you! Thelma, go and pack your stuff. You, Marian, sit down."

Thelma disappeared hastily into the bedroom, but Marian stood pat, her hands on her enormous hips. "I don't take orders from any *man*. I will not sit down."

"All right, you can stand on your head as far as I'm concerned. Just stop shrieking like a fishwife. You have neighbors, neighbors have ears."

"She insulted me. You heard her, she *insulted* me."

"You insulted her first."

"But she deserved it, she asked for it. After what she's done to you, how can you stand there and take her part?"

"She's my wife."

"Wife. A fine word, but that's all it is, a word. She's used you, deceived you, made a fool of you. And she intended to do the same thing to me. To think I was taken in by that sweet smile of hers and that soft 'Sit down and have a cup of tea, Marian, it will do you good.' As if she *cared*. Lies, lies. The soft-talkers, they're the worst. I've been taken in by them before. You'd think I'd have learned my lesson."

Her voice broke and spots of color blotched her face and her neck. In a moment of perception Harry realized that she was not so much angry as disappointed. She had been looking forward to having Thelma around for a while to alleviate her loneliness and lend her life a little excitement. Thelma's visit would have meant a transfusion of vitality; now the transfusion had been stopped almost before it began. Marian had closed the valve herself: she could not accept the blood of a slut, she would prefer to die.

"The girls at the office," Marian said, "maybe they're silly, yes, even malicious, but there's not one of them bad like her. Not one of them's ever gotten into that kind of trouble."

Harry found himself saying, without conviction, "Thelma's not bad. She made a mistake."

"When people make a mistake they're *sorry*. They're not proud of it like her. They don't go around bragging about a trip to California. I want to go to California too, I've dreamed of it for years, but you can bet I'll choose a more respectable way of getting there."

"I'm sure you will." The dry irony of his tone added, *I'm sure you'll have to.*

"This man she called Ron. Who is he?"

"I'm afraid," Harry said, "that it's none of your business."

"News like that gets around. I'll find out."

"I'm sure of that, too." Not only would Marian find out. Once Ron's disappearance hit the newsstands, the whole city, the whole country would find out, and Thelma would have to get used to stronger words than bastard and slut. Harry wondered, with weary detachment, if anyone dared print the word cuckold.

Thelma came out of the bedroom wearing the navy blue coat and hat she'd bought for Easter and carrying a rawhide suitcase which had been a wedding present from Ralph and Nancy Turee. She ignored Marian who was standing tense, braced for the next round, and said to Harry, "I'm ready. We can go now."

"And good riddance," Marian said.

"The same to you."

Harry interrupted quickly, "Come on, Thelma. I'll take you home."

"I'm not going home. You can drop me at a hotel."

"The house is yours. You need it more than I do. I won't bother you."

"I wish you'd stop being *noble*. I can't stand it!"

"I'm not being noble. It's just that I'd feel better if I knew you were looking after yourself properly. Me, I can stay anywhere, with Ralph, or Billy Winslow or Joe Hepburn. I'm used to bumming around. You're not. You have to take care of yourself, now more than ever."

She bit her lip in indecision, weighing her pride against her common sense and her concern for the baby.

"I won't bother you," he repeated. "I'll just take you home and pack up some of the things I'll need."

"All right." Her voice was tight and squeaky. "Thank you, Harry."

Harry took her suitcase and opened the door, and she walked out into the hall with quick, impatient steps. Harry hesitated, as if he wanted to say something pleasant to Marian before he left, but Marian had turned her back, and it was like the closing of a steel safe to which he didn't know the combination. No one did.

Outside a spring rain had begun to fall, lightly and steadily. Neither of them seemed to notice. They walked in silence for a time, unaware of any weather but their own, inside.

"Harry?"

"Yes."

"Where will you stay? In case anything happens and I have to get in touch with you. . ."

"I don't know. I haven't decided yet. With Ralph and Nancy, perhaps."

"But they have four children."

"Yes, I know," Harry said quietly. "I like children."

TWELVE

The private day school which the two Galloway boys attended had been closed for two weeks because of an epidemic of measles. One of the ways Esther had devised to keep them busy, and presumably out of mischief, was to give them certain duties and responsibilities previously assigned only to adults. The particular duty the boys enjoyed most, since it involved a rare freedom, was that of collecting the mail. They were allowed to walk all the way down to the end of the driveway, unescorted except by the little dachshund, Petey, and wait at the gate for the postman.

When the postman handed them the day's mail, they assumed it was a gift, and so they usually took him a gift in return, a cookie coaxed out of the housekeeper, Mrs. Browning, or a new drawing by Marvin or the prize from a box of cereal. On Monday they had a special gift for him, the first angleworm of the season, a scrawny specimen elongated by considerable handling and rather dried out after a time spent in Greg's shirt pocket.

The boys arrived early and the postman was late, so they had plenty of opportunity to indulge in the usual arguments and fights about who was to present the gift, who was to carry the mail into the house and who was to occupy the place of honor at the top of the iron gate. But on this particular morning neither of the boys seemed inclined to fight. Their energies were directed not against each other but against the mysterious tensions which now seemed to dominate the household. The boys had not been told, or allowed to overhear, anything about their father's absence. They had no means of understanding their mother's strange preoccupation, Mrs. Browning's snappishness, Annie's sudden lapses into silence, or the unusual permissiveness of old Rudolph, the gardener who lived over the garage. Rudolph, the most continuous male contact the boys had, loomed large in their lives. When the holes Petey, the dachshund, had dug in the rose bed on Sunday afternoon were filled quietly and without comment, both of the boys realized that something was the matter.

Their reaction was instinctive. Instead of remaining brothers, each jockeying for position in the household, they became friends, joined together against the world of adults. They climbed to the top of the iron gate and stuck out their tongues in the direction of the house and chanted derisive insults.

"I'm the king of the castle," Greg sang, and named individually the people who were dirty rascals: Annie, Mother, old Rudolph, Mrs. Browning. Marvin was all for including Daddy, but Greg reminded him sharply that Daddy had promised to bring them a new dog when he came home, and shouldn't be listed among the dirty rascals.

"What if he forgets?" Marv said. "He'll be a dirty rascal, then can we sing him in it too?"

"He won't forget. He'll bring something. He always does."

"A cat maybe, huh? I wouldn't say no to a cat."

"Petey would. Petey hates cats. Petey's a real cat-killer."

Petey, who had never seen a cat, responded to his new, unearned distinction with a happy yelp. This settled the matter as far as the boys were concerned. They couldn't possibly keep a cat, and if Ron brought one home by mistake they would simply hand it over to old Rudolph to trade in on a dog. Until the previous day they'd been willing to settle for any kind of dog, but now, sensing that a very large one would be more annoying to the adults, they decided on a Saint Bernard.

"We can teach it to bite Annie," Greg said. "When she makes us go to bed we'll say sic 'em, and then *boiiing,* Annie gets bit."

Marv laughed so hard at this delightful picture that he nearly fell off the gate. "*Boiiing,* Annie gets bit. *Boiiing, boiiing,* Mrs. Browning gets bit. *Boiiing, boiiing,* everybody gets bit."

" 'Cepting us."

" 'Cepting us."

They screamed with laughter and the gate shook and Petey broke into excited yelps. By the time the postman arrived, the boys' faces were red as tomatoes and Marv had started to hiccough as he always did after a laughing fit.

"Mr. Postman! Hi, Mr. Postman!"

"Hello boys." The postman was long and lean, with a weather-cracked smile. "How come you're not in school this morning?"

"Measles."

"You shouldn't be out here if you got measles."

"*We* don't got measles," Marv explained. "The other kids got them."

"Well, I declare. I was never that lucky when I was a boy. The whole town could be dying of plague but they never closed the school, no sir." He put down the heavy mailsack, propped it against the fence, and stretched his arms high in the air. "That's how I got an education. Force. I didn't want one."

"What's a plague?" Greg asked, climbing down from the gate.

"Like measles, only worse."

"You got something for us in your bag?"

"Sure thing."

"We got something for you, too."

"Well, how about that."

"You want to guess what it is?"

"I guess it's a cookie."

"No."

"An apple."

"No. You can't eat it. A human bean can't eat it, I mean."

"What does a human bean do with it?"

"Keep it as a pet."

"Oh. Well, I'm just about ready to give up. What is it?"

"Let *me* tell him!" Marv shouted. "Let *me!* It's an angleworm!"

The postman took off his cap and scratched his head. "An angleworm, eh? Let's see it."

The angleworm, now fairly moribund, was duly produced from Greg's pocket and placed carefully in the postman's hand.

"Well, now, isn't he cute? I must admit no one's ever thought of giving me an angleworm before."

"You'll take good care of him?" Greg said anxiously.

"You bet I will. I think I'll put him in my garden where he'll find other angleworms to play with. There's nothing worse than a lonesome angleworm, so I've been told."

"How do you know he'll meet the kind of angleworms he likes to play with?"

"They're not fussy." The postman opened his sack and distributed the mail as impartially as possible to the two boys. "Well, I've got to be on my way now."

"Someday," Greg said, "can we come with you and carry the sack?"

"Someday, sure. So long, fellows."

"So long."

They watched him until he turned the corner, then they set out for the house. Usually they hurried at this point. It made them feel important to hand over the mail to their mother or Mrs. Browning. But this morning their feet lagged and they kept glancing back at the gate as if they half expected the postman to reappear and offer to take them along on his rounds.

Their mother was waiting for them at the front door. "What a lot of mail. It must be heavy."

"I could carry the whole sack," Greg said, "if I wanted to. Someday I will, he said I could."

Marv put up an immediate protest. "He said both of us, me too."

"That will be very nice, I'm sure," Esther said and began glancing through the mail, putting the bills in one pile on the hall table and the circulars in another. There was only one letter.

For a long time Esther stood staring down at the handwriting on the envelope. Then she said in a cold, quiet voice, "You boys had better go to Annie."

They were afraid of this voice, but they couldn't admit it, to each other or to themselves.

"I hate Annie," Marv shouted. "I don't want. . ."

"Do as I say, Marvin."

"No! I won't! I hate Annie!"

"I hate her too," Greg said. "We're going to teach the new dog to bite her."

"Boiiing!"

"Boiiing, boiiing, Annie gets bit."

"Boiiing, boiiing, old Rudolph gets bit."

"Stop it," Esther said. *"Please.* Please be good boys."

"Boiiing, boiiing, everybody gets bit."

" 'Cepting us."

"Boiiing..."

"Oh God," Esther said and turned and ran across the hall into the library.

Her sudden flight and the loud shutting of the door stunned the boys for a minute. Then Marv said, tentatively, "Boiiing?"

"Oh, shut up. You're such a baby. Shut up."

Marv began to cry. " I want Mummy. I want my Mummy."

The letter postmarked Collingwood, was addressed to Esther in Ron's handwriting.

She knew in advance that it would contain bad news and she tried to prepare herself for it by imagining the worst, that he'd left her for another woman and wasn't coming back.

She was only half right.

Dear Esther:

By this time you may know the truth, that Thelma is carrying my child. I won't try to excuse myself or explain,

I can't. It happened, that's all I can say. I didn't know about the child until tonight. It was a terrible surprise, too terrible for me to face. My God, what I've done to you and Harry.

I don't ask your forgiveness. I give you instead my promise that I will never hurt you or anyone ever again. I'm not fit to live. I'm sick in mind and body and soul. God help me.

                                                                    Ron

She did not faint, or cry out, or weep. She stood like a stone; only her eyes moved, reading and rereading the words on the page.

She was not aware of the door opening and when she looked up and saw Annie her eyes wouldn't focus properly. Annie seemed misty and remote as if she were surrounded by ectoplasm.

"Mrs. Galloway?"

"Please don't—don't bother me right—right now."

"But I can't do a thing with the boys. They've both gone wild, screaming and laughing and carrying on. And Marvin just bit me." Annie exhibited her wounded wrist. "I'm not sure but what they're coming down with something. Do you think I should phone the doctor?"

"All right."

"You don't look so good yourself. Mrs. Galloway. Maybe you're coming down with the same thing. Can I do anything for you?"

"Yes," Esther said. "Call the police."

"The police?"

"I've had a letter. From my husband. I think he's killed himself."

Marvin came bouncing into the room, screaming, "Boiiing! Boiiing, boi-iing!"

Esther turned with a sob and picked him up in her arms and held him tight. Too tight. There seemed to Marvin only one logical thing to do and Marvin did it. He bit her.

THIRTEEN

While the two Galloway boys were waiting for the mailman in Toronto, little Aggie Schantz was on her way to the small country school she attended near Meaford. In the winter when Aggie had to follow the road because snowdrifts made exploring foolhardy, if not impossible, she took the quick and direct route. But it was spring now, and the only snow left lay in crevices between rocks, in the hollows of tree trunks along the snow fences sagging under the weight of winter.

Aggie was a quiet child of eleven. She behaved decorously at school and obediently at home, and no one ever suspected what an adventurous spirit lurked behind her brown braids and black bonnet, or what itchy feet were buckled inside her canvas galoshes. Aggie came from a family of Mennonites whose outside contacts were limited and whose meager amount of traveling, to and from church or from one farmhouse to another, was done by horse and buggy. Aggie dreamed of a larger world. Sometimes when she was looking at a map in geography class, she grew quite dizzy thinking of all the hundreds, the thousands, of places she wanted to visit. They were all places of extremes—the highest mountain, the largest ocean, the biggest city, the oldest country, the hottest desert, the highest waterfall, the fastest rapids—Aggie intended to see each and every one of them.

While her dreams were wild, her plans for escape showed both common sense and resourcefulness. As a farm child she knew enough about horses to realize that they were a slow and unsatisfactory means of transportation. Horses had to be fed and watered and sheltered and rested and groomed. Trains and buses were equally impossible since she had no money. And so Aggie's eyes turned to the lake, to the fleets of fishing boats and the passing freighters that were so large one small stowaway wouldn't be noticed. She couldn't stay away from the lake, she scanned it constantly as if she were shipwrecked on an island, waiting, cold and hungry, for rescue.

As soon as the spring sun melted the snow from the cliffs above the lake, Aggie began taking an indirect route to school. Carrying her books and her lunch in a gray canvas bag, she climbed up to the top of the cliff and then down to the beach by a special steep path used only by agile children and venturesome dogs. The beach along here was very narrow, six feet at its widest, and strewn with boulders and rocks of all sizes. To keep from getting wet she was forced to leap from one boulder to another, but this proved tiring work and she sat down for a minute to rest, tucking her legs modestly under her long full cotton skirt. Her time sense told her she was going to be late for school, and her conscience warned her she'd better do something about it.

"There'll be hell to pay," Aggie said aloud, and the sound of the forbidden word was as intoxicating as a strange tropical drink. "Maybe I'll go there. It's the hottest place."

Half-shocked, half-delighted with her own wit and daring, she began to giggle self-consciously, turning her face sideways so that it was almost hidden by the folds of her black bonnet. And it was then, out of the corner of her right eye, that she spotted the red and black plaid cap wedged between two rocks.

She often found things on the beach, especially in the summertime, sometimes a piece from an old tire, a soaked and dilapidated shoe, a rusty tin can, or an empty bottle, but these were all worthless thugs, discarded by the owners and battered by the waves. The cap was dry, and no one would ever have discarded it because it was brand-new. It had a plastic visor at the front and a scarlet pompon on the crown, and to Aggie, who had never owned anything bright colored in her life, it was a thing of beauty. She pushed back her bonnet, letting it hang from her neck by its strings, and put the plaid cap on her head. It came down grotesquely over her ears and eyes, but Aggie did not know that this wasn't correct. Nor did she, like most eleven-year-old girls, long for a mirror to see how she looked. Mirrors were banned in the house she lived in, and the only glimpses of herself she ever caught were chance and fleeting reflections in a sunny window or in the pond behind the barn on a still day. Therefore she didn't realize that she looked foolish; she knew only that the cap was beautiful, and so it must look beautiful on anyone, anywhere.

But because it was beautiful, it was, by the same token, forbidden. She looked around to check her privacy, and finding it complete, she took off the cap, compressed it as carefully as possible and tucked it inside her waist blouse. Under her bulky clothes it was barely noticeable, and it might have escaped detection entirely if Aggie herself had not been so extremely conscious of its presence, partly from pride in its possession and partly from discomfort over its location.

By the time she reached the small brick schoolhouse the final bell was ringing and the pupils were already lined up to go inside. Red-faced and panting, holding her arms across her chest, Aggie slipped into her place in line, and began marching into the smaller of the two classrooms.

Here Miss Barabou taught, or tried to teach, the four upper grades. They were a mixed group, not only in age and ability, but in background and religion. Miss Barabou herself was a Presbyterian of French Canadian ancestry, and among her pupils she counted Anglicans, Baptists, Mennonites, Christian Scientists, Methodists, and even two Doukhobor children from Alberta. Like many teachers, Miss Barabou chose her favorites principally on the basis of their obedience. The Doukhobor children were wild and unruly, often disrupting the class or flouting authority, and with them Miss Barabou was sharp and critical and sarcastic. On the other hand the Mennonite children were quite docile, they never questioned adult authority or criticized adult behavior or expected adult privileges. While Miss Barabou disparaged the Mennonite religion, she was often grateful for its results, and Aggie was her special pet. Aggie's position was not entirely enviable, however, for Miss Barabou expected a great deal from her special pets and easily became exasperated when she didn't get it.

After the class had bowed their heads and mumbled the Lord's Prayer in unison, they sat down at their double desks and began removing their books from their school bags. Miss Barabou took her place at the front of the class. She was large and majestic, and though she seldom punished her pupils, most of them stood in awe of her.

"Spring is here," Miss Barabou announced with satisfaction, as if she'd had a personal part in its arrival. "Did anyone see a robin on the way to school?"

Hands were raised and seven robins counted. An American eagle was offered by Boris, the Doukhobor boy, but was turned down on grounds of improbability.

"We do not have American eagles in this part of the country, Boris."

"But I saw one."

"Indeed. Describe it,"

Boris described the eagle with such complete accuracy that Miss Barabou was visibly shaken.

But she was also determined. "We do not have American eagles in this section of the country. Ever. Now will someone please mark our seven robins on the bird chart? You, Agatha?"

Aggie sat motionless and mute.

"Agatha, I am addressing you. Do you know where we keep the bird chart?"

"Yes, ma'am "

"Will you kindly mark our seven robins?"

"I can't."

"Indeed, and why not?"

"I can't find my crayons."

"Well, stop squirming like that and take another look."

"I can't."

"Which do you mean, you can't stop squirming or you can't take another look?"

Aggie didn't answer. Her face was burning and her tongue felt fuzzy and dry.

"If you have an itch, Agatha, kindly go into the cloakroom and relieve it,"

Miss Barabou said in exasperation, thinking, *the awful way they dress their children, it's no wonder they itch. I'll bet she's got on six layers of clothing at least.* She added, more gently, "Agatha, is anything the matter?"

"No, ma'am."

It was at this point that Miss Barabou noticed Aggie's empty desk. "Where are your books, Agatha?"

"I—don't know."

"You lost your school bag, is that it?"

"I don't know."

The rest of the class had begun to titter and whisper behind their hands. Miss Barabou ordered them brusquely to start work on their book reports, and went down the aisle to Aggie's desk, her heavy step warning the class to behave. She was positive now that something was the matter with Aggie; the child's face was such an odd color and she was trembling. *Maybe she's coming down with something,* Miss Barabou thought. *That's all I need right now is an epidemic. Oh well, if it gets bad enough they may close the school and I'll have a holiday.*

"Do you feel ill, Agatha?" Miss Barabou asked, somewhat heartened at the idea of a holiday. "Stick out your tongue."

Aggie stuck out her tongue and Miss Barabou studied it with a professional air. "I can't see anything wrong. Does your head hurt?"

"I guess so."

"Let's see, you had measles and chicken pox last year. No mumps yet?"

"No, ma'am."

"Well, think of a lemon."

"A what?"

"Pretend you're eating a lemon. Or a pickle. Can you pretend that?"

"I guess so."

"All right now, does your throat feel queer on both sides just under your chin?"

"No, ma'am."

"Perhaps you're not pretending hard enough. Keep picturing that pickle, it's very, very sour and you're eating it. Now do you feel anything?"

"No, ma'am."

Sylvia Kramer raised her hand to announce that she had a real dill pickle in her lunch box and would gladly offer it for the sake of research. Miss Barabou replied that that wouldn't be necessary, and led Aggie into the cloakroom for further and more private diagnosis.

"Has any of your brothers or sisters been ill, Agatha?"

"Billy has the toothache."

"That's not catching. Why are you squirming and clutching your chest like that?"

Aggie shook her head.

"Do you have a pain there?"

"No, ma'am."

"Honestly, the way they dress you children, it's a crime. Are you still wearing your long underwear?"

"Yes, ma'am."

"I've a good notion to write a note to your parents. It's hard enough teaching without having to teach itchy children. For all I know, you have lice."

Tears welled in Aggie's eyes. She blinked them away, hard. "Agatha," Miss Barabou said quite gently, "now tell me truthfully, what is the matter?"

"I lost my school bag."

"Perhaps you forgot and left it at home."

"No. I lost it. On the beach."

"When were you on the beach?"

"This morning on my way to school."

"The beach isn't on your way to school. Besides, all you children have specific instructions not to go near the beach by yourselves. A lonely spot like that, you can't tell what will happen." Miss Barabou paused, significantly. "*Did* anything happen?"

Aggie merely looked up at her in helpless bewilderment, and Miss Barabou realized that the child didn't understand. She tried to explain patiently that little girls didn't go to lonely beaches by themselves because there were some bad men in the world who might do nasty things to them. "Did you see any men down there?"

"No."

"I hate to be suspicious, Agatha; or to nag. But I have the distinct impression that you're not telling me the whole truth."

Though Miss Barabou's voice was kindly, her eyes burned with such intensity that Aggie had the feeling they were looking right through her waist blouse at the red and black plaid cap.

"What occurred down at the beach, Agatha?"

"Nothing!"

"You know how important the truth is. What happens at home when you don't tell the truth?"

"I get the strap."

"As you very well know, I don't have a strap, and wouldn't use it if I had. Now you're not going to *cry*, are you?"

Aggie was, indeed. Tears spilled out of her eyes and she had to wipe them away with her sleeve. It was when Aggie raised her arm that Miss Barabou noticed the extra bulk under her clothes.

"What on earth have you got stuffed in the front of your blouse? So that's what you've been fidgeting about. You've got something hidden in there. What is it, Agatha?"

Aggie shook her head, helplessly.

"You won't be punished if you tell the truth. That's a promise. Now stop crying and tell me—no, better still, show me what it is."

"It's—nothing. I found it."

"Nobody finds a *nothing,*" Miss Barabou said dryly. "It's impossible factually, as well as grammatically. What did you find?"

"A cap. An old cap somebody left on the beach that didn't want it any more."

"Well, why didn't you say so before? All this fuss and fume about an old cap. Honestly, I sometimes wonder what kind of home life some of you children have that makes you afraid to speak up. Now remove the cap, and we'll leave it here on the shelf in the cloakroom, and you can take it home with you after school."

Aggie turned her back, removed the plaid cap from under her waist blouse and handed it to Miss Barabou.

Miss Barabou appeared surprised. "What an odd-looking thing. I've never seen one like it. Where did you find it, Agatha?"

"Between two rocks, just sitting there. I guess somebody just threw that old cap away."

"It isn't old. It's hardly been worn at all."

"It looks old to me."

But Miss Barabou seemed to have lost interest in Aggie. She was examining the inside of the cap, and when she spoke again it was more to herself than to Aggie. "There's a label. Abercrombie & Fitch, New York City. Funny. There aren't many Americans around at this time of year. The thing's new, no doubt about it. Expensive, too. Abercrombie & Fitch, I think they sell sporting goods. I wonder what kind of sport this would be worn for. Curling, perhaps, except that I've never seen a curling cap with a sun visor. Or golf. But the golf courses won't be open for ages. I'm not even sure if it's a man's cap or a woman's."

"Miss Barabou..."

"You may go back to your desk, Agatha."

"Is it my cap if I found it?"

"I can't promise you that," Miss Barabou said thoughtfully. "I better consult with Miss Wayley."

Miss Barabou escorted Aggie back into the classroom, pronounced her free of disease, assured the pupils they could associate with her without fear and warned them not to start getting symptoms out of the blue. Then, leaving the class in charge of one of the seniors, she made a beeline to Miss Wayley's room next door.

Social visiting between the two teachers during school hours was forbidden by the school inspector. But the inspector was miles away and not due for another month.

Miss Wayley, upon being apprised of the situation, put her entire class, including those who hadn't yet learned to write, to work on a composition entitled "How I Will Spend My Summer Vacation." Then she and Miss Barabou retired to the tiny room at the rear of the school where they ate their lunch and made coffee during recesses and conducted their private business in general. The room was cold and cramped and ugly, but it had two distinct advantages: a lock on the door which had so far resisted even the expert picking of Boris, and a telephone installed the past winter after a bad storm left the school marooned for nearly twenty-four hours.

Miss Wayley lit a cigarette, took three quick, furtive puffs, and butted it before any of the smoke could seep under the door and cause alarm or suspicion among the students. She saved the butt in an empty Band-Aid box inside the first aid kit.

"I think," Miss Barabou said, "we should phone somebody."

But Miss Wayley was busy trying on the cap in front of the yellowed, broken mirror hanging on the wall, "Don't I look sporty, though? Say, this is kind of cute. I wouldn't mind having one myself. Makes me feels years younger."

"Be serious."

"I am."

"It looks like a man's cap to me. Have you seen any strange men around town lately?"

"If I had," Miss Wayley said cheerfully, "I'd be on leave of absence tracking him down, believe you me."

"Be *serious*."

"I can't. I feel sporty. Here, you try it on, Marie."

"I wouldn't dream of..."

"Go on. See how it looks. Just for fun."

Miss Barabou took a quick glance at the door to make sure it was locked, then she, too, tried on the plaid cap. For one instant, in the cracked mirror, she did indeed look sporty, but the instant was overwhelmed by years of common sense. "It's ridiculous. I wouldn't be caught dead wearing such a thing."

"Well, I would. I can just picture myself whizzing along in some snazzy convertible..."

"Why a convertible?"

"Because that's what the cap's for, riding in a convertible with the top down. I've seen them in the movies."

"That's how it happened, then."

"What did?"

"Someone was riding along the cliff road in a convertible and his cap blew off and landed on the beach where Agatha found it."

"It couldn't blow off, easily, anyway. That's what the elastic band at the back is for, to keep it tight-fitting so the wind won't blow it off."

"How odd," Miss Barabou said, and for the first time she appeared disturbed by the possibilities. "I know it sounds silly, but—well, you don't suppose there's been a *crime* committed?"

"No such luck."

"Please be serious."

"I am. I said no such luck and I mean it. Nothing ever happens around here."

"There's always a first time."

The noise from the two unattended classes was increasing by the minute—thuds, screams, laughter, whistling—but neither of the two teachers paid any attention. Din was a part of their lives and a few decibels one way or another didn't matter.

"I'd feel like a fool," Miss Barabou said, "if I called in the police and it turned out to be absolutely nothing."

"Call anyway." Miss Wayley selected one of the dozen or so cigarette butts she kept stored in the first aid kit, and lit it with a reckless air. "We might as well whip up a little excitement while the whipping's good. Here, help yourself to a butt."

"No thanks. It wouldn't be sanitary."

"Sorry I can't offer you a fresh one. Gee, it'd be wonderful to buy cigarettes cheap the way they do in the States."

"I'm not sure whom to call."

"The local constabulary. What a marvelous word, constabulary, isn't it?"

"The way you chatter, I can't *think.*"

"You don't have to think. Let the local constabulary do the thinking. You and I, we're teachers, we don't get paid for thinking, we get paid for teaching, and what a whale of a difference there is."

"Oh, *stop* it, Betty."

Miss Barabou picked up the phone.

Constable Lehman arrived at the school about nine-thirty, a small, droll-faced man in his fifties who took his work, but nothing else, quite seriously. He came in his own private car, an old Buick, a device intended to allay the curiosity of the students. Through no fault of his own the device backfired. A good half of Miss Barabou's class, and even several members of Miss Wayley's lower grades, recognized him immediately and such excitement spread through the school that a recess had to be declared.

The children, with the exception of Aggie Schantz, were herded into the yard like wild ponies, and a conference was held in Miss Barabou's room with the plaid cap on exhibition on her desk. Instead of being nervous, as Miss Barabou had expected, Aggie luxuriated in the special attention she was receiving. She told her story in full detail, and Lehman, who'd had experience with children of his own, did not interrupt her even when she included such nonessentials as what she had for breakfast and how many robins she saw en route to school.

"We count robins," Miss Barabou said by way of apology and explanation. "For the bird chart. Natural history, you know."

Lehman's nod indicated that he understood perfectly, and was, in fact, an old hand at counting robins himself.

"I see more than anybody," Aggie said, with becoming modesty, "mostly because I have a longer way to go to school. Boris saw an American eagle."

Lehman pursed his lips. "Did he, now? Well, they say more and more American people are coming up this way every year, why not eagles, too, eh? Can you show me this special path you take down to the beach, Aggie?"

"I can *show* you. You can't go down it, though."

"I can't, eh? Why not?"

"You're too old."

"You may have something there," Lehman said, and sighed for Aggie's benefit, and winked for Miss Barabou's.

Miss Barabou, who was not accustomed to being winked at, blushed in confusion and turned to Aggie. "Of course you'll show the Constable the path, Agatha. I'll excuse you from school for the rest of the morning. You go with Constable Lehman."

"I don't want to."

"Get your coat and galoshes on."

Aggie didn't move.

"Agatha, did you hear me?"

"I don't want to go without you."

"You know perfectly well I have to stay here and supervise my class."

"You could send them all home," Aggie said hopefully. "They wouldn't mind."

"No, I'm sure they wouldn't. Neither would I, until it came time to explain to thirty howling parents. Why on earth don't you want to go with the Constable?"

"The bad men."

"What bad men?"

"That do nasty things to little girls on beaches."

"Oh, for heaven's *sake*." Miss Barabou's blush had spread to the tips of her ears and down her neck to the collar of her jersey dress. "I was only trying to—oh well, it doesn't matter. I give up. I'll go along, there's no point in arguing."

Miss Barabou sat in the back of the Buick alone, holding herself stiff and resistant to the feeling of adventure that was growing inside her with every turn of the road and every glance at the Constable's face half visible in the rear-view mirror. *He's really quite a nice man. Humorous, too. Betty said she heard he's a widower, all his children are grown and he lives by himself. He needs a haircut.*

She tried to discipline her thoughts by planning the next eighth grade British History assignment, but she could not seem to concentrate properly. The scarlet pompon on the plaid cap which lay on the seat beside her seemed to be taunting her: *Come on, live now. The Magna Charta is very old; King John is very dead. Be sporty.*

She looked sternly, ponderously, out of the window, though her head felt quite light and empty, as if giddy little bubbles were whirling around inside, released by some strange alchemy she did not understand.

"We're almost there." Aggie's voice pealed with excitement. "Right around the next corner."

"Roger," Lehman said.

"What's that mean?"

"It means right-ho. Roger, dodger, you old codger, I'm a major too."

"Oh, you make me laugh."

"I aim to please."

He stopped the car on the side of the road and all three of them got out, Aggie still giggling behind her hand, Miss Barabou very sober and dignified as if to make up for the levity of the others. Looking down at the water a hundred feet below, and the path by which she was expected to descend, she offered up a short silent prayer.

Lehman said to Aggie, who was impatient to start down the path, "Hold your horses a minute, lass. Now when you found the plaid cap, was it directly below here?"

"No sir. I walked along a piece first until I got tired and sat down and then I found it."

"About how far did you walk?"

"I don't know. I can show you down there."

"Show me up here first."

"I don't know if I can."

"Try. Start walking."

They began walking single file up the road with Aggie in the lead like a general with delusions of troops.

The road was not a main one, and though it was marked on maps as "improved," the improvements had long since disappeared in the throes of winter. The surface had buckled in places and some of the potholes were as large as Aggie's head.

Lehman appeared to be watching his footing very carefully, paying no attention to Miss Barabou struggling along in the rear. Aggie was skipping on ahead, not looking down at the road at all but avoiding every bump and hole as if she had made a complete mental map of the route and knew its every pitfall.

"I'm beginning to get tired," Aggie said, "so I guess it was right about here."

She looked up expectantly, as if awaiting Lehman's commendation, but he seemed too preoccupied to notice her. He was staring down at the mud along the side of the road, his eyes narrowed against the morning sun.

"Well?" Miss Barabou said when, out of sorts and breath, she finally caught up with the others.

"Look here, ma'am."

"I can't see anything out of the ordinary."

"No?"

"Some tire marks, that's all. It's a road, you'd expect to find tire marks, that's all. It's a road, you'd expect to find tire marks."

"Not ones leading over the top of the cliff." Lehman turned to Aggie, who was bouncing all over the place. "Be a good lass and stay out of the way. In fact, how about you going back and waiting in the car?"

"But I haven't showed you anything yet."

"You've shown me quite a lot more than I expected."

"Tell me what."

"Well, stand still a minute. See these marks here? They were made by the tires of an automobile, a new one and a heavy one, my guess is a Lincoln or a Cadillac. Now where do they lead?"

"Nowhere. They just stop."

"Exactly. They just stop."

Lehman walked to the edge of the cliff and Miss Barabou followed him, wide-eyed and nervous. "What does it all mean?"

"It means there's a car down there, perhaps with people in it."

"*People.* But we've got to do something right away, help them..."

"I'm afraid it would be too late. The marks aren't fresh and the water's deep."

"Perhaps you're being too pessimistic. It could be that some people just stopped here for a look at the view and went on again. That's more likely than..."

"There's no sign that the car turned around."

Miss Barabou's hand moved to her throat. "I'll—I'd better take Aggie back to the car."

But she stood peering down at the water below, as if she hoped to distinguish the outlines of a car, the contours of people. The glare of sun on water dazzled her eyes and she stumbled back half-blinded.

Lehman caught her by the arm. "Watch it. That's a long fall."

"Yes."

"It's a city car, I'll bet you that."

"How can you tell?"

"Around these parts a person driving an expensive car would still be using snow tires at this time of year. The kind of winters we have up here, we need them. But in a city where the roads are kept clear, snow tires wouldn't be necessary." He paused. "I wonder."

"You wonder what?"

"What makes a person drive over a cliff."

Lehman drove Miss Barabou and Aggie back to school and left them there with instructions to say nothing to anyone. Then he called the Provincial Police and returned to the cliff. Three police cars were waiting for him when he arrived, as well as the resuscitation squad of the local fire station, all ready to go into action.

No action was necessary.

Two barges, sent down from Meaford with winches and dredging equipment, located the car in twenty feet of water just below the cliff where Lehman had found the tire tracks. The car was barely damaged, the windows and windshield were unbroken, and Ron Galloway was still inside, fastened snugly to the driver's seat by his safety belt.

FOURTEEN

Ralph Turee returned to his office from his eleven o'clock seminar feeling hungry and exhausted. He had got up too early for sufficient rest and too late for breakfast. Harry had spent the night at his house and the two men had talked until after three in the morning. Talked and talked and settled nothing beyond what was already settled—Galloway was missing, and Thelma was waiting for him to come back and claim her as his future wife.

He sat down at his desk and was unpacking the lunch Nancy had made for him when the door opened and Nancy herself appeared.

Turee looked up in surprise. It was not a rule that Nancy should stay away from his office during working hours, but her visits were so infrequent that she looked strange in the surroundings, like a new graduate student perhaps, or someone who'd lost her way in the corridors and merely stopped by for directions. She was a small pretty woman with a round cherubic face and rather short sturdy legs—"practical" legs, Turee called them, in contrast to what he considered her impractical mind. She was wearing her new violet-colored Easter suit, which meant that the occasion, whatever it might be, was important.

He rose and kissed her briefly on the forehead by way of greeting. "How did you get here?"

"Took a cab."

"A *cab.* My God, Nancy, I told you we're short of money this month after those Easter outfits you bought for the kids and..."

"Save your lecture. This is an emergency."

Her tone rather than her words stopped him. "Has one of the kids been..."

"Nothing like that. Esther called. She wants me to spend the rest of the day with her."

"Why?"

"Ron's been found."

"Dead?"

"Yes."

Something inside Turee that had been stretched tauter and tauter like a violin string, broke suddenly with a twang. Along with a dozen other sensations he felt a sense of relief that the suspense was over. Ron was, in a way, now safe; safe from Esther's cold scorn, and Thelma's demands, and Harry's reproach, and the ridicule of the world. "How did it happen?"

"He drove off a cliff into the bay, somewhere not too far from the lodge. He had the convertible with the top down. Esther said the policeman who came to tell her said Ron mightn't have been found for days, or weeks even, if he hadn't had his safety belt fastened." Her lower lip projected childishly and began to tremble. "I don't know, there's something so f-f-funny about that, Ron was always p-playing it s-s-safe."

"Don't cry."

"I can't help it."

"All right then." He watched with detachment while she dabbed at her eyes, wondering for the hundredth time at what peculiar things roused a woman's emotions. The fact that Ron drove over a cliff to his death didn't seem to bother her as much as the safety belt being fastened. "Ron did it intentionally?"

"Yes. Esther had a letter from him this morning—he'd posted it Saturday night in some little town up north. She told me about it on the phone."

"And?"

"Well, this will come as a great shock to you, Ralph, but—well, Thelma's pregnant. By Ron. It's incredible, utterly incredible, he and Harry were such good friends. I can't *believe* it. Can you?"

He turned away deliberately, without answering.

"You don't even seem surprised, Ralph. You mean you *knew?* All along? And you didn't tell me?"

"We'll go into that another time."

"But you..."

"How is Esther taking it?"

"I don't know. She sounded calm enough. She seemed anxious for me to come and stay with her, though, so I will."

"Good girl."

"I couldn't very well refuse. Oh yes, and I've made arrangements with Mrs. Sullivan to go and meet Janie's school bus. The other kids are big enough to look after themselves for a while."

"They won't have to. My last class is a two o'clock. I'll be home before four."

"No, dear, you won't."

He looked exasperated. "What the hell does that mean, no-dear-you-won't?"

"I've been thinking it over. Somebody has to tell Thelma. It wouldn't be humane to let her hear on the radio or read it in the newspaper. Someone has to drive to Weston and tell her in person."

"Meaning me."

"You're the logical one. I thought of Harry, but it's so difficult locating him when he's on the job going from office to office. Besides, having Harry tell her wouldn't be very—well, delicate, would it? So that leaves you."

"Obviously."

"You don't mind very much, do you?"

"I mind like the very devil."

"Someone has to do it. I'd volunteer, but I don't trust myself. I'm angry with her, bitterly angry, I couldn't even pretend any sympathy."

"Can I?"

"No, but you can *feel* it," she said earnestly. "You're much kinder than I am about human frailties."

When he reached Weston it was five o'clock and his nerves were rubbed raw by traffic tensions and anticipation of his errand. At the very outskirts of the city he was still thinking up excuses to turn around and go back, or to call Bill Winslow or Joe Hepburn and pass the buck to one of them.

Though it was still bright and sunny, the blinds were already drawn on the windows of the square red-brick house where Thelma lived. Turee had to ring the doorbell half a dozen times before Thelma finally appeared.

Freshly scrubbed, without make-up, and with her long fair hair combed straight back, Alice-in-Wonderland style, she appeared younger and more vulnerable than Turee remembered her. Although he had talked to her on the telephone, he hadn't seen her since the last time the fellows had gathered at Harry's house a month ago, and on that occasion, as on other similar ones, she'd been unobtrusive and efficient, quietly refilling glasses and passing sandwiches, more like a good maid than the mistress of the house. Looking at her now, Turee tried to recall whether at any time during that night she'd paid special attention to Galloway, whether hands had touched briefly, or significant glances had passed back and forth, or knowing smiles been exchanged. The only incident Turee could think of happened late in the evening: Galloway had dropped and broken his glass and Thelma had cleaned up the mess. No one thought anything of it at the time, no one saw anything significant or symbolic in Thelma's kneeling docilely at Galloway's feet, picking up the pieces of glass and blotting the carpet with paper towels. Galloway had not offered to help. He'd seemed, in fact, stunned by the accident, as if he'd broken some valuable crystal by Steuben instead of an ordinary tumbler from the dime store.

"Hello, Ralph."

"Hello, Thelma. How are you?"

"Fine. I think, fine." She was carrying a man's blue and white striped shirt and a threaded needle. "Come in, won't you? I'm just sewing."

The three lamps in the living room were turned on but the room still looked gloomy, and the atmosphere was cool and damp as if the place had been shut up all day and used as a refuge by someone hiding from the sun or the neighbors.

Thelma sat on the chesterfield beside a pile of men's clothes, socks and shirts and undershorts. "Harry called at noon. Thanks for letting him spend the night with you."

"He's welcome to stay any time. The kids are crazy about him."

"Oh."

"He likes them, too. He doesn't even mind them climbing all over him at six-thirty in the morning. That's a true test."

"Is it?"

"My own opinion is that Harry would make a very fine father. He's got all the..."

"You're wasting your time," she said, flatly and finally. "Harry is not the father of my child. I couldn't possibly go on living with him, pretending that he was. If that's what you're suggesting."

"I'm not merely suggesting, I'm strongly urging you to reconsider. Harry and I talked it over last night. He's willing, he's actually eager to assume responsibility for the child. He loves you, Thelma."

"I know that. But I don't love him. And if I had to continue living with him under such false pretenses I might grow to hate him. No child should be brought up in a house of hate as I was. No, Ralph, don't argue. The future is settled."

"Is it?"

"Yes. Oh, there'll be a lot of talk, a lot of scandal, but it will blow over. Then Ron and I can move somewhere else and start a life of our own." She spoke quickly, glibly, as if she had said these exact words to herself many times, perhaps because she believed them, perhaps because she was mere-ly trying to believe them. "You don't mind if I go on sewing, do you? Harry's coming for his things after be finishes work and I want them to be in order. He won't have anyone to look after him for a while."

"For a while?"

"He'll get married again some day... I know he thinks his love for me is unique and undying and so on, but I understand Harry pretty well. Some nice woman will come along and give him the kind of life he wants."

"You've given him the kind of life he wants."

"He's easily satisfied. I'm not."

"You put up a good front."

"I have my pride. Oh, I guess you think that word sounds peculiar com-ing from me, but what I said is true. I couldn't very well go around telling people like you and Nancy that I was bored and lonely sitting around this house all day, knowing the future would be exactly the same. The only per-son I ever told was Ron. He told me things too—that Esther was smarter than he was and he was always embarrassed when they went out togeth-er and she dominated the conversation and everything. He said it made him feel as if he were her idiot son whom she dragged along out of duty."

It was, to Turee, a rather bizarre picture of the Galloways' relationship, and yet he realized instantly that it showed some true colors and some bold, clear lines.

"I told him he needn't fear anything like that from me, I'm not very smart. Or if I am, nobody's ever mentioned it."

Suddenly she put down her sewing and flashed him a glance so sharp and direct that he blinked trying to meet it. "What are you doing here, Ralph? You're usually home by this time. I know you and Nancy eat early because of the children. Did you just come to hear me chatter?"

"No.."

"I knew as soon as I opened the door and saw you, I knew there must be a reason. An important one. Is it about Ron?"

"Yes."

"If it were good news you'd have told me right away. So it's bad news. How bad?"

"He's dead."

"You're not—there can't be any mistake?"

"No."

She bunched forward until her forehead rested on her knees and stayed there motionless, as if she'd lost the will to move. Street noises seeped in through the cracks of the windows and streaks of light past the edges of the drawn blinds. Turee wished he were outside with the noise and the light, instead of in this room where everything seemed to have died, not even a clock ticked or a fly buzzed.

Thelma spoke finally, her voice muffled by the folds of her skirt. "The car."

"What about the car?"

"He had an accident?"

"There is reason to believe," Turee said cautiously, "that the act was intentional."

"What reason?"

"He posted a letter to Esther before he died."

"To *Esther.*" Her head snapped up like a puppet's jerked by a string. "Not to me. Why not to *me?* Why not to me? I'm the one who loved him. I gave up everything for him, my home, my husband, my good name, and I'd have given up anything more I had. Why not to me? Why not... Oh God, I can't stand it. Ron, Ron, Ron. Oh God, come back, Ron, come back. Don't leave me alone. I'm scared. I'm scared."

"Thelma. Please . "

"Ron, Ron, Ron darling. Oh, my God!"

She kept on moaning, her teeth pressed into her lower lip until the blood began to run, as if she were consciously inflicting mutilation on herself as punishment. Presently the metallic taste of the blood made her cough, and the moans turned into a fit of coughing. She held one of Harry's shirts against her mouth to stifle the sound. When she put it down again it was stained with blood and tears, and Turee thought what a sharp piece of irony it was that Harry, who had done nothing against anyone, should have to sop up the tears and wipe off the blood.

"Let me fix you a drink, Thelma."

"No!"

"Well, perhaps Harry has some pills lying around that will help calm you down a little."

"Pills!" She spat the word into the center of the room as if she were aiming at an invisible cuspidor. "Harry has a million pills lying around. Go take them all as far as I'm concerned."

"Damned if I wouldn't if I could find them," Turee said, rather pleased by her fit of temper. It meant that she wasn't too submerged in her grief to react to ordinary stimuli.

She held Harry's shirt to her mouth again, and if Turee hadn't known better he might have taken it for a gesture of affection. "What was in the letter he wrote to—to Esther?"

"I don't know."

"You haven't seen it?"

"No."

"Then she could be lying, deliberately lying, pretending there's such a letter to make me feel bad."

"That's not very reasonable, is it?"

"You don't know Esther."

"Only for ten years."

"Nobody knows what goes on inside somebody else."

"There's the circumstantial evidence of their actions and words. When you see a man obviously enjoying his dinner you can assume he feels hungry and thinks the food is good."

"Assuming and knowing—there's an appalling gap between them. And I fell into it." Fresh tears spilled down her cheeks and she jabbed at her eyes viciously as if they were traitors betraying her. "The night—Saturday night—when I told Ron about the baby I could see he was surprised, shocked even, but I thought he was pleased too, pleased because he loved me, and the baby was the bond of our love, and we would all be together in the future. That's what I *assumed*. What I know now is that he didn't want any future with me in it, he'd rather die. He'd rather *die*."

"Don't blame yourself so much, Thelma."

"There's no one else to blame." Her lower lip was beginning to puff and her eyes had swollen and reddened. "How could he have done it, deserted me, left me to face everything alone?"

"Thelma..."

"I thought he was a man, not a nasty little coward. No, no, what in God's name am I saying—he wasn't a coward! He—I don't know. I don't know! Oh Ron. Oh *Ron!*" She seemed to be clinging wildly to a pendulum that swung between the extremes of love and hate, grief and fury. "I can't stand it. I can't go on living without him."

"You must."

"I can't, I can't do it."

"You have to think of your child."

She folded her arms across her abdomen as if she suddenly had a notion that the fetus was already aware and must be protected from the sight and sound of strangers who might be hostile. "What will happen to us, Ralph, to him and me?"

"I don't know."

"I had such high hopes, such wonderful plans."

This was Thelma stripped down to essentials, like a hot rod with its top removed, its fenders missing, its engine exposed and unmuffled and its twin pipes roaring, *I* and *me*. All of Thelma's high hopes had been built on deceit and her wonderful plans made entirely at the expense of other people.

Something struck the front window and landed on the porch with a plop. Thelma jumped, as if the little sound had been loud as a cannon, aimed at her.

"Probably the evening paper," Turee said. "I'll bring it in if you like."

"I don't like. I—will it be in, about Ron?"

"Perhaps."

"And me?"

"I'm not sure who knows about you, except for Harry and Esther and myself." A few minutes later he was forced to add, silently, *and the entire police department.*

The account of Ron's death was headlined on the front page of the paper, PROMINENT TORONTONIAN FOUND DEAD IN GEORGIAN BAY. Esther had apparently refused to provide a recent photograph of Ron, so some newspaperman had scrounged around in the file room and came up with a picture taken several years previously at a New Year's Eve party at the Granite Club. Ron was grinning self-consciously into the camera, serpentine entwining his neck and bits of confetti clinging to his hair and his dinner jacket. Both the picture and the caption, Galloway in a Gayer Mood, were in incredibly bad taste. Turee had a futile hope that Esther wouldn't see it. That Thelma should see it was inevitable, but somehow this seemed more fitting to Turee, since all of Thelma's recent actions indicated her lack of the sense of propriety that was so strong in Esther.

Although Thelma hadn't wanted him to bring in the newspaper in the first place, she was now watching him with nervous impatience, twisting and untwisting her small plump hands. "Well, what does it *say?*"

"Read it for yourself."

"No. I can't. My eyes hurt."

"All right. First, there's a factual account of how and where he was found. I see no point in reading that aloud, it will only upset you."

"Go on from there, then."

" 'An autopsy has been ordered. Authorities are still investigating the possibility of accidental death, although the present evidence points to suicide. A letter received this morning by his wife, the former Esther Ann Billings, allegedly indicated Galloway's intention of killing himself. This letter is now in the hands of the police, who, because of its delicate and personal nature, refused to release its contents to the press.' "

"She gave the letter to the *police?*" Thelma's tone was incredulous, and Turee's would have matched it if he'd spoken. It seemed incongruous to him that Esther should have handed such a personal letter over to the police. The locker rooms of a police department could spring as many leaks as locker rooms anywhere else, and Esther was sophisticated enough to know this. Perhaps she'd had no choice and the police had demanded the letter as evidence of intent to commit suicide. Or perhaps Esther had meant, without thinking of the consequences to herself or her children, to involve Thelma, immediately and publicly.

Thelma said, "I'm in the letter, I suppose?"

"Yes.

"By name?"

"I think so."

"So it's only a matter of time until everybody in town knows. My God, how can I face it?"

"You have friends."

"Ron's friends, and Harry's. None of my own, not one."

"There's still a solution," Turee said. "If you'll accept it, if you'll be reasonable."

But she turned away, closing off the face of reason as if by a stone door. "I won't."

"You haven't even..."

"Hide behind Harry, that's your solution?"

"Harry's willing, I told you that. Don't underestimate him. He's a fine man, a generous man."

"Oh, I know. Good old Harry, always willing to give his last shirt to a friend—or lose it to him in a poker game. Harry's such a good loser, is that why everyone likes him so much? He loses so gently and gracefully. But he loses. He always misses the boat. Why?"

"Maybe he doesn't want to go any place."

"Well, I do. And I will. Anything will be better than going on living with Harry, in this house, in this town."

Her tone was final, and as if for emphasis she picked up her needle again. In and out of the holes of a button her hand moved, quick, precise, without a tremor. Either the pendulum had stopped swinging, or Thelma had let go of it.

Turee rose and crossed the room, awkwardly and painfully. His legs had gone numb and his feet felt as if they were being pierced by a thousand needles, all sharper than the one Thelma was wielding. She looked up and met his questioning gaze. "Stop worrying about me," she said bluntly. "I'll be all right as long as I keep busy, keep doing things. Tomorrow I'll start on the baby's layette. Everything will be sewn by hand.... You're not leaving, Ralph?"

"It's getting rather late."

"I was hoping you'd stay until Harry comes for his clothes. He's probably seen the papers and he'll be very upset. He's terribly emotional about things—friends, home, mother, lost dogs. "

"Aren't you?"

"Me? I haven't any friends, and I never had either a home or a mother or owned a dog. Does that answer your question?"

"Not very satisfactorily."

"How you love to analyze people, Ralph, but please don't try it on me."

Turee remembered Harry's saying similar words early Sunday morning while they were driving from Wiarton back to the lodge: *Just don't start analyzing Thelma. I love her the way she is. Let her have her dreams.*

Well, she had them, Turee thought dryly. What a blind fool Harry had been. Not like a husband, but like a too-permissive parent, overly ready to cover up a child's errors, and eager to accept the most comfortable explanations.

"I'll make you some tea, Ralph. Perhaps you'd like a sandwich, too?"

"No thanks to both. I'll wait for Harry, though."

"That's good of you." She picked up the pile of clothes from the chesterfield and rose, a little clumsily, as if she were not yet used to the new proportion of weight in her body. "If you'll excuse me, I'll finish Harry's packing.'"

"Where is he going to stay?"

"He told me he's taking a room at a hotel. I don't know which one. I didn't ask."

"Will he keep on with his job here?"

"I didn't ask that either." She paused in the doorway. "I keep telling you, but you still don't seem to understand. Harry and I are through. He is part of the past. We must both start right now forgetting each other. I've made my decision—it wouldn't be fair to Harry if I kept in touch with him, if I fostered any hope in him that we would get together again. I don't want to know where he's living or what he's doing. I wish him good luck, that's all. And happiness too."

"How magnanimous."

She missed the irony. "I bear no grudge against Harry. Why should I? He did his best."

After she'd left the room, Turee picked up a magazine, but it was impossible for him to read. He found himself listening to Thelma's step, on the stairs and along the hall, heavy and uncertain as if she were dragging something behind her. He could hear her moving around in the bedroom directly overhead, opening drawers, closing them, mumbling to herself now and then, muted sounds that disintegrated before they could reach Turee as words.

She's frightened silly, he thought. If Harry could force himself to take a really firm stand with her, she might be willing to give in, to lean on him. Thelma's repeated protestations of independence seemed to be covering up a real need to lean. Perhaps the reason she couldn't yet do it was her fear that Harry might not be able to bear her weight. It was now up to Harry to prove his strength.

The telephone began to ring in the next room and Thelma came downstairs to answer it, quite slowly, as if she knew in advance that the call couldn't be important, all the important things had already happened to her.

"Hello.... Yes, this is Mrs. Bream.... Is he hurt?... Oh, I see.... No, I can't come myself, it's impossible. I'll see if I can get somebody else... Thank you for telling me. Good-bye."

Turee met her at the door of the living room. "Harry's been injured?"

"Not badly. He jammed the back of a street car on College Avenue and he has a few head cuts. He's in the emergency ward at Toronto General. They're going to keep him there overnight."

"Why, if it's nothing serious?"

"Why?" The corners of her mouth twisted in bitterness. "Because he's too drunk to go anywhere."

FIFTEEN

The curtained cubicle was so small that Turee barely had room to stand beside the bed. Harry lay on his back, his eyes closed, his entire head bandaged very tightly, so that the skin of his forehead had contracted into a petulant frown.

"Harry..."

"He's out," the nurse said. She was a type Turee recognized, stout, middle-aged, efficient, with a false front of maternality that wouldn't deceive a child but had fooled many an adult. She added, "He talks a blue streak, then passes out, and a minute later he's talking again."

"I thought he was only slightly hurt. All those bandages..."

"They don't mean anything. Head cuts bleed a lot so the doctor usually applies a pressure bandage for a day or two in case of hemorrhage. Actually he's only got eleven stitches. He'll suffer more from the hangover. And other things."

"Such as?"

"As soon as he's released from here they'll take him down and book him for drunk driving. He'll get a stiff fine. Too bad, him with no job and his wife pregnant. Maybe that's why he did it."

"Did what?"

"Drank so much. Some men get all emotional over their first baby. I guess it strains their sense of responsibility. Do you want to stay here with him for a while?"

"Yes."

"Good. I have things to do. If he gets rambunctious, just give me a buzz."

"All right."

"I'm Miss Hutchins."

Turee stood in silence at the foot of the bed, observing the differences that lack of consciousness emphasized. Harry's affability seemed to be unmasked as weakness, his urge to please as anxiety. And this is what Thelma sees, he thought, Harry with his guards down. This is what she based her decision on. She can't afford to lean on a straw.

"Harry."

Harry shook his head back and forth on the pillow as if he was trying to shake off the sound of his own name nagging him back into a world he wanted to forget.

"It's Ralph, Harry. You don't have to talk. I just want you to know I'm here."

"Thelma?"

"She's all right. She's at home. The next door neighbor is staying with her, a Mrs. Mal—somebody."

"My head hurts. Wanna sit *up.*"

"I'm not sure you..."

"Wanna sit up."

"All right." Turee cranked the bed up halfway. "That better?"

"Nothing's better. Nothing's better in the whole world." His slurred speech and glassy, unfocused eyes made it clear that either Harry was still drunk or under the influence of a sedative. "*Nothing.* See?"

"I see. Sure."

"You're a good head, Ralph. There's no better head than you, nowhere. See?"

"Sure, sure. Now take it easy."

Harry closed his eyes and lapsed into incoherence for a time. Only the odd word was distinguishable, but his angry, guttural tone and his bellicose expression indicated strongly that Harry was telling somebody off.

Turee moved up to the head of the bed and put his hand lightly and firmly on Harry's shoulder "Harry, can you hear me?"

"Can't hear you. Go away."

"What's bothering you?"

"I bumped into a street car. Damn thing wouldn't move. I was in a hurry."

"Where were you going?"

"No place. No place to go."

"Before you hit the street car, Harry, what happened?"

"I had a little drink."

"I know that."

"One little drink. 'S what I told the policeman. 'S what I'm telling you."

"I thought you were at work. You don't usually drink between office calls."

"No office calls. No more office calls."

"What do you mean?"

" 'Take your goddam pills,' I said, 'I quit.' I said, 'The whole bloody bunch of you can go jump in the lake.' Lake." He repeated the word, wincing, as if it had pierced his consciousness like a needle. "Lake. I was in a bar. I heard them talking about a lake. Ron. That's what Ron did. Jumped in the lake. Isn't that funny, hah? Isn't that funny?" Tears were streaming down his face, and he had begun to hiccough. "Wanted to jump in the lake too. Couldn't find it. Couldn't find the bloody lake."

"You can find it some other time," Turee said dryly. "Right now you're supposed to take it easy."

"Street car in my way. Wouldn't move. 'Giddyap,' I said, 'giddyap,' and I stepped on the gas. Didn't mean to hit it, just wanted to push it along, get it started. I was in a hurry. I was—where was I going? Can't remember."

"It doesn't matter."

Harry wiped his face on a corner of the bed sheet, then held it against his mouth to stem the flow of hiccoughs. "My head hurts. I broke something. Did I—broke something?"

"No." He wishes he had, Turee thought. It would be easier on him if he could misdirect his misery at something physical. But all Harry's breaks are in places no doctor could reach to use a splint or apply a cast. "You've got a hangover," Turee added bluntly. "How much did you have to drink?"

"Just one little..."

"Come off it. I'm not a policeman. How much?"

"Don't, don't, don't. I can't remember."

"All right."

"I needed a drink. I quit my job."

"Why? You've always liked your job."

"No wife any more, no home, might as well have no job, start from scratch."

"That's pretty childish logic. How do you expect to live?"

"I don't know. I don't care."

"Do you think the company will take you back? You've been with them for years."

"I'm not going back."

"You could apply for a transfer to another city."

"No wife, no home, no job."

"Also no friends, if you want to play it that way."

"Friends." Harry spit the word across the room as if it had a foul taste. Then he turned and buried his face in the pillow and started to curse. He kept it up for a long time.

"You're beginning," Turee said finally, "to repeat yourself."

"Shut your goddam..."

"All right, all right, all right."

"How the hell did you get here anyway? Who asked you to come?"

"Thelma. I was with her when the hospital phoned."

"Doing what? Or is that too personal?"

Turee, white with anger, explained in very elementary language what he was not doing with Thelma. "Now is that clear enough for you or shall I draw pictures?"

"Goddam you, shut up! Shut up, shut up!"

As if on cue, Miss Hutchins, the nurse, reappeared. She wore the professional smile which she picked up outside the door like a surgical gown and left there when she departed. "Just what is going on in here? Do you want to wake the whole hospital? How does your head feel?"

Without waiting for any answers, she began adjusting the tray holder on Harry's bed. "Here we are. Some nice Cream of Wheat. And a cup of chocolate with a marshmallow—one of the new dietitians is bugs on marshmallows, puts them in everything. And two little pills to help with the jitters."

Harry glanced briefly at the pills. "Chlorpromazine."

"Now how did you know that?"

"Never mind. I won't take them anyway. I want my clothes."

"What for?"

"I've got to get out of here. Where are my clothes?"

"Where I put them. So let's not have a hassle, Mr. Bream. In a hospital when the doctors says you stay, you stay. Might as well pretend you're a guest and be polite about it"

"I have to talk to my wife. It's urgent."

"Look, Mr. Bream, even if you managed to get out of here, you wouldn't be allowed to go home. You were driving while drunk and involved in an accident. You'll have to be taken down to the jail and booked. There's a policeman at the desk now waiting to question you about the accident. This isn't the Royal York Hotel but it's better than a cell in the local pokey."

"Bail. I could get bail. Ralph, how much money have you got?"

"Here?" Turee said. "About a dollar and thirty-five cents. In the bank, a little more."

"Well, there's Bill Winslow or Joe Hepburn. Or Esther. No, we couldn't bother Esther. But Bill would..."

"Bill won't," Miss Hutchins said bluntly. "Not tonight, anyway. Now if you behave yourself, you can stay here. You're warm, comfy, well looked after. But if you start throwing fits they'll haul you up to the psycho ward. Some of the beds there have cages around them. Now do you want to spend the night locked up like a monkey in a zoo, or are you going to be a good boy, eat your Cream of Wheat, take your pills and stop arguing?"

Harry peered at her resentfully from under his bandages. "You're very *rude.*"

"Am I now?" Miss Hutchins' smile for the first time was one of genuine amusement. "Well, I've been handling drunks for thirty years. I guess it's not the best way in the world to learn manners. Think you can feed yourself?"

"Of course I can feed myself."

"Try."

Harry tried. He picked up the spoon and dipped it in the dish of cereal, but his hand was shaking so badly he didn't attempt to raise the spoon to his mouth. He lay back and closed his eyes. "I'm not hungry."

"None of you are," Miss Hutchins said dryly. "But some protein helps with the shakes. The pills ought to help, too. Are you going to take them?"

"I—guess so."

Miss Hutchins gave him the pills in a tiny paper cup and Harry swallowed them like an expert, without any water.

"There now," Miss Hutchins said. "I'll take your tray away and we'll try eating again later after you've had a little rest."

"Chlorpromazine never affects me. I've had it dozens of times."

"Is that a fact?"

She removed the tray and cranked down the bed. Within a few minutes Harry was asleep again, snoring heavily through his open mouth.

Turee followed Miss Hutchins into the corridor. "Should I stay around?"

"Oh, there's no reason to. He'll be fine. It's nearly eight o'clock, he may sleep clear through the night."

"I hope so," Turee said, wishing he could do the same, sleep through the night right up until noon the next day. By noon some things would be settled. Harry would be free, and Esther would have weathered the first day of widowhood. Perhaps, too, the autopsy would be completed and any uncertainty about Ron's death dispelled. Turee wondered, and felt a little shocked at himself for wondering, if Ron had made a will, and if he, or any of the rest of Ron's friends, were mentioned in it. *I can't help it. I have a dollar thirty-five in my pocket.*

"...a funny thing about Mr. Bream," Miss Hutchins was saying. "Before I took in his tray, I checked the result of the blood alcohol test they ran on him. It was only one-tenth of one percent. In a normal person that's not even intoxication level, yet Mr. Bream was almost dead drunk when they brought him in. I guess he's the kind who can't hold his liquor."

"I guess he is."

"Or else he's under some severe emotional strain which aggravated the effect of the alcohol. It's odd his wife didn't come to see him." Miss Hutchins' tone was casual, there wasn't the faintest emphasis on the word *wife*. But her eyes gave her away. They were honed sharp as a fortune teller's on the lookout for some slight reaction that would indicate she was on the right road to her client's secrets. "When I talked to her on the telephone she sounded quite cool and collected, just the kind of person you'd think would rise to an emergency."

Noon. Noon tomorrow, Turee said to himself as a child says Christmas. *By noon some things will be settled and Miss Hutchins will have faded into the past and good riddance.*

He had no reason to suspect that a long time later Miss Hutchins would reappear in his mind, her features distinct, her voice persistent, her outlines as precise as they were now while he was watching her bustle off down the corridor to the nurses' station.

Turee began walking in the opposite direction toward the exit door. The policeman Miss Hutchins had referred to was waiting at the registration desk, talking to a young man wearing a crew cut and a trench coat.

As Turee was about to pass, the young man turned and his face brightened with recognition. "Why, hello, Professor."

"Good evening."

"I guess you don't remember me. I'm Rod Blake. I was in a poli sci course of yours a couple of years ago."

"Blake. Of course." He recalled Blake now as a brash youngster whose good opinion of himself had been considerably higher than his grades. "What are you doing this year, Blake?"

"A little of this and that. I've got my sights set on a job. A good one. Why start at the bottom, I always say."

"Well, good luck."

Turee was impatient to leave, but the young man took a step to the left, blocking his way. It was an unobtrusive and expert motion, as if Blake were accustomed to people trying to get away from him and had practiced means of circumventing them.

"Nothing the matter with your family, I hope?" Blake said.

"They're all well, thank you."

"That's good. I thought your being here in this ward might indicate..."

"I was visiting a friend who had an accident."

"Nothing serious, I trust?"

Turee glanced at the policeman who appeared bored, either by the conversation, his job, or Blake. "Nothing serious, no. Well, good night, Blake."

"It was a real pleasure bumping into you like this, Professor."

They shook hands, firmly, like old friends or secret enemies, and Turee went out into the spring night.

The cold wind evaporated the moisture on his brow and spread a chill through his entire body. *I flunked him in the course. He hates my guts. I wonder what his angle is.*

SIXTEEN

It was characteristic of Blake that when he wanted something badly he went after it with such tactless determination that he weakened his own chances. The job at the *Globe and Mail* was a case in point.

He had decided on journalism as his field because it apparently offered glamour and excitement and a chance for advancement "Wait'll I'm editor," he'd told one of his girl friends. And he had chosen the particular newspaper, the *Globe,* because it was old, established, solvent, and the news editor was a man named Ian Richards whom Blake respected as much as he could respect anyone.

Every day or two, for the past month, he'd been dropping in at Richards' office, trying to prove, by means of story ideas, plans for a new sports column, revamping the front-page format and so on, that the Globe had tired blood and needed a quick transfusion of Blake. He oversold himself. Richards' preliminary interest had turned into dislike, his amusement into acidity. Yet no matter how clearly Richards indicated these changes, Blake seemed to remain obdurately unaware of them.

Late Tuesday afternoon he appeared at Richards' office in an elated mood. Richards didn't pay much attention to the mood. He'd seen samples of it before, and it usually meant only that Blake had been thinking beautiful thoughts of himself again.

"I'd ask you to sit down," Richards said, "but I'm busy."

Blake grinned. "I can talk on my feet."

"You can talk on your head, I'm still busy."

"You'll be sorry if you don't listen. I'm on to something."

"Again?"

"This time it's big. You've been following the Galloway case?"

"I read my own newspaper, naturally. What about it? Suicides are a dime a dozen."

"And the stories behind them?"

"I'm sure they're all very interesting, but it's not the kind of thing we print."

"You might want to print this one. You, or some other newspaper. I'm giving you first chance. Nice of me, eh?'"

"Dandy," Richards' mouth puckered as if he'd bitten into something sour. "Just dandy."

"Well, the whole thing started in kind of a chancy way. Last night I dropped in at the Emergency Ward at General. It's a good place to pick up things, there are always policemen around waiting to question accident victims and so on. Anyway, I was just standing there minding everybody else's business when I happened to see an old prof of mine from U. C., Ralph Turee. He handed me a bum deal in his course but I figured, let bygones be bygones. Besides, I had a hunch—it seemed like the last place in the world you'd meet a guy like Turee. I mean, he's just not the type you associate with accidents or emergencies or the like. He's cold, and cautious, probably never even had a parking ticket in his life—maybe a little like you, eh, Richards?"

"So you had a hunch. Go on."

"It seems Turee was in the ward, visiting a friend of his who had an accident. That much I got from him, the rest got from the nurse in charge. I had no trouble at all. Nurses always go for me. I gave her the treatment and she opened up like a flower. The friend Turee was visiting was a guy named Harry Bream who'd been brought in drunk after hitting a street car. Bream did a lot of ranting and raving during which he dropped some names. Galloway was one, Ron Galloway. As soon as I heard that, bells started to ring."

"Same old bells, or new ones?"

Blake brushed away the sarcasm as he would a fly, with sweep of his hand. "So I began checking. First the records at City Hall, then your file room downstairs. When Galloway was married, nine years ago, to his present wife, Harry Bream was his best man. And get this, he was also best man at Galloway's first marriage to the heiress, Dorothy Reynold. The conclusion's obvious: Bream and Galloway have been very good friends for a very long time."

"So?"

"Well, Bream now has a wife himself. They were married about three years ago, no children, live out in Weston. Her name is Thelma. Mean anything to you?"

"Not a thing."

"You should get around, Richards. Like me. That suicide note Galloway left—well, let's put it this way: I've got a pretty good friend in the police department."

"He let you see the note?"

"No, but he told me what was in it."

Richards looked grim. "For how much?"

"Not a cent. He likes my pretty blue eyes."

"I suppose policemen find you as irresistible as nurses do?"

"You might," Blake said with a smile, "put it like that, yes."

"You're a fresh kid, Blake. Full of ideas, some of them good, full of stories, some of them true. But mostly full of you-know-what. I wouldn't give you a job here even if I could. You're trouble."

"Trouble or not, I have some very valuable information."

"My advice is, take it to the *News.*"

"The *News* has no class. Besides, I hear it's going to fold. I don't want to start a trip on a sinking ship. I can't swim."

"You'd better learn."

"O.K., the hell with you, Richards. Let a silly personal prejudice cut you off from a scoop."

"We don't depend on scoops for our circulation."

"All right, but would you turn one down?"

Richards hesitated, drumming his pencil on the desk.

"Listen, Blake, if you've got a story, I might buy it. I won't buy you."

"How much?"

"That depends on the story. If it's good, if it's true. And if it's printable."

"I'd print it, if I were news editor."

"We don't always think alike. Let's hear the story."

"Not yet. I have to check out one more thing before everything's positive. Oh, it'll check, don't worry. My methods may not come under the Boy Scout rules, but they work." He perched on the edge of Richards' desk, clasping his hands together as if he were congratulating himself. "You know, that's the trouble with this paper, you need a live wire around with some high voltage."

"You might blow the fuses."

"Think it over. I've got guts, energy, youth, a nose for news. . ."

"What makes you hate yourself so much?"

"I've got to talk myself up. Who else will do it?"

"Haven't you got a mother?"

"Oh, come off it, Richards. How do you pick reporters around here, for their modest smiles and the way they sweet-talk you? Anybody can do that. Oh, you're a great man, Mr. Richards, sir, I don't really deserve to work for such an outstanding newspaper, sir, but I'll do anything, I'll scrub floors, I'll wash out the cuspidors..."

"Beat it, Blake. I told you I was busy."

"O.K., but I'll be back. Unless I get a better offer somewhere else."

"If you do, take it." He picked up a piece of copy from his desk and began reading.

Blake craned his neck to look at it. "The autopsy report on Galloway, eh? You know what I bet you'll do with it? Take your little red pencil and reduce it to something as dull as a stock quotation."

"That's my business."

When he had gone, Richards took off his spectacles and rubbed his eyes. They felt gritty, as though he'd been bucking a strong and dirty wind. He felt more distaste for than interest in Blake's promises. If the police department had so many leaks that a kid like Blake could find out the contents of a supposedly secret suicide letter, this was a story in itself, perhaps a bigger story, in the long run, than any Blake could dream up.

He replaced his spectacles and turned back to the autopsy report. It was, as far as Richards was concerned, considerably duller than a stock quotation: death had been caused by drowning, water was found in the stomach and lungs, and foamy mucus in the trachea, and the blood chlorides on the left side of the heart were thirty percent lower than those of the right, a positive indication of drowning in fresh water.

The report revealed only one surprise, that Galloway had made a previous attempt at suicide in the earlier hours of the night, Saturday, that he had died. Considerable amounts of a barbiturate compound were found in the stomach and other vital organs. When questioned about this point, Dr. Robert Whitewood, the pathologist who performed the autopsy, stated that it was fairly common to discover traces of previous suicide attempts, which he compared roughly to the "hesitation marks" frequently found on victims of suicide who had used razors, knives, or other sharp instruments.

Nothing in the early part of the report affected Richards—water in the lungs, chloride content of the heart, mucus in the trachea, these meant only that Galloway was a dead man. But the phrase, hesitation marks, conjured up a live one.

"Hesitation marks." Richards repeated it aloud, thinking, Galloway was a man, like himself, going through all the motions of living, until one day he no longer felt any incentive to move. He had tried to kill himself, and failing, had tried again. Between the two attempts there was the time of hesitation. At what point had he written the letter to his wife?

And who, Richards wondered, was Thelma?

SEVENTEEN

Thelma seldom read the newspapers. She was not actually concerned about other people, and though she had her share of female curiosity Thelma's ran round and round on a limited track like a toy train stopping only at certain junctions, responsive only to the lever of Thelma's immediate interest.

On the front lawn the morning paper lay unopened, already yellowing under the sharp spring sun. For several hours Turee had been trying to reach her by phone to warn her about the small but strategically placed paragraph on the second page of the *News,* headed MYSTERY WOMAN HINTED IN GALLOWAY DEATH. Thelma had heard the phone ringing and had refused to answer. She was practically certain that the caller was Turee and that he merely intended to repeat what he'd been telling her for the past two days, that, in the interests of good taste if nothing else, she was not to attend Galloway's funeral. Thelma had resisted this advice with voluble obstinacy. For one reason, quite unconscious, it presented her with something definite to rebel against, and so helped to take the edge off her grief. Turee's interference served as a counter-irritant, and the time she spent resenting and opposing it was time she would otherwise have spent in self-pity and regret and guilt.

The funeral was scheduled for three o'clock that afternoon at the Galloway home, and though it was not yet one, Thelma was already dressed for the occasion in an old black wool suit that didn't quite accommodate her new proportions. She had bathed her eyes to reduce the swelling and used powder on the lids to hide their blisterlike transparency. She wore no other make-up, and her light hair was pulled back from her face into a small tight knot. She looked more like a sorrowing widow than Esther could have looked after a month of practice. She was aware of this fact, too, and it gave her a grim sense of triumph.

But the thought of Ron brought tears to her eyes and she was on the point of breaking into sobs when the telephone began to ring again, and, almost simultaneously, the front-door bell.

"Damn you," she whispered. "Damn you, leave me alone!"

Then she turned deliberately away from the ringing phone and, wiping her eyes on her sleeve like a small girl, she went to answer the front door.

On the threshold stood a good-looking young man with a crew cut, a handful of pamphlets showing the advantage of owning a water-softener, and such a fast opening spiel that Thelma didn't even hear all of it.

"...not more than a few pennies a day, ma'am, and the luxury of rain water right out of your tap."

"It's no use wasting your time. I simply haven't the money right now."

"A softener will save you twice that amount in soap and detergent, water bills, wear and tear on clothing, and what's more, it will conserve your water heater. If I could just step inside a minute and show you the actual figures..."

"Well, I don't know."

The young man took quick advantage of her hesitancy. Feigning clumsiness, he dropped one of the folders he was carrying, and in bending down to pick it up he changed position expertly so that when he rose again he was inside the house. The maneuver was so smooth that Thelma couldn't help admiring it. At one period of her life she'd sold cosmetics from door to door and she knew some of the tricks, but this one was new to her.

Thelma closed the door behind him, somewhat amused at the idea of playing dumb and letting the young man think he was getting away with something. It did not occur to her that he actually was, that until an hour ago he'd known no more about water-softeners than a baby and the pamphlets he was presenting to her were distributed free at the Hydroelectric office.

"My name is Blake, ma'am. Rod Blake."

"I'm Mrs. Bream. Sit down if you like."

"Thanks. Now about this water-softener, of course it may seem like a large initial expense, but in the long run it will more than pay for itself, believe me. Now take this model. Begging your pardon, ma'am, but if we could have a little more light..."

Thelma pulled open the drapes, unaware that Blake wanted more light so that he could study her more carefully. Observing the bulge beneath the shabby black suit, the pallor of her skin, her tear-swollen eyes, he felt no pity at all, only a glow of exultation that his hunch had been right. This was the woman. He was more sure of it than ever when he noticed the framed tinted picture on top of the piano. A wedding picture, obviously, and the self-conscious, stiffly smiling bridegroom was the man he'd seen in the emergency ward at General Hospital on Monday night. The bride was Thelma, looking ten years younger than she did now, though Blake knew the Breams had been married for only three years.

"My house is so small," Thelma was saying. "There wouldn't be room for it."

"Ah, that's the story I hear all the time. It usually turns out that there's some corner nobody's thought of. Mind if I take a look for myself?"

Thelma didn't answer or turn from the window. She was staring out at the street, her small plump hands clenched rigidly together like desperate lovers.

"Ma'am? I asked if I could..."

"Be quiet."

Surprised, Blake followed her gaze. He could see nothing extraordinary, nothing even worth watching: a couple of children having a tricycle race, an elderly lady walking slowly between two canes, a young mother wheeling a pram, a man painting his porch, a trio of small, giggling girls lurching along in their mothers' high-heeled shoes.

"Mrs. Bream..."

"Is that your car parked in the middle of the block facing this way?"

"I don't have a car. I'm just getting started in the business."

"The car—I don't see very well these days—is it a Buick?"

"I think so."

"About five years old?"

"About that, I guess. I don't under—"

"Is there a man in it? My eyes—all this crying—I'll go blind if I don't stop... Is there a man in the car?"

"Yes."

"Oh, my God, he's watching me. Maybe he's been there for hours, all morning... My God, what will I do? Why can't he leave me alone?"

Blake shifted uncomfortably. What had started out, on his part, as a kind of lark was disintegrating before his eyes, like a sawdust doll spilling its insides. "I think maybe I'd better be on my way. If your kitchen's too small and all that..."

"You can't go now."

"But I..."

"He's getting out of the car, he's heading here. You can't leave me here alone with him."

"It's none of my business."

"God knows what he's thinking, seeing you come into the house. He may believe that you and I—oh, I don't know. But you can't leave now, without explaining to him that you're just a salesman. You must have some card or identification from the company you work for."

Blake had begun to sweat. "I'm new at the job. This is my first day. The company's just trying me out."

"You can tell him that."

"No, no. I mean, I don't work for any particular comp—"

"The pamphlets are from the Hydroelectric Company."

"Yes, but..."

"All right, you work for the Hydroelectric Company. You needn't be afraid," she added contemptuously. "Harry can be unpleasant but he'd never hurt anyone."

"Why drag me into it for Pete's sake?"

"You dragged yourself. No one invited you."

Harry knocked on the door, and when Thelma didn't answer it immediately he let himself in with his own key...

They met in the hall.

"Hello, Harry," she said. "So you got out of the hospital. How are you?"

He peered at her through the dimness, blinking, like a man accustomed to wearing spectacles, who without them finds the world strangely altered. "You're dressed funny."

"Am I?"

"I don't remember that suit."

"I had it before we were married."

"Black... You're going to the funeral?"

"Yes. Are you?"

He shook his head. "Turee says it would be bad form if either of us went, under the circumstances."

"Turee says this, Turee says that... Well, Turee can run your life for you but he's not running mine. I'm going to the funeral. I have a *right* to go."

Harry smiled at her sadly. "We all have rights we don't, or can't, use. Technically, I have a right to come into my own house, kiss my own wife, make love to her if I want..."

"Is this another of Turee's ideas?"

"No. My own."

"Well, you can stop that kind of talk, speaking of bad form. If you and Turee pretend to have such fancy manners, why don't you practice them?" She turned away. "Besides, I—we have a visitor."

"I'm aware of that."

"He's nothing, nobody. A man selling water-softeners. Claims they save money. I wonder if they really do."

"I wonder." Harry still wore his smile but it seemed oddly changed. It was sly, wary, incongruous, a cat smile on a cocker spaniel. "You have a perfect right to have visitors, to buy water softeners... But then, as I said, I have rights too. It's when our rights conflict that there's bound to be trouble."

"I'm not afraid of your threats."

"You're trembling."

"Oh, I admit you make me nervous, only it's like walking in front of a small boy with a supply of snowballs—the idea of being hit by a snowball makes me nervous. But even if one should hit me it wouldn't be so bad. It's only snow. So go ahead. Throw one."

"It's spring. There's no snow. Small boys might switch to rocks."

"Oh, stop all this talk. Do what you came to do and get it over with!"

"I will. I thought I'd better explain myself first. I've appealed to you in various ways, Thelma, to save us both. I've begged for your mercy, and I've asked for your pity. But no matter what words were used it always amounted to me asking you. Now I'm *telling* you."

She looked at him, silent and sullen.

"My bags are out in the car, Thelma. I haven't unpacked since I left here on Monday afternoon."

"Why not?"

"Because I'm coming back," he said calmly. "I'm moving back into my house with my wife."

"Stop talking like a fool."

"I'm not a fool. Or a small boy. And I have something in my pocket more authoritative than a snowball or a rock."

"What?"

"A gun."

"You must be cra—Harry! Harry, listen to me..."

She put out her hand to stop him, but he brushed past her and went into the living room. She could see, quite distinctly, the contours of the gun in the lower left pocket of his suit coat.

Blake was standing in the far corner of the room, clutching his pamphlets as if they were a passport to the outside world. Drops of sweat wriggled down his temples and behind his ears, leaving moist, shiny trails like slugs.

"Hello there," Harry said brightly. "About this proposition of yours, I think my wife and I might be interested. Tell me, does soft water make shaving any easier?"

"I—I don't know."

"Come, you're old enough to shave, surely? How old are you?"

"Twenty-one."

"A mere boy. Do you throw snowballs?"

"I..."

"Never mind. You must excuse my wife and me for ringing you in on our private little difference of opinion. My wife hasn't been well lately. We're expecting a child in a few months, our first. Say, that's going to mean a lot of extra washing, isn't it? I think a water-softener might be a good investment. How about it, Thelma?"

"Harry," she said dully. "Don't. Stop."

"Go take a pill, Thelma. You're not well." He turned back to the young man who had managed one surreptitious step toward the door. "You look familiar to me. Have I seen you before?"

"No," Blake said, thinking, it's true. He couldn't have seen me, he had his eyes closed when I was talking to the nurse. She said he was out, out like a light...

"What's your name?"

"Rod Blake."

"Funny, I'd have sworn we met some place. A hospital—have you been in a hospital recently?"

"No."

"Well, no matter. Tell me more about your product."

"We have—several models."

"Go ahead, talk about them. Speak your piece."

"Well—well, as I was just saying to your wife, this is my first day on the job."

"So?"

"I don't know much about it yet." Though he was still pouring sweat, he had begun to shiver, as if a cold wind was blowing through the house up from the basement of the past. "I—I've thought of a good idea."

"Let's hear it."

"Perhaps I could leave these folders with you and you can study them for yourself, facts and figures and so on. Then when you decide..."

"I've already decided. We'll take one."

"Which—which model?"

"Any model."

"But. . ."

"Any model," Harry said graciously. "All we want is enough soft water for the baby's clothes. I'll probably be doing some of the washing myself, so my motives aren't entirely unselfish. Are you married?"

"N-no sir."

"Ah well, you've plenty of time. I was well over thirty when I got married—took me that long to find the right girl. I found her, though, I found her. And I don't intend to lose her."

"Well—ah, I'd better be going now."

"What's your hurry?"

"I—the fact is, I have to get hold of an expert to come and measure—measure things."

"I can see you're a real eager-beaver. Ever see a beaver dam, by the way?"

"No sir."

"Highly interesting. You should go out of your way to find one some time."

"Yes sir. I will."

"Industrious lot, beavers."

"They certainly are." Blake began moving toward the door, breathing heavily, as if he had just completed building a dam entirely by himself with no help from any beavers. "I'll—I'll put your order in right away and see about installation."

"Oh, there's no great rush about it." Harry smiled fondly at his wife. "We can't hurry Mother Nature anyway."

"Harry. Listen to me."

"Now, dear, don't be embarrassed or upset about a perfectly natural process."

"Be quiet." Thelma watched Blake approach her and she stood squarely in the middle of the doorway, so that he couldn't pass her on either side without pushing her away. "We don't want a water-softener. My husband is merely amusing himself at your expense and mine. He's probably been drinking."

"Not drinking," Harry said. "*Thinking.*"

"Drinking," she repeated to Blake, softly, as if she were confiding a secret. "And he has a gun."

"I know, I know, but what the hell am I supposed to do? I want to get out of here."

"You can't leave me alone with him."

"You said before you weren't afraid."

"I didn't know about the gun then."

"Sweet Jesus," Blake whispered, and he felt his knees buckle like a sick colt's. *Let me out of here in one piece and I'll go to church every Sunday for a year.*

"Thinking," Harry went on, as if he had not heard the exchange or else considered it too trivial to bother about. "Yes, my dear, that's what I've been doing, a lot of plain, common sense thinking. And I've decided that you're in no condition to make the decisions for the family, now that there are going to be three of us. You're too emotional to be allowed a freedom of choice. It's up to me to take a firm stand, and I will. I'm head of this house, it's time you realized that. *I* will decide the future. You hear that, Thelma?"

"Yes," Thelma said. "I hear."

"I'm glad you're coming to your senses. I don't want to hurt your feelings, but the fact is, you've always been a little unstable."

She looked grim. "Have I?"

"So it's up to me to take over, to make all the decisions. Now the first decision I wish to make is about the water-softener. I want a water-softener and I intend to get one. Is that clear?"

"Yes."

"You see how easy your role is going to be from now on? All you have to do is agree."

"Yes."

"Actually, it will save you trouble, it will be easier on you if I shoulder the burden of responsibilities. It puts too much of a strain on a woman, making decisions, being boss. It puts a strain on anyone." He passed the back of his hand across his forehead. "A great strain. I'm—I'm really quite tired. Haven't been sleeping much. Working all day, thinking all night, thinking..."

"You should lie down here, Harry, and get a good rest." She crossed the room and began arranging the pillows at one end of the davenport. "Lie down, Harry."

He didn't have to be told. He sank back among the pillows, limp with exhaustion. "Lie down with me."

"I can't right now. I have to go out."

"Not to the funeral? You're not..."

"Of course not. If you don't want me to, I won't. You're the boss, Harry."

"Where are you going, then?"

"To the store. Now that you're moving back into the house I have to stock up on groceries. What would you like for dinner?"

"I don't know," he said, closing his eyes. "I'm so tired."

"Fried chicken?"

"I don't know. Kiss me, Thelma."

Her lips touched his forehead briefly. It felt hot and dry, like something cured in the sun, or slow-baked in an oven. "You rest now, Harry. It's such a strain, all this thinking and being boss, it's given you a fever."

His eyes snapped open, painfully, as if he had been pierced by a splinter of irony from her voice. "You don't care. You don't care about anything."

"I do care, very much."

"No... You listen to me, Thelma. I'm the boss. I want fried chicken for dinner tonight. Hear that?"

"Yes."

"I make all the decisions from now on. Is that clear?"

"Of course."

With a sound of desolation he turned and buried his face in the pillows. She stood looking down at him, tight-lipped, cold-eyed. "I'll need the car keys if I'm going to do the shopping. Are they in your pocket?"

He didn't respond. She waited for several minutes, still as a stone, until Harry began to snore. Then she bent over him, and, moving with delicate precision, she took the car keys from one pocket and the gun from the other, and put them both in her purse. Blake watched her from the doorway with the awed expression of a man witnessing the dismantling of an unexploded bomb.

When she turned and saw that Blake was still in the house she seemed surprised and displeased. "I thought you'd left."

"No."

"You're free to go any time." She went into the hall, closing the door behind her, and began putting on her hat, arranging the black veil over her face, tucking in wisps of hair. There was a mirror built into the hall rack but she didn't even glance toward it. "You're free to go," she repeated. "You were so anxious to leave a few minutes ago."

"Naturally. What did you expect me to do, tackle a crazy man?"

"He's not crazy. He's emotionally exhausted."

"Same difference, as far as I'm concerned. You'd better watch out for yourself, Mrs. Bream." He appeared reluctant to leave, as if he had misgivings about his behavior and wanted to confess and apologize but didn't know how to go about it. "What are you going to do about the gun?"

"I have no idea. What does anyone do about a gun?"

"Unload it, that's the first thing. Let me see it."

She opened her purse. She knew nothing about guns but it seemed odd to her that it wasn't heavier, more substantial.

"It's not real," Blake said, in a high, tinny voice.

"Pardon?"

"It's a toy, a cap pistol." The color of shame and fury spread across his face. "A cap pistol. And I was taken in. I was..." *I was a coward. I was scared by a toy gun and a little man years older than I am. Scaredy-cat, scaredy-cat.*

"I'm so relieved," Thelma said. "I should have guessed, of course. Harry just isn't the type to harm anyone even if he wanted to. People can't get away from their own type no matter how hard they try."

"Can't they?"

"Poor Harry. A toy gun. Well, I suppose we'll all look back on this some day and laugh. I mean, there was I, scared out of my wits, and you—I thought you were going to faint, you looked petrified."

"I wasn't frightened in the least," he said, and giving her a look of hatred, he turned and opened the door and ran down the porch steps, fleeing from his own identity, pursued by his own shadow.

Thelma started to call after him, to tell him not to bother about the water-softener, but at that moment the telephone began ringing again. This time she answered it promptly because she didn't want Harry to wake up.

"Hello?"

"Thelma, this is Ralph. I've been trying to reach you for hours."

"I was out." I don't even have to lie, she thought. I was out. Out of patience. "Is anything wrong?"

"Maybe. Harry came to my office this morning. He looked in terrible shape, as if he'd been on a binge for a week. I know that can't be true, though. He's afraid to drink since he had to pay that two hundred dollar fine after the accident."

"Why worry about him?"

"He was talking—well, pretty unrealistically. About you, and going home, and how he intended to get a firm hand on the reins, that sort of thing."

"So?"

"I thought you should be warned. He's a hell of a good guy, Thelma, it's up to us to keep him out of trouble."

"Not us," Thelma said dryly. "You."

"What does that mean?"

"He's here now. Sleeping. After making a delightful scene in front of a total stranger. It's the last straw. If he's going to be kept out of trouble you'll have to do it, you and Bill Winslow or Joe Hepburn. You're his friends. *I'm not.*"

"What are we supposed to do?"

"I'm going out now, to Ron's funeral—and you can start raving and ranting about bad form or anything else, but it won't do any good. I'm going.
And when I get back, I want Harry out of here, out of this house. If he's
still here when I come back, I'm going to phone the police and have him
arrested for threatening me with a gun.

"A gun?"

"Oh, just a cap pistol, as it turned out. But the threat was real and I have
a witness. Harry can be arrested."

"You wouldn't..."

"Wouldn't I? Listen, I'm fed up. I'm sick and tired and fed up. These
scenes are tearing me apart. I have my health to consider, and my baby. I
need peace and quiet, relaxation. How can I get any, with him barging
around like a maniac? I would do anything to get rid of him. And I will, if
you don't prevent it."

"I'll do my best."

"He won't be here when I come back?"

"No."

"Promise?"

"Yes."

"I suppose I should thank you in advance, only—well, whatever you do
will be for Harry's sake, not mine. I ask no favors from anyone."

"I understand that. Go-it-alone Thelma, as usual."

"I'm not quite alone." She hung up.

In the living room Harry lay crushed among the pillows, dreaming of tri-
umphs and defeats, the rhythm of his gentle snoring broken now and then
by a catch of his breath, a pause, a sigh.

What long eyelashes he has, Thelma thought. Then she said softly,
"Good-bye, Harry."

EIGHTEEN

Harry remained at home and slept through the funeral, partly from a desire to escape it, partly from genuine weariness. By the time Turee and Bill Winslow arrived at the house, he was awake and sitting up on the davenport, though still dazed.

"How did you fellows get here?"

"Thelma left the door unlocked," Turee said.

"No, I mean, what brought...?"

"Action now, explanations later. Come on, Harry."

"Come on where?"

"To my house."

"I don't want to go to your house. I'm staying here. I'm waiting for Thelma."

"Thelma's not coming back until you leave."

"But she has to. She promised to make me fried chicken for dinner. I *commanded* her to."

"Oh, great, great," Winslow said. After the funeral, he'd had three quick, long martinis which had submerged his sorrow but left a lump of anger sticking in his throat like an olive pit. "You *commanded* her to. Fine. With a toy gun. Even better. What makes you pull such damnfool stunts?"

"I was only trying to prove..."

"What you were trying to prove and what you proved are a couple of light-years apart. You threaten a woman and she gets frightened. But after the fright goes away, what's left? Revenge."

"Not Thelma."

"Exactly Thelma. Get it through your thick skull that she wants you to get lost, or else. All these damnfool antics of yours, I don't blame her. Now let's hurry up and shove out of here. I need a drink."

"Well, gee whiz," Harry said plaintively. "What's everybody so sore about?"

"Who's sore?"

"You are."

"The hell I am."

"Quiet, both of you," Turee said. "Come on, Harry. Bill has his car, he'll drive us over to my house."

"Where's my car?"

"Thelma said she'd leave it at the house for you. Nancy's expecting us, let's get going."

"I don't want to go. I'm not a child. I can't be ordered around."

"You are and you can."

"I thought you were my friends!"

"If we weren't your friends, we'd both be home having a nice quiet dinner. Now let's go."

"All right, *all right.*"

Harry got up and went out the door, muttering to himself. He paused at the bottom of the veranda steps and glanced back at the door as if he had an irrational hope that Thelma was going to appear and ask him not to leave.

Mrs. Malverson was out on her front lawn watering a bed of daffodils. She spotted Harry and waved the hose playfully by way of greeting.

"Hello there, Mr. Bream."

"Hello, Mrs. Malverson."

"Beautiful weather for daffodils, isn't it?"

"I guess so." He hung back while the other two men approached the car parked at the curb. "Mrs. Malverson, I'm—well, I won't be around for a while. Business, you know how it is. I was wondering perhaps if you could drop in on Thelma now and then, cheer her up a bit. She hasn't been well lately."

"I know. I told her that myself only last Sunday. Child, I said, you look as if you've been up all night, and crying too. I'm sure it was Sunday. Yes, it was, because I remember now I asked her to go to church with me for the reading of the flowers. She dropped a bottle of milk, she was that nervous. And all this week she's been avoiding me. Me, her friend. Of course that's what you can expect from a woman at certain times."

"Certain times?"

"Oh, come now, Mr. Bream. Surely you've suspected that a little stranger is coming into your life?"

"Stranger? Yes. Yes, that's the right word." He turned so abruptly that he almost lost his balance, and walked toward the waiting car.

Mrs. Malverson stared after him, her mouth open in surprise. *Now what does that mean? Maybe I shouldn't have blurted it out like that, but my goodness, these are modern times. People don't hide things like a baby, they go around shouting it from the housetops as soon as they're sure. Unless...*

"Oh, that's ridiculous," she said aloud, with a violent tug on the hose. "Never have I seen a more devoted wife than Thelma Bream. Keeps the house spotless, airs the mattresses every second Thursday. And never a cross word between the two of them. She's always quoting Harry, Harry this, Harry that, as if he was some kind of god instead of an ordinary little man that sells pills, and some of them no darn good either. And every morning when he leaves for work out she traipses to the car to kiss him good-bye. A real womanly woman, if I ever saw one."

Unless...

"Absolutely ridiculous," Mrs. Malverson repeated weakly. "I ought to be downright ashamed of myself."

When they reached Turee's old Three-story house on Woodlawn, Nancy came to the door to greet them. Though she looked red-eyed and worn, she spoke cheerfully: "Hello Harry—Ralph... Where's Billy? Isn't he coming in for a drink?"

"Not tonight," Turee said. "His wife has a cold and he wants to go home and catch it, so he'll have an excuse to cry."

"What a time to try to be funny."

"I'm quite serious."

"Well shush, anyway. Harry, where's your suitcase?"

"In my car. Wherever that is."

"Thelma left it for you in the driveway. Here are the keys. Now go get your suitcase."

"I can't stay here. I've been enough bother..."

"Nonsense. You're perfectly welcome to sleep on the sun porch. This is practically the only time of year it's usable. You won't freeze and you won't stifle. Now how's that for an offer?"

"Well..."

"Of course you'll stay. It'll be just like old times, before you were mar- rie—"

Nancy's tactlessness was sometimes as overwhelming as her hospitality, and Harry stood silent and embarrassed in the face of both, looking down at the carpet which was muddy with the tracks of children and worn in places right through to the padding.

Nancy touched his arm in gentle apology. "I'm always saying the wrong thing. Without meaning to. Come on, I've got dinner ready for you. Ralph will get your suitcase later."

The children had already been fed and sent upstairs with instructions to amuse themselves, no holds barred, and the two men were left alone at the round oak table in the big old-fashioned kitchen. They were both preoc- cupied and hungry and the meal was disturbed only by the sounds from upstairs, sometimes loud, sometimes muffled, running feet, squeals and giggles, stifled screams, an occasional howl.

There was a hectic quality in the children's playing, as if they knew something secret and strange and terrifying had happened and they were combatting the knowledge with hysterical denial. "Uncle Ron is dead," Nancy had told them calmly. "Now if you have any questions I'll answer them as best I can." It was like asking a roomful of grade-schoolers if they had any questions about the mechanism of a hydrogen bomb. No ques- tions were asked, out loud.

Death. A sacred word, yet an evil one, a beginning and a finality, heaven and hell, streets of gold and pits of fire, angels and demons, bliss and brimstone. *If you have any questions...*

The din from the second floor grew louder and more frantic. Nancy's voice plunged into it, sharp as a scalpel. "What are you four doing up there? Avis? Sandra? You hear me?"

Sudden and complete silence, as if all four, simultaneously, had been anesthetized.

"I want an answer. What are you doing?"

A girl's voice, brassy with defiance, "Nothing."

"It doesn't sound like nothing."

"It's *nothing.*"

"Well, please do it more quietly."

Whispers. A gasp. A frightened giggle. Then the muted chant of children:

> "Galloway was laid to rest
> In his Sunday pants and vest.
> Galloway was laid to rest..."

The sounds floated down into the kitchen and Harry shivered and turned white. "I missed it."

"Missed what?"

"Ron's funeral."

"That doesn't matter. Barbaric custom, anyway."

"Thelma, she was there?"

"Yes."

"There wasn't any scene, any trouble? I mean, with Esther?"

"The ladies," Turee said with some irony, "are ladies, and don't make scenes at funerals."

"I was just wondering."

"You wonder too much."

"Yes."

"You've got to stop it."

"I know."

"Start thinking on the positive side. You're young, healthy, competent, you've got a future."

"I can't see it."

"Not with your eyes closed and pictures of Thelma pasted inside the lids. Start looking around. The sky hasn't fallen. The city is still here. The blood is still bouncing around in your veins. Here, have some of this port. An uncle of mine sent me a dozen bottles. He had to choose between his wine cellar and his ulcer."

Harry eyed the glass of port with suspicion, then shook his head gravely. "No thanks. I haven't had a drink since Monday."

"Why not?"

"I was afraid it might interfere with my thinking."

"Something should have." Turee sipped at his port and made a wry face. "No wonder the old boy developed ulcers. This stuff's god-awful. Try it."

Harry tried it. "It's not so bad."

Nancy came into the kitchen to ask Turee to go upstairs immediately and discipline the children.

Turee seemed unperturbed at the request, as if it was a very familiar one. "What do you want me to do?"

"I don't know. Something, anyway."

"Be more explicit."

"I can't. All I know is, if I'm expected to do all the disciplining in the family, the children will grow up thinking I'm an ogre. They'll have complexes."

"Ogress. And they'll have complexes anyway."

"Sandra's the instigator of this whole thing. I feel like spanking the daylights out of her."

"Go ahead and do it, then."

"You're no help at all!"

Turee rose, kissed her on the left cheek, and pushed her gently toward the doorway.

The wine, the warmth of the kitchen, the playing-out of the little domestic scene, all combined to cast a flush across Harry's face. He fidgeted with his empty glass, rolling the stem back and forth between his palms, and a glint of moisture shone in his eyes. "I can't stay here, Ralph. I wish I could. But seeing you and Nancy—and the kids—well, I guess I couldn't stand it. You understand."

Turee was grave. "Make your own decision. I was only trying to help."

"No one can help me. I've got to go it alone."

It was the same sentiment Turee had heard Thelma express, and he wondered how deeply either of them meant it and how far either of them would go alone. Together, leaning on each other, entwined in marriage, they'd been able to remain upright, as cornstalks in a field can withstand a high wind.

"What you suggested on Monday," Harry continued, "about leaving town, applying for a transfer, it's beginning to make sense to me now."

"Good."

"I'm sure they'll give me a transfer. I'm a good salesman and there's nothing in the record against me, except that business on Monday. Maybe if I go away for a while Thelma will actually miss me, eh?"

"Maybe."

"She might even change her mind. I could always send for her then, her and the baby, couldn't I? I mean, it's not impossible, is it?"

"Not at all."

"She's always wanted to leave this town anyway."

Not with you, Turee thought, refilling Harry's glass. "I realize that."

"Say, you know something, Ralph? For the first time in days I'm beginning to feel that things are making sense again. Don't you feel that, Ralph? Things will work out?"

"Certainly."

"I guess I was practically going off my rocker for a while there, staying up all night, thinking, trying to figure things out, not eating, not seeing anybody. I feel quite different now. Almost *hopeful*, you know?" He paused to sip at his wine and wipe the beads of moisture from his face with the back of his hand. "Now why did I say *almost*? I don't mean it. I mean very. Very hopeful. You were right, Ralph. I've got a future. I've really got a future, haven't I?"

"Of course." Turee saw Harry's bright new smile, and the bright new confident look in his eye, and anxiety began to gnaw at his mind with the teeth of rodents. Harry was on his way up again, the long erratic journey up, like a crazed bird, or a misguided missile darting wildly in and out of the orbits of meteorites. "Harry. Listen. Don't get too high."

"Now that's a funny remark. A few minutes ago you were trying to cheer me up and now that I'm cheered up, what are you trying to do? Puncture me? Well, you can't, old boy. I feel wonderful, see, I feel..."

"Harry, before you leave town, I think you should hire a lawyer."

Harry's jaw dropped in astonishment. "Lawyer? What for?"

"For Thelma."

"So she can divorce me? Is that what you mean?"

"No, no," Turee said impatiently. "She's going to need someone to protect her interests, that's all."

"Why? *I'm* going to protect her interests. I'll send her every cent I can spare."

"I know that. But suppose something happens to you—you become sick and can't work, you get hurt in an accident—what then? Thelma would be left alone with a child to support."

"I don't see how a lawyer would help that."

"You're not thinking straight, Harry. The child is Ron's—he's admitted paternity—therefore his estate should be made responsible financially for the child's upbringing."

"Thelma would never take a cent from Esther. She's too proud."

"Pride be damned. There should be nothing personal in this situation. Thelma may be proud, Esther may be reluctant, you may be all churned up, but the fact remains that the child has a legal right to support. That's where the lawyer comes in. He'll act in the child's best interests. His own, too. I understand in cases like this where a considerable amount of money is involved, they work on a percentage basis."

"What exactly do you mean, a considerable amount of money?"

"I didn't mean anything exact. All I'm saying is that Thelma should have a lawyer."

"But then there'd be a lawsuit. Everything would come out in the newspapers."

"If Esther's lawyers advise her to fight the case, there'd be a lawsuit, yes, but I don't think they will. And if they did, I don't think she'd accept their advice. At the moment Esther's pretty bitter about Thelma, but she's not really a vindictive woman. She'll simmer down between now and the time the child is born."

"What it boils down to, then, is begging Esther for money. Well, I won't do it. To hell with it. I can support Thelma and the child, and no *begging* necessary."

"Oh, be reasonable, Harry. Why deprive the kid of its legal right? I know how willing you are to support it, but it's going to grow up, to need things, housing, clothing, education. Ask me, I'm an expert. I've been broke for fourteen years and no doubt will continue that way for another fourteen. Kids are expensive. They don't always stay in the cradle, wearing diapers and living on milk. They need shoes, dolls, new suits, bicycles, baseball mitts, piano lessons, there are doctors' bills, dentists' bills..."

"All right," Harry said listlessly. "Don't go on. You're telling me I can't afford all those things."

"No. I'm telling you you don't *have* to. Thelma and the child are entitled to be kept in comfort and there's no sensible reason why they shouldn't be, except your pride and Thelma's, if pride is the right word."

"I don't need charity."

"Keep yourself out of it, Harry. Because you're not really in it. You'll have to face that squarely." Turee paused, pressing his fingertips against his temples as if to press his thoughts into the right phrases. "You're not really in it," he repeated. "I think you've been daydreaming this past week, Harry. I think you've half convinced yourself that nothing took place between Ron and Thelma, that the child is actually your own. Don't keep on like this, Harry, it's dangerous."

"But suppose..."

"There's no supposing about it. The child is Ron's. Now accept the fact and go on from there. If you keep setting up delusions to stumble over, you'll get nowhere. Why can't you face the truth?"

"I guess—I'll have to." The long erratic journey up had ended for Harry. The crazed bird had grown weary, the misguided missile had struck a meteorite and was falling through space. "I couldn't give her the child she wanted. I tried. God knows I tried. I've been going to a doctor for over a year without telling her. I covered up for myself by pretending that I didn't want her to have a child because of her health, her age."

"Why didn't you tell her the truth, Harry?"

"I wasn't sure, at first. Then when I was sure, I was afraid to tell her. After that, when I began taking treatments and pills—well, I kept hoping things would change. They changed all right," he added grimly. "In a way I never thought possible. My best friend, and my wife."

"It's happened before."

"Yes, but didn't they ever stop to think of Esther, of me?"

"There are times," Turee said, "when people don't stop to think of anything."

NINETEEN

As far as the newspapers were concerned, the Galloway story died on the obit page, but rumors were flying wildly around town like kites without tails. One of them got entangled in Esther's telephone wire: an anonymous caller accused her of murder and demanded five thousand dollars as the price of his silence.

After this episode, Esther refused to take any calls or to see anyone except the lawyers concerned with the probate of Ron's will. It was a curiously simple will for a wealthy man to make. No trust funds or other safeguards had been set up for the children; except for a few minor bequests, everything was left outright to Esther, as if Ron had had greater faith in her good judgment and common sense than he had in his own. The lawyers came with papers for her to sign, and went away again, and came back with more papers. These visits were, for a time, Esther's only contact with the outside world.

She stayed indoors, wandering from room to room of the huge house, trying to find things to do, straightening pictures that weren't crooked, dusting ash trays that hadn't been used, moving chairs that had been moved only a few hours before, reading aloud to the two boys in a new gentle faraway voice which had a strangely quieting effect on them. The extremes of unexpressed grief and rage, which characterized the early period of her mourning, began gradually to moderate with the passing of the days, leaving behind a kind of acceptance, and a broader perspective. She came to realize that she was not the only injured and bereaved person, that it was Thelma, perhaps, who would ultimately suffer more than anyone else. She had a growing urge to call Thelma, partly out of pity, partly out of curiosity, but she was a little timid about doing it directly, since she couldn't be sure how Thelma would interpret such a call.

As a compromise she tried to get in touch with Harry at his office. She was informed that Harry had left the country a week previously and his present location was unknown since the head office in Detroit handled all transfers to the United States.

The following afternoon she received a badly typed letter from him, postmarked Kansas City, Missouri.

Dear Esther:

I tried to say good-bye to you but I was told you were ill. I hope you are feeling better by this time and bearing up under the terrible strain. As you probably know by now, Thelma and I decided to separate, and I applied for a transfer and landed here, of all places. It's a lot like home, even the climate, though I guess it's warmer here because there's no lake.

I feel the way I did when I first left home for boarding school, like a mass of jelly inside from sheer homesickness. The nights are the worst. In the daytime I keep busy. I have to. This is a big city and I have to get to know it the way I know Toronto, if I'm to be any good to the company. They've given me a company car to drive, by the way, and everyone is very nice, so I've really nothing to complain of, jobwise. If I could only get over this sick, empty feeling inside.

I have just reread the first page of this letter, and for a guy who has nothing to complain of, I certainly complain! Forgive me, Esther. You have your own sorrows, I'm a dog to add to them.

I've sent Thelma three special-delivery letters but she hasn't answered. I know you two aren't likely to go out of your way to meet each other, but if you hear any news of her through Ralph or Billy Winslow or Joe Hepburn, please let me know.

I have so many things to say to you but somehow I can't say them. I want you to know one thing, though—I accept full responsibility for what happened. It was entirely my fault, I should have been more alert, more suspicious, more everything, I guess. I can't go into the details, they are too personal, but I repeat—it was all my fault and mine alone. Ron would be alive today if it weren't for my weakness and vanity. Last night I dreamed I was a murderer, so I guess this is how I really feel inside.

I will try to be more cheerful next time I write. Meanwhile, take care of yourself, Esther. Love,

                                        Harry

It was the second time within a week that the word murder had come up.

She reread the last part of the letter, thinking how simpleminded Harry was to believe that a catastrophe could be caused by any one person. A lot of people were involved, not just the leading characters, but the bit players, the prop man, the stagehands, waiting in the wings.

In the same mail a letter, with an imposing letterhead of six names and the address of a law firm, contained an incongruously informal message:

Dear Esther: I'd like to drop in early Friday morning. No papers to sign, but a few matters to discuss. Yours,

                                        Charles

Charles Birmingham was a tall, austere man in his early sixties with a strong British accent which he had picked up at Oxford and managed to retain for forty years, intact. His too-formal manner of dressing gave the impression that he was always on his way to a wedding or a funeral, and his cold fishy eyes indicated that it didn't matter which.

Esther didn't like him, and he considered her a fool, so there was little room for a meeting of minds.

He came to the point of his visit without any preliminary niceties. "Mrs. Bream has retained an attorney."

"Yes, I just had a letter from Harry yesterday telling me he and Thelma have separated."

"I'm afraid you miss the point." *Women always do,* his tone implied. "This has no bearing on the separation. It concerns Mrs. Bream's unborn child. If Ron hadn't been so idiotic as to write that letter and you hadn't been so precipitate about handing it over to the police, we'd have an excellent chance of winning our case."

"Winning our case? You intend to fight?"

"To the best of my ability. As your attorney, it is my job to protect your financial interests."

"Have I any say in the matter?"

"Naturally, but it's customary for clients to take the advice of their attorney."

"Is it, indeed?" Esther's smile was chilly. "Well, I don't always do the customary thing."

"I'm sure you don't. However, in this case, I do hope your negativistic attitude toward me personally won't interfere with your better judgment."

"I don't like the idea of going into court, not one bit."

"If you're sued, you'll have to."

"Well, fix it so I won't be sued. Why can't the whole thing be handled in a friendly, civilized manner?"

Birmingham's lifted brows indicated his low opinion of this suggestion. "My dear Esther..."

"I don't want any scandal or fuss."

"There already is scandal."

"I know that." She remembered the soft, queer voice on the telephone, and her own terror, so paralyzing that she couldn't answer, couldn't even hang up. "It's got to be stopped. I'm afraid to go out, afraid to send the boys to school. I have this feeling that we're being watched."

"By whom?"

"I don't know."

"What do you propose we do about it?"

"Offer Thelma money to leave town. Once she's gone, the rumors will die down, people will forget, I can begin to live again."

"How much money?"

"Fifty thousand dollars. It would be worth that much to me to see the end of her."

"Suppose she refuses?"

"I don't see why she should. She has nothing to gain by staying here, except shame and humiliation and ridicule."

"Perhaps that's what she wants, self-punishment, self-debasement."

"Thelma's too sensible for that."

"My dear Esther, one of the things you learn early in my profession is that you can't tell from the outside who's sensible and who's not, and a great deal of the time you can't tell for certain what's sense and what's not. As far as I was able to gather, Mrs. Bream is not the usual femme fatale with a string of extramarital affairs behind her. She's an ordinary virtuous woman who has committed the kind of sin which ordinary virtuous women don't permit themselves to commit. If they do, they suffer. Mrs. Bream is suffering, suffering doubly because of the drastic consequences of her infidelity. In such a frame of mind she'd be unlikely, I think, to accept the kind of pay-off you suggest."

"Why?"

"It might seem to her a reward for having done something she loathes herself for."

"You read too much psychology."

Birmingham permitted himself a small tight smile. "Not at all. I practice it."

"I still think you're wrong about Thelma."

"Quite possibly. I talked to her only once, yesterday, in the presence of her attorney. She said very little, seemed uninterested, detached. Finally she complained of feeling ill, stomach cramps, dizziness, and so on. Purely psychosomatic, of course."

"Have you ever," Esther asked coldly, "been pregnant, Mr. Birmingham?"

"Fortunately, no. When I left, Mrs. Bream was trying to get in touch with the doctor, and her attorney was hopping around the office like a nervous stork. I deplore such excitements. Her attorney, by the way, hinted delicately at a small monthly stipend from the estate until the baby is born. This is impossible, naturally."

"Why?"

"Any payment—including the one you suggested—would be a virtual admission that your husband was responsible for the child. Then, later, when the child is born, we wouldn't have any grounds to fight the case. Mrs. Bream, or rather, her attorney, who will probably receive twenty-five percent of any settlement, would be in a position to make some pretty stiff demands." He added on a note of cheer, "Of course there's always the possibility that Mrs. Bream won't carry the child to term, or that it will be born dead, in which case our responsibility ends."

"What an inhuman remark to make." Esther had turned white with anger and her hands trembled as she lit a cigarette.

"It wasn't intended as such. You have an unfortunate tendency to over-emotionalize the issue. A natural womanly reaction, of course, but it increases the difficulty of my position."

"What is your position, to distort the facts?"

"My dear Esther..."

"You know the truth and so do I. Let's face it."

"Facing the truth," Birmingham said bluntly, "is going to cost you a heap of money."

"All right. I've got a heap of money, haven't I?"

"Considerable, yes. You also have two arms, but that's hardly a reason for discarding one of them."

"A very poor analogy. Look, Mr. Birmingham, let's get this straight. I hold no brief for Thelma. I don't like her and never have. But I feel a certain obligation toward her because I..." She hesitated, coloring slightly. "Because I understand her position. It could happen—has happened—to other—other women. I don't intend to fight any claims she makes on the estate. My conscience wouldn't allow it."

Birmingham had not been Galloway's lawyer at the time of his divorce, but he remembered the case and Esther's role in it and be began to realize that it was futile to argue with her. Whether or not she liked or approved of Thelma Bream, she had made a very strong identification with her: *There went I. Only I was luckier.*

"Very well," he said. "We'll let the matter ride for the present."

You will, I won't, she thought. But aloud she said cordially, "Of course. I'll see you to the door."

"That won't be necessary."

"It will be a pleasure."

She stood at the door watching his departure. He walked stiffly down the broad stone steps of the veranda and crossed the driveway to his car with ponderous dignity, like a penguin crossing an antarctic waste, never missing the warm places of the world because he did not know they existed.

Though she had disliked Birmingham for years, she had never before openly opposed him. Now, like a child who has suddenly issued a declaration of independence, she felt a new power and vitality, as if some secret well of energy had been tapped. She ordered old Rudolph to check her car and bring it around to the front of the house. Then she went upstairs to dress for town. For the first time in a month she passed the closed door of Ron's room without the increased heartbeat of fear and guilt.

"You're out of practice," Rudolph said. "You better let me drive you, Mrs. Galloway."

"No thanks. You can stay and help Annie with the boys. Tell them," she added, "tell them they'll be going back to school tomorrow."

Usually, when Esther drove downtown, she avoided the heaviest flow of traffic. Today she deliberately sought it out, feeling a pleasant, reassuring sense of anonymity. She was a woman in a car among hundreds of other women in cars. There was nothing special about her to attract attention. No one would bother watching her. No one but some crank on a telephone would believe she murdered her husband.

At the Bank of Commerce, on the corner of King and Yonge, she withdrew from her checking account two hundred dollars in twenty-dollar bills, sealed them in an envelope and addressed it to Thelma. It was not an act of kindness or of pity, but one of compulsion, and the emotions behind it were deeper and stronger than kindness or pity.

Whatever the reasons, it was, for Esther, the first step back into the flow of life. Others followed, as spring passed into summer. She met friends for lunch at the King Edward or the Royal York or the Plaza. She and Nancy took their combined brood of six to Sunnyside for a day of rides. She wrote to Harry, cheerful, impersonal letters which he answered in the same vein. She went to dinner at the Winslows' house and to several outdoor concerts with Joe Hepburn who was tone-deaf but liked fresh air and crowds. The first week in July she drove the two boys and Annie up to the lodge near Wiarton, and promised them a return trip before school started again in September.

Aside from sending the money to Thelma once a month she had no contact with her, but she heard from Turee that Thelma was having a difficult time during her pregnancy. She had rented her house in Weston and taken a small apartment in town to be nearer her doctor in case of emergency. Esther wrote down Thelma's new address in her address book, and the following day, a stifling morning in early August, she drove slowly past the apartment house on Spadina, trying to find enough courage to stop and ring the bell. But the car kept right on going as if of its own volition, and Esther thought, *there was no parking space anyway. And it's so hot. And early—she might not even be up. Besides, I have nothing special to say to her, no comfort to offer her, no special formula, no guarantee.*

Throughout the summer she had been making similar excuses to herself, and while they oiled the surface of her mind, they did not seep down and touch the grit and gravel underneath. She was stoned by dreams of identification in which she became Thelma, harassed and trying to defend herself, accused and trying to justify herself, continually at the mercy of some cold-eyed stranger or some false friend. The accusing figures in the dreams varied—Birmingham, Turee, an unknown policeman who resembled her father, a schoolteacher she had once hated—but the accused was always the same, Thelma-Esther, like a double exposure, one image superimposed on the other.

She took the two boys back up to the lodge again for the final week in

August, and on returning she began outfitting them for the school year ahead.

The meeting which she had both anticipated and dreaded for a long time took place in Eaton's College Street. She had just started up the escalator to the children's wear department when some woman stumbled getting off at the top. There was a little flurry of excitement by the time Esther reached the scene—the escalator attendant had propelled the woman to a chair, a floorwalker was waving his handkerchief in front of her face in the vague hope of whipping up more oxygen, and a clerk had been sent for some water.

The woman, heavy with child, seemed embarrassed at all the fuss, and when the clerk returned with a paper cup full of water she refused it. Instead, she rose with awkward dignity, made her way to the nearest counter and stood there a moment to steady herself.

Esther approached the counter and said, "Thelma?" and the woman turned, squinting, as if she'd been summoned from some dark world into sunlight.

"Are you all right, Thelma?"

"Yes. I'm fine." Her face was puffy, like rising dough, and her legs distorted by swelling. Her maternity dress, soiled around the collar, clung in wet patches between her shoulder blades and under her arms. Perspiration and oil had seeped through her make-up and stood out in droplets along her forehead.

"It's good to see you," Esther said. "I've thought of you so often."

"Have you?" Thelma smiled dryly. "Thanks."

"I—look, couldn't we go some place for a cup of tea? We can't talk here."

"I have nothing to say. Besides, my intake of fluids is very limited. Thanks all the same."

"I'll admit I felt bitter toward you at first, but not any more. I wish we could be friends."

"Do you?" Thelma turned back to the counter which was filled with infants' toys, rattles and teethers and rubber dolls and stuffed animals. "I've gone this far alone. I think I can manage the rest of the way."

"How much longer do you have to wait?"

"Why all the sudden interest?"

"It's not sudden. Listen, we could go over to the Honey Dew for some toasted scones. Or some butter cakes at Child's."

"I'm on a diet."

"All right then, a leaf of lettuce and a dab of cottage cheese."

"Why are you being so persistent?"

"I want to talk to you," Esther said truthfully. "I've wanted to all summer, actually, but didn't have the nerve."

"Nerve?"

"Well, whatever you want to call it. I was—embarrassed, I guess."

"That's a word I'm beginning to understand quite well."

"Have things—has it been hard for you?"

Tears appeared in Thelma's eyes. She blinked them away, obstinately. "Why should you care?"

"I don't know why, exactly, but I do."

"It's been hell."

"I'm sorry."

"Don't, *don't* be sympathetic. It's the one thing I can't stand. Oh, for God's sake, let's get out of here, people are staring, I think I'm going to cry."

She didn't cry, though. By the time they reached the nearest Child's she seemed to have herself under good control. The coffee-break crowd had left and the early lunchers hadn't arrived, so the place was nearly deserted. They chose a table in the corner farthest from the windows, and Esther ordered butter cakes and black tea, and Thelma a chicken salad which she looked at ravenously but barely touched, as if she knew too well the penalties of such a splurge.

"My blood pressure's up," she explained. "The doctor's afraid of eclampsia. I have to count every ounce of fluid, every grain of salt."

"Does Harry know?"

"Know what?"

"That you're not well."

"I *am* well," she said stubbornly. "I have to be careful, that's all. Harry." She repeated the name, frowning, as if she had trouble identifying him. "No, Harry doesn't know. I haven't written to him since June."

"He's been writing to you, though?"

"Oh yes. He sends me money twice a month, more than he can afford, actually—a money order from Kansas City and two hundred dollars from here—I guess he arranges the two hundred through the local office. I don't know why, it seems an odd way of doing things, but I'm grateful for the money. He must have been given a raise in pay."

Esther didn't even blink. "That's very likely. Wages are higher over there."

"His letters have changed recently. Oh, nothing definite you can put your finger on, he still misses me and so on, but I have the feeling—well, that it's only words, that he's doing quite nicely by himself. Or *not* by himself."

"What does that mean?"

"Maybe he's found somebody else," Thelma said in a low voice. "Oh, I don't blame him. I *wanted* it to happen."

"Are you sure it has?"

"No. But I have this intuition. And I know Harry. If some woman ogles him at an office picnic he's not going to run away, he'll stand there and be ogled and love every minute of it."

"I grant you there may be something in intuition, but carrying it as far as an office picnic and an ogling woman..."

"There actually was an office picnic. He mentioned it in his last letter. He said he'd had a very good time. Oh, not that I care. I want him to have a good time, to be happy. He deserves it. Only..."

"Only what?"

"I wish he wouldn't tell me about it. I'm so miserable. I'm so miserable." She dabbed at her eyes with a piece of Kleenex. "Office picnic. To *hell* with him."

"Now don't cry."

"I can't help it."

"Think of the future, the baby. How much longer do you have to wait?"

"Nearly three weeks."

"That's not very long."

"It seems—it feels like an eternity."

"Is there anything I can do to help?"

"No. No, thanks." She took another bite of the chicken salad, then pushed the dish away from her. "The next letter I get from him, I'm not going to read. I won't even open it."

"Aren't you being a little unreasonable?"

"Just as unreasonable as I can get, I know that. I'm a dog in the manger. I don't want Harry back, I could never live with him again. It's just—well, the thought of him carousing around with other women, going to all kinds of parties. . ."

"One office picnic."

"That's all he mentioned. There are probably dozens of occasions he didn't mention." She dabbed at her eyes again. "It's not that I begrudge him anything. I want him to be happy. I'll give him a divorce so he can marry her."

"By her, you mean the woman who ogled him at the picnic and pursued him relentlessly through a round of wild parties?"

"You needn't laugh at me," Thelma said sulkily. "I can read between the lines."

"Some people become so expert at reading between the lines they don't read the lines. You're letting your imagination run riot. You've taken an office picnic and blown it up into a series of orgies."

"No. Harry wouldn't enjoy orgies. He's not like that. He's just the kind of man who should be married."

"He already is."

"No, not any more."

"Someday, perhaps, the two of you will get together again..."

"No. Never."

"How can you be positive?"

"Because I was never in love with him. I was over thirty when we met—I'd never had a real proposal before and I knew it was my last chance to—well, to have a full life, a baby—my God, how I wanted a baby." She looked down at her distended abdomen pressing against the table, and smiled, very faintly. "I didn't dream it would be so difficult."

TWENTY

Thelma's baby was born at the Women's College Hospital on a cold rainy morning during the last week of September. She'd gone to the hospital alone by taxi in the middle of the night without notifying any of her friends or neighbors.

Ralph Turee was the first person outside the hospital to hear of the birth. Thelma's doctor called him just before he left for a nine o'clock class, and told him that Thelma had been delivered of a fine, healthy eight-pound boy. Thelma's condition was "only fair" after two blood transfusions, and she was allowed no visitors for the present, but the baby could be seen through the glass walls of the nursery.

Feeling that something in the nature of a celebration was in order, Turee called a meeting of the remaining fellows for lunch at the Plaza. Over martinis and steak pie, Turee broached the subject of relaying the news to Harry.

"I think we should send him a telegram."

"Why?" Joe Hepburn asked. "To *congratulate* him?"

"Well, no. But he ought to be told Thelma and the baby are all right."

"I don't know, it strikes me a telegram would be in bad taste under the circumstances."

"Harry wouldn't know the difference and it wouldn't matter to him if he did. The only thing that concerns him is Thelma. The poor guy's probably sitting around biting his fingernails."

Bill Winslow spoke for the first time. The combination of the weather, the martinis, and a breakfast quarrel with his wife had put him in a sullen mood. "The hell he's sitting around biting his nails. Poor guy, my eye."

"What does that mean?"

"Never mind."

"I do mind," Turee said sharply. "Come on, what's the big secret? What do you know?"

"Plenty."

"Such as?"

"Such as Harry's not sitting around biting his nails over Thelma. He's not sitting around, period."

"You seem pretty positive."

"Why shouldn't I be? I had a letter from him yesterday. We haven't been corresponding much, I don't know why he picked me to confide in instead of one of you."

"Well, what did he say?"

"Read it yourself. I've got it here somewhere, been carrying it around. Kind of a shock."

The letter was passed across the table and Hepburn and Turee read it simultaneously. Its contents were simple enough: Harry had met a girl, a perfectly wonderful, marvelous girl named Anne Farmer. She was divorced, through no fault of her own; her husband had been a brute, a real cad and so on, but through it all Anne had remained faithful, sweet, kind, and so on. He intended to get a divorce and marry this paragon of virtue as soon as possible, and he hoped that the fellows would wish him luck. Not that he needed it, because Anne was so wonderful, so understanding, et cetera. All the best, Harry.

"Je—*sus*," Turee said and flung the letter down on the table.

Winslow picked it up and replaced it in his pocket. "Nice timing, eh?"

"I just can't believe it."

"Try a little harder."

"In all his letters to me, he's never mentioned another woman. I was led to believe he spent all his time working."

"Does that sound like Harry? Not to me."

"Hooked," Hepburn said gloomily. "Hooked again, and we're not there to protect him. Her husband was a brute. Naturally. All ex-husbands are brutes. All future husbands are angels. *Then* comes the switch."

"Shut up," Turee said. "I'm trying to think."

"The time for thinking is past."

"Listen. We'd better send that telegram to Harry after all. Suppose he suddenly decides to write Thelma a letter like this. The shock might kill her. The doctor said her condition was only fair. That's hospital jargon for anything-can-happen. We've got to warn Harry."

The telegram was drafted by all three men and Turee telephoned it in when he returned to his office: *Thelma delivered of healthy son. Her condition fairly serious. Imperative that you do nothing to upset her. Wait for letter. Ralph.*

Later the same afternoon Nancy took a dozen roses to the hospital for Thelma and stopped at the nursery to see the baby. A masked nurse wheeled the bassinet to the glass wall and pulled the coverlet part way down to reveal the baby's face. He was quiet, but not asleep, a beautiful child with a shock of black hair and brilliant blue eyes.

Nancy tapped against the glass, smiling and cooing. She was unaware that she herself was being observed until a voice spoke suddenly beside her, "Hello, Nancy."

Nancy turned with a little jump of surprise. "Why—why, Esther."

"I came, too. I had to see for myself." Her yellow raincoat and hat were still dripping with rain. "I guess I'm making a mess on the floor."

"You can't help it, in this weather."

"I—he's a lovely baby, isn't he?"

"Yes, very."

"He looks like his father. Don't you agree? He looks like Ron?"

Nancy agreed but said nothing.

"Well, I had to see for myself," Esther repeated, and with one more brief glance through the glass wall she turned and walked briskly down the corridor, her raincoat rustling around her legs like dead leaves.

It was two weeks before Thelma was released from the hospital. She left as she had entered, by taxi, but this time she wasn't alone. She held her son in her arms, with a pride and joy she had never known before, or believed possible.

She moved back into the house in Weston. Her neighbors all knew or suspected the truth by this time, but they were kindly people, especially Mrs. Malverson next door who threw herself immediately into the role of grandmother. She helped Thelma with the shopping, the washing, the cleaning, she clucked and cooed over the baby and took him for long walks in his pram, she measured out the ingredients of his formula with the severe precision of a pharmacist.

Mrs. Malverson believed herself to be Thelma's closest friend and confidante. She was, therefore, extremely surprised when she went over to Thelma's house one afternoon in late October and noticed a For Sale sign posted on the front lawn. She found Thelma upstairs sorting through the contents of an old trunk while the baby slept beside her in his bassinet.

"I saw the sign," Mrs. Malverson said flatly.

"Oh, is it up already? Good. I asked the realtor to hurry."

"You've been crying."

"Not much. Looking over old things always gives me the blues—I don't know why, I'm happier now than I ever have been."

"So you're going to move."

"Yes."

"When?"

"As soon as I can."

"Where?"

"Nevada."

"But that's in the States."

"Yes. I have an appointment at the American Consulate for Friday morning. I'm applying for a permanent visa."

"Well. *Well.*" Mrs. Malverson plopped down on the side of the bed. "I've got to catch my breath. This is all so *sudden.*"

"Not to me."

"Ronnie's too young to travel that far."

"No, the doctor said this is actually the best time, especially if we go by plane."

"But well, there's the lawsuit coming up and everything..."

"It won't be coming up. Esther has agreed to a settlement out of court. I didn't want to take it—she's been so nice about things since that day I met her in Eaton's—but my attorney said I'd be a fool to turn it down. It's quite a lot of money."

"And well it should be." Mrs. Malverson was on the point of asking how much, but she desisted, in the hope that Thelma would volunteer the information.

Thelma didn't. "Anyway, it's all settled now. I signed the papers."

"Nevada. I ask you, why Nevada? I hear it's a wicked spot. Gambling, even on the Sabbath, that's what I heard."

"It's a good place to get a divorce," Thelma said grimly. "Six weeks, and it's all over."

"A divorce?"

"Yes. My husband..." She stumbled awkwardly over the word, and her face flushed. "Mr. Bream called me long distance last night. He wants a divorce. He's in love with another woman."

"Well. *Well.*"

"Don't be so shocked. I wasn't. I've actually been expecting it for some time now. It's almost a relief to have it confirmed."

"You poor child. You poor..."

"*No.* I don't really care. I thought I might when I heard his voice again, but last night on the telephone he didn't even sound like himself, it was like talking to a stranger. Her name's Anne."

"Her?"

"The woman." She slammed down the lid of the trunk, but the gesture, like Pandora's, was a little too late. Too many things had already escaped. She said roughly, "All this old junk of Harry's, I might as well throw it away."

She left the first week of November. Turee offered to drive her out to the Malton Airport but she refused. She said all her good-byes briefly and by telephone, as if she preferred not to risk any display of emotion which might make her change her mind.

She sent air-mail letters to Mrs. Malverson, the Turees and Esther, assuring them of her safe arrival in Las Vegas. The trip had been pleasant and Ronnie a perfect angel all the way, but she didn't like Las Vegas. The countryside was too desolate and the town itself full of very odd people. When her residence requirements were up she intended to move on, perhaps to Southern California. There was no mention of homesickness, loneliness, regret. Or Harry.

At Christmas time she sent large, elaborate baskets of fruit to all her friends, belts of hammered silver and Indian turquoise to the Turee children, and hand-tooled leather holsters to Esther's two boys. On the back of a Christmas card to Joe Hepburn which didn't arrive until New Year's

she wrote that she had her divorce papers and she and Ronnie were staying temporarily in a motel in Pacific Palisades until she decided on a permanent place. She did not give the name of the motel, or the exact location of Pacific Palisades, which Hepburn had never heard of and couldn't
find on the map.

It seemed as though the Breams, who had once lived in such close prox-
imity, were now trying to get as far away from each other as possible. In
Harry's next letter to Turee, in February, he said he had maneuvered a
transfer to Florida. The Kansas City climate was proving too rigorous for
Anne who was inclined to be frail. Enclosed in the letter, almost as an
afterthought, was the formal announcement of his wedding. Mr. and Mrs.
Paul Davis Dugan announced the marriage of their daughter, Anne, to Mr.
Harry Ellsworth Bream.

"Well, that's that," Turee said and passed the announcement and the letter across the breakfast table to his wife.

"Yes. Yes, I guess it is."

"You don't sound very happy about it. I thought you *liked* people to get
married and live happily ever after and so on. What's eating you?"

"Oh, there's something so final about it, seeing it in print like this."

"Let's hope it's final."

"I can't help—well, Thelma and Harry always seemed so right for each
other. I kept hoping things would work out between them."

"You're a great hoper."

Nancy reread the letter, making little snorting noises of disapproval.
"Frail. Huh. She was born and raised in Kansas City, now suddenly she's
too frail. Oh, I bet Harry has picked himself a lemon. A real *lemon*."

"Nancy, love..."

"What's more, I hear Florida is hotter than hell in the summer and people are always getting lost in swamps."

The new Mrs. Bream did not get lost in a swamp. She did, however,
become dissatisfied with Florida rather quickly, and once again Harry
found himself on the move, this time to a new job, obtained through one
of Anne's relatives, with an oil company in Bolivia. Since he knew nothing about either oil or Bolivia, he expected to be extremely busy and would
not have the chance to write as frequently as in the past.

By the time another Christmas rolled around, his letters had ceased
entirely.

TWENTY-ONE

Thelma's Christmas card that year consisted of an enlarged snapshot of her son standing in a shallow wading pool, staring sober and wide-eyed into the camera. He was now some fifteen months old, a handsome child, dark-haired like his father, stockily built like his mother.

The enclosed letter to the Turees was unlike any Thelma had written before. Even her handwriting had altered: it was larger, less controlled, and the lines slanted ebulliently upwards.

Dear Nan and Ralph:
Would you ever have recognized Ronnie? I bet not. He's getting to be so big I can scarcely carry him anymore (23 lbs!), but fortunately, I don't have to. He's very good at getting around by himself, too good, sometimes! It is so long since I've written to you that I hardly know just where to start. First things first, though, so here goes. I am going to be married this week, and if I were any happier I'd burst! His name is Charley, he's a widower with grown children, and he's quite the nicest person in the world. I met him last summer on the beach at Malibu. He was walking his dog and the dog bit me on the leg. Not very romantic! We'll be going to live in Charley's house in Santa Monica. (As a matter of fact, I'm writing this from there—Charley is out in the yard making a swing for Ronnie.) I hope you will find time to convey my good news to Esther and the Winslows and Joe and Mrs. Malverson and to give them my regards. I won't be writing again for a long time, nor hearing from any of you. I'll do my best to explain why, and I can only hope your feelings will not be hurt. Charley knows nothing about my past life. He thinks I am a widow—I told him that on the spur of the moment when we first met, and I've had to stick to my story. Please try to understand my position, and my reasons for not giving you Charley's last name or my new address. He's a wonderful man, and even if he found out the truth about me I think he'd forgive me, but I can't afford to take that chance. I love him too dearly.

I feel that I'm on the brink of a whole new life for myself and for Ronnie. (He needs a father now, you should see the cute way he trails behind Charley!) I can't do anything to endanger our happiness, even if it means no more communications from my dearest friends.

Please try to understand, and give me your blessing. Love,
                                                    Thelma

Nancy was extremely happy over the news. "I think it's terribly romantic."

"Indeed," Turee said. "How do you know he's not marrying her for her money?"

"What money? All she has is the settlement out of Ron's estate."

"Do you happen to know how much it was?"

"No, and neither do you, smartie. Esther won't discuss it."

"Other people aren't so particular. One of the assistant professors in the French Department is related by marriage to Martindale, the attorney Thelma hired. It seems that right after Thelma left town, Martindale bought himself a new house and car with his percentage of the take. So the take must have been considerable."

"Even so, you have no reason at all to believe that this Charley is marrying Thelma for her money. She says right in the letter he has a house of his own, so he can't be exactly poverty-stricken. You're an incurable cynic, that's all."

"Really."

"I *still* consider the whole thing very *romantic.*"

"You needn't shout," Turee said. "Oh, there's one more point that occurs to me. If I were Charley, I think I'd be a little suspicious of my wife having no contacts whatever with her own past."

That spring Turee received an offer of a guest lectureship at the Santa Barbara campus of the University of California for the summer session. The pay was excellent, he couldn't afford to turn it down. Nor, on the other hand, could he afford to transport a wife and four children across the continent and rent adequate housing for them. They were all very eager to go with him and emotions were running at an all-time high when Esther unexpectedly provided a compromise solution to the problem. She decided to take the two boys to Europe for July and August and offered Nancy and the children the use of the lodge while she was gone.

Nancy accepted with gratitude, and the Turee household returned more or less to normal. Tempers calmed down, tears stopped, sulks disappeared, and preparations for the summer began.

Turee departed in early June, traveling by bus as far as Detroit and then by air coach to the West Coast. He intended to live as cheaply as possible during the summer so that he could return home not merely with some memories and experiences but with some hard cold cash. With this objective in mind, he rented a small furnished apartment at the rear of an old house set in the middle of a lemon grove near the campus.

Time passed quickly at first. There was work to be done, and sightseeing, and exploring the strange little Spanish city crushed between the mountains and the sea. The members of the faculty and their wives were friendly and hospitable. They invited Turee to dinner, to concerts, to barbecues; but there were still left some long evenings to spend by himself, especially over the week ends when his colleagues were busy with their own families. It was on one of these evenings, a Friday, that the thought occurred to him of going down to Santa Monica the next day and trying to find Thelma.

He knew that the idea must have been in the back of his mind before he even left Toronto because he had packed in his suitcase Thelma's last letter enclosed in the Christmas card with the snapshot of Ronnie on it. He remembered packing it, surreptitiously, without mentioning it to Nancy, and as he took it out now to reread, he realized that he had intended, from the first moment he'd been offered the appointment in California, to find Thelma. He wasn't certain why, whether he wanted to see her again out of curiosity, or for old times' sake, or merely to make sure she was all right.

He read the letter over twice, looking for facts. Then he got out his AAA tour books, a map of Southern California and a scratch pad to make notes.

Charley. Last name unknown. Occupation: not stated. A preyer on women, for all I know, Turee thought grimly. Age: a widower with grown children, which might place him between forty-five and fifty. Maybe older, but this wasn't likely, in view of Thelma's infatuation. Other facts: he owned a house in Santa Monica, and a dog which bit, and he sometimes visited the beach at Malibu.

Turee checked the map and the tour book. There were miles and miles of beach along Malibu, and the city of Santa Monica, to the south, was listed as having a population in excess of seventy-one thousand. The chances of finding a middle-aged man named Charley who owned a house and a biting dog seemed extremely remote.

The letter, then, was useless, as far as leads were concerned. This left the picture of the boy, Ronnie. It was sharp and clear, and the boy's unsmiling features quite distinct. It had obviously been snapped by someone more skillful with a camera than Thelma. Probably by Charley. Maybe Charley was a camera bug. That hardly narrowed the search down, though; camera bugs were as common in California as bleached blondes.

But as Turee studied the picture he felt a growing sense of excitement, as if an idea had already begun to germinate in the depths of his mind and was trying to push its way up through several layers of consciousness.

A very cute kid, he thought. Looks strong and healthy. Thelma probably watches him like a hawk, and has him checked by the doctor at least once a month. Not just any old doctor, either, but a specialist. A pediatrician.

Pediatricians. Of course. It's so simple, why didn't I think of it before? To hell with Charley, who needs him?

Once again he consulted the tour book—Santa Barbara, population about 50,000—then he picked up the local telephone directory. In the yellow pages, listed under Physicians and Surgeons, he found eight pediatricians. If Santa Monica had a similar ratio, he could expect to find about a dozen.

A dozen pediatricians and a picture of a little boy. Perhaps, with luck, that would be enough.

He checked the southbound bus schedule by telephone, wrote an enthusiastic note to Nancy outlining his plan, set his alarm for five, and went to bed.

That night in a dream he saw Thelma walking along a wide and desolate beach, her long fair hair streaming in the wind. Suddenly from behind a boulder a man appeared with a little dog. The man pointed toward the sea, and Thelma turned and walked slowly and methodically into the water until it covered her head. The man laughed, and the little dog began to bark, and the air was filled with the screaming of gulls and the black whirring wings of cormorants.

He woke up with one alarm ringing in his ears and another, shriller one in the back in his mind.

It was still dark, and the cool foggy air pushed heavily into the room, redolent of lemon blossoms. Turee got up and closed the windows. The smell was sickeningly sweet. Like flowers at a funeral. He thought of Thelma drowning in his dream, and the last letter she had written with its strange alteration of style and handwriting which Nancy had explained away by saying people's writing changed with their moods, that at last Thelma was happy.

Perhaps she had not written that letter at all. Perhaps, even then, she had been dead, and Charley himself had sent the letter to mollify Thelma's friends and at the same time discourage them from trying to find her.

And the boy, Ronnie? He, too, might be...

"No," Turee said aloud. "No. It's those damn lemon trees. The smell makes me sick. The kid's all right."

It was the damn lemon trees.

"The kid's perfectly all right," he repeated, as if someone in the room had denied it.

He reached Santa Monica shortly after nine o'clock, obtained a map of the city at the bus depot, and, with the aid of a telephone directory, made a list of the pediatricians in the area. Checking two of them by phone he learned that they would be in their offices only until noon, since it was Saturday.

That gave him two and a half hours. And a decision to make. He made it, with a silent apology to Nancy: he committed his first extravagance of the summer by hiring a car.

Neither his wife nor his friends considered Turee very methodical or efficient. Working against time, he turned out to be both. Instead of visiting the doctors in alphabetical order, he grouped them according to address. Five he was able to eliminate at once—they practiced in one building as a children's clinic. None of them remembered seeing the boy in the picture.

A sixth was on vacation in Montana. A seventh had gone to Los Angeles to see a patient at Children's Hospital.

It was half-past ten when Turee reached the eighth name on the list, a Dr. Hamilton who occupied an office in a diagnostic clinic. Turee was informed at the main desk that Dr. Hamilton was at St. John's Hospital but expected back any minute. Could his secretary do anything to help? Down the hall, three doors to the left.

Dr. Hamilton's secretary turned out to be a harried-looking blonde wearing spectacles and a snug white uniform. "I'm Miss Gillespie. Are you waiting for Doctor?"

"Yes."

"He should be in any minute. He has a patient scheduled for 10:45. Please sit down."

"Thank you."

He didn't sit down, however. He looked at his watch, picked up a magazine and discarded it, paced the length of the room twice, until finally Miss Gillespie said, "Is there anything I can do for you?"

"Well, perhaps. How long have you worked for the doctor?"

"Over three years."

"My name is Ralph Turee. I came from Toronto in the hope of finding an old friend of mine. I know she lives—or lived—in Santa Monica but I've lost her address. Since moving here she has remarried and I don't know her new husband's name."

"Are you sure you came to the right office? Dr. Hamilton is a *pediatrician*."

"Yes, I'm coming to that. The woman I'm looking for has a little boy. The only hope I have of finding her is through this boy. She sent me a picture of him last Christmas. He'd be nearly two years old now. His name's Ronnie."

"We have dozens of Ronnies," Miss Gillespie said with distaste, as if every single Ronnie gave her a pain in the neck. "Perhaps if I could see the picture? Actually, I know Doctor's patients better than he does. I'm the one who entertains them and keeps them quiet until their turn comes. And if you think that's easy, just come around some afternoon about four when we're running behind schedule and emergencies keep popping in like flies and the kids are all howling and the phone's ringing—well, you get the idea."

"Vividly. I have four of my own."

Turee handed her the picture of Ronnie and she studied it intently for a moment. "Yes, he's one of our patients, I'm sure of it. Comes in quite frequently. He's allergic—chocolate, eggs, milk, and so on."

"Who brings him in?"

"His mother. She's one of these fussy mothers, doesn't care in the least about getting Doctor out of bed at one o'clock in the morning if the kid has the slightest symptom. Overprotective."

It sounded like Thelma. She was not dead. It had been the lemon trees, after all. He said, "What does she look like?"

"Oh, nothing much. I mean, it's hard to describe an ordinary-looking woman. Except her hair, it's really beautiful." Miss Gillespie glanced at the picture again and handed it back with a puzzled frown. "Did you say the boy's name was Ronnie?"

"Yes."

"I'm sure you're mistaken. Or I am. One of us is."

"Why?"

"That boy is little Harry Bream."

TWENTY-TWO

The house lay high in the hills and at the foot of a cliff, behind the city. The mailbox at the beginning of the curving concrete driveway was shaped like an old-fashioned stagecoach. It bore no name, only the street number 2479. The hinged doors were open, and the mail delivered but not yet picked up—a copy of *Life* magazine, nothing more.

A wind was blowing down the canyon. It shook the rows of eucalyptus trees, and the pods struck the roof of the car and rattled off with the sound of scurrying mice.

The house itself was simple and elegant, of stained redwood, with a wide expanse of patio which had recently been hosed down. Steam rose from the flagstones as if secret fires were smoldering underneath. Except for the rising steam there was no sign that the house was now occupied. Turee pressed the door chime, waited, pressed it again several times, but no one answered.

He crossed the patio and picked his way down a steep path through massed geraniums to the rear of the house. Here he found a second patio, more secluded, shaded by a plexiglass roof and decorated with camellias in redwood tubs.

He saw the child first, sitting quietly in a sandbox, completely absorbed in the operations of a dump truck. Then he saw the woman. She may have been inside the house and seen his car stop, or she may merely have heard the door chime and the unfamiliar footsteps on the path. At any rate, she seemed to be expecting him, waiting for him. She was sitting bolt upright, tense, in a canvas sling chair made for lounging. Her hands were pressed tightly against her knees as if they had been frozen there.

"Hello, Thelma."

Her only response to the greeting was a blink of her eyes.

"It's been a long time."

"Not long enough. Not nearly long enough." She watched warily as he approached. "How did you find me?"

"Through the picture of the boy."

"Yes. That was a mistake, wasn't it? Well, it can't be helped now." She leaned back in the chair and looked up at the sky, as if she were making some silent plea. "I was afraid that some day I'd be sitting here just like this and suddenly you'd turn up. Now that it's happening, it hardly seems real."

"It's real."

"Yes."

"How is Charley?"

There was no response.

"And Anne?"

This time, by way of answer, she gave a tired little shrug.

"There never was any Charley," Turee said. "Or any Anne. There never was—a lot of things."

"That doesn't sound very grammatical, but it's true, of course. There never was any Charley, or any Anne."

"Just you and Harry?"

"Just Harry and me."

"And Ron?"

"Ron." She spoke the name as if it were one she hadn't heard or thought about for a long time. "Yes. You'll be wanting to talk about Ron, of course?"

"Won't you?"

She smiled crookedly. "Not exactly. I—sit down, Ralph. I'd better put the baby to bed for his nap." Climbing awkwardly out of the sling chair, she crossed the patio to the sandbox where the boy was playing and held out her arms. "Come on, wee one. Put the truck down for now. It's time for our nap."

Wee one let out a rather perfunctory howl of protest.

"Now, Harry, don't make a fuss. We have company. Come say hello to the man."

Harry crawled out of the sandbox on all fours, grinned shyly at Turee, and ran ahead of his mother into the house, slamming the screen door behind him.

"I won't be long," Thelma said. "He's very good about naps. He's a—I wish . ."

She pressed her hand to her throat as if to ease the pain of the unspoken words. Then she turned and walked swiftly into the house.

Turee wondered what she'd been going to say. *He's a wonderful boy—I wish you'd go away and leave us alone—I wish you had never come...*

Sounds filtered out of the kitchen, the opening and closing of a refrigerator door, the clink of glassware, the whirring of a mixer.

"Here's your orange juice, Harry."

"I want milk."

"Now, dear, you can't have milk, you know what the doctor said."

"I want milk."

"You know something, Harry? When I was a little girl we didn't have oranges the way you do now. Only at Christmas time did I see an orange, and then it looked too beautiful to eat, like pure gold. So I used to keep it in my room, dreaming of the day I'd eat it. But I never did eat it because it got all hard and shriveled and it was no good any more."

It seemed that she was talking not to the child but to Turee, trying to explain, to excuse: the orange of pure gold which she had plucked was shriveled.

"There, you drank it all up like a good boy. Now come on, off to bed with you."

Images rose to the surface of Turee's mind like a series of colliding bubbles, each of them bursting until the final one remained fixed and clear. A figure in white. The nurse at the hospital after Harry's accident, with the phony smile and starched behind.

Miss Hutchins. He'd met her only once, over two years ago. He hadn't expected ever to see or think of her again, yet she had traveled nimbly over the years and miles to reappear on Thelma's sunlit patio and talk about Harry: "...dead drunk when they brought him in—his blood alcohol test showed only one-tenth of one percent—that's not nearly intoxication level in a normal person—he's the kind that can't hold his liquor."

But Harry had always been able to hold his liquor very well. Long after Winslow had slid under the table and Galloway was retching over the railing of somebody's back porch and Turee himself had reached a state of doldrums, Harry would still be bouncing around, the life of the party.

He hadn't been dead drunk, then. He'd been pretending. He'd been acting out one of a series of scenes, expertly timed, carefully planned, with himself in the role of tragic victim to distract attention from the real victim, Galloway. The whole thing had been staged, right from the first telephone call to Thelma from Wiarton, to the final letter about his new job with the oil company in Bolivia. And the gullible audience reacted as they were expected to. Act one, poor Harry, what a terrible break for such a nice guy. Act two, Harry starts on his brave search for a new life and finds it. Act three, Harry gradually fades away into the oil fields of Bolivia.

Bolivia, yet. My God, what fools we all were. We never questioned any of it for a minute. Thelma's renunciation of Harry, his attempt and failure to win her back, her courageous persistence in carrying on alone, her refusal to answer his letters, her reaction to his "marriage"—none of it had been real. All the time the Breams were supposedly drawing farther apart, they were binding themselves closer and closer to each other, not only by ties of love but by the stronger ones of guilt.

Thelma came out of the house. She had put on a sweater and was buttoning it at the neck, as if for her the day had suddenly turned chilly. "I called Harry at the office. He'll be right home."

"He has a job?"

"No. He's at the doctor's. He hasn't been well." She hesitated over the final word, then spoke very quickly to cover the hesitation. "You look fine, Ralph. How is Nancy? And the children? Are they with you?"

"No. They're all up at the lodge for the summer."

"The lodge, how far away that seems, and long ago. I wish—well, it doesn't matter now." She sat down in the green canvas glider and began to swing back and forth, as if, childlike, she found comfort in the motion of rocking. "You came all the way out here to find Harry and me?"

"Not Harry. You."

"You didn't expect to find Harry?"

"No," Turee said, coloring slightly. "I thought—we all thought he was in Bolivia."

"Naturally." She sounded grave, but a trace of sardonic humor flickered in her eyes for a moment. "That was Harry's idea, about the oil job in Bolivia. Harry's very—imaginative."

Once again she hesitated over the final word, as if other phrases had occurred to her first, more damaging and more precise ones which her personal censor refused to pass. She must have realized that her hesitancy had piqued Turee's curiosity, for she added by way of explanation, "It's very hard to describe someone you love deeply. Try it."

"This hardly seems the time or place."

"Perhaps not."

"Who dreamed up Charley?"

"Harry."

"He threw a boomerang. If it weren't for Charley I wouldn't be here. I was suspicious of him. I wanted to make sure you and the boy were all right."

"You came here because of Charley? How funny. How terribly *funny.*" She didn't laugh, though. She merely swung back and forth on the glider, her eyes fixed on Turee's face. "What are you going to do now?"

"I'm not sure. It's a very complex situation."

"Don't hurt Harry. Please don't hurt Harry."

"How can I help it?"

"Blame me. I'm the one responsible. I planned everything."

He didn't believe her but he kept his doubts to himself. "Why?"

"Why? There wasn't any one why. There were dozens, going back years. I'd always resented Ron, the way he had everything handed to him on a platter, the way he used to order Harry around. It rankled to see Harry toady to him." She paused. "Poor Harry, he's always had such bad luck."

Perhaps Harry's worst luck had been meeting Thelma, but apparently this notion didn't occur to her.

"Like your coming here and finding us like this," she said. "Sheer bad luck."

"Someone would have found you eventually."

"No. You were the only person interested enough to try. And you would never have found me if it hadn't been for the picture of little Harry. I wanted to show him off, I couldn't help it. That was my mistake. Pride. Vanity."

"Not pride or vanity. Your mistake was greed."

"I didn't want anything for myself, only for my husband and my child."

"And the child belongs..."

"To Harry," she said sharply. "He is *Harry's* child. Ron never came near me until I was certain I was pregnant. Then, of course, I arranged it. I had to. It was part of our plan, the hardest part of all for me, but the most vital. Ron had to believe sincerely that the baby was his. Otherwise Harry could never have persuaded him to write the final letter to Esther, which was so necessary to the suicide buildup."

"Persuaded?"

"No force was necessary. Ron had been drinking before he arrived, and he had more, some Scotch, with Harry and me. He was always easy to handle when he was drunk. Besides, when he found out about the baby, he was so overcome with guilt and shame he actually *wanted* to confess, to atone, in some way, for what he'd done to Harry and to Esther."

"Harry told him what to write?"

"Harry suggested. Ron was too upset to do his own thinking. He was very fond of Harry, you know. Everyone was. Everyone is, I mean." Color splashed her face. "What a silly mistake, using the past tense like that, as if he were dead or something."

"Or as if he had changed."

"He hasn't changed, not a bit."

But the denial was too quick and too vigorous, and Turee wondered what the years of pretense and deceit, of remorse and guilt, had done to Harry. "The phone call Ron made to Dorothy Galloway's house the night he died..."

"It wasn't Ron. Harry made the call. Like the letter, it was part of the suicide buildup. The idea of suicide had to be so strongly implanted ahead of time that no one would even think of murder. Because if anyone had thought of it, if anyone had started to make a real investigation, Harry and I were wide open. Neither of us could account for our time that Saturday night. Harry didn't make any emergency call at a clinic in Mimico, he was with me, waiting for Ron, waiting to go ahead with our plan. Nor did his car break down, the excuse he gave you and the others for being late arriving at the lodge. He wasn't even driving the car. I was. I was following him so that when the time came he could take over our car and go on ahead to the lodge. It was a tight schedule but we'd planned very carefully. Harry drove me into Meaford and I caught the 10:30 bus back to Weston. I arrived home barely ten minutes before Harry's phone call from Wiarton."

"That was planned too, of course?"

"Every word."

Turee looked bewildered, confused. "I can't—I can't quite believe it."

"I can't quite believe it myself, sometimes."

She turned her head suddenly as if she'd heard a sound she'd been waiting for and knew well. Half a minute later Harry appeared from around the side of the house.

He was a little paunchier, a little balder, than Turee remembered, but his step was still bouncy and his grin still boyish. It looked quite real, as if he was genuinely glad to see an old friend.

He crossed the patio, his hand extended. "Ralph, old boy. By God, you're a sight for sore eyes. You don't look a day older. Does he, Thelma? Sit down. How about a drink, fellow? What would you..."

"Let's not play games, Harry," Thelma cut in sharply. "Please."

"Come now, we've got to be polite, sweetheart. What's the matter with a little drink for auld lang syne?"

"I'm not sure Ralph would accept a drink from either of us."

"Nonsense. He's our friend."

No one spoke, but the words, *so was Galloway*, hung in the air like dust in a shaft of sunlight.

Finally Turee said, "Did Galloway?"

"Did he what?" A fretful little frown appeared between Harry's eyebrows. "I don't know what you're talking about."

"The night he died, did Galloway accept a drink from you?"

"Two, as a matter of fact."

"Loaded with barbiturates?"

"Loaded with nothing more than Scotch."

"How did you manage to drug him?"

"Drug him? Absurd. He came in, he said he was feeling sick and wanted something to settle his stomach. I gave it to him. Maybe I gave him too much. Quite accidentally."

"Harry..."

"Must we go into all this? It's done, it's over, it's been over for years. Besides, I've got a headache. Every time I go to the doctor I get a headache. I hate his guts. All these psychiatrists are quacks and fools."

"Why go to him, then?"

"Thelma insists. There's nothing the matter with me. The whole thing's absurd. I feel fine. I only go to please Thelma. Isn't that right, Thelma?"

Thelma was silent.

"Well, tell him, Thelma. Tell him there's nothing the matter with me, I only go to the doctor to please you, Thelma?"

She sat mute, not looking at him but staring upwards, as if she were lost and alone on an island, searching the sky for signs of rescue.

"Tell him the truth, Thelma. Go on. The truth."

"God help us," she said and turned and began walking toward the house.

"Thelma, come back here."

"No. Please."

"I command you to come back here. You must obey me. I'm the boss. We settled that years ago, didn't we? I'm the boss, aren't I?"

She hesitated a moment, biting the corner of her mouth.

Then she said quietly, "Yes. Sure you are, Harry."

"You mustn't walk out on me like that. It's disrespectful. I don't like it. I won't tolerate it. You hear?"

"Yes, Harry."

He held out his hands toward her, palms up, and Turee saw on each wrist a red scar in the shape of a cross. "You know what I've got to do if you don't treat me right, if you don't behave yourself. And this time I won't fail. I'll cut deep."

"No, Harry. Don't. Don't make me suffer any more."

"You suffer? Thelma, Thelma, you've got it all wrong. I'm the one who must suffer. I must wash away your sins with my blood. Now sit down and be polite. Ralph came all the way down here to see us. We must be hospitable. He's our old friend. Eh, Ralph? How many years has it been, Ralph?"

"About a dozen," Turee said.

"Only a dozen? Ron and I were friends for twice that long. Ron's dead," he added, as if he were imparting a piece of news. "It's my turn next."

"Why do you think that?"

"Thelma and the doctor keep asking the same question. It's not something I think. It's something I know. Some people know things. Without rhyme or reason they just know. There's a special day ahead for me. I will recognize it when it comes. There will be signs, in the sky, the air, the trees, so I will know, *this is it, this is the day.*"

"What about your wife and your little boy?"

"My little boy? So you believed her, too. I don't blame you, it's quite a convincing story she tells. Only it's not true. The boy belongs to Galloway. Thelma lied to salve my ego. She's a very talented liar. For a long time I believed her when she said she was pregnant before Ron ever went near her. I believed her because I so very much wanted to. I managed to convince myself that all the tests I'd taken back in Toronto were wrong, that I wasn't sterile, I was a man like other men. Then one day, when I was giving the boy his bath, I noticed the way his left ear stuck out from his head a little more than the right ear, like Ron's. And the shape of his hands and feet—exactly like Ron's. And I knew then Thelma had lied to me. Oh, her reasons were noble, but she'd lied to me, deceived me, made a fool of me. She'd sinned. I had to do something, I kept thinking something must be done, Thelma must be saved. I tried to wash away her sins with my blood." He held out his scarred wrists. "She didn't understand. She thought it was a mere suicide attempt. She called the fool-doctor and they took me to a hospital. They couldn't keep me there, though. I'm too smart. I was polite, I behaved myself, I answered their questions. They let me go in a couple of weeks. The trick is to tell them enough but not too much. Let them think you're communicating but keep your secrets to yourself. Talk all you want about your childhood but not about your child. Especially if he's not really yours. Thelma."

She raised her eyes to him. They looked pale and pure as if they'd been washed a thousand times with tears. "Don't leave me alone, Harry. I love you."

"I know that," he said wearily. "I love you too. But the time has come when I must know the truth. I have been living with so many lies, I can hardly tell any more what's real and what isn't. Like Charley. Your husband, Charley. I know he isn't real, we made him up together, you and I. Yet sometimes I can see him quite distinctly, sitting in my chair, driving my car, walking into your bedroom and closing the door. And if I listen hard enough I can hear the two of you whispering together, I can hear the creak of bedsprings, and I know you're making love in there, you and Charley, and I want to kill him for the same reason I killed Ron, because he dared to touch you."

"Don't go on, don't think about it."

"You never knew that before, did you, Thelma? I didn't want Ron's money. I wanted his life. I killed him out of rage and hate and jealousy. When he was in the back seat unconscious and I was driving his car, wearing his cap, carrying his wallet, I felt like a man. Funny, isn't it? He wasn't really much of a man. But he had something I didn't, something I wanted. And later when I was strapping him into the safety belt on top of the cliff, and you were waiting on the road in our own car, all I could think of was, you'll never touch her again, Galloway, you'll never touch another woman, cuckold another friend, beget another bastard..."

"Stop. Please stop."

"Not now. This is the time for truth. You're such a natural liar, Thelma. You lie the way other people breathe, without thinking about it."

"No!"

"But you must tell the truth now. There isn't much time. The boy—my boy—he's not really mine, is he, Thelma?"

"I lied for your sake. I wanted you to be happy. I..."

"The boy is Ron's?"

"Yes," she said in a ragged whisper. "Don't hate me for it. Please don't hate me."

"Thelma, Thelma, you are my love, how could I ever hate you? You've told me the truth. That's the first step."

"Step?"

"To atonement, to peace." He looked up at the sky, smiling and composed. "You see that single cloud up there, Thelma? That's one of the signs I've been waiting for."

"It's only a cloud, Harry. Don't imagine..."

"Only a cloud? Ah, no. This is the day."

"Stop."

"Don't you feel how different it is from other days? You, Ralph, don't you feel it, too?"

"It's an ordinary day," Turee said. "How about that drink you offered me a while ago?"

"Not now. You can pour it yourself after I've gone."

"You just got here, don't talk about leaving."

"I must. Look, Ralph. There. See it? A bird flying across the cloud. If I'd had any doubts at all, that would dispel them."

Turee tried to catch Thelma's eye for some hint on how to handle the situation. But her eyes were closed. She seemed to have fallen into a troubled sleep. Her hands twitched and tears glittered on her lashes.

"You can't leave Thelma."

"No," Harry said. "I won't leave Thelma. She's coming with me. She wants to." He reached down and touched her gently on the shoulder. "You want to, don't you, Thelma? We've been down some pretty dreary roads together. This last won't be any rougher."

Turee said, "Stop this foolishness and let me help you."

"It's too late to do anything for me. Help the boy, if you can. He's a good boy. He deserves to be brought up by a good man. You don't have to be afraid he'll grow up to be like me."

"I won't let you walk off like this..."

"You can't stop us. Besides, I don't think you really want to. They still hang people in Canada." He leaned down and kissed Thelma on the forehead. "Come on, dear."

Thelma rose silently, hanging on to his arm.

"For God's sake, don't go with him, Thelma," Turee shouted. "Stop and think."

"I've already thought," she said quietly.

They walked together hand in hand across the patio and up the steep path along the side of the house.

A minute later Turee heard the roar of a car engine. He thought of the cliffs of Santa Monica above the sea, like the cliffs of Wiarton above the lake, and he could see behind the next corner of time the last dreary road Harry had chosen.

They still hang people in Canada, Turee thought. *It's better this way. Better for the boy. He's got a life to live, I must see that he lives it right... My God, I wonder what Nancy will say....*

THE END

DO EVIL IN RETURN

By Margaret Millar

To Faith Baldwin

*"Those to whom evil is done
Do evil in return."*
—*W. H. Auden*

ONE

The afternoon was still hot but the wind carried a threat of fog to come
in the night. It slid in through the open window and with curious, insinuating fingers it pried into the corners of the reception room and lifted the
skirt of Miss Schiller's white uniform and explored the dark hair of the girl
sitting by the door. The girl held a magazine on her lap but she wasn't
reading it; she was pleating the corners of the pages one by one.

"I don't know if Dr. Keating will be able to see you," Miss Schiller said.
"It's quite late."

The girl coughed nervously. "I couldn't get here sooner. I—couldn't find
the office."

"Oh. You're a stranger in town?"

"Yes."

"Were you referred to Dr. Keating by anyone?"

"Referred?"

"Did anyone send you?"

"I—no. I found her name in the phone book." The girl rose suddenly and
the magazine and her cheap brown handbag fell on the floor. "I've *got* to
see her. It's terrible important."

"If you'll let me have your name and address I'll tell doctor you're here."

"Violet O'Gorman, 916 Olive Street."

"Miss?"

"Mrs. *Mrs.* Violet O'Gorman."

Miss Schiller gave her a sharp look before she turned and rustled starchi-
ly into Charlotte's office.

Charlotte had already put on her street clothes but she was resigned to
the idea of a change in plan. It had been years since she'd spent a day without one.

She was adjusting her hat in front of the wall mirror, a tall, slender
woman just past thirty, with an air of calm efficiency.

"Now what?" she said, without turning.

"Someone just came in. She wasn't referred, said she got your name from
the phone book."

"Oh."

"She calls herself Mrs. O'Gorman."

"If that's what she calls herself that's probably her name," Charlotte said
crisply. "And by the way, Miss Schiller, when you're talking on the phone
please say *what is the name,* not *what was the name.* It sounds as if you're
talking to a corpse."

"I try to please." Miss Schiller's tone and her compressed lips implied that Dr. Keating was beyond pleasing anyway.

Charlotte took off her hat again and ran her hand expertly over her smooth brown hair. Miss Schiller frowned faintly in the direction of the hat. She disapproved of the way Dr. Keating dressed after office hours—in big picture hats and sheer dresses and high-heeled pumps. A patient meeting her on the street might easily lose confidence in her, thinking she was on her way to a bridge or cocktail party instead of to the hospital to make her rounds. Miss Schiller herself had never had any confidence to lose. She went to a chiropractor for her lumbago and bought Chinese herbs at a little store downtown to build up her hemoglobin.

"Show Mrs. O'Gorman in, will you?"

"Very well, doctor."

Miss Schiller went out, holding her hand against the small of her back, an indication of performance of duty while in pain. Charlotte smiled. She knew about the chiropractor and the Chinese herbs, she knew practically all there was to know about Miss Schiller, and so she was tolerant. *To know all is to forgive all,* she'd quoted to Lewis once, and she believed it sincerely. Lewis had replied that she was a remarkable woman. She had agreed, without conceit. It was amazing in this day and age to be able to survive at all without nervous tensions or insomnia or any of the obscure psychosomatic symptoms that plagued half the people who came into her office.

Charlotte was both healthy and happy. She drove herself, but not to the point of exhaustion. She was competent at her work, which was general practice; she had a shrewd if not profound mind, and a nice sense of humor. Most of her male colleagues called her Charley and spoke of her behind her back in a friendly, rather sexless way. She wasn't sexless, though. There was Lewis. And eventually—well, eventually something would have to be done about Lewis. They were passing irrevocably beyond the moonlight-and-roses phase. It was sun-and-dandelions now, stronger, earthier stuff. Lewis was becoming urgent, detachment difficult.

She made it a rule not to think about Lewis during office hours. She pushed him out of her mind and fixed all her attention on the girl Miss Schiller brought into the office. Miss Schiller had a firm grip on the girl's arm like a prison matron escorting a possible runaway.

Her face was red and indignant. "Imagine. She wasn't going to come in. Off she ran. Imagine, after all the trouble you've..."

"That will be all, thanks, Miss Schiller," Charlotte said.

"I was so coming in," the girl protested when the door had closed on Miss Schiller. "I only went out in the corridor to find a drink of water. I got this awful thirst."

"Sit down, Mrs. O'Gorman."

The girl sat down apprehensively on the edge of a chair. She was about twenty, dark-haired and quite plain except for the radiance of her eyes and the healthy flush in her cheeks. Though it was a humid day she wore a heavy tweed coat which she held tight over her stomach with both hands. Her forehead bore a long zigzagging scar. The scar had welted and Charlotte wondered if the girl had had any x-ray treatments to make it less noticeable.

"I just got an *awful* thirst. I guess I drink about two gallons of water every day."

"That's good for you," Charlotte said, "in your condition."

The girl let out a little cry. "Oh God. Oh God, does it show? Does it *show?*"

"I'm sorry I startled you. I thought naturally..."

"How could it show *already?*"

"It doesn't."

"It must! You said—you said..." She covered her face with her hands. Tears spilled out between her fingers and dripped off her wrists.

She wore a wedding ring. But then, they all did. They bought them at the dime store. Charlotte thought that for some that must be the worst period of all—even worse than labor—when they went to the dime store to buy their rings. There probably wasn't one of them who hadn't dreamed of being a June bride. Charlotte felt depressed.

She said finally, "Where is your home, Mrs. O'Gorman?"

"In Oregon. Ashley, Oregon."

"Are you married?"

"Yes. Yes. Only I left him. He isn't the one, he isn't the—the father."

"What do you want me to do, Mrs. O'Gorman?... What's your first name?"

"Violet."

"Who sent you here, Violet?"

"No one." The girl widened her eyes in a show of innocence. Charlotte wasn't fooled. She thought, I hope the word isn't around that I perform illegal operations.

"No one sent me," Violet repeated. "Like I told the nurse outside I saw your name in the phone book and I came to you because you was a woman, because I thought you'd understand how it is being in the family way with no husband."

"You don't want your baby, is that it?"

"How can I want it?" Violet asked simply.

"You're young and healthy. If you go ahead and have the child you'll be able to hold your job until the last few days..."

"I don't have a job."

"Well, perhaps the man involved will contribute to your support. If you can prove that it's his child he'll have to."

"I can prove it, all right. I wasn't living with Eddie. He said I was making him nervous so I went to stay with my sister for awhile. That's how he knew the baby wasn't his." She touched the scar on her forehead with the tip of one finger. "He hit me with a lamp. I stood it for two months after that and then I left him. He said such terrible things to me. I didn't mean to be bad."

The girl started to cry again. Charlotte looked at her, crisp and businesslike. ("Does nothing move you, Charley?" Lewis had asked her last week before he left. "In my profession I can't afford to be moved," she had told him. "I would be weeping all the time, and quite useless, don't you see?" He didn't see. In spite of his sophistication he judged the weight of an emotion by the amount of tears or laughter it displaced.)

She said, "I gather that the man involved doesn't want to marry you."

"He couldn't anyway." She fumbled in her coat pocket for a piece of Kleenex. She found one, sodden with previous tears and stained with lipstick. "He's married already."

"Did you know that when you...?"

"Yes. He told me. But I didn't care then. He was so different from anyone I ever met."

"Older than you?"

"I guess, about forty."

"Had you known him long?"

Violet uttered a sound that was almost like a laugh. "I never saw him before in my life."

"Yet you...?"

"Yes. *Yes.* I—oh, you wouldn't understand."

"I'll try," Charlotte said gravely.

"Well, he came in the bar where Eddie works—Eddie's my husband. He began talking about the big redwood trees, how it was such a crime to cut them down. He said some of them were four or five thousand years old and two hundred and fifty feet high, and how they were almost human. I don't remember his exact words but he talked like—like poetry."

Charlotte watched her in silent pity.

"Well, Eddie said that was a lot of baloney about the trees, and when I started to talk he told me to shut up and go back to my sisters. I was scared not to. Eddie is—is tough."

"Tough?"

"He used to be a pro fighter until his appendix burst. I didn't want no trouble, so I left."

"But not to your sister's."

She shook her head. "I went out and waited beside his car. It was the only car there with a California license. I—I really only wanted to apologize to him for Eddie's bad manners. We talked for a while and then he said he had to go back to his motel because he was leaving in the early morning, going home."

"That is, coming here, to Salinda?"

"Yes. I was awful disappointed. I mean, didn't you never go to a big city like Portland and maybe catch someone's eye when you were walking along the street—and you knew right away that you had something in common, a lot in common? I felt like that about him.... I guess you never been to Ashley."

"No." She had never heard of it.

"It's a little town where people never stay. They go through it, heading east or north or south. No one stays." She raised her head and said passionately, "I hate it. I hate Eddie, too."

And out of the hatred, Charlotte thought, had come Violet's union with the man who talked like poetry. To her he was probably a symbol of all the romantic and exciting people who passed through the town, heading east or north or south, but never stayed.

"I don't know how it happened after that. I don't *know*. I—oh doctor, please. You've got to help me."

"I'm sorry I can't, not in the way you mean."

The girl let out a cry of despair. "I thought—I thought being you was a woman like me—being you..."

"I'm sorry," Charlotte said again.

"What I do? What can I do with this—this *thing* growing inside of me, growing and growing, and me with no money and no job and no husband. Oh God, I wish I was dead!" She struck her thighs with both fists. "I'll kill myself!"

"You can't, Violet. Stop now and be sensible."

Miss Schiller appeared. She'd been listening at the door. She liked excitement, and violence was always cropping up in her dreams.

"Did you need me, doctor?"

"Why, no," Charlotte said coolly. "As a matter of fact you may go home. I'll lock up."

"Well, I thought..."

"Good night, Miss Schiller."

The door banged shut again.

Violet's face was blotched with white. "She must of heard me. She'll go around telling everyone."

"She has no one to tell, only her cat."

"C—cat?"

"She has a big tomcat; the two of them gossip together for hours.... Are you feeling better now, Violet?"

"Why should I? Nothing's been changed."

Charlotte felt a little foolish. Ordinary tact seemed silly in the face of such simple and direct reactions as Violet's: How can I want this child? Why should I feel better when nothing is changed?

"Such operations are illegal," Charlotte said bluntly, "unless they're necessary. That is, medically necessary, in the case of a mother's life being at stake."

"My life is at stake."

"You only think that *now*. Later on, when you adjust to the..."

"Please," Violet said. "Please. Give me some medicine."

"I can't. Even if I could it wouldn't work. Your pregnancy is too advanced. How far along are you?"

"Four months."

Charlotte thought of the child secure inside Violet's reluctant body, impervious to the violence of her fists and the animosity of her mind. It would be recognizably human by this time, the arms and legs well formed, the cervical flexure gone, the head nearly straight, the nose and lips and checks already distinct. Four months—how could the girl be sure?

"I'm sure," Violet said. "It only happened once." She raised her head and looked at Charlotte, half-hostile, half-anxious. "I guess you don't believe that no more than Eddie did."

"I believe it."

"Just once, it happened. Just for a minute, and now look at me. It ain't fair. I don't *deserve* it."

"I know... I know... This Eddie you mentioned, your husband... Perhaps your best bet, for the time being anyway, would be to go back to him if he'll take you."

"Oh. he'd take me, all right. He likes to have me around, somebody to cook for him and to bully. Oh, what's the use sitting here talking? You won't help me."

"I can't."

"You *can*, but you won't, because you're afraid. Well, I'm afraid too, worse than you." Violet's eyes were bleak. The crying had washed away their softness; they glared like marbles. "Doctor—you don't know anybody else who'd..."

"I'm sorry, I don't," Charlotte said honestly. There were rumors, of course, about old Dr. Chisholm, but then there were about many doctors, off and on, herself included. Most of the rumors originated with disgruntled patients or chronic cranks.

Violet was watching her, sadly, bitterly. "I guess you've never been desperate like I am."

Charlotte was patient. "Now Violet, let's not make this a contest between you and me, who's more afraid or who's more desperate. This is a practical problem. We can't solve it with emotions. Tell me, have you any place to stay?"

"My step-uncle keeps a boarding house downtown. He's letting me stay in the back room upstairs until—until things are settled."

"What things?"

"He thinks I should get money from this man—the father."

"Have you tried?"

"Yes. But he wasn't home. He was out of town."

"Is he coming back?"

"Yes, tonight, they told me."

"He doesn't know that you're pregnant?"

"No."

"Do you think that he'll admit that the child is his?"

"He's gotta. It *is*. My uncle says I can go to court and make him pay a lot of money. I can ruin him forever, my uncle says."

"I wouldn't think of revenge, Violet—only of doing the right thing for yourself and your child."

There was a long silence before Violet spoke again. "I don't want to ruin him. I got no hard feelings being it was as much my fault as his. I don't even want money. I only want to be the way I was before—without anything growing inside of me. I'll put up with Eddie, with anything, just so's I could be the way I was before."

"I'm sorry," Charlotte said. "I wish I could help you."

The phone rang in the reception room and Charlotte went out to answer it. It was Lewis. She told him, rather brusquely, that she was glad he was back and that he was to call her later at home.

When she returned to her own office Violet was gone. She had slipped out the rear door, and the only evidence that she'd been there at all was the wad of sodden Kleenex left on the chair and the history sheet on Charlotte's desk. The sheet was blank except for the name and address at the top, written in Miss Schiller's librarian's backhand: Mrs. Violet O'Gorman, 916 Olive Street.

She picked up the history sheet and stood holding it in her hands for more than a minute. Then she crumpled it into a ball and hurled it quite viciously at the wastebasket.

TWO

Just as she tried to forget Lewis during office hours, in the evenings she tried to forget her work. She wasn't entirely successful.

"You're jumpy tonight," Lewis said.

"Am I?"

"Could I flatter myself that it's strictly from joy at having me back?"

"You could not."

"You are glad, though? Aren't you?"

"Of course."

"I missed you, Charley."

There wasn't the usual banter in his voice. He sounded tired.

She went over and put her hand on his shoulder. It wasn't often that she touched him first and on her own initiative. She was very proud; Lewis had to be the aggressor, to make the first move.

He was in his early forties now, a tall man, so rangy and loose-jointed that he could never fit into any ordinary chair. The one he occupied he'd bought himself and given to Charlotte. It was red leather and didn't match the gray and lime color scheme of the rest of the sitting room. It stood out, compelled attention. When Lewis wasn't there the chair was a symbol of him, a discordant note in the restful little room, as Lewis was the discordant note in her life.

He twisted his head so that her hand was pressed tight between his cheek and his shoulder. She had an irrational feeling that her hand was caught in a crevice between boulders.

She broke the silence. "Lewis?"

"Yes, darling."

"Perhaps you should have stayed home with Gwen the first night..."

"I couldn't," he said simply. "Let's change the subject."

"All right. How was the trip?"

"Like any trip without you, long and dull." He had gone with two other lawyers on a week's fishing trip in the Sierras. It was an annual, routine affair. Lewis never enjoyed it; he went along merely because it was expected of him. Lewis liked to conform: his defiance of the conventions was purely verbal.

"I'm glad it was dull. I'll seem exciting by contrast." She spoke lightly, but she felt a twinge of pain that was part anger and part jealousy. Minutes with Lewis were few and precious. Yet he had squandered a whole week of them on a fishing trip. I'm getting possessive, she thought. I must watch myself. You can't own people. I own my car, my house, my clothes—that ought to be enough. It wasn't enough, though. The car had to have Lewis at the wheel; the clothes had been selected to please him; and she'd bought the house six weeks after she'd met him, not knowing why at the time, merely thinking that her apartment was too cramped and there wasn't enough privacy.

The house had a high stone wall on three sides. On the fourth side there was a sweeping view of the city and the harbor. From Lewis' chair by the picture window you could look down and see the city spread out below, a tangled network of lights all the way down the hill to the sea. The city was medium-sized, large enough to support half a dozen second-rate night clubs, and small enough to pass the word along if you patronized any of them. She and Lewis never went to night clubs or even to movies together. They met at her house—he hid his car in her garage, or left it a block away—or they drove down to the beach at night, as anonymous in the dark as all the other lovers parked on the blowing sand.

"I like your hair," Lewis said, raising his head to look up at her. "It's brown, plain brown. You don't often see plain brown hair any more; it's usually tinted red.... Charley, you're not even listening."

"I am. You said I had brown hair."

"What I really meant was that I love you. Everything about you is right."

"That's nice."

"Nice." He frowned; his black, bushy eyebrows made him look cruel. "Charley, there's something the matter with you tonight. I've said or done the wrong thing again. Or you're still sore about the fishing trip."

"I'm not sore. I have something on my mind. A patient who came in this afternoon."

"Tell me about him."

"Her. I can't tell you."

"You often do, medical ethics to the contrary."

"I know... Lewis, I think I made a mistake." She stood at the window locking and unlocking her fingers. Somewhere in the city, in the chaos of yellow and red and green lights was the light that belonged to Violet—a dim, flyspecked light in the back room of a boarding house on Olive Street. And Gwen—there was a light for Gwen, too, as she sat waiting for Lewis to come home, patient and sweet as always, with the collies beside her, all of them as gentle as Gwen herself.

"As long as you didn't kill anybody," Lewis said, "by giving them the wrong prescription."

"I don't make mistakes like that. This was an error in judgment. The girl—everything the girl said was right. I was afraid, I still am. But such silly, trivial fears compared to hers... And she said I've never been desperate. I haven't. I've never had anything to make me desperate."

She turned suddenly, aware of a subtle change in the atmosphere. Lewis was lighting a cigarette. She knew from his expression that he was disappointed and angry at the way the evening was turning out. Their first evening together for a week—it should have been perfect, and it wasn't, and Lewis was silently blaming her, as if it were her fault that the two of them couldn't live separate from the rest of the world. She and Lewis would never, could never be alone, in spite of the stone wall on three sides of the house. The fourth side was unguarded, unprotected. Violet crept in, and Gwen and Miss Schiller, even the two men who'd gone with Lewis on the fishing trip.

She said, with a sigh, "I feel depressed and quarrelsome, Lewis. Perhaps you'd better go home."

"Perhaps I had." He ground out his cigarette in the myrtle wood ash tray he'd brought her from up north. "Though I don't like being ordered around like a little boy."

"I didn't mean it to sound unpleasant, darling. I meant, we'll only quarrel if you stay."

"You can sound pretty officious. God, Charley, what do you think I'm made of? You keep me hanging around, you tell me to come, and then you tell me to go peddle my papers. You rant about some silly girl and her fears when we've got a million things to say to each other about us." He got up and grabbed her roughly by the shoulders. "Who cares, who the hell cares? Charley, you haven't changed your mind, you still love me?"

"Yes. Naturally."

"When I hold you, you draw away as if I had a bad smell."

"Oh Lewis, for heaven's sake," she said sharply, pulling away from his grasp. "I told you, I'm not myself tonight. Everything's wrong, out of focus."

He looked grim. "Because of this girl?"

"I suppose that started it."

"Why?"

"She's in trouble. I refused to help her."

"Why should you help her? She's probably just an ordinary tart who got caught."

"No. She's a nice girl, sensitive, and very bewildered."

"You've had cases like that before. Why does this one worry you?"

"Because of us, Lewis. Don't you see...?"

"No."

"If we go on together, if we become lovers, I might accidentally end up in the same boat she's in."

He let out a snort of disgust. "I see now. For some extraordinary reason you've identified yourself with this girl, and me with the man who got her in trouble, the callous, bestial male."

"No, I haven't." She looked up at him, searching his face for some sign that he understood. "What would you do if I got pregnant?"

"Considering our present platonic relationship that's rather funny."

"You aren't laughing. What would you do?"

"Oh, come off it," he said. "You wouldn't get pregnant."

"It's possible."

"Not with the proper insurance."

She smiled, a little bitterly. "That's a funny analogy. When you take out earthquake insurance it means you're protected financially against an earthquake. It doesn't guarantee that there *won't be* an earthquake. The sense of security is false."

"Now earthquakes. God, Charley, what's got into you? You're becoming a neurotic."

"Am I?" She averted her face. "I think you'd better leave."

"Certainly," he said. "Certainly."

He crossed the room towards the door, slowly, giving her an opportunity to call him back. She didn't. She stood at the window until she heard his car roar out of the garage. The furious racing of the engine indicated that Lewis was taking out his temper on the car.

His cigarette was still smoldering. She carried the ash tray out to the kitchen and washed it, moving awkwardly because she was angry. Hers wasn't a hot and immediate anger like Lewis'; it couldn't be satisfied, as his could, by racing the engine of a car or breaking a golf club. Charlotte's anger was slow and cold; it crept gradually through her body, depressing the nerves, making her almost incapable of moving and talking.

She thought of all the things she should have said. Then she said them silently to herself, rephrasing and cutting them until they were sharp and elegant as diamonds. It was the kind of childish satisfaction that she seldom permitted herself.

She looked at the clock. Nine-thirty. Lewis would be home by now, making up a lie for Gwen. Miss Schiller would be putting up her hair and talking to her cat, perhaps even telling it about Violet: *"Today a bad girl came in, bold as you please, and wanted doctor to get rid of the baby—oh, the things that happen! And the people you meet!"*

Yes, the things that happen. Charlotte felt a stab of regret. I should have helped the girl, she thought. I meant to do something for her, but she'd already gone.

She stood at the window, locking and unlocking her fingers. A low gray fog hung over the distant housetops and gave them the contours of a dream. Under one of the housetops was the girl Violet worrying out the night, friendless, penniless, thinking of death.

916 Olive Street. The address had stuck in her memory as the girl's grief and terror had stuck in her throat.

With a decisive movement Charlotte turned from the window and went to the hall closet for her coat and hat.

THREE

Olive Street threaded north-south through the city. At one end there was an imposing hotel that rented ocean views at twenty dollars a night, at the other a flour mill. In the center, once a select suburb, the grandiose old three-storied Victorian houses had been gradually debauched by slums and abandoned. The slums had pushed ahead like an army of grasshoppers destroying everything that grew in its path. Nothing would ever grow again in that concrete wilderness except people. More and more people, whites and Negroes, Mexicans, Chinese, Italians. They kept alive and multiplied. They worked on the dock or at the freight yards; they were gardeners, busboys, charwomen, bookies; they took in washing and roomers; they sold tamales, green tea, religion, firecrackers, used furniture, souvenirs, rose bushes, and Mexican silver jewelry.

Olive Street was never empty or quiet. It had no set hours of work and rest like the middle-class parts of town. It was awake all day and all night. After dark there were fights and crap games, police sirens and recriminations.

Charlotte knew the section well. She had two regular patients within a block of 916. Though she wasn't apprehensive about visiting Olive Street, she took the precaution of locking her Buick and removing the radiator cap that the garage man had fixed so that she could take it off and put it on herself. (She'd lost two before she caught on to the fact that you couldn't make people trustworthy by trusting them. It was better to withdraw the temptation.)

916 was a relic. Built to last, it had lasted stubbornly through sixty years and a major earthquake and a succession of owners and tenants.

The present tenant, according to the crudely printed sign in the right front window, was Clarence G. Voss. The sign read, in full: CLARENCE G. VOSS. PHRENOLOGY AND PALMISTRY. FRESH-CUT FLOWERS FOR SALE. PIANO LESSONS.

Inside the house someone was playing, not a piano, but a harmonica, with brash inaccuracy. An elderly Italian sat rocking on the front porch, his hands pressed tight over his ears.

Charlotte nodded and said, "Good evening."

He lowered his hands, scowling, "What's that?"

"I said, good evening."

"Cold and noisy."

"Perhaps you could tell me if Mrs. Violet O'Gorman is at home,"

"I pay no attention to other people."

He replaced his hands over his ears and withdrew into his world of silence. He kept his eyes on her, though, as if there was a remote possibility that she might do something interesting.

Charlotte pressed the doorbell.

"Out of order," the Italian said.

"Thanks."

"Nobody fixes anything around here."

"I think the button is jammed."

"You're wrong."

It was jammed. She fixed it in three seconds with a bobby pin while the Italian watched her with grudging approval.

Inside the house the harmonica stopped abruptly at the sound of the bell.

A man opened the door, a small, middle-aged man with a red baseball cap pulled down over his forehead. His ears jutted out from under the cap, extraordinary ears, pale as wax and enormous. His chin and nose were elfin and sharp, his eyes were like small black peas. Charlotte could see the outline of the harmonica in the pocket of his Hawaiian-print shirt.

Charlotte didn't smile or even attempt to look pleasant. He was the kind of man who would immediately construe a smile from a strange woman as an invitation to intimacy; a man as quick to take offense as to take liberties.

"I'm looking for Violet O'Gorman. Is she at home?"

"I don't know." He had a surprising voice for his stature, deep and resonant. "Who wants her?"

"I do."

"Sure, sure, I know that, but what name will I say is calling?"

"Miss Keating."

"Keating. Come inside and I'll go see if Violet's home."

She went in, showing none of the hesitancy she felt. He closed the door by giving it a shove with his foot. The hall smelled sour. In the light of an old-fashioned beaded chandelier Charlotte saw that the linoleum on the floor was grimy and split with age. Dust grew in the corners like mold, and the paint on the woodwork had alligatored.

He stood with his hands in his pockets, his eyes narrowed. "What did you want to see Violet about?"

"A personal matter."

"My name is Voss. I'm her step-uncle."

"I thought so."

"Violet and me've got no secrets from each other. She's one swell little kid, believe you me. Anybody'd harm a hair on her head I'd strangle him with my bare hands."

"I'm in rather a hurry," Charlotte said.

He hesitated, then swung round suddenly and skipped up the stairs, quick and neat as a cat.

Charlotte lit a cigarette and wondered if she'd been wise in giving Voss her name.

She wasn't afraid of him, but the house made her uneasy. It had an air of decadent resignation, as if so many things had happened there that one more wouldn't even be noticed.

She could hear Voss whispering upstairs. What is there to whisper about, she wondered. Violet is in or she's not in, there's no need for secrecy.

But the whispering went on, and the ceiling creaked faintly under the weight of cautious feet. She raised her eyes and caught a glimpse of a face peering down at her through the rails of the banister. The face drew back into the shadows so quickly that she wasn't sure whether it belonged to a man or a woman. She had only the impression of youth and a picture in her mind of a flat, crooked nose that looked as if it had once been broken.

She called out sharply, "Voss!"

Voss appeared at the head of the stairs. "Violet's not in. She must have went to a movie or something."

"You might tell her that I was here and that I'll call her early tomorrow morning."

He came slowly down the steps, tracing a pattern on the banister with his forefinger. "Of course, if I knew what your business was, maybe I could help you. I've had a lot of experience one way or another in my lifetime."

"Thanks, I don't require any help." She opened the door. "Good night."

"Good night."

She breathed in the cool, crisp air, feeling such an overwhelming and irrational relief that her knees shook a little. She was angry at herself for being too imaginative about the house. A house could be old and dirty without becoming the scene of a tragedy. And Voss, while he was a sleazy character, might live a fairly respectable life.

She crossed the dimly lit street to her car. The old Italian whom she'd talked to on Voss's porch was sitting on the curb out of sight of the house, eating potato chips from a cellophane bag.

He watched her silently as she took the radiator cap out of her purse and replaced it on the car. Then he said, "Voss is a no-good bum."

"Is he?"

"I see by your car you're a doctor, eh?"

"Yes."

"Voss doesn't need a doctor, he needs an undertaker," the Italian said gloomily. "He needs one bad."

Charlotte unlocked the front door of the car.

The old man got up suddenly, spilling the bag of potato chips in the gutter. "Wait a minute," he said. "I could ride down the road a piece with you."

"Why?"

"I'm not going anywhere else."

"That's not a very good reason."

A small black and white mongrel appeared and began to eat the potato chips one by one in a leisurely manner. The old man reached down and stroked its dusty back. "I have a good reason," he said. "You want to know about Violet, don't you?"

"Yes."

"Well, then... We can't talk here. Voss is watching. He hates me, we have a great mutual hate."

Charlotte unlocked the other door. The old man climbed into the car, running his hand over the upholstered seat with a sigh of satisfaction. "This is the life, yes sir, this is where I ought to be sitting, a big shot. And I would be too if it wasn't that years ago I got an ulcer. A peptic ulcer, the doc called it. Sometimes I suffer—how I suffer! Right now I feel good. My name is Tidolliani, by the way. Tiddles, they call me."

"Mine is Keating."

"I know. I heard you tell Voss. I was listening at the window."

"Why?"

He looked surprised. "Why? Well, I like to know what my enemies are doing so I can outwit them."

Charlotte pulled away from the curb. She suspected that the old man, Tiddles, wasn't entirely sane, but he seemed harmless and, besides, he had put into words her own feeling about Voss. (She thought of how angry Lewis would be if he ever found out. He was always trying to make her promise not to pick up hitchhikers, and he'd even bought her a gun to keep in the glove compartment of the car. Though she was flattered by Lewis' concern, she'd refused to accept the gun.)

"You can stop anywhere now," Tiddles said.

She turned off the next side street and parked the car. She asked abruptly, "Where is Violet?"

"I don't know, but Voss does. He knew she wasn't up in her room. He took her away himself in a car two hours ago, him and another man, one of the new roomers.

"*Took* her away?"

"Well, she acted like she didn't want to go. The other man was driving the car, an old blue coupe with an out-of-state license."

"Did she have a suitcase with her?"

"No. The three of them drove off together, and pretty soon Voss and the roomer came back. Voss had two bottles of muscatel with him, and didn't even offer me a drink. As if I cared," he said bitterly. "As if I cared."

"Violet didn't come back later on by herself?"

"No. Maybe she never will."

"Why do you say that? Of course she'll come back," Charlotte said firmly. "And when she does, I want you to tell her that I'll call her tomorrow morning, in case Voss forgets."

"He won't forget, but he won't tell her." He glanced at her slyly out of the corner of his eye. "You might think I exaggerate about Voss, eh, because I hate him? Wrong! I don't! He is a cheap crook that ought to be in jail. When I think of the people they put in jail nowadays, and here is Voss running loose on the streets! I have a friend who committed a murder. He had a record so clean you could eat off it, he never even put a slug in a pay phone, but he got sent up for life. They ought to have let him go. He'd learned his lesson, he'd never do it again. Besides there was only this one person he ever wanted to murder, his wife it was. A very nice lady but she made him nervous. Take a man like Voss, now. He would do anything for a dime, anything that was mean and petty and miserable and low enough. Yes. Yes, he even thinks he can play the piano and the harmonica!"

The old man was getting drunk on words and hate.

Charlotte said, "I'll drive you home now."

"All right," he said with a sigh. "All right."

"It was kind of you to go to all this trouble."

"Think nothing of it. It was a pleasure."

He got out at the corner nearest Voss's house. Though he seemed tired, he had obviously enjoyed his little conspiracy with Charlotte against Voss.

"Voss," he said, "Voss will think twice before coming in with two bottles of muscatel and not even offering me a drink."

"Thanks for your help, and good night, Mr. . ."

He spread his hands. "Such a hard name. You can call me Tiddles like the rest."

"Good night, Tiddles."

"I'll wait up for Violet."

He shuffled up the street, his head bent against the wind.

She thought about the old man all the way home. He was getting senile. The only thing that kept him alive was his hatred for Voss.

She put the car away in the garage, glad to be back again. The sight of her wide-windowed cheerful house raised her spirits. She thought, I was silly to get upset and worried over Violet. I'll phone her tomorrow, help her in some way. The old man must have been exaggerating about Voss...

She was raising her hand to pull down the garage door when the blow struck her. She had no time to duck, or even to be aware that she'd been hit on the side of the head.

She dropped stiffly like a felled tree.

FOUR

In the dream she was riding in a long, gray bus with Lewis and Voss and Violet and the old man, Tiddles. The rest were quarreling fiercely, and Charlotte kept trying to pacify them, to reason with them. But the words that came out of her mouth were terribly wrong:

You must calm down and regurgitate yourselves. You must stop this synthetic acne and parturition. I'll call the police and you'll all be incarcinomated. Stop the bus, I say, stop the pus!

When she regained consciousness she was lying on the davenport in her own sitting room. Lewis was kneeling beside her, urging her to drink from the bottle of Scotch he held under her nose as if the fumes alone were medicinal like smelling salts.

She grimaced and pushed the bottle away. "No—no..."

"Charley... Darling, are you all right?"

"Yes." There was a painful area on the side of her head, but no swelling and the skin wasn't broken; her coronet of braids had softened the blow.

"I found you in a faint on the driveway. I keep telling you, Charley, you're overworking."

She sat up, feeling dizzy and nauseated. "Someone hit me," she said in a surprised voice. "On the head."

"Lie down, darling."

"No..."

"You hit your head when you fell."

"No. Someone else—where's my purse?"

"Purse? I don't know."

"Didn't you find it?"

"I didn't look for it, naturally," Lewis said, frowning. "I came back to apologize for being irritable and found you on the driveway."

"Lewis, get me the flashlight."

"Why?"

"I want to see if my purse is out there."

"You shouldn't move around. I'll go and look."

"No. Let me."

"Do you have to be so damned independent? Can't I ever do anything for you? Hell, Charley..."

Her face was set and stubborn. He found the flashlight in the utility drawer in the kitchen and they went outside together to look for the purse. There was no sign of it.

Lewis said, "How much money was in it?"

"Forty dollars or so."

"You'll have to report it to the police."

"In the morning," Charlotte said. She didn't point out to him what she observed in front of the garage door where she'd fallen. It was a dribble of moist sand. She hadn't been to the beach for a month and there was no way the sand could have come there accidentally. Moist sand packed in a stocking or a sock, she thought. A neat home-made blackjack, except that it sometimes left traces.

They returned to the house and Lewis bolted the door. "As a lawyer I advise you to phone in a report to the police. Armed robbery is a serious business."

"I can't, not tonight. They'll come out and ask questions and I don't feel up to answering them."

She was rather relieved that the purse had been stolen. There had been a series of petty robberies in the neighborhood recently and she wanted to believe that this was simply one of the series and that the man who did it had no connection with Voss or Violet or the face between the rails of the banister. It was only chance that her visit to the house on Olive Street coincided with the robbery.

Lewis was looking at her sharply. "What were you doing out there on the driveway, anyway? I thought you were going to bed when I left."

"I had a call to make."

"Emergency?"

"I think so."

"You're holding something back."

"I can't discuss my cases with you, Lewis."

"I don't believe this was a case."

"He was an Italian," Charlotte said. "An old man about eighty." It wasn't quite a lie; Tiddles was a case, in a way. Lying to Lewis, even a little, pained her, but he sometimes made lying necessary by his extreme reactions to the truth. He would disapprove of her visit to Violet.

Lewis had some old-fashioned ideas about women. Gwen was, in a way, his ideal: she loved her home, she kept the place meticulous, the dogs clean and obedient, the garden neat, fragrant. But Lewis never stayed home to enjoy any of it. Gwen bored him to death, while Charlotte very frequently shocked him. It was a blow to his male pride that a woman could be as emotionally and physically independent as Charlotte. She was a competent physician and supported herself in comfort; she witnessed with detachment the most harrowing kinds of death and disease; she drove alone through the roughest sections of the city picking up hitchhikers when she wanted to, out of interest or pity; she paid calls to houses where the children slept five to a mattress on the floor. Such activities should be limited to men, in Lewis' opinion. While it was all right for a woman to be a doctor, her practice should be confined to people of a certain level of society, within a certain income bracket. He would never understand that her background was different from his. She was fitted, by temperament and training, for the work she did. She enjoyed meeting all classes of people and she met them with an impersonal ease, and without pretensions of any kind.

"You shouldn't stay here alone for the rest of the night," Lewis said. "Call Miss Schiller and ask her to come over."

"Oh no! She'll be in bed."

"She can get up again. Be reasonable, Charley."

"She'll fuss around all night."

"Even so."

"All right, Lewis," she said wearily. "I'll call her."

Miss Schiller arrived by taxi five minutes after Lewis left.

She tottered under the weight of a suitcase the size of a trunk. Her face glowed with night-cream, and in the bun of hair at the nape of her neck was stuck a pair of steel knitting needles. Miss Schiller was in a state of wild excitement.

"Imagine," she kept repeating. "Just imagine!"

Among Miss Schiller's friends things were always happening—people got engaged, sick, fired, married, divorced—these were common enough. But it wasn't every day that someone she knew got hit on the head by a burglar and left to die in the night.

She was a little disappointed at the size and seriousness of Charlotte's injury. You'd expect at least a lump at the hands of a ruthless burglar that attacked defenseless women and left them for dead. No lump, and not a drop of blood. Miss Schiller swallowed her disappointment and reminded Charlotte that a criminal usually returns to the scene of his crime. Her tone implied strongly that very likely this one would be around during the night to finish the job.

"You can't tell," she said. "He might be watching us through the window this very minute."

"He must have x-ray eyes then. The blinds are drawn."

"I've never liked Venetian blinds," Miss Schiller said decisively. "I know for a *fact,* anyone can see in through those cracks."

She refused to accept Charlotte's suggestion that she sleep in the guest room. After she'd turned out Charlotte's light she took up her position on the davenport. From here she could watch all the windows and all the windows could watch her.

She removed the knitting needles from her hair and put them within easy reach on the coffee table. The needles were not, as Charlotte had supposed, for knitting, but for defense. And in the big suitcase at her feet were some of Miss Schiller's more valuable possessions.

(If there was one burglar in town there was very likely another, and she was taking no chances.)

Miss Schiller spent a restless but satisfying night. She investigated noises, diagnosed shadows, patrolled the house and suffered frequent hot flashes which necessitated her getting ice water out of the refrigerator. Every ten or fifteen minutes she crept into Charlotte's room to ask Charlotte if she was sleeping and to assure her that all was, temporarily, well.

Listening to Miss Schiller make her rounds was worse than listening to a dozen taps dripping or a couple of tomcats fighting outside the window. Towards morning Charlotte fell asleep with bitter thoughts of both Lewis and Miss Schiller.

FIVE

After breakfast Charlotte dropped Miss Schiller and her suitcase at the office and went on to Mercywood hospital to make her morning calls. Lack of sleep never bothered her. When she pushed through the heavy swinging doors of the hospital she looked fresh and alert.

In a private phone booth in the corridor downstairs she looked up Voss's number and dialed. Though she heard the phone being lifted off the hook at the other end, no one answered.

"Hello. *Hello.* Is this 2-8593?"

"Yes." It wasn't Voss. This voice was high and quavering, the voice of someone very old or very frightened; "Violet? Violet?"

"No," Charlotte said. "It's Violet I want to speak to" "

She went away."

"She went away *where?*"

But the line was dead. Charlotte hung up impatiently. Damn the girl, she thought, I've wasted hours on her already. I have work to do.

It was half-past ten by the time she finished making her rounds of the wards. When she returned to her office she found that Miss Schiller had done nothing in her absence; she hadn't even opened the mail. It was quite obvious that Miss Schiller had spent the morning telephoning all her friends, telling them what had happened and probably a few things that hadn't.

Flushing under Charlotte's gaze, Miss Schiller picked up her appointment book.

"The little Wheeler boy's coming in at two," she said. "His mother says he didn't pass and she thinks it's because he's so self-conscious about his warts. She wants you to take them off."

Charlotte made a noncommittal noise. The Wheeler child's only trouble was an hysterical mother.

"Oh, and Mrs. Ballard phoned, doctor. She had one of those palpitating spells during the night and she wants you to come over before office hours this afternoon."

"Call her back and tell her I won't be able to make it before five-thirty or six."

"I told her you were booked straight through practically and you weren't feeling well."

"I'm feeling perfectly well," Charlotte said. "And I wish to God you'd forget about last night."

Miss Schiller looked injured. "Well. Well, I *must* say."

"Have you a list of the house calls I have to make before lunch?"

"Here it is."

Charlotte looked over the list. The patients were all women. The majority of her patients were women and children, a fact that irritated her, since she wanted a more general practice. She said, "I'll be seeing Mrs. Connelly last. You can get in touch with me there if anything turns up."

"Yes, doctor."

"After that I'll have to go down to the city hall and report the loss of my purse."

"You could phone, right from here."

"If I do they'll send a policeman out."

"Oh. That wouldn't *look* nice, would it?"

"Not particularly."

"I'll call Mrs. Ballard then, doctor. A lovely person, isn't she?"

"Yes."

"Just *lovely*, I think."

Charlotte gave her a sharp glance. It wasn't possible that Miss Schiller knew...? No, of course not. She was just chattering, as usual. To Miss Schiller, Mrs. Ballard was simply a regular patient whose husband paid her bills promptly and in person, and sometimes dropped in to talk with the doctor about his wife's condition. Having Gwen as a patient was becoming more and more unbearable. But it had to be borne; there was no way of getting out of it. Charlotte had suggested to her several times that she consult another doctor, a nerve specialist, but Gwen had been sweetly adamant: "Oh no, Dr. Keating. I have the greatest faith in you!"

I won't go, Charlotte thought. I'll send someone else—Parslow or James—I refuse to go.

When she passed the mirror in the corridor on her way outside she saw that her face was pale and pinched-looking; it was beginning to show the strain, not of the past night, but of the coming afternoon.

The police department occupied the rear half of the city hall.

Charlotte knew by sight the sergeant on duty at the desk, a man named Quincy. His wife had been in a traction cast at Mercywood for several weeks and Charlotte frequently met him in the corridors looking rather ineffectual and down at the heel. In uniform, behind his desk, he seemed larger, and his tone was brusque and officious.

He reprimanded Charlotte for her delay in reporting the stolen purse.

"We might have picked the man up last night," he said, frowning.

"You might have. It's not likely that he'd hang around afterwards, though."

"You can't expect protection unless you co-operate with the police. The least people can do is report things on time." He tapped his knuckles irri-

tably with a pencil, as if he wished they were hers. "You say you were closing the garage door when the assailant struck you from behind and ran off
with your purse."

"Yes. I wasn't seriously hurt, as you can see."

"It's assault, anyway. Did you see the weapon?"

"No, but I think it was a blackjack made with wet sand."

He frowned again. "That's just an amateur deduction, isn't it?"

"Yes."

"I'd better mark it, weapon unknown. What did this purse look like?"

"Brown lizard with a gold clasp." She described the contents, and esti-
mated her total loss at seventy-five dollars.

"Next time something like that happens, phone the police immediately,
Miss—" he consulted his report—"Miss Keating. Haven't I seen you somewhere before?"

"At the hospital."

"Oh. Oh yes. You're a nurse?"

"A doctor."

"A doctor." His expression was bitter. "I've seen so many doctors lately
you'd think I'd be able to spot one at a glance. My wife..."

"Yes, I know about her. She's had a rough time."

"Plenty rough."

"These bone operations are tricky, but she ought to be out soon."

"I..." He seemed a little dazed by her sympathy. It was as if he intended
to deliver a speech against doctors and illness and medical bills, and had
somehow missed his cue. "Well. Well, I'll get in touch with you if we discover anything."

She went out, her heels tapping briskly on the marble tiles. Everything
in the building seemed to be made of marble or iron or stone; hard, cold
materials that symbolized the hard, cold quality of impersonal justice.

At the end of the corridor an old man was standing half-hidden behind
a pillar, as if he wasn't certain whether to advance further into the building, or to dart out again. He took a bandana out of his coat pocket and
wiped his face and stepped back behind the pillar so that only a part of his
sleeve was visible.

Charlotte said, "Tiddles?"

The old man stared at her, white with surprise.

"What are you doing here, Tiddles?"

"Nothing."

"You weren't arrested or anything?"

"NO—no..." He wiped off his face again and put the bandana back in the
breast pocket of his coat leaving the tip of it sticking out very nattily. He
had on a brand-new green suit and a bow tie. He'd combed his hair and
shaved. The suit was too big for him—the sleeves touched his knuckles

and the trouser cuffs brushed the floor—and he kept fingering the bow tie nervously as if to assure himself that it was still there, that it hadn't dropped off or been stolen. He smelled of bay rum and wine and moth balls.

"You're all dressed up," Charlotte said.

"Do I look good?"

"You look fine."

"You have to look *good* to come to a police station. Otherwise—well..." His shoulders moved eloquently under the pounds of padding. "I got the suit from a friend of mine, he had to buy it to go to a classy wedding last year. You have to look respectable at a police station. The police don't like me. I've been picked up a couple of times, nothing serious, just making a little noise and having a few too many. Even so. Even so, they hold things against a man." He looked at her anxiously. "This tie is a little young for me."

"Not at all."

"People are judged by their clothes. If you look like a bum you get treated like a bum. They won't believe anything you tell them."

"What are you going to tell them?"

"About Violet," he said. "About how they murdered her."

"Why do you think that?"

"She never came home. And Voss is nervous. Nervous as a cat."

"I see."

"And this morning he said to me that I'd have to move out, he wasn't going to rent rooms any more. Take my word, Voss is nervous. And the two of them..."

"Two?"

"The roomer, name of Eddie. The two of them talked all night down in the kitchen where I couldn't hear. They're suspicious types, always figuring that someone is spying on them."

There was a moment's silence before Charlotte spoke again. "I wouldn't tell the police that Violet was murdered. They'll ask for evidence and you haven't any."

"The evidence of all my senses."

"Tell them only what you know for certain—that she didn't come home last night."

"You think that's best?"

"Yes. If you make a wild accusation that you can't prove they might consider you a crackpot."

"Which I'm not."

"No."

"Never have been and never will be a crackpot."

He walked off down the hall, his trouser cuffs picking up the dust from the marble floor.

Charlotte had an impulse to follow him, to lend her support to his story, but she held back. He could tell it alone. Her presence might only raise questions: *Back again, Miss Keating? Oh, it's a disappearing girl this time. And what's your connection with the girl and with this old man?*

Tiddles was all right. He could manage by himself.

On her way back to the office she drove past Voss's house. The windows and doors were closed, the blinds drawn. Someone had taken in the rocking chair from the porch and removed from the window the sign that had said, CLARENCE G. VOSS. PHRENOLOGY AND PALMISTRY. FRESH-CUT FLOWERS FOR SALE. PIANO LESSONS.

She stopped the car and got out and walked up to the house, rapidly, as if she were trying to keep ahead of her better judgment.

The doorbell had jammed again but she didn't bother fixing it this time. She pounded on the door with her fist. Half a dozen Negro children gathered on the sidewalk to watch her, curious and silent, their eyes popping with questions.

The door opened slightly and a woman's voice said roughly through the crack, "What do you want?"

"I'm looking for Violet O'Gorman. "

"She's not here."

"Well, is Mr. Voss in?"

"He ain't around, either." She opened the door far enough to stick her head out, and yelled at the children on the sidewalk. "You kids beat it, see? I don't want none of you niggers hanging around here."

The children departed, hiding their mortification under wide white grins.

"Are you Mrs. Voss?" Charlotte asked.

"Yeah, not that it's anybody's business." She stood with her right hand on her hip, and her left on the door, ready to slam it shut. She had a dead-white skin with a heavy blotch of rouge running from each cheekbone to the hairline above her ears. Her thin mouth had been fattened with lipstick. It looked grotesquely young and voluptuous growing on the ageing face. "I don't get the point of *standing* here," she said bitterly. "If you want Violet, look for her. I ain't the little sneak's mother."

Charlotte raised her eyebrows. "Sneak?"

"I said to Clarence, get that creepy kid out of here before I go batty. No, he says, no. He's got an angle, he says. Ha. He's got more angles than a pretzel and not one of them's ever paid off. Money. Money, that's what I want. Just *once* before I die I'd like some *money!*"

Poverty and disease had desiccated her mind. Nothing would ever grow there again.

Charlotte was repelled by the woman but she felt, too, a sense of compassion. (Lewis was sometimes annoyed by this compassion. He distrusted it, he couldn't believe that it wasn't some kind of neurosis: "Naturally you can afford to make excuses for and feel sorry for people, Charley, because you're not involved. No one could ever really touch you.")

Watching Mrs. Voss's ruined face Charlotte realized that money was the only thing for her to hope for. She couldn't ask for the return of her beauty, her health, her youth. Money was the symbol and substitute for all three. And it was possible. There was money all over the place—a dime in a slot machine at the right time, a tip on the right horse, the right number on a lottery ticket, the right angle.

Charlotte wondered about Voss's angle on Violet. There must be money involved, but it wasn't Violet's. *"My uncle says I can go to court and make the man pay a lot of money,"* Violet had said in the office yesterday. *"My uncle says I can ruin him forever."* That must be Voss's angle. But Violet, instead of going to court, had run away.

"Well, what do you think you're staring at, anyways?" Mrs. Voss muttered. "I don't have to stand around being stared at."

The door slammed so hard that the porch shook and a frightened jay flew out squawking from under the eaves.

SIX

When she returned to her office after lunch the Wheeler boy and his mother were already waiting in the reception room. The boy was sitting silent over a comic book while Miss Schiller talked to his mother. Miss Schiller always attempted to diagnose, advise and cure the patients in the reception room before they even reached Charlotte's office.

"...castor oil," she was saying. "I've seen some of the most frightful warts disappear with castor oil—oh, here's doctor now. Good afternoon, doctor."

"Afternoon," Charlotte said. "You can come right in, Mrs. Wheeler, and you, Tommy."

The boy was a handsome twelve-year-old, small for his age, and timid. His mother was a giant of a woman. When she sailed into the office with Tommy behind her she looked like a three-masted schooner towing a dinghy.

"Sit down, Tommy. Up here on this table."

He sat down. He was trembling.

"Troubled with warts again, are you? Let's have a look at them."

She held a magnifier over the boy's hands. The warts had multiplied in clusters all over his knuckles and the joints of his fingers.

"Let's see now. I took off two of these with an electric needle about a year ago, didn't I?"

He said in a whisper, "Don't do that again."

"I won't. There are too many this time." She turned to Mrs. Wheeler. "I think we should try some bismuth shots."

"Shots?" Mrs. Wheeler's mouth gaped. "Oh no! Tommy's scared to death of shots. Aren't you, Tommy?"

The boy let out a whimper.

"See? He's just terrified of needles, he's always been from the time he..."

"Nobody likes shots, Tommy." Charlotte touched his shoulder reassuringly. "Have you ever given yourself a good hard pinch?"

"I guess."

"That's about how much this will hurt."

He pinched himself on the forearm, thoughtfully. "That'll be O.K. I guess."

He was reasonable, Charlotte thought, but he'd been exposed to so much emotion at home that it was only a matter of time before he got out of control.

She worked as fast as she could, talking to distract his attention. But in the end she had to call in Miss Schiller and all three of them held the boy forcibly on the table while Charlotte inserted the needle into his hip. When it was over Miss Schiller was sweating and Charlotte had a scratch on her wrist and Mrs. Wheeler was like a huge flabby ghost.

"He gets another shot in a week," Charlotte said. "And next time I'd let him come alone. He can ride his bicycle over."

"He hasn't got a bicycle," Mrs. Wheeler said. "I consider them too dangerous."

"Most things are, if you want to worry about them," Charlotte said crisply. "Tommy's a big enough boy to come here by himself, aren't you, Tommy?"

He put his sleeve over his eyes in shame, and his mother led him out.

There were two people waiting in the reception room, a woman with a tiny baby, and a good-looking man about thirty-five with bright blue eyes that were slightly narrowed as if in amusement. Though Charlotte had never seen him before, she had a sense of recognition. A moment later she realized, with a kind of pleasant shock, that he looked enough like her to be her brother.

He saw the resemblance too, and one corner of his mouth turned up slightly in a half-smile. Then he dropped his eyes and kept them fastened on the large manila envelope that was lying across his knees.

Charlotte turned to the woman with the baby. "Mrs. Hastings, you can go inside with Miss Schiller now. I'll be with you in a minute."

When the door had closed behind them the man got up and crossed the room. "Dr. Keating?"

"Yes."

"My name's Easter. I'm from the police department."

"Oh."

"You reported the loss of a purse."

"Yes."

"We've found one. It doesn't exactly fit the description you gave but it had a card inside with your name on it."

"One of my professional cards, you mean?"

"No. Your name and office address were typed on it, not printed."

"There was no card like that in my purse."

"Take a look anyway," Easter said. He put the manila envelope on Miss Schiller's desk and opened it. The purse slid out. It was brown but it wasn't lizard, and instead of a gold clasp it had a plastic zipper and a shoulder strap. It gave off an odor that Charlotte couldn't immediately identify, a kind of sea-smell.

"It's not mine," she said.

"But you recognize it?"

"No I don't."

"Your friend did."

"Friend?"

"The old character who calls himself Tiddles. He says this purse belongs to Violet O'Gorman."

"Perhaps it does." She tried to look casual under his curious stare.

"According to this man, Tidolliani, Mrs. O'Gorman was a friend of yours, in fact you were trying to locate her last night and you couldn't."

"She wasn't a friend. She came to me yesterday afternoon as a patient."

"What was the matter with her?"

"She was pregnant."

"Married?"

"She'd left her husband."

"Did she want you to look after her during her term and delivery?"

Charlotte looked at him dryly. "Not exactly."

"I see."

"I refused to help her, in that sense. But I intended to do as much for her as I could."

"Intended?"

"I had a phone call and while I was answering it Violet left by the rear door. That's why I went to see her last night. She seemed pretty desperate in the afternoon. She wasn't mature enough to realize that her situation wasn't particularly unusual or hopeless. People would have helped her, and there are several agencies that..."

"Look," he said with a satiric smile. "You're trying to persuade yourself, not me. I didn't write the laws dealing with unwanted kids."

From inside the office came the sound of Miss Schiller's voice, strangely different, talking to the baby: "She's so sweet. She's *sutz* a wee dumpling!"

Charlotte said, "What happened to Violet?"

"She's dead."

"How?"

"She came in with the tide this morning. Or most of her did, anyway. Part of her right arm is gone."

"Are you deliberately trying to horrify me?"

"I'm just telling you. You should be used to that sort of thing."

"You never get used to it," she said simply. "Each time it's new."

He looked away, his face grim. "As for her purse, a couple of kids found it caught on one of the pilings down at the wharf. There was nothing in it but the card with your name on it. Which is odd, considering the number of things women usually carry around. Maybe the kids who found it helped themselves, but I doubt it. They would have dropped the purse back into the water if they'd taken anything out of it, instead of bringing it to us." He slid the purse back into the envelope. "Well, I'll let you get on with your work."

"There's no rush. Please—I'd like to hear more about Violet."

He let out a queer, muted chuckle. "Doctor, there isn't any more. She was in a spot, she killed herself, she's in the morgue. End of Violet."

Charlotte glanced up at him with dislike. "A neat summing up. Does dealing with death make you so callous?"

"I hate it. I'm afraid of it, too." He picked up the manila envelope and put it under his arm. "Have you noticed, by the way, that we look alike?"

"No."

"We do. I hope it doesn't turn out that we're long-lost siblings. That," he added with a long deliberate stare, "would be a damn shame."

Charlotte turned abruptly and went into her office. Violet was dead, in the morgue. *"People would have helped her and there are several agencies that..."*

"Look, you're trying to persuade yourself, not me."

The Hastings baby was lying on the table kicking her legs and waving her arms. Charlotte picked her up and held her against her shoulder—the Hastings baby—or Violet's baby—or Violet, herself.

SEVEN

The Ballards lived in a canyon below the fogline. By five-thirty, when Charlotte arrived, the fog had already covered the sun and the air was moist and cold.

Three of the collies met her at the door. They didn't bark because Gwen had told them to be quiet, but they sniffed Charlotte's medical bag and her shoes, and one of them, a huge, handsome sable, planted his feet on her chest and studied her face with grave curiosity. His gold and white nose was at least five inches long. Charlotte stroked it gently.

"Oh, that Laddie," Gwen said, laughing. "Down, Lad."

She was wearing a blue silk housecoat that brushed the floor, and though she seemed a little nervous, she looked as well as she usually did. She had always been tiny and very thin. She traded on her size and made sure she kept it. She wore little heelless slippers and she dieted constantly, dulling her appetite with gallons of hot, strong tea.

"Down, Laddie boy," Gwen repeated. "I just can't teach him to stay down. He won't listen. I guess he knows I love him best." She took the dog's front paws and lowered him to the floor. "He's my baby. Shake hands with Dr. Keating, Lad."

All three of the collies sat down and offered their paws with an air of polite boredom. Charlotte shook hands with each of them, feeling, as she always did when she came to this house, that she was entering an unreal world where values were reversed and the dogs kept Gwen as a pet.

"Are you feeling better?" Charlotte asked.

"Oh yes. Much."

"Good."

"I've made tea.... I *love* tea."

Charlotte left her medical bag in the hall and followed Gwen into the sitting room. The dogs came too; they went everywhere that Gwen went.

The room belonged to Gwen; there was nothing of Lewis here or anywhere in the house except his study. Gwen had braided the oval rugs herself, woven the textile for the slip covers, made the pieces of petit-point and sewed the ruffled chintz drapes. Milk glass and pewter, chintz and maple suited her, and the furniture was scaled to her size. Everything was small and fragile, and Gwen looked both picturesque and right sitting in the spindly maple chair with one foot resting delicately on a petit-point footstool. (No wonder Lewis bought me the big leather chair, Charlotte thought. There's no place here for him to sit.)

The tea table was set with Gwen's best Spode, and the tea was already

made, the pot protected against the chill of the fog by a yellow wool cozy
Gwen had made herself.

The dog, Laddie, came and put his chin on Gwen's lap. She stoked his
heavy white ruff as she talked. "In fact, I feel so much better really, I guess
it was silly of me not to cancel your call. But..."

She put her head on one side, in a kind of winsome, you-know-me gesture. Her fair hair had thinned and sallowed, and her fine white skin was
loose beneath her chin, but she had the mannerisms of a woman who had
once been beautiful. Her history was written on her face and illustrated
by her artful, fluttering hands. At eighteen she had had the world at her
feet—she was the most popular debutante in Louisville; she had clippings
to prove it—but the world had gradually deserted her. She had had nothing to offer it but her youth.

At forty she lived for her house and her dogs, and sometimes in the middle of the night she had spells of terror. Her pulse was so fast it couldn't be
counted; her body twitched; her head took fire. Twice Charlotte had been
called in the night and found her like this and given her a sedative. There
was nothing organically wrong with Gwen's heart. Her symptoms were
typical of the cardiac neurotic and couldn't be tracked down by a doctor
who had had no special psychiatric training.

"Was this attack like the others?" Charlotte felt for the pulse in Gwen's
wrist. It was still rapid, nearly a hundred.

"A bit worse, I think. Oh, I was frightened—what's my pulse?"

"Just about normal. Have you been taking the capsules and medicine I
prescribed?" The medicine was a sedative and the capsules contained
estrogenic hormones, but Gwen wasn't the kind of patient you could tell
these things to. She would certainly misinterpret the hormones, Charlotte
thought grimly.

Gwen looked vague, and a little hurt. "I *try*. I take them when I can
remember. But I have so much on my mind. Winkie's having pups again
in six days. It's going to be a huge litter, perhaps a dozen. She's so heavy
she can hardly..."

"You should be especially careful to remember the capsules. After all,
you're more important than Winkie or her pups."

Gwen let out a little cry. "Why, that's just what Lewis says! He's always
telling me, look after yourself, darling. Remember you're much more precious than any dogs."

Precious. Darling. The words stung Charlotte's ears. She's lying. He
wouldn't call her... But why not? They were married: they lived together
day after day; there must he some tender moments. Perhaps some very
tender ones, though Lewis claimed there weren't.

She said, without expression, "It might be a good idea to cut down on
stimulants like tea and coffee and coke."

"I try, I really do. But then I love my tea so much... It's ready now if you'd like some, doctor..."

"Thanks, I would."

The tea was lukewarm and so strong it coated Charlotte's tongue and the roof of her mouth. She drank it fast and put the empty cup on the table.

Gwen's hands had a bad tremor. Because she fluttered and fussed so much by nature the tremor wasn't noticeable until she picked up the empty cup to refill it. The cup rattled in the saucer like hail against a window.

"Are you still dieting?" Charlotte asked.

"Well, not very *much*. I have to, a little bit. I'm so tiny every pound shows. I mean, one avocado and there's an inch around my hips."

"You're underweight. I advise you to skip the diet, for a while."

"I'll try."

"I can't do anything for you, Mrs. Ballard, if you won't help yourself. There's not much use in paying me five dollars for a prescription and then leaving it to gather dust on the bathroom shelf."

Gwen clapped her hands with delight like a child. "Oh, that's what I like about you, doctor. You're so outspoken and so *honest.*"

"Am I? Thanks."

The dogs sensed something, a tension, an excitement in Gwen's laugh. They crowded her, raising their noses for attention, their wagging tails sweeping across the teacups and the ashtray. They were more than Gwen's dogs, Charlotte thought. They were part of Gwen herself—each of them like a separate sympathetic nervous system, feeling everything that Gwen felt.

"Mollie, you bad girl," Gwen said. "You've spilled the ashes. Settle down, now, all of you, and behave yourselves, or I'll put you out in your dog run."

The dogs quieted but they wouldn't leave her. They followed her around the room as she turned on the lamps, as if they were expecting something out of the ordinary.

Charlotte rose, too, and began brushing the silky white collie hairs from the front of her dress. "Though it sounds pretty hackneyed, I think your real trouble may be nerves, Mrs. Ballard."

"Oh, please call me Gwen. After all, we've known each other nearly a year now."

"Nervous disorders aren't really in my field and I suggest that you consult someone else."

"I *won't* be shunted off to some so-called specialist. You're too modest, doctor. You don't realize how much good you do me. Why, after one of your visits I feel just wonderful. Lewis notices it too. He said one day, Dr. Keating's a regular tonic for you, Gwen darling."

Gwen darling. "That only proves my point. I don't actually do anything for you. I'm a kind of emotional sedative, a reassurance."

"Why, I believe you're right."

"That's why I recommend a—nerve specialist."

"You mean a psychiatrist?"

"Yes."

Gwen smiled. But the smile wasn't real and the dogs knew it; they stood with their plumed tails between their legs and watched and waited.

"But I don't want to," she said. "I can never do anything I don't want to."

"There's no longer any stigma attached to going to a psychiatrist, you know. As a matter of fact it's become a mark of distinction—only rich people can afford to."

Gwen's tone was playful. "Now doctor, you're only trying to get rid of me, 'fess up. You think there are so many really sick people in the world that you're wasting your time on me and my silly old spells."

"Not at all. When I can't treat a patient to my satisfaction I recommend someone else."

"Well, I won't have anyone else, so there. Imagine me at a nasty psychiatrist's, telling him *everything*. Oh, I'd die!"

Charlotte drew on her gloves. Throwing words at Gwen was like throwing bubbles; they burst before they got anywhere. "I'm glad I was able to help in some way," Charlotte said. She felt such tension and weariness that she was ready to weep. *You're so honest, doctor, so honest...*"Take the capsules and the medicine and try not to worry too much about the spells. I don't think they're serious."

She went out to the hall and picked up her medical bag, and Gwen and the dogs followed, Gwen looking a little hurt by her departure, like a disappointed child.

"Oh, it's a shame you have to leave, doctor. Dinner's ready, and it would be easy as pie to set another place. Lewis will be home any minute now."

"Thanks. I..."

"Another time, perhaps?"

"Yes."

"I know," Gwen said gently, "that Lewis would *love* to have you."

"That's—nice."

"Good-bye, now."

"Good-bye."

Outside, the fog had thinned, but the sky was darkening.

EIGHT

She had a late dinner at home alone. The house was dead and quiet. She put some records on the Capehart to drive away the silence, but the silence stayed in ambush underneath the music waiting to spring at her between records.

She hadn't heard from Lewis all day. (Such a long day, she thought. It seems a week since I had breakfast with Miss Schiller this morning and saw Tiddles in his green suit at the police station.... A long day for me, and a long night for Violet, a long, dark forever . . Don't think, don't think about it. It wasn't your fault.)

Lewis always phoned her once or twice during the afternoon. They didn't talk long—they were both busy—but the calls reassured Charlotte. They made her feel that she was loved, that she wasn't just playing around with a married man: she was in love and so was Lewis, and it was their bad luck that he was already married when they met.

She hadn't called him at his house for a long time; she had to look up the number in the telephone directory before she dialed.

Lewis answered, sounding falsely genial as he always did before he identified a caller. It was part of his public personality. "Hello. This is Lewis Ballard."

Charlotte spoke fast. "I want to see you. Can you come over?"

"Sorry, you must have the wrong number."

"Does that mean you can't?"

"That's right. This is 5-5919."

"Darling—Lewis, I..."

But he'd already hung up.

It wasn't his fault, she thought. He had to hang up; Gwen was there listening. Even so she felt rejected, and a little cheap. *"Sorry, you must have the wrong number, toots." "Maybe I have, bud."* She went over and sat in Lewis' chair, holding the palms of her hands over her eyes.

The front door was still open, as she'd left it to air out the house after she'd cooked dinner, and the wind slid across the floor and chilled her legs.

She went to the door to close it. Two men were coming through the gate into the walled garden. The taller one bolted the gate carefully behind him and wiped his hands on his trousers. The other man was small. He moved through the shadows with furtive delicacy like an elf and his ears stuck out from his red baseball cap, pale enormous blobs of wax silhouetted against the dark trees.

He flitted across the flagstones toward the light of the open door, a moth of a man. It was too late to close the door. Too late and too futile. The little man could fly through a window, drop from a chimney, crawl out of a crack and scamper through an evil dream.

"Remember me? Eh?"

"You're Mr. Voss."

"Sure, that's right." He jerked his thumb towards his companion. Charlotte saw that both men were wearing crudely sewn mourning bands on their sleeves. "This here's my pal, Eddie O'Gorman."

"I've seen Mr. O'Gorman before."

O'Gorman stepped into the circle of light. Though he was still young his face was a record of violence and neglect, the nose broken, the left ear a mash of tissue, the cheeks pitted with acne scars.

He held his fists clenched against his heavy thighs.

"You seen me *where?*"

"At Mr. Voss's house. You were watching me through the rails of the banister."

"Yeah? What's so wrong about..."

"Now, now, Eddie," Voss said and turned to Charlotte. "Poor Eddie's upset. He got bad news today, real bad. Didn't you, Eddie?"

"Yeah." Eddie touched the mourning band on his sleeve with a convulsive gesture, as if he wanted to rip it off.

"His wife died," Voss said. "Killed herself. But maybe you already heard about Violet."

"Yes, I have."

"Poor little Violet. Who'd of thought she'd of done it the way she did? It came as a terrible shock to Eddie. Didn't it, Eddie?"

"Sure."

Voss explained to Charlotte, "He don't talk much anyway, don't talk at all when he's grieving, he gets speechless, he..."

"What do you want?" Charlotte said. "Why are you here?"

He looked a little injured by her abruptness. "Well, I figured, me and Eddie figured, that maybe you hadn't heard about Violet, and being you were so interested in her you'd like to know before you read about it in the newspaper."

"Well, you've told me. Thanks, and good night."

"Now *wait* a minute." Voss's face creased in a malevolent little pout. "Now that's no way to treat a couple mourners. Is it, Eddie?"

Eddie coughed, holding one hand over his chest. "We could talk better inside. This night air ain't so good for my bronichal tubes."

"It won't kill you," Charlotte said. "It's the same as day air."

"Say, you're a doctor. Say, what's it mean when you get up in the morning and cough and cough and then maybe an hour later you're O.K. again? Do you think that's serious?"

She stared at him through the screen door. This was Violet's husband. *"He hit me with a lamp"* Violet had said.... *"He'd take me back, he likes to have me around, somebody to bully."* She glanced at the telephone ten feet away, hoping it would ring so that she could establish contact with someone. It didn't ring, and she was afraid to go over and pick it up; the action might precipitate trouble.

"Well?" Eddie scowled. "Is it serious? You think maybe I'm a lunger?" His mouth twitched nervously at one corner. Eddie was scared to death, and violence was the denial of his fears.

"No," Charlotte said. "The cough is probably caused by a post-nasal drip. That is, when you're sleeping phlegm accumulates at the back of your nose and drips into your throat. In the morning you cough it up."

"What's that word again, what I got?"

"Post-nasal drip."

"How about that. Say, Voss, this dame knows her stuff, takes one look at me and says post-nasal drip, just like that."

"Oh, shut up," Voss said. "For Christ's sake I got symptoms, too, only I don't yap about them when there's business to be done."

Charlotte repeated, "Business?"

"Not business, exactly. You see, poor Violet didn't have many friends, only Eddie and me and the wife, and you. Violet was one swell kid, she don't deserve to have a pauper's funeral, no flowers or nothing. Funerals come high nowadays. I was around pricing them this afternoon, and boy, those undertakers are sure raking in the coin. Though some of those caskets were real beautiful. Weren't they, Eddie?"

"Sure."

"We thought of a white satin casket with maybe a great big horseshoe made of purple violets."

"Gee," Eddie said, "that'd be pretty." He touched his nose tenderly. He felt swell. Here, all this time he'd been worried about being a lunger and it was just his post-nasal drip.

"So," Voss said, "that's why Eddie and me came here. We figured Violet had a few friends, maybe we'd take up a little collection, buy a couple wreaths, stuff like that."

"How much?" Charlotte said flatly.

"I hate to think about cold cash, with Violet where she is. Still"—he shrugged—"that's what makes the world go round. Who am I to try stopping it?"

"How much?"

"Say $300."

There was a long silence before Charlotte spoke. "That would buy a great many wreaths."

"Sure, but consider the casket."

"I haven't got three hundred dollars."

"You can get it. You have a friend."

"I have quite a few friends."

"One special friend, though."

"Several."

"One *very* special."

"Stop it," Charlotte cried. "You must be crazy to think I..."

"Three hundred dollars wouldn't mean a thing to him. Or to you. Think of poor Violet."

"I only saw the girl once in my life."

"But you helped kill her," Voss said, quite pleasantly. "She came home yesterday and she says. I've been to the doctor only she won't help me, I wish I was dead."

"I think you'd better leave," Charlotte said, trying to keep her voice steady. "This sounds like extortion."

"Now *wait* a minute, that's a nasty word. Ain't it, Eddie?"

"It sure is. I don't like it."

Voss fingered the mourning band on his sleeve. "We came here as Violet's friends because we wanted to give her a good send-off. Christ, we even got to pay a minister. How far do you think three hundred dollars will go?"

"I don't know or care."

"Don't act so snotty or you will. You'll end up caring plenty." He turned to Eddie. "Extortion, she says. How about that?"

"How about it, that's what I say."

A mockingbird began to chatter from his perch on the lemon tree, abusing the invaders.

"You'd both better go home," Charlotte said, "and start thinking up some new angles."

"We don't have to," Voss said. "The angles are all there, and they ain't nice, lady, they ain't nice at all."

"You're very vague."

"I don't have to be vague. I can spell it out for you in straight ABC's. There's you, y-o-u, and there's him, B-a-l-l-a-r-d. And then there's my poor little Violet. Quite a threesome, eh? Eh?"

"Be more explicit," Charlotte said. "You want me to pay you three hundred dollars because of Mr. Ballard and because you think I'm partly responsible for Violet's suicide. Is that right?"

"Maybe. Maybe you haven't figured the angles, though."

"What angles?"

"Think about it." Voss turned to his companion. "Come on, Eddie."

"But she didn't give us the money," Eddie protested. "We didn't get the three hundred..."

"You heard the lady. She don't want to give us the money."

"You said she would."

"She will. She's got to have time to figure, is all. Maybe she's a little slow in the head. Come on, let's go "

"Wait," Charlotte said. She was assailed by an obscure and terrifying feeling that the little moth of a man was threatening to eat away the fabric of her life. Already she felt naked, unprotected.

Voss turned his indeterminate eyes on her, squinting against the light that shone above the door. "You changed your mind?"

"No." She reached her decision suddenly. "I've had enough of this. Get out of here or I'll call the police."

Eddie began to edge towards the steps, but Voss still faced her: "I don't think so. You pore over what I said, and when you change your mind you know where I live. Only you better make it soon. I got lots of important business in the fire, see? Maybe I don't look it but I'm a big shot, I'm a very important..."

"You're a cheap crook," Charlotte said. "Get out of here."

She slammed and bolted the door and stood with her back against it until she heard the squeaking of the gate as it opened and closed again. Then she picked up the phone and dialed police headquarters. She acted on impulse, without planning what she would say or thinking of the consequences.

"Police headquarters. Valerio speaking."

"H—hello?"

"What's your trouble?"

"I need some kind of—protection."

There was a voice in the background, a whining voice made harsh by whisky—"lost every damn cent of it, and then comes crying to me about it..."

"Oh, can it for minute," Valerio said. "I'm talking on the phone. Hello? What's your name and address?"

"Charl..." Her throat constricted, pressing back the words: Charlotte Keating, 1026 Mountain Drive. I'm being blackmailed. The men involved are potentially dangerous, they should be arrested. No, I can't give evidence. No, I can't tell you why I'm being blackmailed, but it's nothing criminal, nothing bad. I've been seeing a married man...

She could picture the two of them grinning knowingly if she told them, Valerio and the man with the whine, snickering together: "*Seeing* a married man, that's a hot one, that's a lulu..."

"I didn't get the name," Valerio said.

She hung up quietly.

She switched on the floodlights in the yard and went out to her car.

NINE

She phoned Lewis from a small café at the foot of the breakwater where they sometimes met.

"I'm down at Sam's, Lewis. I have to see you."

"Aren't you the same person who phoned here before? You still have the wrong number."

How quick-witted of Lewis, Charlotte thought. Gwen might be suspicious of two wrong numbers so close together. Pretending the calls were from the same blunderer was clever to Lewis. Too clever. It suggested practice in easy deceptions.

"Please hurry, it's important for both of us," she said quickly and hung up before he could reply.

She waited outside in her car, watching the boats at anchor inside the breakwater. A whole city of boats, like a city of people, all kinds, all classes; sleek and lavish yachts with their riding lights twinkling, sturdy fishing sloops, spruce little starboats fast as arrows, flatties and snowbirds, and weathered dinghies barely afloat.

A car drove past slowly and pulled to a stop a few yards ahead of her. Lewis got out, his shoulders hunched against the wind. She hardly recognized him. He wore a topcoat and a fedora and he had a scarf drawn high around his neck.

They walked in silence towards the lighthouse at the end of the breakwater.

"I didn't even know you owned a hat," she said at last.

"Now you do."

"It's quite a—disguise, isn't it?"

"I couldn't find my false whiskers. The hat will have to do."

"Oh *Lewis*."

There was no one else on the breakwater, and the only lights were feeble, from the three-quarter moon and the green signal that flashed off and on from the top of the lighthouse.

She clung to his arm, hiding her face against his sleeve. *"Lewis."*

"What is it, darling? Here. Here, sit down."

He drew her down to one of the stone benches that lined the breakwater. The bench was wet from the spray of the tide that was now ebbing, but neither of them noticed.

"Let's have it," he said, smoothing back her hair with his hand. "What's the matter, Charley?"

"I'm in trouble."

"Sorry."

"So—are you."

"That's nothing new," he said wryly. "I've been in trouble ever since I met you a year ago."

"This is worse."

"Tell me."

"I don't know how to begin."

"Begin at the beginning and go on until you come to the end."

Her smile was faint, sad. "That's from *Alice in Wonderland,* isn't it?"

"Yes."

"I wish I were Alice."

"Why?"

"Then I could wake up and find it was all a nightmare, that I never really met..." She lapsed into silence, listening to the cruel crash of the water on the rocks below. "I'm being blackmailed."

"Why?"

"Someone knows about you and me."

"Well," he said quietly. "Well. Who is it?"

"Two men."

"Strangers?"

"Not exactly. I knew one of them before. I met him last night."

"On that 'call' you made after I left?"

"Yes. Partly."

"It wasn't actually a call, was it...? No, don't turn away. Answer me. Was it, Charley?"

"I went down to see if I could find the girl who was pregnant, the one I told you about last night."

She had to tell him everything then, about Voss and the old man Tiddles, and Violet and Eddie; about Easter's visit to her office with Violet's sea-stained purse, and the ugly scene on her veranda when Voss asked for the money for Violet's funeral.

When she had finished Lewis said, "The girl killed herself?"

"The police think so."

"Don't they *know?*"

"It's too early for an autopsy report. She was only found this morning."

"I see." He took his cigarette lighter out of his pocket and began playing with it absently, flicking it off and on in unconscious rhythm with the lighthouse signal. "That's quite a group of characters you're messing around with."

"I guess."

"I've warned you before about that informal way you have of picking people up. Well." He sighed. "I suppose it's too late for one of my maiden-aunt talks. What are you going to do?"

"I don't know."

"It's illegal to pay blackmail."

"I know. I—in a way I'd like to give him the money and get it over with. Three hundred dollars isn't very much to pay for my peace of mind. If I could only be sure that it would end there . . "

"You're talking crazy, Charley." He peered down at her, half-puzzled, half-angry. "You're afraid of this man. Aren't you?"

"A little, I guess."

"Why?"

"I'm not sure." Though candor was her habit, she felt unable to speak out, to voice her doubts. The moving sea, which she had always loved, had become a threat to her, and the concrete breakwater seemed insecure, adrift.

Lewis' hand on her shoulder was strong and steady, but it wasn't a strength she could lean on, it was a strength that could be used against her.

"Listen to me," he said harshly. "If you're willing to pay three hundred dollars to everyone who finds out about us you're going to end up broke. At least a dozen people already know. It's not a criminal act..."

"You wore a hat and scarf tonight."

"It's windy, it's cold."

"Not that cold."

She turned her face away. The rocks below the seawall were slimy with eel-grass exposed by the ebbing tide. She couldn't see it in the dark but she could smell it presence. The smell reminded her of Violet's purse and of death.

"You haven't told me everything," he said. "What else has Voss got on you?"

"Nothing definite."

"But he implied something?"

"Yes."

"Tell me."

"He..." She watched his face while she spoke. It was white and blurred. "He said I'd better think over the angles, that Violet and you and I made— a threesome."

"A threesome?" His jaw dropped in genuine astonishment. "What in God's name did he mean by that?"

"I don't know. I thought perhaps he meant that you—that you knew Violet in some way."

"I never even heard of the girl until you mentioned her last night."

She knew he was telling the truth. She felt suddenly light-headed, as if a physical pressure had been removed from a section of her brain. "I wanted to be sure, Lewis. Don't get angry."

"How can I help it," he said simply. "This Voss must be crazy. He's got to be stopped." He rose from the stone bench and pulled his coat collar up around his neck. "Where does he live?"

"Olive Street, 916. What are you going to do?"

"See him. Talk to him. I won't stand for him bothering you like this. I'll scare the bejesus out of him if I have to."

"There won't be any trouble, will there?"

He looked down at her grimly. "Of course there'll be trouble. What do you expect? The man's blackmailing you and I'm going to stop him."

The breath caught in her throat. "I'd rather pay him the money than have you get into a brawl."

"Going soft on me, Charley?" His smile was uglier than a frown. "That's your trouble. You get involved with people like Voss and O'Gorman, and then you don't know how to deal with them. You haven't any defenses because they don't fight with your weapons."

In spite of the brisk onshore wind, he was sweating. His face was streaked with moisture, and when Charlotte reached for his hand to be pulled to her feet, his palm was clammy. She knew that he was nervous, perhaps even afraid. His legal practice had nothing to do with crime or criminals; it was confined to wills and trusts and estates, and an occasional discreet and very expensive divorce. She realized what a great effort it had been for him to undertake to go and see Voss himself.

"I'm coming along," Charlotte said.

"What for?"

"Because I want to. Because..."

"Haven't you gotten into enough of a mess already?" he said. "Look. You can't deal with a crummy gang like that. You're sensitive, you're a woman. You ascribe to these people feelings and thoughts and morals they don't have. You've fallen among thieves, Charley, and you're a nice, gentle girl for all your knowledge."

"I'm coming along," she repeated.

"Stubborn, aren't you?"

"A little. I have to be."

"Why do you want to come along? Don't you trust me?"

She hesitated briefly before she answered. "I don't trust your temper, your mood."

"I see. You think the situation is going to call for a woman's soothing influence."

"Perhaps. Why should that make you angry?"

"I'm not angry."

"You are.... Did you have a quarrel with Gwen?"

"Gwen doesn't quarrel," he said heavily. "She sits around looking very, very pained."

"I saw her this afternoon."

"She told me."

"I can't go on treating her any more," Charlotte said. "Get me out of it, Lewis."

"How?"

"Tell her you've heard rumors that I drink or something. Anything."

"That's absurd," he said. "I refuse."

They walked back towards the café in strained silence, Charlotte keeping a little ahead of him, her step firm and stubborn.

He put her in her car. "I suppose there's no use reasoning with you? You're coming?"

"Yes, I am. Don't you see, perhaps I can help, perhaps I can..."

"Perhaps, perhaps, perhaps. All right, I won't argue." He closed the door of the car. "I'll meet you there in twenty minutes."

"It *won't* take that long, will it? It's only on Olive Street."

"I have to stop at my office. I have some business to attend to first."

"At this time of night?"

"Yes. It's something Vern asked me to look after and I forgot about it." Vern Johnston was his partner in the law firm. "He wanted me to put some more food in the aquarium."

"I see." She knew he was lying; Vern would never dream of letting anyone else feed his precious fish. "Meet me in twenty minutes, then."

"All right."

"And park on Junipero Street," he said. "There's no point in advertising our visit."

He stood for a minute looking down at her through the open window, his head bent. She thought he was going to kiss her. She wanted him to. Instead, he turned suddenly and walked back to his car.

TEN

On Olive Street the adolescent Vosses and Eddies flocked sheeplike in front of the bars and poolrooms, crept singly down alleys like hungry cats, pressed together for love or warmth like rabbits in the dark between the walls of shacks.

But the people on Olive Street were not animals, as Lewis seemed to think. Charlotte had made calls among them by day and night, and knew them. They're people like myself, she thought, only they haven't had my luck, so I owe them something. I owe them tolerance, understanding and even faith. Faith in Voss and his wife, in Eddie? No, no, it was too late. They were already too crippled for therapy; the damage was done, the muscles atrophied, the nerves degenerated.

She turned off on Junipero Street and parked in front of a brown wooden cabin. There were no blinds on the windows and she could see the family inside—a withered little Mexican woman ironing, and a young couple dancing without music, oblivious to the woman and the ironing board, the girl lean and lithe, the boy with his hair worn long and parted sleekly in the middle all the way to the nape of his neck.

Lewis' blue Cadillac slid up behind her, looking as conspicuous in that neighborhood as the little Mexican would look at the opera with her ironing board. Charlotte stepped out of her car and they came together on the broken sidewalk.

"Did you—feed the fish?"

"Fish? No." He avoided her eyes. "Vern was there. He stopped by to check up on one of the black mollies. He thinks she's pregnant."

Bubbles of laughter rose suddenly in her throat and stung her eyes to tears. She clung weakly to his arm and pressed her face against the sleeve of his coat.

"What's so funny, Charlotte?"

"I don't know. Everything. Vern fussing over a pregnant fish... I'm sorry. I'm sorry I laughed."

"Here." He gave her a handkerchief. "Wipe your eyes. You weren't laughing."

"I was. I was laughing."

"I don't think so." They were talking in whispers, as if Voss might be in ambush behind a tree, or hidden in the trunk of one of the cars, listening. "Are you ready?"

"Yes."

"Come on, then."

He held her arm as they crossed the street.

Except for a square of flickering light in the attic, Voss's house was dark, a corrupt monster with one dying eye. The porch smelled of wet wood, and where the warped planks slipped towards the center there was a small puddle of water. Within the past hour someone had hosed down the porch and it hadn't had time to dry. Charlotte leaned over the railing. The hose had been flung into a pyracantha bush and it was still connected, still dripping water through the tiny thorny leaves. Someone (Voss?) had washed the porch in a hurry and then run away or gone into the house to hide in the dark.

No one answered Lewis' knock. He rapped again and waited, jabbing his hands nervously in and out of his pockets.

"Lewis..."

"Yes?"

"You've got a gun in your pocket."

"Are you surprised?"

"Very," she said in a whisper. "Very surprised."

"I carry it to improve my morale." He rapped on the door again. "Sometimes it sags."

"Lewis, don't threaten these men, it wouldn't work. Voss is a psychopath, he's dangerous when he's cornered or frightened or feeling inferior..."

"All right, I'll tell him what a hell of a fine fellow he is, then I'll hand him three hundred dollars as a slight token of my esteem."

"I hate guns," she said passionately. "I hate violence."

He turned away with a little shrug of his shoulders. "Go ahead and hate it, but don't pretend it doesn't exist."

A long, lean, gray cat appeared out of the shadows and swaggered along the splintered railing of the porch waving his tail contemptuously. Charlotte reached out her hand to stroke him. He spat at her and leaped off the railing, vanishing in a spidery tangle of geraniums.

"This is a waste of time," Lewis said. "No one's hone."

"We could try the back door."

"Why bother, if nobody's here?"

"There's a light in the attic, and other people live here besides Voss and Eddie—the old Italian that I told you about. Probably others too. It's supposed to be a rooming house."

"God," Lewis said.

Charlotte's eyes had adjusted to the dark and she could see quite distinctly as she went down the porch steps and around to the side of the house. Here, the stench of decaying garbage fought and overpowered the fragrance of night-scented jasmine.

The path that led to the back yard was tangled with weeds and littered with rubbish. It was as if every roomer and tenant and owner who had ever lived in the house had flung his debris haphazardly out of doors and windows. There were piles of newspapers and empty bottles and rusted foul-smelling cans; a legless chair, two tarnished picture frames lying across the corroded springs of a bed, an old automobile headlight with the glass shattered, and an abandoned wardrobe, its cardboard belly bulging with age. There were even evidences of children; the frame of a box kite, a doll—the glass eyes sunk into its head as if pushed by exploring, curious fingers—and a wicker baby carriage with the front wheels gone, so that it seemed to be down on its knees praying.

All the broken, useless things, the scraps and parings and rinds of living.

"God," Lewis said again. "Have you had enough?"

"I—guess so."

"Then let's get out of here."

"All right."

She turned to go back, and in turning, she looked up at the window in the attic with its flickering light. A woman's face was pressed against the pane, contorted, weirdly white and luminescent like a fish in the blue-black depths of the sea.

There was a sudden smash of glass, followed by a series of silvery tinkles as the fragments struck the roof of the porch.

The woman began to scream. "Help, help! Let me out of here, let me out!"

"We're coming," Charlotte answered. "It's all right, Mrs. Voss, stop screaming."

"Let me out! Let me out! Let me out! Let me out!"

Two boys passing on the street turned their heads briefly and then walked on. Screaming women were common on Olive Street; the boys knew better than to interfere, to be around if and when the police arrived.

The back door of the house was half open. Lewis went in ahead, fumbling his way along the wall until he found the switch and turned on the lights. The kitchen table bore evidences of a drinking-party—three empty bottles of muscatel and four smudged glasses and half a bag of potato chips. A number of potato chips were scattered over the floor as if someone had become drunkenly playful and started throwing them around like confetti. The table and the drainboard of the sink were silvered with cockroaches.

Mrs. Voss's screams continued, muted by the massive old walls.

The attic was four flights up. At some time it had been partitioned to serve as a separate apartment; Mrs. Voss was locked in the tiny room that had once been the kitchen. The key was in the lock, turned sideways so that Mrs. Voss couldn't push it out with a hairpin and maneuver it through the crack at the bottom of the door.

Charlotte opened the door. Mrs. Voss stopped in the middle of a scream, her mouth gaping, both hands clutching at her throat. She was sitting on the floor with her legs sprawled out in front of her. Her skirt was slit to the hip where she'd torn at it in her frenzy. A little red Christmas candle was burning in one corner of the room—the light bulb had been removed from the ceiling months or years ago, and tiny house spiders lived like kings in the empty socket.

"I didn't have nothing to do with it!" Mrs. Voss shrieked. "I didn't have nothing to do with anything! I didn't even hear nothing. I didn't, I didn't!"

"Of course you didn't," Charlotte said. "Of..."

"They wouldn't let me go along, they wouldn't take me, they locked me here to die!" She began beating the floor with her fists and shaking her head back and forth. The candle flame flickered, leaning away as if in fright. "They said I talked too much, I can't keep my mouth shut. They said I got hysterical alla time. Me, me, me, hysterical!" She drew a long shuddering breath. "They wouldn't take me along."

"I can't understand you when you shout like that," Charlotte said softly. "No one's going to hurt you. Take it easy."

"They said I got hysterical alla time. I don't, I don't! I never did!"

"Easy now." She turned to Lewis who had remained outside the door. "There's some brandy in my car. Would you get it?"

"And leave you here alone with..."

"Of course. Mrs. Voss realizes that I'm her friend, I'm going to help her."

"Yes," Mrs. Voss sobbed. "Yes, yes! You're my friend! You're my friend!"

Tears spurted out of her eyes as if something had suddenly smashed inside her. Charlotte knelt down and put her arm around the woman's shoulders. She could hear Lewis going down the stairs, very swiftly, as if he was glad to get away.

"I didn't have nothing to do with it, I didn't." She dabbed her eyes with the hem of her torn skirt. Even after all her shouting and weeping, her face was still white. "They can't put me in jail. I'd die if I was put in jail. I'm sick anyways, I'm sick."

"I know."

"You can see in my face I'm sick. Maybe I'm going to die, anyways."

"That's nonsense. You need some good, nourishing food, and a nice rest in the hospital."

"No, no, I'm scared of hospitals. I never been in one."

"That's why you're scared.... Here, hold onto my arm and we'll go downstairs."

Mrs. Voss was still breathing heavily and rapidly, but she was no longer hysterical. She had enough presence of mind to remind Charlotte to blow out the candle before they went downstairs.

In the huge barren living room Mrs. Voss lay down on the couch and Charlotte took off her coat and wrapped it around Mrs. Voss's legs.

"What happened that you had nothing to do with?" she asked.

"I don't know nothing."

"Yes, you do. I can't help you if you won't tell me anything."

"They was fighting, they was all arguing down in the kitchen after I went upstairs."

"Who was?"

"Eddie and Clarence and the old man."

"Tiddles?"

"Yes, Tiddles."

"What were they arguing about?"

"A purse. Something about a purse."

Lewis returned with the brandy and Charlotte mixed an ounce of it in half a tumbler of water. She wasn't sure what effect brandy would have on Mrs. Voss; too much, undiluted, might send her back into hysterics.

"They were arguing," Charlotte said, "and then what?"

Mrs. Voss began to cry again, softly, exhaustedly. "Oh. I can't tell. I don't know."

"Something happened."

"I think—I think Tiddles—died."

"Do you mean they killed him?"

"No—oh, I don't know. I didn't see. I just know there was blood, a lot of blood. I heard Eddie on the porch talking about it, he's ascared of blood. He kept saying they got to wash it off. I started to come downstairs to see what'd happened, only Clarence saw me. That's when they took me up to the attic and locked me in. They wouldn't take me along, they said I couldn't keep my tonsils from flapping. 'Good-bye, sweetheart,' Clarence says, 'good-bye sweetheart, it's been hell knowing you.'" She turned her face away and pressed it against the brown mohair upholstery to hide her shame and humiliation.

Lewis had gone out into the hall again. Charlotte could hear him walking around on the creaking floor, walking and walking, like a man exploring the possibilities of escape from a cell.

Charlotte said, "What makes you think Tiddles is dead?"

"The quiet. They was all arguing in the kitchen first, afterwards on the porch. And then suddenly there was a quiet, a long, dead quiet before Eddie started to talk about the blood and washing it off with a hose. That's when I started to come downstairs and Clarence heard me. 'Something has come up,' he says, 'Eddie and me are going on a little trip.'"

"Where do you think they went?"

"Somewheres in Eddie's car, I don't know where. Maybe they took the old man away."

"Maybe."

"I'm tired, I'm so tired."

"I know. I'll see what can be done."

She found the phone in the dining room and dialed the County Hospital. When she had finished talking she went out into the hall. Lewis was sitting on the bottom step of the staircase rolling an unlighted cigarette between his fingers. He looked grimly amused, as if it had just occurred to him how funny it was that he, Lewis Ballard, should be in such a place.

"Now what?" he said.

"I thought you could drive Mrs. Voss out to the County General. They're expecting you..."

"Why me?"

"I have to go to the police. I think there's been a murder and it's better if you stay out of it entirely."

He was no longer amused, no longer anything but frightened. He said, "Christ," and wiped his forehead with the back of his hand.

"You needn't come into the picture at all," Charlotte said, keeping her voice low so that Mrs. Voss wouldn't overhear. "I'll tell them that I came here alone and found Mrs. Voss locked up and hysterical and that I phoned a friend to come and drive her to the hospital."

"Your story's not going to match hers."

"She's confused. She may not even remember that we came here together."

"I hope to God not."

"Take her around to the back of the hospital—there's a door with 'emergency' printed on it. The doctor on duty is a friend of mine. I told him what to do. Just drive her there. Don't stay, get home as fast as you can."

"Christ."

She went back into the sitting room and told Mrs. Voss that she was going to be driven to the hospital.

"I don't want to go," Mrs. Voss moaned. "No. I'm scared."

"There's nothing to be afraid of. You'll have a good sleep tonight and tomorrow morning I'll come in to see you. We'll try and get you back to normal again."

Lewis brought his car around to the front of the house and he and Charlotte half carried Mrs. Voss out and put her in the back seat.

Mrs. Voss was weeping again, hiding her face with her hands. Good-bye sweetheart.

ELEVEN

When the car was out of sight she went back into the house and called Easter. The phone rang eight or nine times before he answered.

"Mr. Easter?"

"Yes."

"This is Charlotte Keating. I don't know if you remember..."

"I remember."

"I'm down at 916 Olive Street. Something pretty bad has happened. I don't know exactly what. Could you come and have a look around?"

"I'm in bed."

"You can get out of bed."

"If I had a reason."

"One reason is that I'm asking you to."

He was there in ten minutes. She couldn't force herself to stay alone in the house, so she was waiting for him on the porch when he arrived.

He crossed the front yard slowly, taking his time, looking up at the windows of the house, the shattered glass on the roof of the porch. In the half-dark his eyes looked peculiar, intensely penetrating, as if they could see more than eyes were meant to see.

"What's up?"

"I'm not sure, but I think the old man, Tiddles, has been murdered."

"Why didn't you call headquarters and tell them instead of me?"

I couldn't."

"Why not?"

"I—well, I didn't like the way the policeman sounded over the phone."

"Then you *did* call headquarters?"

"No—I mean I called earlier. About a different matter."

Easter leaned against a pillar, attempting to look casual, but his eyes betrayed him. "What matter?"

"It has nothing to do with—with this. Why do you stand there asking me such silly questions?"

"Because I'm getting such silly answers." He glanced at the front door of the house where the big wooden numbers 916 had been nailed. "This is where Violet O'Gorman lived. What are you doing here?"

Her hesitation lasted only a fraction of a second, but he noticed it. One eyebrow shot up in an amused, skeptical way.

Charlotte said, "I came to see if there was anything I could do for Violet's relatives."

"It's after eleven o'clock. Do you always get your charitable impulses at such awkward times?"

"I get all kinds of impulses at all hours of the day or night."

"Sounds inconvenient."

"I didn't ask you to meet me here so we could discuss my impulses. In fact I'm sorry now that I called you at all."

"Are you?"

"Naturally. I didn't expect you to go into that hammy tough-cop routine. I'm not on trial for anything."

"Then why the lies?" Easter said, gravely.

"Lies?"

"You called the police earlier but on a different matter. You hung up because the policeman's voice wasn't pretty enough. Then you came here to offer your help to Violet's relatives. I've met Violet's relatives, O'Gorman, and Voss and his wife, and the only kind of help anyone would offer them is help to drop dead. Now let's be more reasonable, Miss Keating. Whatever's going on around here, you're mixed up in, perhaps innocently, perhaps not so innocently. I don't know much about you. When I came to your office this afternoon I was impressed. I thought you were a remarkable woman. But that may have been simply because you look like my kid sister."

"You're very frank."

"Setting a good example."

"I don't know whether I can trust you."

"You can try," he said. "I've never met anyone I can trust completely, but maybe you'll be luckier."

"I came to—because Voss wanted some money from me."

"What for?"

"He has some information I don't want generally known."

"A man."

"Yes."

"Married."

"Yes."

"How much? Not how much married, how much blackmail?"

"Three hundred dollars."

"Cheap enough."

"I wasn't going to pay him. And my relationship with this man isn't what you're thinking, Mr. Easter."

"It's pure as the driven snow."

"*Yes.*"

"Good." He smiled at her suddenly, a very warm and friendly smile. "You know, I believe you. Lying doesn't come natural to you. You have a lot of guts."

The praise was so unexpected and so sincere that she felt herself blushing. She turned away, annoyed at herself, and at Easter too, for the easy way he'd gotten the information he wanted. Yet there had been nothing else for her to do but tell him. Someone had to know the truth. Better Easter than another policeman less intelligent and less honest.

"All right," he said. "You came to see Voss and then what?"

"No one answered the door. Mrs. Voss was locked in the attic. She broke the window with her shoe to attract our attention."

"Our?"

"Mine."

"Editorial our, eh?"

She didn't answer.

"When you were a kid," he said, smiling, "did you ever have to write fifty times on the blackboard, *Charlotte Keating told a fib?*"

"No."

The lean, gray cat had returned. Charlotte could see his lustrous green eyes staring at her between the leaves of a hibiscus bush no more than a yard away. He began to wash himself, very fastidiously, as if he was showing his contempt for the squalor in which he lived and meant to rise above it. Both of his paws were black with blood.

"The cat," Charlotte said.

"Where?"

"Under the bush. He has blood on him."

"May have caught a rat."

"He wouldn't get in such a mess just killing a rat."

Easter went to his car and brought back a flashlight. A trail of bloody paw prints led to the side of the house, vanished in a clutter of broken bottles and appeared again across the top of the discarded wardrobe with its bulging sides.

She saw then what she had missed before. Behind the wardrobe, half-hidden by weeds, was the foot and part of the leg of a man. The shoe was black, newly polished but split across the instep, the sock striped with yellow, the trouser leg green splattered with red; gay Christmas colors.

She thought of Tiddles in all his borrowed finery, anxious to show the police that he was no bum, but a solid, respectable citizen. Tiddles was dead now. It no longer mattered to him what he had been in life and what people thought, or that he was lying in a foul pile of rubbish and a cat had walked in his blood.

Charlotte picked her way through the rubbish and leaned over Tiddles. He was lying on his back staring up at the sky, his eyes fixed in terror, though the terror had long since passed. He was covered with blood, so much blood that it was impossible at first glance to tell where he had been wounded or how. It had squirted from his nose and gushed from his open mouth, smelling sour of vomit.

Easter lifted one of the old man's hands; the fingers were cold and already beginning to stiffen. "It's going to be hard to fix the time of death."

"Mrs. Voss knows. She heard the argument Tiddles was having with the other two men, and then the sudden quiet."

"Argument about what?"

"A purse."

"Where's Mrs. Voss now?"

"I sent her out to the County General. She's ill, perhaps very ill, I don't know yet."

"What happened to your friend?"

"He drove her there. I don't want him to be..."

"And Voss and O'Gorman?"

"They went away in O'Gorman's car."

Easter turned the flashlight on the old man again. "There are no head wounds and none of his clothing is torn. All the blood seems to have come from his nose and mouth. Notice the smell?"

"Yes."

"Damn funny." The flashlight moved restlessly up and down the body, across the wardrobe with its bloody cat prints, and down to the tarnished picture frames lying on the broken bedsprings. Under the bedsprings, a yard or so beyond the reach of Tiddles' left hand, was a brown lizard purse with a gold clasp. Charlotte recognized it as her own.

She took a step forward, but Easter had seen the purse too and realized her intention. He put a restraining hand on her arm. "Don't touch it, don't touch anything. I'll go and call headquarters." He hesitated. "You'll have to stick around for a while. I suppose you know that."

"Yes."

"About your friend—I'll do my best to keep him out of it. For your sake."

"Thank you."

"For his sake," he added softly, "I'd like to bust his jaw."

TWELVE

The following noon, when she returned to her office after making rounds at the hospital, she found Easter talking to Miss Schiller. Easter looking like an alert young salesman with a zippered briefcase under his arm; Miss Schiller pleased and flushed, giddy as a girl.

"Oh doctor, Lieutenant Easter has just been telling me some of the most fascinating things about fingerprints. Did you know that my fingerprints are different from any fingerprints in the world?"

"No, I didn't. Are they?"

"Absolutely different, absolutely unique. It changes one's whole outlook on oneself. Here I always thought I was just like everyone else."

"You needn't have worried," Charlotte said.

The phone rang in Charlotte's office and Miss Schiller went in to answer it, making little clucking noises of disappointment.

"Have you had lunch?" Easter said.

"No."

"The two autopsies were performed this morning. I thought we could discuss the reports over something to eat."

"It's the first time I've ever been invited to lunch to discuss autopsy reports."

"I specialize in being absolutely different and unique, like Miss Schiller's fingerprints."

"In that case..."

"You'll come? Good."

"Where shall we go? I have to leave a phone number with Miss Schiller."

"The Green Onion."

"All right."

The Green Onion, in spite of its name, was a good French restaurant in the heart of town. They sat in a back booth and Charlotte ordered an omelette and a green salad from a waitress who spoke with a phony French accent and called her Madame.

Easter said he wanted chops.

The waitress raised a pair of impossible black eyebrows. "Choaps? What kind of choaps, Monsieur?"

"Any kind. Lamb, pork, veal. Doesn't matter."

"Well reely," the girl said and moved away with an indignant swing of hips. (People never acted so peculiar back home in Buffington Falls, Iowa.)

"Did you get any sleep last night?" Easter said.

"Enough."

"I'm sorry the police routine took so long."

"It wasn't your fault." The last she remembered of the routine was a policeman in uniform putting a waterproof tarpaulin over the place where Tiddles had lain—over everything, the wardrobe and the bed springs, the tangled weeds and rusted cans.

Easter put the briefcase on the table and took out several typewritten sheets of paper and a dozen enlarged photographs.

"Why are you taking the trouble to tell me about the autopsies?" Charlotte said.

He raised his head quickly. "I though you'd be interested."

"Is that all?"

"What do you mean, is that all?"

"I thought—I imagined you had some other motive."

"No other motive, no."

But she didn't like the way he smiled. She had the feeling that he was setting a trap for her, and she couldn't elude the trap because she didn't know why or where it was being set.

"Violet's autopsy was done first," Easter said, "so I'll tell you about it first. It's a fairly clear case of suicide."

"Why?"

"I'll give you the main evidence. The first picture here is one of Violet when she was found."

Charlotte looked at it. Violet, but not the Violet she had seen two days before, and not the smiling pretty girl whose picture had been printed in the morning paper. This Violet was hardly recognizable because the lower half of her face was covered with white foam like soapsuds.

Easter's eyes were on her. "I know you're a doctor," he said, "but I don't know how much personal experience you've had with violent deaths like drowning."

"Very little. You won't hurt my feelings by being too explicit, if that's what you mean."

"Good. The foam is typical of death by drowning. It's part mucus from the throat and windpipe, and part sea water. If she was dead or unconscious when she entered the water the foam wouldn't be there. It's indicative of a violent struggle for air. In attempting to breathe she gasped in some sea water. The irritation to the membranes caused the mucus, which mixed with the water and got churned up into foam by her efforts to breathe. The fact that her mouth is open is also typical of drowning deaths."

The waitress returned with the order. Charlotte put her fork into the omelette; it was light and very fluffy, like fine foam. She pushed it away.

Easter hadn't even noticed the indeterminate-looking chops that had been placed in front of him. He said, "The next picture is a close-up of Violet's left hand—the right, as I told you before, was missing; it may have been eaten by a shark or amputated by the propeller of a big boat. Since it was obviously a post-mortem injury we didn't bother trying to fix the cause."

Violet's fist was clenched, and a long thread of sea-grass was caught between her second and third fingers. She still wore her wedding-ring.

"When we opened the fist," Easter added, "we found a small pellet of tar from the underwater oil wells, and also deep indentations made by her fingernails on the palm of her hand. A drowning person clutches at anything. In the next picture..."

"Please. I don't think I want to see any more pictures right now."

"Sorry." He put the photographs back in the briefcase. "I didn't mean to spoil your lunch. We won't talk about Violet until later." He smiled, that oddly warm and unexpected smile that always surprised her, made her feel friendly when she was on the point of antagonism. "It's funny, the only thing we've ever talked to each other about is death. I don't know whether you go to the movies or what kind of books you like, or whether you clean your teeth before or after breakfast, or how you like your eggs fried."

"Our relationship isn't a personal one."

"Perhaps not. But I think it is." He hesitated, his fork in mid-air. "Well, *do* you go to movies?"

"When I have the time."

"Would you go with me?"

"I don't know," she said, honestly. "I don't really know."

"Why not?"

"I feel that I shouldn't."

He broke open a roll and buttered it. He had immense hands that moved with precision. "I see. You're being true to Ballard."

"Bal...?" Her mouth opened, closed again. A pulse heat in her temple, fast and hard. "How did you—find out?"

"My Gestapo works night and day. Besides, you should be more careful to destroy his letters."

"Letters?"

He took an envelope out of his coat pocket and flung it on the table with a gesture of contempt or of anger. "This was in the brown lizard purse last night. I removed it before anyone else had a chance to see it. Accept it with my compliments."

It was the letter—the only letter—that Lewis had written to her while he was fishing in the Sierras. She had kept it in her purse to reread when she felt lonely, not thinking that the purse would be stolen, and that the letter had been written on Lewis' office stationery.

Easter began to quote, word for word, his tone suddenly soft and venomous: "Charley dearest, what a rotten time I'm having without you. Everything is bleak and empty..."

She tore the letter into pieces. "Do you always read other people's mail?"

"When I have a reason."

"You're a fraud and a cheat."

"I don't think so," he said simply. "I'm human, and I guess I'm suffering from a very common human frailty—jealousy." When she didn't respond, he added, "It's a sucker's racket, Charlotte—playing around with another woman's husband."

"It's my business, not yours."

"I'd like to know how Ballard did it. I might pick up a few pointers."

"Pointers?"

"On how he got you to fall for him so hard, I meant. I'd like to do the same thing."

"You're insulting..."

"I don't intend to be. I admire you. You're a strong woman. It would take a lot of strength to live with you. I have it. You'd never lean on me, but I don't have to be leaned on to feel superior. I feel superior anyway."

"And you always will," she said bitterly. "Your ego will take care of that nicely."

He looked grave. "It wouldn't be very smart to latch onto someone without an ego. He'd make too many demands on yours."

"I won't—I won't discuss the—the matter."

"Very well. Just let it creep into your subconscious now and then. That's good enough for the present."

The waitress came with the coffee. Easter changed the subject, his voice and glance impersonal again, as if he had the ability to turn her on and off in his mind like a faucet. "There was a wallet found in your purse too—no money left in it, of course. That accounts for the wine-party in the kitchen. Four glasses, four merrymakers; we can presume they were Voss and his wife and O'Gorman and the old man Tidolliani."

"Voss and Tiddles hated each other." *We have a great mutual hate,* Tiddles had told her the night they first met.

"My guess is," Easter continued, "that Tidolliani was snooping and they found him snooping and decided to play it friendly, over three bottles of wine. They got the old man drunk, probably, but they got themselves drunk, too and the argument began about the purse. I think we can assume that Tidolliani found it where Voss or O'Gorman had hidden it, perhaps in the rubbish pile.... I went to see Mrs. Voss early this morning."

"So did I."

"Is she putting on an act?"

"No," Charlotte said. "She doesn't remember anything about last night. She's disoriented to some degree. She has an idea that she's going to have her tonsils out and that Voss is coming to see her any minute." She sipped her coffee, thinking of Mrs. Voss lying in the hospital bed, looking quite relaxed and contented, but with that strange vagueness in her eyes: Voss hadn't deserted her, no, quite the opposite. *She* had deserted *him,* had come to the hospital like a real lady to have her tonsils removed, and Voss would come to see her during visiting hours. "I got bad tonsils," she'd told the nurse.

Charlotte said, "Why did Voss want to steal my purse? I live way out on Mountain Drive, there must have been a hundred purses more readily available than mine."

"They weren't after your purse," Easter said, but he refused to give his reasons for the statement.

Charlotte persisted. "It had something to do with Violet?"

"Yes."

"But you think Violet killed herself, she wasn't murdered?"

"That's what the evidence says," Easter replied with a shrug. "In addition to the external evidence I've given you, there were internal signs, too— foam in the windpipe and the bronchial tubes, water in the stomach, the lungs and the duodenum, water containing algae and other minute particles of sea life. Lungs distended, heart dilated on one side."

"All that," Charlotte said quietly, "isn't evidence that she committed suicide. It's only evidence that she died in the water."

"You're hard to convince."

"Perhaps."

"The final point is circumstantial evidence only—the fact that she was despondent over her pregnancy. She didn't want the child." He saw the question in her eyes. "It was a boy."

A boy. She thought of the inexplicable craftsmanship that had gone into the making of that dead boy—the delicate precision of the cells, the network of nerves and veins, the interplay of glands, the gradual growth, just so much and no more, all marvelously balanced and molded from one tiny ovum and one infinitesimal spermatozoon.

Easter's question came, as unexpected as a blow. "Who was the man involved with Violet?"

"I don't know. How could I know?"

"She could have told you something."

"Only that he was married, that he was away when she called him but that someone told her he was returning that night. She intended to see him."

"Some day," Easter said grimly, "I intend to see him myself."

"If you find him." (The father of Violet's baby, she thought. The most important figure in the case, because without him there would have been no case—yet the most shadowy figure, unknown and unreal; perhaps even quite innocent of the train of events to which he had given the initial push.)

She repeated her thoughts aloud, but Easter said, "Innocence is no more of an excuse than stupidity or ignorance."

"I see. You don't make excuses for people?"

"Sometimes. But to excuse, to explain, isn't enough. You don't correct a neurosis by eliminating it, you have to offer an acceptable substitute. The positive approach: here's a gumdrop, junior, now stay out of the ant paste."

She raised her brows. "I didn't realize you were a philosopher."

"Philosophy is for poets," he said curtly. "I deal with people, dead or otherwise." He pushed his coffee cup aside and the muddy liquid splashed over the side like a wave breaking over a sea-wall. "I think the real reason you don't want to believe that Violet killed herself is that it would leave a scar on your conscience."

"That's what a conscience is made of, scar tissue," Charlotte said. Little strips and pieces of remorse sewn together year by year until they formed a distinctive pattern, a design for living.

"If Violet was murdered it was by someone she trusted—not Voss, who had no reason, not O'Gorman, whom she feared. O'Gorman had reasons to kill her, but fists are his weapons—there's nothing fancy or subtle about Eddie. No. The person who might have murdered Violet would have to be someone she liked or trusted well enough to accompany out to the pier near the point where her purse was found. Someone like you, for instance."

"She didn't like or trust me. And you surely can't be serious about suspecting that I..."

"I'm curious. I'm curious about the card she was carrying in her purse with your name and address typed on it."

"All I can tell you is that I didn't give it to her."

"Some day," he said, "I'll find out who did. It might be interesting." A fly circled the table, came to rest on his knuckles. He didn't brush it off. He watched it explore the hill of one knuckle and walk gingerly into the valley between his fingers. "Have you ever walked out on the pier late at night?"

"Sometimes."

"I went down there last Friday after midnight looking for a fisherman who'd stabbed a man in a bar. I didn't find him. I didn't find anyone, in fact. There wasn't a soul on the pier and every boat was dark. But it was noisy. The sea was noisy and the wind was noisy and there was a loose piling that kept rubbing against the planks at every wave and shrieking like a gull. A good place for a murder. A push, a drop of fifteen feet into the water, perhaps a scream. But, as I said, there are natural noises out there. They might cover the scream as the night would cover the murderer." He had been sitting, tense, on the edge of the seat as he described the pier. He leaned back now, visibly relaxing. "Well, that's what could have happened. And probably didn't."

The fly had discovered the coffee cup and was walking cautiously around the rim like an explorer at the edge of a crater.

"As for the old man," Easter said, "there's no question of murder."

"No *question?*"

"His death was natural. No signs of any blows or wounds. He died of an acute peptic ulcer that eroded through a blood vessel and caused a fatal hemorrhage. The argument he had with Voss and O'Gorman probably precipitated the hemorrhage but there's no way of proving that. Voss and O'Gorman are technically innocent as lambs."

She looked incredulous. "You mean you're not even going to try and find them?"

"Oh, there's a warrant out for their arrest, certainly. But not in connection with Violet's death, or the old man's. We can't prove anything there; we can't prove any charge of attempted extortion; we can't even prove they locked Mrs. Voss up in the attic. All we have on them is suspicion of armed robbery in connection with the purse they stole from you. Sad, isn't it?"

"Yes."

"There's no justice. Go on, say it."

"There's no justice," she repeated. "But there should be."

"Certainly there should be," he said ironically. "There ought to be a law. Say that one, too—there ought to be a law."

"Well, there ought to be!" She spoke in such a loud, angry voice that the man in the next booth turned to stare at her, half anxious, half hopeful, as if he'd like to witness a good quarrel, providing it didn't get too rough.

"Looking for someone?" Easter asked.

"Me?" The man coughed. "Well, no. Not at all."

His head disappeared like a turtle's.

"Nice girls don't raise their voices in public," Easter said. "Or tangle with blackmailers. Of course, there's always the possibility that you're not a nice girl, that my eyes have been bedazzled. They are, you know. Absolutely bedazzled. It's the damnedest thing. Are you interested?"

"No."

"Then you don't have to blush if you're not interested."

"If I'm blushing, it's because I'm embarrassed by your impudence."

He smiled. "Blushing or unblushing, you look fine... Where was I? Oh yes, at my bedazzlement. Well, that covers everything, actually. There you have it."

"What am I expected to say?"

"Oh, you don't have to say anything. Just blush now and then. It encourages me."

"You're—you're insufferable."

"Only at first glance," Easter said, patiently. "Second and third glances reveal my sterling, less obvious qualities."

"I don't care to see them."

"You will, though. I'll be around."

She looked at her watch, attempting to appear cool and indifferent. "I have to get back to my office."

"I'm sorry."

"Don't bother driving me. I can walk." She got up. "Thank you for the lunch."

"I hope there'll be others."

"That's unlikely."

"Other autopsies, other lunches," Easter said. "By the way, there's one thing I forgot to mention."

"What is it?"

"Any time you and Ballard need a chaperon, give me a call."

THIRTEEN

At five o'clock Miss Schiller started making preparations to go home. Ever since lunch, when she'd read in the newspaper about Violet's death, she had been talking continually to a succession of patients, enlarging now and then on the truth: "There she stood in the doorway, looking so *alive,* you know what I mean? Yet I knew, I *knew* by her eyes that something was up."... "It's a blot on the city, but then of course she wasn't a *native.* She came from a little town in Oregon, it says in the paper."

A rich, a full, a satisfying afternoon, marred only by an occasional black look from Charlotte and the fact that some patients selfishly preferred to discuss their own symptoms.

Miss Schiller combed her hair and replaced the net over it. With the net on, it hardly looked like hair at all but like a fuzzy gray cap under which the real Miss Schiller hid, bald as an egg.

The newspaper that she'd bought at lunchtime lay on her desk folded so that she could glance at Violet's picture whenever she felt the excitement beginning to deflate inside her. *Mrs. Violet O'Gorman, of Ashley, Oregon, whose body was found this morning on West Beach apparently a suicide...*

Miss Schiller was reading the report all over again, with the intense fascination of one reading about herself, when Charlotte came out of her office dressed for the street and carrying her medical bag.

Miss Schiller hurriedly turned the paper over and said in her most alert, efficient voice, "Yes, doctor?"

"How many house calls to make?"

"Only three. Here they are."

"Lord," Charlotte said. She leaned against the desk and closed her eyes for a moment. The thought of even three house calls appalled her.

"It's none of my business, doctor, but I must say you haven't been looking at all well the past few days."

"No?"

"Haggard, you look, real haggard."

"Thanks."

"I was reading only the other day that doctors die sooner than people in any other profession. Now this new herbal tonic I'm taking, really, it's so invigorating."

"The stuff's probably loaded with alcohol. No wonder it peps you up."

"Alcohol?" Miss Schiller blanched. "Oh no. They wouldn't dare..."

"Cheer up. It won't kill you," Charlotte said.

"But I don't drink. I don't *believe* in alcohol."

"Well, maybe the tonic will help you change your mind."

The phone rang, but Miss Schiller was too perturbed to answer it. In her imagination she was already an alcoholic, doomed to a drunkard's grave, through no fault of her own. The vicious stuff was right this minute churning around in her bloodstream, corroding her will, destroying her character. That's what they told her when she took the pledge—that one never knew when one's will was being corroded until it was too late. Oh dear. She felt quite giddy.

"Charley? Bill Blake."

"Hello Bill," Charlotte said.

"I have to go out of town the beginning of next week. I thought we'd try a switch again, if you're willing."

"Certainly."

"If you haven't anything critical on your books, I could take over your practice for the rest of this week, and you take mine next Monday, Tuesday, Wednesday."

"That suits me."

"Swell," Blake said. "Dare I hope that Miss Schiller has quit and gone into a nunnery?"

"You dare not."

"All I can do is keep her under ether, then. I'll see you, and thanks, Charley."

"Good-bye." She hung up and turned to Miss Schiller. "Dr. Blake sends you his love."

"He *does?*" Miss Schiller bounced out of her drunkard's grave with the single-minded agility of a rabbit. "Well, I must say I'm flattered. Dr. Blake is such a *sweet* man."

"Yes. He'll be around now and then for the rest of the week. Any calls that come in, just relay to his office. And in the morning you'd better phone the patients who have appointments and send them to Dr. Blake, or else make new appointments. The charts are all in order?"

"Of course." Miss Schiller was offended. "Well, I mean, *really.* I've been in this business for..."

"No offense meant." Charlotte picked up her medical bag from the desk where she'd put it when she answered the telephone. It seemed heavier than usual. She realized that for the first time in years she felt exhausted. She moved slowly, as if part of her brain tissue had been destroyed like a spastic's, and each physical move she made had to be thought out and the muscles forced to obey.

"What a nice coincidence that Dr. Blake phoned," Miss Schiller said. "Now you can have a good rest for a few days. Go down to the beach and lie in the sun."

"Perhaps I will." She wondered, briefly, about the "nice coincidence," and then forgot about it as soon as she reached the street and got into her car.

It was nearly seven and the sky was showing its first stars, when she arrived home. Even before she turned into the driveway she could hear her phone ringing, a shrill rising, falling, like the sound of tree toads. The ringing stopped as she was unlocking her front door and began again a few seconds later.

She thought it might be Lewis calling and when she answered the phone she tried not to sound tired. Lewis hated her to sound tired; it always started an argument about her working too hard.

"Hello?"

"You work late," Easter said.

"I wish you'd stop bothering me."

"Who's bothering you? I have a new lead in Violet's case and I thought you'd like to hear about it."

"What is it?"

"I've just learned that Violet has an older sister who lives in Ashley, a war widow by the name of Myrtle Reyerling. Violet may have confided in her about the man we're after—let's call him Mr. B."

"Why Mr.—B?"

"No reason. I'm driving up to Ashley tomorrow, unofficially, to have a talk with Mrs. Reyerling. Do you want to come along?"

"No thanks."

"Think it over."

"I've thought."

"The trip will do you good," Easter said. "Fresh air, etcetera."

"There's fresh air here."

"But the Oregon fresh air is said to have therapeutic qualities for nervous women—a sort of gaseous Lydia Pinkham's Vegetable Compound."

The door chime pealed. "I've never been nervous in my life and my doorbell's ringing."

"I hear it."

"So if you'll excuse me..."

"I will, but I don't want to."

"Thank you for the invitation."

"Keep thinking it over," Easter said, and hung up. As she was going towards the door it occurred to her that Easter's invitation was oddly coincidental with Dr. Blake's offer to take over her practice for a few days. There was no connection, of course, but it worried her. She wondered about Easter's motives, whether he was falling in love with her as he pretended, or whether he thought she knew more about the case than she had told him.

Before she opened the door she glanced out of the little window at the top and saw that her caller was Lewis.

For a moment he looked to Charlotte like someone she had once known well and hadn't seen for years. His face was grim, his mouth a tight bitter line. There were dark gray circles under his eyes like smudges of soot.

"Hello, Charley."

"Lewis—Lewis, are you ill?"

"No." He kissed her on the cheek; his breath smelled of brandy.

She withdrew from his embrace, holding him at arms' length so that she could see him better. "You haven't been drinking too much, or anything?"

"I am not ill and I haven't been drinking." He crossed the room and flung himself wearily into the red leather chair. He was wearing the hat and topcoat he'd had on the previous night when they'd met on the breakwater. He leaned his head against the back of the chair and the hat slid off and rolled on the floor. He didn't seem to notice. "At least I've been drinking only enough for medicinal purposes, to keep me from strangling my wife."

The words jarred her. "You mustn't talk like that."

"If I didn't talk it I might just go ahead and do it.... Have you seen the papers?"

"Yes."

"It's the same girl, the one who came to you?"

"Yes."

"Well, I'm sorry," he said. "Sorry for the girl, and sorry you had to be mixed up in it." All during dinner Gwen had talked about it: *"Oh, the poor child, how lonely she must have felt! I know so well what loneliness is. Sometimes when you're not here, Lewis, when you stay away in the evenings for hours and hours, I almost feel like—like killing myself."* Gwen, sitting across the table from him, an animated little doll with the big dogs pressing their noses moistly against her arm begging for attention, for a scrap of meat. He had felt a murderous rage, a terrible desire to stop those white fluttering hands, that gentle voice: *"That poor, poor girl. Think how the man must feel who got her into that condition."*

He covered his eyes with the palms of his hands.

Charlotte sat on the hassock at his feet. "I tried to call you this afternoon at the office."

"I wasn't there."

"I know."

"I went to a movie."

"I didn't think you ever went to movies," she said, half lightly.

"I don't. I was tired. I thought I'd go to sleep from boredom, but I didn't.... I need some sleeping pills, Charley."

"I have a couple of nembutals I can give you."

"Thanks. Thanks a lot."

She brought the capsules out of the medicine chest in the bathroom. "Don't take them until about twenty minutes before you go to bed."

"All right."

"Lewis, is anything the matter?"

"Not a thing."

"I'm glad, Mr. B."

He looked very surprised, and pleased. "You haven't called me that for a long time. Remember?"

"I remember."

"I love you, Miss K."

"Darling, it's nice to see you smiling again."

"I'm out of practice."

"I know. Things will be better for us someday, wait and see." She gave him a cigarette and lit it for him, feeling happy that she was able to help him when he was tired. Her own tiredness was nearly gone. "I'm taking the rest of the week off, Lewis."

His hand tightened on her arm. "Sudden, isn't it?"

"The chance came up. I thought that I'd take a little trip in the car, perhaps."

"A trip where?"

"Oh anywhere. You know I've always liked driving to new places."

He hadn't taken his eyes off her, hadn't even blinked. "New places such as where?"

"Well, I haven't seen much of Oregon," she said. "They say it's very nice in the summer."

"Who says?"

"I thought perhaps..."

"Stop that thought-perhaps business. Your mind's made up. It always is. Where are you going in Oregon?"

"Ashley."

"Where the girl lived?"

"Yes."

"Haven't you gotten into enough trouble already?"

"Please, darling..."

"Don't go," he said. "Don't go, Charley."

"I want to. I feel that I should."

"Why should you? It's none of your affair."

"The police are going."

"Police?"

"I want to get there first. I don't like the lieutenant in charge of the case, Easter."

"I know him," Lewis said. "He's a troublemaker."

"He rang me up tonight and asked me to go with him to Ashley and talk to Violet's sister. I refused. I think he was trying to set a trap for me. I know I haven't done anything, but the feeling is there that in some obscure way

I'm deeply implicated in Violet's death."

"Don't go, Charley," he said again.

"But I want to. I'm not afraid of Easter. I'm just curious."

"Just curious. Oh God."

"Besides, driving rests me, the trip will do me good."

"It might do us both good. A world of good."

He got up. When he leaned over to pick up his hat from the floor he staggered slightly, and she wondered if he had had more to drink than he admitted, or if he was simply exhausted.

He kissed her at the door, a long kiss that seemed to Charlotte to be sad and bitter. She felt suddenly like weeping.

"Good-bye, Charley. Good-bye, darling."

"Lewis, you'll take care of yourself?"

"Of course. Have a nice time."

"Wait. Lewis, if you don't want me to go, if you have a reason..."

"Reason?" he repeated. "No. No reason except that I'll miss you."

"I hope you will."

"Good-bye, Charley." The words had an air of finality, as if he never expected to see her again.

The door closed.

FOURTEEN

She left the following morning long before sunrise. For the first hundred miles she drove along the coast where the road meandered like a concrete river following the curves of the sheer, barren cliffs, blanketed by fog. As the sun rose it swallowed the fog, leaving only a few undigested wisps hiding in the hollows and dips of the road.

The highway turned suddenly inland beyond the reach of the sea, where the heat lay thick over the fertile valley. Here the barren cliffs seemed remote and Charlotte could hardly imagine them only a few miles away from this sudden profusion of growth: acres and acres of silver-green lettuce—greengold, the farmers called it—and groves of oranges too huge to look real and miles of fat tomatoes reddening on the vines.

But the valley ended with the same finality as the cliffs. The road ascended, and the area of the redwoods began, trees so high, so ancient, that their origins dazed the imagination. There was a clearing where the trees had been ruthlessly cut down and hauled away, and from here Charlotte could see two mountains to the northeast, their snowy caps untouched by changes in the weather or by the footprints of men. It was as if nature—and the department of highways—had collaborated to give the tourist the whole scope of California in a few hundred miles.

When she crossed the border into Oregon she had to cut her speed because the noon sun, pressing down through the huge trees, made such brilliant patterns on the road that it was difficult to see any distance ahead or to distinguish the real from the shadow. Now and then she heard a mountain stream chortling furiously, violently, as if nothing could ever stop its mad, hilarious descent to the Pacific.

She reached the outskirts of Ashley a little after two o'clock. A sign informed her that she was about to enter Ashley, the Friendliest Little Town in the West, Population 9,394, Come Early and Stay Late.

She stopped at the first AAA motel that she came to. It was built in a small clearing of trees, two hundred yards off the highway, and it was so new that it still smelled of fresh wood.

A fat man in shirt sleeves was sitting on a kitchen chair tilted against a door marked "office," fanning himself with a comic book. A dozen other comics were scattered around his chair, half of them without covers, the others brand-new, *True Love Comics, Teen-Age Romance, I was Jilted, Western Love and Romances.* The fat man's face was as innocent and devoid of thought as a marshmallow. He was probably laughed at in school as the fat boy, Charlotte thought. Now he's getting back, he's the hero of all the comic books, the lover who jilts, the cowboy who rides roughshod over women's hearts. Poor man, poor boy.

"Any vacancy?" she said.

"Yes, ma'am. Number Four over there. Bath and shower, Beautyrest mattress. Six dollars a night."

"That will do."

She parked her car in front of Number Four, and came back to register at the office her name and address and the make and license number of her car. A card on the desk identified the fat man as Mr. Roy H. Coombs, Mgr., La Siesta Motel.

"You a doctor, eh?" Mr. Coombs said. "I see by your car."

"Yes."

"I never saw a lady doctor so close up before. In the movies I have, though. Ingrid Bergman was a doctor in a movie once, fell in love with Gregory Peck, only Peck happened to be..."

"Yes, I know. 'Spellbound.'"

"Yes, yes, that was it. 'Spellbound.' I don't know what she saw in Gregory Peck. He's skinny as a broom, besides being a nut—in the picture, I mean."

"Have you a phone book?"

The question took him by surprise. He had to stop a moment to make the transition from romance to phone books. "Well, sure we have."

"I just want to look up an address."

"Oh. Sure." He searched around the desk and under the counter for the phone book and couldn't find it. He stood up, panting from the exertion, and wiped his forehead with the sleeve of his pink shirt. "Somebody must have swiped it off of me. That's low, stealing a phone book." (But there was a dreamy look in his eye; the fat boy was Dick Tracy, out for revenge, on the trail of the thief who took the telephone book. On his slender wrist, a two-way radio. In his head, a photographic memory.)

"Perhaps you can help me locate someone," Charlotte said crisply, and Mr. Coombs's eyes snapped back into focus.

"I should be able to, lived here in town all my life."

"Do you know Mrs. Myrtle Reyerling?"

"Myrtle? I sure do. Why, Sergeant Reyerling's one of our war heroes, got his name on a plaque in the First National Bank, corner of Third Street. Myrtle lives in an apartment above Woolworth's. You can't miss it. Drive straight into town and there it is."

"Thanks."

The Woolworth store had a bright new facade but the apartments above it were dark and airless and smelled of last month's grease and last week's cabbage.

Charlotte paused before a door marked, in pencil on a torn slip of paper,

M. Reyerling. The transom was open and there were sounds inside the room, not sounds of quarreling, but of two women vociferously agreeing with each other about a third who wasn't present.

"I told her. I told her time and again."

"I know you did, you bet you did."

"But no, no, she was headstrong. Always believing the best of people. The *best*. Huh. I know now there's no *best* in anyone. Only better. And them damn little better than the worst."

"You're absotively right, Myrtle, but don't let it get you down."

It was Myrtle Reyerling who opened the door, a tall, thin woman in her late twenties, with a six-inch pompadour that listed slightly to one side like a schooner in a high wind. Her mouth was pinched-looking, her jaw hard, but there was something pathetic about her eyes; they were questioning, bewildered.

"Mrs. Reyerling?"

"Yes."

"I'm Charlotte Keating, a friend of Violet's."

The woman turned away, swallowing, swallowing again, before she spoke. "I guess you know about her then?"

"Yes, I do."

"Come in if you want to. This here's my girlfriend, Sally Morris."

A dark-haired young woman with a wiry body and big muscular legs acknowledged the introduction with a nod.

"It's all over town," Mrs. Reyerling said. "Whisper, whisper, whisper, about how Violet was in the family way and not by Eddie. I don't believe it. Violet was a good girl. My kid sister was a good girl and don't anybody say different."

"Now take it easy, Myrt."

"She was a *good girl.*"

The young woman called Sally made a little gesture of impatience. "Oh, for heaven's sake, good girls can do a lot of the same things as bad girls. I just told you, I saw her with my own eyes. She was in that bed, sleeping. And there were signs—know what I mean?"

"No!"

"Now Myrt, you know me, I'm no gossip, but I'm no dumbbell either. I've been working around there long enough to know the *signs.*"

Charlotte interrupted, "Signs of what?"

"Well, you know." There was an embarrassed silence before the girl broke out again: "In the *first* place what was she doing there, sleeping at eight o'clock in the morning in a man's room? The man was already checked out—he left the key in the lock outside like it says on the door to do when you check out. Well, I saw the key and I figured I'd get the room made up early. I went in, and there was Violet sleeping peaceful as a baby. I didn't say anything. It wasn't any of my business. I just walked out again and rapped on the door real hard to wake her up. Then I beat it. I didn't even tell Myrtle about it until today. She always made so much fuss when Violet did anything wrong, even when she took a drink or smoked a cigarette."

"I didn't mean to," Mrs. Reyerling whispered. "I didn't. I had to look after her, she was my kid sister. I wanted her to grow up to be a lady."

"Sure. Sure, I know, Myrt. I'm not blaming you. It's life, is all. We all got to take it on the chin."

"How many times do I have to take it? How many chins you think I've got?"

"Now, Myrt." The girl turned to Charlotte. "I work at a motel, see? Rose Court, it's called; on the other side of town. That's where I saw her, in this guy's room."

"Do you remember the man?" Charlotte asked.

"I didn't see him. But when I was making up the room afterwards I found a tie he'd left behind in the john. I never saw a tie like it before. It was blue with gray coins on it and little wee dice with red eyes. I thought I'd hook it to give to my old man, maybe it'd bring him luck in a crap game. But I got cold feet, and turned it in to my boss, Rawls. Rawls is as honest as the next guy, which isn't saying much, because he started to wear the tie himself, instead of mailing it to the man who'd left it behind." She hesitated a moment. "I'm not saying anything *against* Rawls, exactly. If he found a wallet he'd probably turn it in to the police minus a few bucks for his trouble. But this tie—he couldn't resist it. He thinks he's a pretty classy dresser. Around town they call him Adolphe Menjou."

Mrs. Reyerling had gone to the window and was looking down into the street below, her arms folded across her breasts.

"Here's how I figure it," Sally said. "If it happened once it could have happened plenty of times, so maybe this man who left the tie had nothing to do with Violet's being in the family way."

"It never happened at all." Mrs. Reyerling didn't turn. She addressed the window pane as if it was some kind of impersonal umpire. "The kid was Eddie's. He said it wasn't because he was sick of Violet. He was playing around with somebody else and he wanted to drive Violet away."

Sally didn't argue. She made a little grimace at Charlotte to indicate that Myrtle was beyond reasoning.

Charlotte said, "Perhaps if I could talk to Mr. Rawls, he might remember..."

"Now *wait* a minute. You think he'd admit anything? Not on your life! He'd swear black and blue there wasn't any man or any tie or even any motel. How could he admit about the tie without admitting he's a crook? Why, if he did, they might take away his AA Approved card. Those AAA people are fussy. They don't stand for stuff like that. They're always snooping around to see if I changed the bath mats and the shower curtains and swept under the beds." She paused. "Rawls won't tell you a thing. Besides, I might get fired, see?"

"I see, of course."

"You won't go to Rawls, then?"

"No."

"I should have kept my yap shut, anyway," Sally said with a trace of bitterness. "I don't know what gets into me, to talk so much. I just came over here to help Myrt, to cheer her up."

Mrs. Reyerling turned a flat gaze on her. "Cheer me up.... Tell me lies about my own sister."

"Now listen, Myrt. Don't go turning against *me*."

"Bad lies."

The girl was beginning to get angry; a red flush crept gradually up her neck like the colored mercury in a thermometer. "You better look into your own conscience. Who was it that got Violet going around with Eddie in the first place? Who was it kept saying, 'Eddie's a nice dependable guy. He'll make some girl a good husband.' Who was it said, 'Looks aren't everything.' Hell no, looks aren't everything, he may look like a chimpanzee with smallpox but you'll get used to it, Violet. Once you got Mrs. in front of your name...'"

"I didn't," Mrs. Reyerling cried. "I didn't force her to marry him. I didn't even ask her to. She liked him."

"You told her to like him." Her mimicry was sharp, cruel: "'Marry Eddie and love will come later, and maybe he'll even get over those little habits of his, like pulling the wings off flies.'"

"Stop! Stop it!" Mrs. Reyerling put her hands over her ears and ran into the bedroom.

They could hear the thud of her body as she flung herself across the bed. She didn't weep, but heavy, anguished breathing rose and fell in the humid air, the breathing of a wounded animal.

Sally's belligerence was gone. She stood scratching the side of her neck where the flush had been, looking ashamed of herself. "I guess I ought to keep my temper more."

"I suppose we all should."

"What I said was the truth, but not the whole truth. The whole truth—well, that's hard to get at, the why of everything. I guess Myrt had her reasons for wanting Violet to be married, to be settled down and safe. It's not her fault that she judged Eddie wrong." She lapsed into silence.

"I'd better leave," Charlotte said. "If there's anything I can do to help Mrs. Reyerling, I'll be at the Siesta Motel."

"I know it. It just opened. We already got so many nobody's making money any more."

"Perhaps I can drive you back to work."

"No thanks. I'm through for the day. I'll stay here and make Myrt some tea. She'll snap out of it. I looked after her the day she got the telegram about Tom dying." She added, with a sad little sigh, "Maybe we don't act like friends, sometimes, but we are."

Charlotte stepped out into the hall. She had the feeling that the girl had spoken the truth. She and Myrtle had a bond of friendship that would survive the bickerings, as well as the tragedies, of day-to-day existence.

On the street below, the rays of the late afternoon sun shot through the plate-glass windows of stores and ricocheted off the sidewalks and the white stucco walls of buildings. The heat was palpable, like a layer of jelly, through which the cars crawled and the pedestrians moved sluggishly.

Only the children hurried, boys on bicycles weaving through the traffic with careless ease, and grade-school girls, intent and purposeful, impatient for the next minute, the next week, the next year.

Charlotte unlocked her car. She thought of Violet walking up and down this same street, softer than the other girls, not quite so forceful, so decisive. (And Mrs. Reyerling had known this about Violet, perhaps—had tried to protect her and blundered.)

She had a feeling of discontent, of failure. The further she plunged into Violet's life, the murkier and more diffuse it became. It was like diving into a strange lake, diving deeper and deeper and gradually realizing that the lake had no bottom, only a constantly moving silt that would never settle. One could reach out and grasp at the silt—as Violet herself had reached out and grasped in her final moments—but when the fist was opened it contained only a few grains of sand and the marks of fingernails on one's own flesh.

FIFTEEN

She turned the car around and headed back in the direction of the motel. She wondered if Easter had arrived in town yet and what he was up to. Perhaps the girl Sally would be too afraid of losing her job to tell him about the tie Rawls had kept. Or perhaps he wouldn't see Sally at all. She might be gone by the time he reached Mrs. Reyerling's apartment and it was unlikely that Mrs. Reyerling would tell Easter about her and give Sally a chance to repeat her story.

She felt obscurely pleased that Easter might never find out about the episode in the motel but she didn't understand why she should feel this way. The episode didn't involve her personally. It concerned only the nameless, faceless man who had left a tie in a motel bathroom and the seed of a child in Violet's womb. She realized that she was afraid of Easter. Though he couldn't harm her, couldn't even touch her, the fear was growing, stupidly, irrationally. What had he said on the telephone last night...? That he was driving up "unofficially." This could mean that, officially, the case was closed. She suddenly hoped that it was closed and filed away forever in a steel drawer.

She had an early dinner at a drive-in on Main Street. When she arrived back at her motel the sun was settling into a pillow of pink clouds and Mr. Coombs had turned on his red neon vacancy sign. He was still sitting in the kitchen chair, looking strangely dwarfed by the background of huge trees. He had finished his comics for the day, piled them neatly on the wooden step with a stone on top to keep his dreams from blowing away. Captives, they fussed and fluttered in the rising wind.

Mr. Coombs nodded, and tipped an invisible hat. "Evening."

"Good evening."

"Cooling off some. Still too hot inside, though. If you want to sit out for a spell, I'll bring you a chair."

"No thanks, don't bother."

Mr. Coombs slapped at a mosquito on his forearm. "You get in touch with Myrtle Reyerling all right?"

"Yes."

"Her kid sister died. A genuine tragedy."

"I heard about it."

"O'Gorman, her name was. I know her husband, we went to school together. He worked in a bar about a quarter-mile up the road, but I hear he blew town."

"What bar?"

"Sullivan's. Sullivan's been dead for ten years, but they still call it that."
He stopped, looking a little embarrassed. "If you should want a drink there
are places better than Sullivan's. I mean, it's not a very high-class estab-
lishment, that's what I mean."

A car with a skiff strapped to its top turned in from the highway and Mr.
Coombs waddled over to meet it.

The sign, Sullivan's Log Cabin, was hung between two posts just off the
highway, but the building itself was set a hundred yards back from the
road in a grove of redwoods. There was a cleared space for parking to the
left of the sign. Charlotte left her car there and began walking up the foot-
path to the bar. There had once been a string of lights along the path but
the bulbs had worn out or been broken; only the wires and empty sockets
remained, and fragments of glass that crunched under Charlotte's feet.

In spite of the brisk wind a sour smell rose from the ground, as if a long
succession of drunks had tottered down the path, paused to be sick, and
gone on. In the east a full moon was rising but its pallid light couldn't pen-
etrate the trees, and Charlotte had to feel her way timidly along the path.

She stopped suddenly and looked back over her shoulder—an instinctive movement; she'd heard nothing behind her, but she had an overwhelming impulse to look around.

A man stepped out from behind a tree, a tall man with massive sloping
shoulders that gave his body an aspect of menace.

"Hello. Charlotte."

"Oh. I—you startled me."

"I hope so," Easter said. He sounded angry. "Quite a fast one you pulled,
coming here ahead of me."

"I didn't intend it as a 'fast one.' I merely drove up to. . ."

"Get some fresh air. I know. Well, now that fate and a mutual interest in
fresh air has brought us together, let me buy you a drink."

"No thanks."

"Weren't you on your way into Sullivan's?"

"No."

"Just out for a stroll, eh?"

"Yes."

"Don't snap. It's unbecoming." He took her arm. "Come on, Charlotte.
You and I have some things to discuss."

"What things?"

"Things," he said vaguely.

His hand on her arm was firm and surprisingly reassuring. She realized
that this strange, somber place frightened her, and her fear of Easter was
lost in the more immediate fear of walking alone up the dark path.

He matched his step to hers. "I talked to Mrs. Reyerling. She told me about the 'nice-looking lady' who claimed to be a friend of Violet's."

"Oh?"

"About the only additional fact that I learned about Violet was that she couldn't swim. But—there was a girl with Mrs. Reyerling in the apartment, a Miss Morris. She seemed very quiet, very nervous."

"Well, I didn't make her quiet and nervous, if that's what you're implying."

"I didn't imply it. But, it's a thought—maybe you did."

"How?"

"Why don't *you* tell *me?*" Easter said.

"I like to see you guess, you're so good at it."

"All right, I'll guess that she gave you some information and you asked her not to tell me for some reason. You're quite a devious character, Charlotte, in spite of that honest pan, that let's-put-all-our-cards-on-the-table look."

"You're awfully quarrelsome, aren't you?"

"I don't think so. I get along all right with other people."

"So do I. By the way, I don't very much like being leaped at from behind trees. It's cute and boyish and all that, but it gives me a pain."

His teeth gleamed white in the darkness. "I'll have to keep on giving you a pain if I can't get any other reaction."

Sullivan's was a long narrow building made of logs, with *Acme on Tap* written across the front window in green neon. Inside, a middle-aged man in levis was playing two nickel slot-machines, alternating between them with such quick precision that he seemed to be working a machine in a factory rather than enjoying himself. At the bar two men were studying a racing form, checking selections with a pencil, conferring in whispers, checking again. Sullivan's had an air of deadly earnestness.

The bartender was young and bored.

"Beer for me, please," Charlotte said.

"Make it two." Easter flipped a coin on the counter. "Things slow tonight, eh?"

"Slow every night at this time. It's too early. The afternoon drunks haven't had a chance to sober up and come back again."

Easter sipped his beer. It tasted metallic. "I see O'Gorman's not around any more."

"He quit last week. You a friend of his?"

"We have a lot in common."

"I heard just tonight that he's back in town," the bartender said.

"Good. I'd like to catch up with him again."

"I figure it's just a rumor, though. This guy that claims he saw him said O'Gorman was driving a new Ford convertible. O'Gorman's car was an old Plymouth that couldn't do fifty if it was going downhill. You don't get rich tending bar, believe you me."

"Funny if he's in town and didn't call me. I'm kind of disappointed."

"Yeah?" The bartender blinked. "I wouldn't be too disappointed."

"If he shows, tell him Easter is looking for him, Jim Easter."

"He won't show. He stuck me with a bum check for ten dollars. That and the convertible don't make sense, unless the car's hot."

"Maybe it is."

"A cop, aren't you?"

"Yeah."

"I don't want any trouble here."

"You won't get any."

"That's a promise. I hope." He ambled down to the other end of the bar and began talking to the two men who were bent over the racing form.

"So that's the real reason you came up here," Charlotte said. "Not to talk to Violet's sister, but to look for O'Gorman and Voss."

"Both. There was an off-chance that O'Gorman might be stupid enough to come home. In fact, he may not even know there's a warrant out for him and Voss. The last report I had on O'Gorman was that he was heading north. He sold his '38 Plymouth at Crescent City for a hundred and fifty dollars. That's about fifty dollars less than the list price, and after the deal was closed the new owner got a little suspicious about it. He called the local police and they called us." He drained his glass. "This is the first I've heard about the Ford convertible, though. It makes it fairly certain that he's around here someplace, not to stay, probably, but to do a little showing off in front of the home-town folks."

"How could he buy a new car? He had no money."

"He has now. What I'd like to know is where he got it. Any ideas?"

"No."

"Sure of that?"

"Of course I'm sure."

"Not even one tiny idea?"

"No! What are you getting at? I—you're confusing me. You don't think that I gave O'Gorman the money? I didn't. When I went there, he and Voss had already gone."

"Let's be confused together," Easter said lightly. "You know, I went to a lot of trouble for the privilege of buying you a beer."

"Trouble?"

"Of course I didn't think it would end up the way it did. I'm an incurable optimist. I figured that you would drive up here with me and give me a chance to parade my wit and charm etcetera, and we would return home, you with the first flush of love on your cheeks, and me feeling the same way as I did when I started. As I do now. Well," he added, "it didn't work out."

"I'm beginning to see a little light."

"Yes? Tell me about it."

"It concerns a doctor I know called Bill Blake."

"Blake? Yes, I believe I know him too." He was smiling. "In fact we went to college together. I introduced him to the girl he married."

"You also introduced him to the idea of calling me up and offering to..."

"Well, don't get sore about it."

"I'm not sore. I'm boiling."

"You ought to be flattered."

"You planned everything."

"Not quite everything," he said dryly. "I underestimated your obstinacy, or whatever quality a woman like you has that makes it impossible for her to see what's good for her."

"You're good for me, are you?"

"I am," he said. "Ballard isn't."

"Please leave him out of this."

"How can I? You think you're in love with the man."

"I think so and I am."

"You intend to marry him."

"When it becomes possible, yes, of course I'll marry him."

"The thought makes me sick." He ordered another beer, but when it came he didn't drink it. He kept tracing a letter with his forefinger on the mist that appeared on the outside of the glass. B, B, and then again, B. "I have an interesting theory about you, Charlotte."

"Have you?"

"I think the reason you picked Ballard is because you unconsciously wanted to avoid marriage. By falling in love with a man who couldn't marry you anyway, your problem was solved for you, at least temporarily. Until his wife dies. Or something."

"What do you mean, *or something?*"

"Just or something." He erased all the B's from his glass with one swipe of his palm. "People do die, you know. Like Violet."

She stared at him, her eyes hostile. "If you're implying that Gwen Ballard might possibly kill herself, I assure you you're wrong. She isn't the type."

"You know her, then?"

"She's been a patient of mine for a year."

"Well," he said. "Well. That's very interesting. I don't suppose you've ever been tempted to slip a little prussic acid in her cough medicine."

"No," she said steadily. "I've never been tempted. And I consider the remark incredibly boorish."

His face had gone suddenly grave. "I'm glad it shocked you. It was intended to. If anything ever happens to Mrs. Ballard, you'll be hearing lots of remarks like that. You're asking for them. You're not only her doctor, you're her husband's girlfriend. That's boorish too, eh?" When she turned away without answering, he added, "I suggest, very seriously, that you turn Mrs. Ballard over to another doctor."

She was too proud to tell him that she had already tried. "Thanks for the advice."

"You have a lot to lose, Charlotte. Stop leading with your chin.... Now I suppose you're sore again."

"I've never stopped. You're simply—simply impossible."

"Now that's a silly remark," Easter said patiently. "I'm the most possible man you know."

"I want to leave."

"The door's open." He saw her hesitation. "What's the matter, afraid of the dark?"

"No!"

"Well, go on. Leave."

"Thanks, I will."

"By the way if you want to get in touch with me, I'm staying at the Rose Court Motel. That's where Miss Morris works. I thought it would be a nice place to stay. She's such an interesting character."

Charlotte walked to the door. She felt Easter's eyes on her back, and she wondered if her stocking seams were straight.

SIXTEEN

At the motel, there was a light in Mr. Coombs's office but the door was closed and the blinds were drawn. A radio was turned on inside, a crime program, Charlotte thought as she drove past and heard the loud, heated voices and the eerie background of organ music.

She parked the Buick in the carport beside Number Four. She was still breathing hard, angrily, as she unlocked the door of the cabin and fumbled for the light switch on the wall. Before her hand reached the switch the light clicked on, as startling as a flash of lightning.

"Surprise," Voss said with a low satisfied chuckle. "Hey look, Eddie. She's surprised all right, ain't she?"

"She sure is." Eddie grinned self-consciously and stroked the lapel of his green and brown plaid coat. They were both wearing brand-new outfits that were almost identical. Plaid suits, with vests, and brown suede loafers, and ties with the picture of a half-naked woman hand-painted on each.

With a motion so swift that Charlotte had no time to forestall it, Voss reached behind her and slipped the bolt into place across the door.

She didn't try to unbolt it. She made no physical movement at all.

"Surprised, eh?" Voss repeated. "I kind of thought you would be."

"Get out," she said, "or I'll call the manager."

Voss made a half-circle around her and sat down on the luggage rack at the foot of the bed. "The manager? That's a hot one. Why, Coombs is an old school chum of Eddie's. That's how we come here. Eddie wanted to drop in on Coombs and say good-bye, and maybe show off his snazzy new outfit."

"Who's a show-off?" Eddie muttered. "Say that again. Who's a show-off?"

"Oh, take a joke, can't you, and stop interrupting me. Like I was saying, we came to pay Coombs a little social call, and I just happened to glance at the register in his office and see your name. I figured I better wait around and find out what's your angle." His eyes roamed the room. "Not a bad little dump, eh, Eddie? But this is peanuts compared to how we'll be living some day." His gaze returned to Charlotte and settled there. "We're leaving the country, Eddie and me."

"Good."

"Came up here to say good-bye to the folks, and then we're heading for better climes, like they say." He paused, frowning. "Hey Eddie, take off your hat. Ain't you got no manners? And offer the lady a chair—she looks like she could use one."

Eddie took off his hat. He had a new duck-tailed haircut, the kind affected by some of the gangs of juveniles Charlotte had seen on Olive Street. She said, "I'll stand, thank you, and Eddie looks better with his hat on."

"Don't act so snippy. Remember, we still have some information about you that wouldn't do you much good if it got around the right circles." But he didn't say it threateningly. He was smiling, in fact, and the smile broke into a chuckle, as if he had some secret and wonderful joke. "The right circles. Oh dear, oh dear. I guess my sense of humor gets the best of me sometimes."

Eddie was laughing too, in a feeble, puzzled way, as if he didn't know what the joke was, but was willing to go along for the ride.

"Yes, sir," Voss said. "It's better climes for Eddie and me."

"Where did you get the money?"

"We earned it. That's a good one, eh, Eddie? We *earned* it."

The two men began laughing again, gleefully, like a couple of boys who had outwitted a parent.

"I don't claim to be extra smart," Voss said at last, wiping his eyes. "Just lucky. For once I was in the right place at the right time and I got the right answers."

"Answers to what?"

"I'll tell you. I'll tell you exactly how it happened. Eddie and me was walking up the street and suddenly the guy in front of us started to toss thousand-dollar bills in the air, and Eddie and me picked them up. How's that?"

"Fine," Charlotte said. "I wouldn't count on those better climes, though."

"Yeah? Why not?"

"There's a warrant out for your arrest. Easter's looking for you."

"Easter? The cop?"

"Yes."

Voss's face crinkled up in incredulity and outraged innocence. "We haven't done anything. What would he be looking for us for? We're innocent."

"Maybe about the old man," Eddie said. "Maybe the old man died."

"We didn't touch the old man," Voss said. "We was out on the porch having a friendly little argument when suddenly, oops, he starts to vomit, the vomit got bloody." He broke off, frowning. "Damn near turned my stomach. So the old man died, eh?"

"Yes."

"Well, they can't pin any rap on me. I wouldn't demean myself bumping off a two-bit pickpocket like Tiddles. Murder's a sucker's racket."

"So is robbery. You stole my purse."

"Purse?"

"You didn't plan to steal it, you meant only to frighten me. When I went down to Olive Street that first night to see Violet, you were afraid that I'd changed my mind about helping her dispose of the baby. That baby was valuable to you; as long as Violet was carrying it she was a means of making money for you. So you headed me off while I was talking to the old man Tiddles. You were waiting for me when I got home, intending to scare me off. But when you saw my purse you couldn't resist stealing it, could you?"

"I didn't steal any purse," Voss said, with a sly glance at Eddie.

The cigarette hanging from Eddie's lip gave a nervous wiggle. "Me neither! Me neither, I tell you."

"Who said you did?"

"You *looked* at me."

"Sure, I looked at you. I look at everybody. I got eyes, ain't I?"

"You don't have to use them creepy."

"O.K. O.K. I apologize that I got creepy eyes. That suit you?"

"No, it don't suit me. You looked at me like I stole that purse. I don't like it."

"Stop flapping your tonsils. That's what this dame wants, don't you get it? She wants you to talk your way into a trap."

Eddie turned his scowl towards Charlotte. "Where's this trap?"

"There is no trap," Charlotte said. "I told you the police are looking for you. If you're sensible, you'll give yourselves up. You'll have a chance to prove your innocence."

"How can I prove my..."

"Shut up!" Voss yelled at him. "Shut *up!*"

"Sure. But how can..."

"Come on, let's get out of here." Voss was almost hopping up and down in his excitement. "Come on, step on it."

"Sure. Sure."

"You're making a mistake," Charlotte said. "But you've made so many already that one more won't matter."

"Yeah?" Voss unbolted the door. "You make your mistakes, sister, and I'll make mine. Come on, Eddie, get the lead out of your scat."

"Where are we...?"

"Shut up!"

Voss closed the door very quickly as if he was afraid that Charlotte would follow them out, screaming. Ten seconds later she heard the car shoot past with a grinding of gears. She opened the door and went out, in the hope of catching the license number. But Voss had cut the car lights; she couldn't even tell which direction he took on the highway.

Mr. Coombs trudged, yawning, out of his office. "Thought I heard a car."

"So did I."

"Some friends of yours were here a while back. They get in touch with you?"

"Yes, thanks."

"Local boys who made good, from the looks of them. Funny thing, I never thought Eddie had the brains to make good. It goes to show... Well, about time for me to be closing up and getting my beauty sleep, ha ha."

"I'd like to use the phone first, if I may."

"Private call?"

"Yes."

"I'll stay out here then. I never like to eavesdrop. Bad business, eavesdropping. Bad business, and bad *for* business."

She called Sullivan's bar, but Easter had already left, and the man who answered the phone at the Rose Court Motel told her that Mr. Easter, in Number Twenty-one, hadn't come back yet.

There was nothing to do but wait. She sat down at Mr. Coombs's desk and picked up the current issue of *Thrilling Love Comics*. She felt like weeping, for the innocents like Mr. Coombs, and Violet and Gwen, and for the lost and twisted people like Voss, and the angry, stupid ones like Eddie O'Gorman.

SEVENTEEN

She left the motel at sunrise the next morning and by eight o'clock she was at the California border. Here, inside a bridgelike structure were three gates guarded by state inspectors in uniform.

Charlotte slipped into the empty middle lane and stopped. At the gate on her left a woman with four children and a dog were standing beside an old station wagon with a New Jersey license. They were all, including the dog, eating cherries out of a box as if their lives depended on it.

Between bites, the woman registered her complaint. "You can take cherries from Wyoming to Idaho. You can take cherries from Idaho to Oregon. But you can't take cherries from Oregon to California. No. California, *they* take cherries from *you.*"

"Madam," the inspector said, "we've gone into that already. We did *not* take any of your cherries. We gave you the privilege of eating the cherries here at the border."

"I paid for those cherries and there's no reason why I shouldn't take them with me. It's a free country. Just who does President Truman think he is? Either he steals my cherries, or he forces my kids to eat them so fast they maybe'll get the colic."

"It is not President Truman, madam. It's the fruit fly. These diagrams on the wall here illustrate the life cycle of the fruit fly..."

"Fruit fly. Now I've heard everything. Hurry up, Tommy, Janet.... Not one of us moves an inch till all those cherries are eaten. *Fruit* fly. Next maybe you'll start searching my dog for fleas. Maybe the dogs in California don't have fleas. They got butterflies, maybe, gold butterflies.... Hurry up, Tommy."

The little boy addressed as Tommy, after a sly glance at the inspector, cautiously slipped half a dozen cherries down the front of his shirt. He caught Charlotte's eye and instantly assumed an expression of unassailable virtue.

Charlotte turned away, suppressing a smile. She noticed then, for the first time, the car that had stopped at the third gate. It was Easter's car, but Easter wasn't in it. He was standing beside a poster, watching her. She didn't look at him. She looked at the poster. It showed how many millions of dollars of damage a pair of fruit flies could do.

He said, "Cute kid, that Tommy."

"Are you following me?"

Easter shook his head. "If that isn't just like you, Charlotte—there's one main north-south highway and you think everyone behind you is deliberately following you."

"I don't think *everyone* is. Just you."

"My dear Charlotte, I have to get home, too. I was hoping 101 would be big enough for both of us."

An inspector approached, opened the back door of the car, and glanced around. "Any citrus fruits, lemons, oranges, limes...?"

"No fruit at all."

"How about that box of cherries you bought at Grant's Pass?" Easter said. "Cherries are teeming with fruit flies."

"I didn't buy any cherries," Charlotte told the inspector. "This man is just trying to delay me."

"I have to check up anyway," the inspector said. "May I have your trunk keys, please?"

She handed him the keys, and he went around to the back of the car and opened the trunk.

"See you later," Easter said, and climbed back into his car. He honked the horn as he went past, and waved his hand at her.

She kept the speedometer at seventy-five for the next hundred miles, but she didn't catch up with Easter. She didn't even know why she wanted to, except to prove to him that though she was a woman she was just as efficient and skillful a driver as any man.

She gave up the attempt at Eureka where she had to stop for gas and for lunch. She ate at a hamburger stand. She was amazed at herself for trying to overtake Easter, and at all the other rather childish things she'd said and done since she met him. The poise, the self-control, that she'd cultivated for years seemed to slip away when she was with Easter, leaving her as gauche as a high-school girl, quick to blush, quick to be angered or take offense.

If I can't catch up with him, Charlotte thought, I will lag away behind. I will make him wonder what's happened to me. No, no, that's absurd. I mustn't even think of such a thing. I must be myself, not this half-aggressive, half-coy female. I will drive home in the ordinary way, as if Easter didn't exist. I should be home by five.

It was nearly eight when she turned into her driveway.

In the headlights of the car the overhead door of the double garage loomed, a blank wall of white. The door was closed, and she'd left it open. Fear alerted her senses, quickened her imagination. The night wind, which only a moment ago had felt fresh against her skin, now seemed to have a treacherous softness about it. A laughing bird taunted her from his perch on a telephone wire.

She had left the garage door open and now it was closed. It was puzzling, but there was no reason to he afraid. She tried to convince herself that anyone could have closed it—Lewis, Miss Schiller, the postman, a child playing in the neighborhood, perhaps even Easter, trying to startle her as he'd startled her when he stepped from behind the tree at Sullivan's—but common sense told her that none of these was a real possibility. Easter was no cruel practical joker and neither Lewis nor Miss Schiller had any reason to come here, knowing she was away. The child, the postman—she had thought of them only because she wanted quite desperately to believe that the closed door meant nothing, held no secrets.

She left the headlights on. As she walked towards the garage she remembered Easter's picture of Violet's face lathered with death-foam. But the sea is far away, she thought, not even visible at night like this; and I can swim. I can swim a mile if I have to.

It was the first time since she'd become involved in the case that she was afraid of physical violence directed against herself. Her vague diffuse fears (of Easter, of the old house on Olive Street) had synthesized into something so tight and compact it could fit on the point of a needle and pierce her spine.

The door was unlocked and, she saw now, not even fully closed. There were three or four inches of space at the bottom, as if someone in urgent haste had slammed the door down and it had bounced up a little and stuck there.

She had to strain to open it, breathing hard, her whole body tensed, braced against attack. But there was no attack, no one in the garage at all. Only a car, parked on the right side where Lewis always parked his—a small convertible with the top up.

She turned on the ceiling light and walked over to the front of the convertible. It was a blue Ford. She had seen many of them on the streets, but she didn't know anyone who owned one and she could think of no reason for the car to be parked in her garage. It had been driven at high speed— gray and yellow blobs of insects splattered the windshield and the headlights and a small dead bird was caught in the chromium grillwork. She felt the hood of the engine with her hand; it was cold. The car had been standing there for some time.

A Ford convertible, the kind of car Eddie was said to have bought. But Voss and Eddie were miles away by this time, perhaps already out of the country, as they had planned. *"It's better climes for Eddie and me."*

She got into the front seat and turned on the dashboard lights. The ignition key was gone; the car had been left there to stay in her garage. There was no way of getting rid of it except to push it upgrade by herself, which was impossible, or to call the Auto Club for a tow truck.

She turned sideways to step out of the car and a glint of metal on the back seat caught her eye. She leaned over the edge of the seat and saw that Voss and Eddie had reached their better climes.

They were curled up on the floor like a pair of lovers in a fatal embrace. Voss's head was buried against Eddie's chest; there was nothing to show

how he had died. But Eddie's face was upturned, pinned against the door, and on his forehead two neat dark holes had been bored. Death had come to him more easily than to Violet. He looked peacefully asleep except for the extra eyes on his forehead.

On the seat lay an ordinary jackknife with the large blade pulled out, a knife like the one Eddie had used the previous night. He'd taken it out of his vest pocket, and flipped the blade open and cleaned his fingernails while Voss was talking. The knife lay now on the back seat of the car, a childish, impotent weapon of defense against the swift certainty of a gun. Eddie had had no chance to use the knife; its blade was unstained, gleaming blandly in the light of the garage.

She stumbled out of the car, half paralyzed, not by the shock of seeing two dead bodies, but by the realization that there was no way now that she could get rid of the car and the bodies. They were hers, they were hanging from her neck like the mariner's albatross. A scream died in her throat.

Outside, the bird was still laughing at her from the telephone wire.

EIGHTEEN

A car passed on the road, not speeding as cars usually did on Mountain Drive at night, but groping along, as if the driver was searching for a certain house, a certain person. The car paused, reversed gear, and braked to a stop outside her house.

She ran out of the garage and pulled down the door just as Easter stepped through the wooden gate into the yard. He didn't speak for a minute. His eyes traveled from her face to the Buick with the headlights still on, to the closed door of the garage.

"I'll open the garage for you." he said.

"No." She made a convulsive movement of protest that stiffened her whole body, like an electric shock. "No, thanks."

"All right, do it yourself." He added something under his breath that sounded like "damn emancipated females."

"I—I'd prefer to leave the car out." Her voice was unnatural, high and tight, as if hands were squeezing her larynx. "I never know when I'll have to make a call."

"Blake's taking your calls."

"Stop arguing with me. I'm—tired. If you don't mind, I wish you'd go away."

"You're always wishing I'd go away. It's painful to me. Easter, Easter, go away, don't come again some other..."

"Please. I really am tired."

"I know. I won't keep you. I came to see whether you got home all right."

"Well, I did. I *did*. You can *see* that."

"I can see a lot of things," he said slowly. "You're nervous as hell. What's up?"

"Nothing. You—you didn't really come here to see if I arrived safely. You're spying on me."

"Why should I?"

"Because you think that I'm mixed up in all these terrible things."

"They're not so terrible—a suicide, a natural death—no murder." He repeated, "No murder," in an insinuating tone as if he expected her to contradict him. She said nothing.

He walked over to her car, turned off the headlights and removed the key ring from the ignition. He tossed it to her. It fell in the grass at her feet and she watched it dully, as if her mind were too dazed to understand the concept of catching something that was thrown at her.

"Your keys," Easter said.

"Keys? Oh. Yes, of course."

They knelt, simultaneously, to pick up the key ring and their arms touched. She drew back as if he'd aimed a blow at her.

He picked up the key ring first. "I'm poison to you, eh?"

"No. Not poison." A jackknife, a gun, foam.

"You won't be making any calls tonight. I'll put your car away for you and bring your luggage into the house."

"No! I won't let..."

"What's the matter? Is there something in the house you don't want me to see?"

"No."

"Ballard, perhaps?"

"There's nothing in the house," she said contemptuously. "Come in and see. Snoop all you want to."

"Since you put it so charmingly, I will."

He got her week-end bag out of the car while she unlocked the front door.

She turned on all the lights in the sitting room: "There. See anything?"

"No."

"No guns or b—bodies?"

He looked at her quizzically. "I hardly expected to find any guns or bodies. Just Ballard."

"Why do you want to see Lewis?"

"For one thing, his wife reported him missing this morning."

"Missing? *Lewis?*"

"But that's just one thing. There are other things.... Where is he?"

"I don't know. And if Lewis wants to go away, it's not my business, and it's certainly not yours, Mr. Easter."

"You might be surprised."

"You have nothing against Lewis except that I love him."

"The way I feel, that's plenty to have against a man. Even if it were all."

His intensity disturbed her. She didn't know what to say or do. She stood near the door, her hat and gloves still on, her handbag under her arm. She said finally, "Sit down and I'll find something to drink."

"I'll stand, thanks. I feel more like a policeman when I'm standing and less like a guy calling on the woman he loves. I'm both. But right now I'm standing. Where's Ballard?"

"I don't know. I haven't seen him since the night before last at dinner-time. I told him I was going to drive up to Oregon."

"Did you tell him why?"

"Yes."

"And he didn't want you to go?"

"He didn't care."

"You're lying."

"He didn't care much."

"Plenty."

"Stop beating around the bush like this," she said passionately. "If he cared at all, it was because the trip meant that I wouldn't see him for a couple of days. What other reason would he have for caring whether I went to Ashley or not?"

"I can think of several."

"You. You can think of anything against Lewis. He told me that's what you were—a troublemaker."

"That's what I am." He lit a cigarette. There was no draft in the room. The smoke moved directly, purposefully, to the ceiling. "By the way, I have news for you about Voss and Eddie."

She felt the blood draining out of her face. She turned and began taking off her gloves and her hat, fussing with her purse—any kind of quick movement to distract his eye from her pallor.

"They've disappeared. Sunk without a trace. I'm a little disappointed about losing them. I was hoping to ask Eddie a few questions about where he got the money to buy his new car."

You can still ask him. But he won't answer.

The telephone began to ring. She looked towards it, dazedly, as if she'd never heard a phone ring and was surprised that the curious black object could make such a noise.

"Answer it," Easter said. "Or I will, if you like."

"No. No. I will." She crossed the room and picked up the phone. "Hello?"

"Dr. Keating, it's me, Gwen Ballard. I've been trying to get you all day. Miss Schiller kept telling me to phone Dr. Blake. But I wouldn't. I said, no, Dr. Keating's my doctor, I *won't* see anyone else."

Charlotte glanced over her shoulder at Easter. He hadn't moved, but his body was tense as if every nerve cell was straining to help him hear what was being said at the other end of the line. She put her hand over the receiver and said, "This is a private call from one of my patients. You wouldn't be interested."

He didn't speak, just looked at her, unblinking.

She took her hand away from the receiver. "Is there anything the matter?"

"I've had another attack." Gwen's breathing was labored, her voice faint and tremulous. "I'm alone. I'm afraid."

"There's nothing to worry about. Take it easy and..."

"I must see you. Please come, Dr. Keating—Charlotte—I must talk to someone, a friend."

A friend. Gwen, alone and in terror, calling to her, of all the people in the city, as a friend. Charlotte felt a nausea rising from her stomach, souring her throat. "Has anything happened?"

"He tried to kill me. Yes! He tried to kill me! He said he hated me, he'd always hated me!"

The pitch and volume of Gwen's voice had risen. Charlotte saw that Easter had heard, not the words perhaps, but the notes of hysteria. She had to quiet Gwen before Easter got suspicious. She said, "I'll be right over. Ten minutes."

"Oh, thank you, Dr. Keating, thank you."

Charlotte replaced the phone. "I have to make a call."

"So I heard."

"If you'll excuse me now..." She looked pointedly towards the door.

Easter raised one eyebrow. "You want me to leave?"

"It's customary."

"Suppose I like it here. It's cozy and warm, and I expect Ballard to call."

His reaction was something she hadn't foreseen. She'd thought he would leave when she did, giving her a chance, later, to plan what to do about Voss and O'Gorman. There was no way of forcing him to leave except— and the irony stung—to call the police.

Silently, she picked up her hat and purse and went out the door. She didn't look back, and Easter didn't speak.

As she backed her car out of the driveway she saw that she had made a fatal error.

In her hurry to close the garage door when she heard Easter's car, she had forgotten to turn out the light. Its beams shone gaily out of the little window at the side of the garage, as if inviting anyone to come in and see for himself.

NINETEEN

Nine o'clock. An offshore wind was blowing and the palm trees cringed and leaned away from it, waving their frantic arms.

The Ballard house couldn't be seen from the street. It appeared suddenly, at a curve in the cypress-lined walk, a handsome house of oiled redwood set in a formal garden. Charlotte had always disliked this garden. The flower beds were too meticulously planned; they seemed to have no connection with nature any more. They were Gwen's and not the earth's. The lawn, too, was so immaculate that it was impossible to imagine real people walking on it.

And real people never did, Charlotte thought. The lawn wasn't to be walked on, but to be admired from the dining alcove or from the picture window in the living room. Even the collies, whom Gwen loved best, were not allowed on the grass. They had their own yard behind the house, fenced runways and miniature houses and a brooder for the bitches with new pups.

A light was kept on for them all night. Charlotte could see several of the dogs watching her cautiously through the wire fencing, their tails half raised, as if they weren't sure yet that she was a friend.

She spoke to them softly and one of the tails began to wag, slowly, with dignity, like a feathered fan waved by a condescending duchess.

The other dogs, Gwen's three favorites, were upstairs with her in her bedroom. They lay beside her bed, a protective phalanx. Gwen had told them to lie down and they had obeyed; but their eyes were restless, they followed Charlotte's every move, they searched Gwen's face for reassurance, and now and then the big sable-colored male let out a whimper like a child.

"Doctor—doctor, I can't breathe."

"You're trying too hard. Relax."

"I will. I'll relax. I won't—choke?"

"No. The attack's nearly over. See for yourself. Put your fingers here on your wrist. There, feel your pulse?"

"I guess so."

"It's not much faster than mine."

"It isn't?"

"Of course not."

Gwen's breathing had steadied as soon as her attention was no longer focused on the necessity of breathing. Charlotte often encountered the same reaction in children who were afraid to go to sleep because they might stop breathing.

Gwen's head sank back among the lace-trimmed pillows. Charlotte saw, then, the bruise on the side of her neck, a recent bruise, still blue, about the size of a thumbnail.

Gwen saw her staring at the bruise, and she touched it with her finger, gently. "He tried to kill me. He said he would, some day, and now he's tried. But he got frightened, perhaps the dogs frightened him with their growling. He let go of me suddenly and went up to his room and I haven't seen him since. It was the night before last, just about this time."

"The bruise isn't serious." She thought, not as serious as the bullet holes in Eddie's forehead, the acrid choking water that Violet had swallowed in her fight for air. No, the bruise wasn't serious, but the intent behind it was. She remembered what Lewis had said the last time she'd seen him: *"I haven't been drinking. Or at least only enough for medicinal purposes, to keep me from strangling my wife."* She wanted to say something to reassure both herself and Gwen, but all she could think of was, "People do odd things in moments of anger."

"He wasn't angry. I did nothing to make him angry. He came home that night, and I said, 'Hello darling, where have you been?' And he said, 'In hell, I've been in hell.' I was so surprised. Lewis always tells me where he's been."

No, he doesn't, you fool, you pathetic fool. You make me hate myself, hate Lewis, hate life itself.

Gwen said softly, "You know my husband."

"Yes."

"You know him as he appears to you, but you can't know him as he is. He's a cruel man. He has no feelings. Other people are stones to him; he can pick them up or toss them aside or kick them around. He never thinks they're human and can feel pain and despair just as he can."

He's not like that, Charlotte wanted to protest. He's a good man, but he's been warped by your narrowness, soured by your eternal sweetness. Don't blame Lewis, or yourself either. It's nobody's fault. Fate tricked you both, and me, and even Easter. A four-ply trickery.

Given's tiny mouth was twisted in perplexity. "It's such a funny kind of cruelty he has. The more I do to please him, the more he despises me. He looks at me across the table at dinner and my heart turns cold. I try to be bright and amusing the way wives are supposed to. I even read a book about little stories to tell and interesting facts and things like that. But"... One slender arm rose and fell, in a gesture of futility. "The funny things I say aren't funny, and the stupid things sound so much stupider when he's watching me like that—as if I were a worm he'd like to crush under his heel."

"You've never told me any of this before."

"I have my pride," Gwen said stiffly, "my reputation."

"Of course."

"No one will ever take that away from me, though Lewis tries." She fussed with the pillows; they were tiny, scaled to her size, like everything else in the room. A little girl's room, Charlotte thought, looking at the teddy bear propped on the chifforobe, the smiling French doll sitting at the window. The years were passing, but the little girl was afraid to grow up. Here, in her own room, she was immune to time. Though she no longer played with the teddy bear, it was there ready to be picked up, its soft furry body a comfort, a symbol of security and innocence. But the little girl was ageing, and with age came fear. Fear of the dark, fear of stopping breathing; other nameless fears that her heart knew—and it beat in futile frenzy like the heart of a frightened bird.

"I know you don't believe that Lewis tried to kill me," Gwen said. "But he did, and I know why. He has another woman. Why, you look surprised, Dr. Keating, almost as surprised as I was when I found out. I guess I shouldn't have been surprised, though. It happens in the best of families. The husband gets tired of the wife and takes up with anyone he can find, a waitress or a shopgirl or any kind of cheap slut with no more morals than a cat."

Charlotte's face was like stone.

"Do I sound bitter, Dr. Keating? Well, I am. It's terrible, it's a terrible thing knowing about this woman, yet not knowing who she is so I could go and talk to her, make her realize."

"Realize what?"

Gwen blinked. "What? Well, that she's breaking up a home, a marriage."

She's not, *I'm* not, breaking up anything, Charlotte thought. The home belongs to you and the dogs, and the marriage was broken long before you introduced me to Lewis, here in this very house. Nor am I a slut. I'm a respectable woman; I work hard, and when I'm lucky I even do some good.

"I think that's where he is now," Gwen said. "With *her. I* didn't tell the police that when I called this morning. I was ashamed to. I just told them that my husband was missing. Then, late this afternoon, a policeman came here to the house. He said he wanted to look around, to see if he could find any evidence of where Lewis might have gone. He had an unusual name—Easter. Do you know anything about police work, Dr. Keating?"

"Very little."

"I just wondered. It seemed to me that this policeman behaved very oddly. He went up to Lewis' study and I heard him typing. Isn't that odd? Why would he want to use Lewis' typewriter?"

"I don't know," Charlotte said. But he had a reason, he always has a reason.

"Then when he came downstairs again he asked me all kinds of funny questions."

"Funny?"

"I thought they were. He asked about any trips that Lewis and I have taken since Christmas. Well, of course, I don't take trips. There's my heart, for one thing, and for another, I love my little home. I'm happy here. I don't need the excitement that Lewis seems to crave.... I told the policeman that. He said he wanted to know about the little trips and holidays that Lewis took because Lewis might have gone to one of the same places again. People repeat themselves, he said." She twisted a strand of her fair hair with thin, nervous fingers. "I didn't tell him that Lewis choked me. I have my pride."

There was a long silence. Charlotte thought of Easter, prowling around Lewis' study, his eyes sharpened by hate.... Easter, waiting for her at home, perhaps wandering out to the kitchen and from there seeing the light in the garage.

"If I knew where he is," Gwen said, "I could sleep, I could stop worrying like this. But he's been acting so strange nearly all week. The last dinner we had together two nights ago he hardly spoke at all. I was trying to make conversation so that Mrs. Peter wouldn't suspect anything was wrong—she's the cook and she loves to gossip. Well, I'd just read in the paper about that girl who drowned herself and I mentioned it to Lewis because I thought he'd be interested, but he told me to shut up, right in front of Mrs. Peters.... That was a terrible thing, about the girl."

"Yes."

"I wonder, did she—suffer?"

"She must have."

"But it was quick, wasn't it? Of course. It must have been. Very quick. Oh, I hate to see things suffer. I could never be a doctor, like you. But I guess doctors get used to seeing suffering and death."

"In a sense."

"I never could. I'm too sensitive." Her lower lip began to tremble. "At least the girl is dead. She's out of things now. She has no more troubles. Oh, I'm so tired. So awfully *tired.*"

"I'll give you a sleeping capsule."

Gwen's eyes widened in quick panic. "No. No, I won't take anything. I must be alert, in case he comes back, in case he tries..."

"There's little danger of that. But I could call Mrs. Peters and ask her to stay with you for tonight."

"No. She has her own family, her own worries. Doctor—Dr. Keating, what would you do if you were in my place?"

"I don't know. Go to a hotel, perhaps."

"But the dogs. There's no one to look after them."

"I can't advise you anyway," Charlotte said slowly. "Personal problems can't always be worked out by objective reasoning. What I would do might be the opposite of what would be good for you to do."

"That's right, isn't it? My, you're so sensible and intelligent! I wish you knew my husband better. He likes intelligent women, maybe because I'm so stupid." One corner of her mouth curved in a sad little smile. "I wish I had everything under control in my private life, the way you must have. I bet you have no problems at all."

For Charlotte, it was the final irony. She looked at the French doll on the window seat. Its painted smile was knowing.

TWENTY

Easter was waiting for her. There was no need to ask him if he had found Voss and Eddie: The garage was dark.

He looked at her across the room. All the lamps were still burning and every line and angle of his face was distinct, grim.

"You've got a bad case of trouble, Charlotte."

In silence she went to the big window where Lewis' chair was, and stared down at the lights of the city. It was only five nights ago that she'd stood in this same place and wondered which of the city lights belonged to Violet. She had told Lewis about Violet that night, she'd said, *"Lewis, I think I made a mistake."*

Well, the mistake had grown, cancerously; its wild, malignant cells had spread from life to life until it covered them all, Violet and Eddie, Voss and his wife and the old man Tiddles; Easter and Lewis and Gwen and Mrs. Reyerling. Her mistake had infected each of them, but its final victim was herself, Charlotte Keating.

She said, without turning, "Have you reported it?"

"Not yet."

"You will, though."

"I have to."

"I suppose you know it will mean the end of my life here, my work."

"Yes."

She closed her eyes. The lids felt dry and dusty. "It's ironic, isn't it? I meant only to help Violet when I drove down to Olive Street that night. My duty seemed so clear, so inescapable. I didn't *want* to go to that house. I was afraid of it. I remember thinking so many things had happened there that one more wouldn't even be noticed. I was wrong. I've done quite a few wrong things, I suppose; pushed the wrong buttons, knocked on the wrong doors."

"You still have a chance," Easter said, "if you can find Ballard."

"Do you hate him so much you must try to drag him into this?"

"He's not big enough to hate. And he's getting smaller by the minute."

"You talk so oddly."

"It will make sense if you'll listen. Or don't you want to listen?"

"I'm not sure. I'm—mixed up. All these hints about Lewis..."

"I've tried to let you down easy, Charlotte. You wouldn't come down. You were treading clouds, still are. When a cloud gets too heavy, it rains. Stormy weather."

"Talk straight, please."

"Trying to," Easter said. "Ballard didn't tell you he knew Violet?"

"He didn't know her."

"He did. He sent her to you."

"No! I won't believe it!"

"You must. It's true. The child was his. He sent her to you knowing how you felt about people in a jam, hoping you'd help Violet get rid of the child, help Violet and save his skin at the same time."

"No." The feeble denial stuck in her throat. "He told me—the night I met him on the breakwater—he said he didn't even know Violet. I believed him. He was telling the truth, I'm sure of it."

"He may have been telling the truth, as far as he knew it. Maybe he didn't remember the girl; maybe he never even knew her name, until he saw her picture in the paper the next day, her picture and the name of the little town she came from. He knew then."

There was a long silence, broken only by the ticking of the clock on the mantel, the passing of the restless minutes.

"I'm not guessing," Easter said. "I know he sent Violet to you because. your name and address on the card found in your purse were written on the typewriter in Ballard's study."

"You're framing him. You're manufacturing evidence against him."

"I don't operate like that," he said flatly, "even for the love of a lady. Want more proof?"

"No."

"You could use it." He took a folded piece of paper out of his pocket and opened it for her to see. It was a photostatic copy of a sheet from the register of the Rose Court Motel, Ashley, Oregon, C. Vincent Rawls, Owner and Manager. Date, Feb. 26/49. Name, L. B. Ballard. Address, 480 Corona del Mar, Salinda, California. Make of car, Cadillac, License, California 17Y205.

She couldn't take her eyes off the name on the photostat. It had been written very carelessly and quickly, and she wasn't sure whether the writing was Lewis' or not. She said, "It doesn't look exactly like Lewis' writing."

"It is."

"And it proves nothing except that he stopped at Ashley for a night."

"On February twenty-sixth."

She didn't reply, though she knew the significance of the date. It was the beginning of July now, and Violet had been four months gone with child when she died. But how could it have happened? Lewis wasn't like that at all, Charlotte thought. He would never have looked at Violet—she was young enough to be his daughter, young and ignorant and not even pretty; and Lewis was a respectable man, a little stolid, a man who valued his place in the community and his reputation. Lewis and Violet. The thought made her sick. It stuck in her throat; it couldn't be swallowed; it couldn't be coughed up. Lewis and Violet. And the baby boy that had died with Violet was Lewis' child; it might even have grown to look like him, walk like him—the son that he'd always wanted, now in a garbage can in the morgue or already burned to dust in an incinerator. Poor Lewis, she thought. But running through her pity was an iron stripe of bitterness.

Easter was watching her, narrow-eyed. "I'm not interested in bringing Ballard to trial on moral grounds. That's woman's work. What he does with his spare weekends in Ashley or Cucamonga is no business of mine."

"You've managed to make it your business. Do you also break into locked hotel rooms and peer over transoms and creep under..."

"I'm after a murderer," Easter said. "Not a four-bit Romeo."

She leaned her forehead against the window to steady herself. The lights of the city whirled, slowed, stopped. "Lewis is neither," she said at last.

"He's both."

"No. You have no proof."

"I can't prove that he killed Violet. But he's made it easier for me by shooting Voss and O'Gorman and leaving the bodies in your garage."

She turned to face him. "He wouldn't do such a thing. Even if he were desperate, he wouldn't involve me in such a mess. He loves me. You can laugh at that, but it's true. He loves me."

"He loves himself, too, and that's the big passion. You're running a poor second, Charlotte."

She repeated stubbornly, "He would never do such a thing."

"I admit it's a pretty stupid idea to drive a convertible containing two bodies into your girlfriend's garage. But I figure that he didn't expect you back for a few days, and he intended to use the time to think himself out of the jam. When you look at it like that, Ballard was playing it smart. Your garage was practically the one safe place in town where he could hide the bodies until he planned a way to dispose of them."

Lewis and Violet. Lewis and Voss. Lewis and Eddie. Three deaths already, and Easter with death in his eyes.

Easter's mouth moved with a question, but she hadn't heard it.

"I repeat," Easter said. "Ballard had a key to your garage?"

"I left the door open."

"But he had a key?"

"I don't see what difference it..."

"Did he have a key?"

"Yes!"

Both their voices were raised, but Easter's had lowered in pitch, and Charlotte's was high and shrill.

"Do I have to squeeze everything out of you?" Easter said. "Don't you know I'm trying to help you?"

"I don't want your kind of help."

"You can't be choosey at this stage of the game. You'd better take all the help you can get while you can get it. You've got a car with two very dead men out in your garage, and I have to report it. I have to report it to the chief, to the D.A., to the sheriff. I should have reported it half an hour ago, but I gave you a chance. Where's Ballard?"

"I don't know."

"And even if you knew...?"

"I wouldn't tell you."

"The loyal-little-woman role, eh?" An ugly smile crossed his face. "Well, come on, loyal little woman, I have something to show you."

"I don't have to..."

"Come on. I want to see that loyalty explode right in your two blind eyes."

She felt a surge of violence. She wanted to reach out and hit him. It was the first time since childhood that she had wanted to strike someone, to hurt. "You're—you're a contemptible..."

"Bully," he said. "Cad. Yeah, I know all that."

"My—my loyalty isn't as absurd as you seem to think it is. There's no proof that Lewis is guilty of anything."

"Not enough for a court of law. It might take a month, two months, to line up the witnesses and the ballistics and medical experts and to organize the evidence. But right now I'm convinced, as the judge puts it in his instructions to the jury, I'm convinced beyond a reasonable doubt and to a moral certainty, that Ballard killed all three of them, Violet, O'Gorman and Voss."

Beyond a reasonable doubt and to a moral certainty.

Heavy, somber words, like a funeral sermon.

Easter glanced at his watch before he opened the front door. "You haven't much time. Coming?"

"Where are you going?"

"Just to the garage."

"I don't want to."

"Afraid you'll be convinced?"

"No."

"Come on, Charlotte."

"No."

Easter made an impatient gesture. "If I have to convince you that Ballard is a murderer before you'll do anything to help yourself out of this mess, you must come out to the garage and see for yourself."

"See what?"

"The gun."

"Gun?"

"You're in a worse spot than you think you are, Charlotte. The evidence indicates that the shooting was done in the convertible, perhaps right in your garage." He paused. "'Coming?"

"Yes." She wanted to see the gun. She even had a sudden hope that she would be able to say definitely that it didn't belong to Lewis. Lewis had a target pistol, a pair of them, in fact. She remembered the day she'd first seen them. She thought back to the time when she and Lewis were having a picnic on a remote stretch of beach near Pismo, and Lewis was trying to explain to her the difference between a revolver and an automatic pistol.

"These are revolvers. Now an automatic works differently. The cartridges are loaded into a clip that fits into the handle and the recoil mechanism discharges the empty shell and throws a new cartridge into the chamber. But a revolver like this has a revolving cylinder which—you haven't even been listening, Charley."

"I have so."

"All right, what is this in my hand?"

"It's a .38 calibre Colt target pistol. Darling, the sun's making me sleepy. Anyway, what is a calibre?"

"You actually don't know what a calibre is?"

"I actually don't."

"You are an amazingly ignorant but lovable woman," Lewis said solemnly. He had leaned over to kiss her, one of the pistols still in his hand.

It had been a happy day. She thought of it now as she followed Easter silently out to the garage. The beach, the sun, the happiness, were as remote as a dream.

Easter beamed his flashlight into the back seat. It pointed like an accusing finger at the gun on the floor beside Voss's knee. "See it?"

"Yes."

"Recognize it?"

"No—I don't know—I'm very ignorant about revolvers."

"You can't be very ignorant or you wouldn't have called it a revolver."

"I—I thought guns and revolvers were the same."

"Did you?" The light hadn't moved off the gun; it was mercilessly steady. "Well, it is a revolver and a very interesting one. Note the ramp built up along the barrel. That's for more accurate sighting. Know anyone who goes in for target shooting?"

"No."

He made a sound of disbelief. "The gun's a common make, a Colt .38. What makes it uncommon is the fancy hand-made grip, and the fact that it's one of a pair. And the other one of the pair is in Ballard's study. I saw it there this afternoon."

She turned away. The ceiling light of the garage was on, and she could see, in sharp contrast to the convertible and its contents, the ordinary items of her everyday existence: her gardening tools, the canvas gloves she wore to protect her hands, the trunkful of woolen clothes she had stored away for the summer, the old bicycle she used sometimes for exercise. They all seemed remote, like the day at the beach with Lewis. It was as if she would never again be able to take up her life where she had left off. The stitch had been dropped, and even if she could return to pick it up, the pattern had already, and inexorably, been changed.

She spoke wearily, "I have a legal right to say nothing."

"That's true."

"I think I'll—go in now."

He followed her back into the house. His face was unnaturally red, the face of a man trying to control himself and restrain his anger. He walked the length of the room and back again, slowly, heavily, his full weight on every step.

"Charlotte..."

"You'd better make your report."

"Not yet. I can hold off for a few more hours. You've been away, understand? You've been away and you haven't come back yet."

"I wish I hadn't. I wish I'd never gone. I wish I'd never met any of you, Violet or Eddie or you or..."

"Take it easy." He went out into the kitchen and found a bottle of Bourbon and poured her some in a water glass. "Drink it."

"I don't want any."

"Afraid you'll talk too much? Look, Charlotte, this is no longer a matter of loyalty. It's a matter of trying to protect yourself from being ruined."

"I can't protect myself. They're there, Voss and Eddie. I can't get rid of them."

"I know you can't." He put the glass of Bourbon on the coffee table. "But you can minimize the importance of their being found in your garage. As the case stands now, that's the point the newspapers are going to concentrate on. Double Slaying in Garage of Prominent Physician—they'll give it the business, and whether you're guilty or innocent, you're going to be smeared. You'll be accused and tried, not by a jury of your peers, but by a couple of newspaper reporters who want a juicy story, a deputy D.A. who likes to have his picture in the paper, several hundred housewives who resent your position as a doctor, a few disgruntled patients, some of your friends who 'knew it all the time,' a couple of W.C.T.U. members who saw you drink a beer once in 1943, and the usual assortment of religious cranks, neurotics, sadists.... There's your jury. Like it?"

"No." Her throat felt raw, as if she'd been chewing glass.

"What we've got to do now is to change the emphasis," Easter said. "Where Voss and O'Gorman are found won't seem so important if the man who killed them is found first. If he is found and confesses." He looked at his watch again. "You haven't much time to decide. Where's Ballard?"

"I don't know."

"You know who his friends are?"

"Some of them."

"Where would he be likely to hide out?"

"I don't think he'd be hiding anywhere near here."

"Use your head," Easter rasped. "He's got to be near here. He didn't drive that car into your garage and intend to leave it there. He intended to come back, to get rid of it. But I don't know when, and time is running out."

"What am I expected to do?"

"Find him. I'll give you three hours."

"What if I can't?" Her legs and arms felt cold, brittle as twigs.

"Try. You know his habits, his friends, the places he likes to go."

She hesitated. "If I find him, what will I do?"

"Tell him to stop running, the race is over."

"Where—where will you be?"

"Me?" His mouth moved in a smile, but his eyes didn't change. They looked flat and hard as coins. "I'll be waiting here. If Ballard turns up I wouldn't want him to get lonesome."

She knew from his face that that was what he wanted—for Lewis to come for the car, and for him, Easter, to be waiting, like a lion waiting at a watering hole in the certainty that the antelope would turn up. He didn't expect her to find Lewis; he was only trying to get rid of her so the two of them could meet alone. A trickle of fear ran down her spine. I must get to Lewis first, she thought. No matter what he's guilty of, I must warn him against Easter.

She looked across the room at Easter. She felt a surge of hatred for him—for his arrogance, his power, his obsession against Lewis. When she passed him on her way to the door, her fists clenched, ready to strike.

He saw them. His smile vanished. With a swift, violent movement he reached out and grabbed her wrists and held them together against his chest with one hand. With his other hand gripping the back of her neck, he leaned down and pressed his mouth against hers.

He let go suddenly, and she fell back a step, holding the back of her hand over her bruised mouth.

"That's for nothing," he said. "That's for no encouragement, no co-operation. That's for no pretty smiles, no soft looks, nothing."

"You're a cheap, rotten..."

"Beat it," he said quietly. "Find Lover-boy. My patience is wearing thin."

TWENTY-ONE

At some time in the past hour a Santa Ana had begun to blow from the desert on the other side of the mountain—a hot, dry, choking wind that harried the trees, hurled the dust down the city streets, swept the people into their houses or into the shelter of doorways where they huddled coughing, shielding their eyes with their hands. Bits of refuse fluttered up and down the road like bold birds, clung convulsively to the windshields of cars for a moment and swooped off again.

The wind was tearing up the city, emptying the streets, stripping the trees, a crazy, confused wind that blew in all directions at once. Charlotte felt that she was a part of it, sharing its wild confusion. She didn't know where Lewis was or how to find him. She didn't even know if he was alive.

The moon leered through the leaves of the giant oaks, veiled, provocative, like a half-told secret: *Is he alive? Perhaps, maybe. Where? Somewhere, here or there.*

She had no hopes, no plans, but she had to start somewhere. She drove to the building where Lewis had his office. There was a light on the second floor behind the partly closed Venetian blinds. Lewis often worked at night and she had often waited for him, sitting in her car or standing in the entrance hall downstairs pretending to read the directory beside the elevator. H. M. Morris, Electrolysis. Salinda Rental Association. C. Charles Tomlinson, Broker. Ballard and Johnson, Attorneys...

The elevator was locked for the night. An elderly Negro with a white woolly cap of hair was mopping the tiled floor, mopping the same place over and over again, as if his thoughts were far away, dwelling on softer things than tile.

"Hello, Tom."

"Yes, ma'am."

She knew he didn't remember her. People walked in and walked out, traded names, traded faces, wore each other's clothes—so many people they lost their identities in Tom's mind, and he erased their footprints with his mop.

"Fine clear evening, ma'am," Tom said. Though it rained, or the city was smothered with fog or mauled by a desert wind, the evenings were always fine and clear to Tom. He stayed inside, slept in the basement, and ate his meals sitting on an upright chair in the broom closet while he read the Bible, or at least held it open on his lap. ("He can't read," Lewis had told her once, in front of Tom. "But he's very religious and he likes to pick out the words he knows, like God and heaven." "God and heaven is fine words," Tom said with dignity.)

"Tom..."

"Yes, ma'am."

"Is—have you seen Mr. Ballard tonight?"

"No, ma'am, I don't r'lect seeing him."

"There's a light in his office."

"Might be. I didn't r'lect to turn it off."

"I'll go up and see."

"Elevator's closed, ma'am. Have to walk up."

"That's all right, Tom."

"Steps is wet, you walk easy."

"I will."

The corridor upstairs was dim, and smelled of soap and chlorine. The door of Lewis' office was half open and she could see part of the reception room—the luxurious gold satin love seat and the tropical aquarium that had been built into the wall. The aquarium lights were on, and the miniature fish moved silently behind glass, striped angel fish and velvety black mollies and brilliant neons as tiny as tacks.

She knew, as soon as she saw that the aquarium lights were on, that it couldn't be Lewis in the office. He paid no attention to the fish; they belonged to Vern Johnson who fed and fussed over them with the same care Miss Schiller gave her cat.

She rapped on the door and said, "Vern?"

"Who is it?"

"Charlotte."

"Well, come in, come in, Charley."

She went in and closed the door behind her. Vern Johnson was a big moon-faced man with thick horn-rimmed glasses that gave his face a false aspect of vagueness. She had known him for years, had gone to school with his sister, and turned down his somewhat boozy and brotherly proposals. It was at one of his parties that she had her first personal talk with Lewis, a week after Gwen had introduced him to her. *"You know, I asked Vern to invite you, Miss Keating." She didn't like the approach. She said distantly, "Did you?" "Yes. I wanted to talk to you. I've been planning for two days what I'd say but now I've forgotten all of it. The general idea, though, was to impress you with my mind." "Why should you want to do that?" "Damned if I know, except that you look so competent and superior I'd like to show you that I'm competent and superior, too." He spoke with a kind of rueful candor. "And are you, Mr. Ballard?" "I've always thought so." She changed the subject, then, with deliberate abruptness. "Mrs. Ballard's not with you tonight?" "No." "I hope she's not ill." "No, she's not ill." He turned and walked away, and a little later Vern came and told her that Lewis had left. "What did you say to him, anyway?" "Why, nothing, nothing at all." "He's a hell of a good guy, Charley. Which is a miracle, considering his wife."*

"Sit down, Charley," Vern said.

"Thanks."

"Looking for Lewis?"

"I... Yes."

"That makes three of us. Gwen's been calling all day."

She didn't sit down. She said, "I won't disturb you if you're busy, Vern."

"I'm not busy." He picked up a small glass bowl from the table and held it up to the light. It contained a single black mollie, no more than an inch and a half long. "See this little lady? She doesn't look much like it but she's about to become a mother. The trouble is, her feeding instincts are considerably stronger than her maternal instincts, so I have to wait around and see that she doesn't eat her offspring."

"Vern—when did you see him last?"

"Three days ago."

"Hasn't he phoned?"

"Yesterday morning. He was drunk."

"Drunk?"

"Sounded like it." He put the glass bowl back on the table, but he kept his eye on the mollie as he talked. "What gives with Lewis, anyway?"

"I can't tell you."

"Won't tell me."

"Both."

"Top secret, eh? My guess is that Gwen is kicking up a row because she's found out about you and Lewis. Our Gwen isn't as dumb as she looks. She's nutty as a fruitcake, but she's not one hundred percent dumb."

"She hasn't found out. This has nothing to do with Gwen. It's more—serious."

"I see."

"Vern, when he phoned did he tell you where he was?"

"No. All I know is that it was a local call and that he wasn't phoning from a booth. There was a lot of noise in the background, people talking and dishes rattling, and the sound of a cash register. He must have been in some café or bar where they had no private phone booth."

"Didn't you ask him where he was?"

"Certainly. He didn't answer. Apparently he'd had some kind of quarrel with Gwen, because he asked me to call her up and tell her he was sorry but not to try and find him. I called her, but by that time she'd already phoned the police. Gwen has a pretty talent for doing the wrong thing."

The mollie dropped her first offspring. It looked like a quarter of an inch of narrow black velvet ribbon, but it was alive and it was complete. It began immediately to swim around the bowl, as indifferent to its mother as she was to it: spending its first moment of life as it would spend its last—in the pursuit of food.

Vern's face was excited. "Well, here we go again. By God, isn't he a cute little fellow? You know, last time she had twenty-two of them. It took her over four hours."

She looked at the mollie who had just demonstrated with the bored ease of an expert the miracle of birth. She thought of a human baby, itself a fish, but helpless, boneless, blind and deaf and fed through a cord—its growth slow; its birth cruel. And between the two violences, the shock of birth and the shock of death, its life was incalculable.

The mollie spotted her offspring, circled it, and lost interest because she had already eaten.

"Charley," Vern said.

She looked up at him, wearily.

"Charley, for nearly a year, off and on, I've been thinking that I should apologize to you."

"Why?"

"I guess I shouldn't have fooled around playing cupid. Remember the first night you met Lewis at my house?"

"Yes."

"I didn't think things would turn out the way they have."

"No one did."

"I thought—well, damn it, I'm so fond of you both, and I wanted you to get together. You seemed a natural, you know? And I hoped—well, I guess what I really hoped was that Gwen would drop dead or something. What a dreamer I am, eh?"

"I've had a happy year," Charlotte said. "I should thank you for it."

"Well, don't," he said sharply. "I feel responsible."

"You shouldn't. I was ready to fall in love and I did. I had never loved anyone before."

He smiled then, a friendly, but rather sad little smile. "Not even me?"

"No."

"My trouble is that I've got to wait around for a woman who likes fish, or who likes me well enough to get to like fish." He saw her glance towards the door and said, "Don't leave yet."

"I have to."

"If he doesn't want to be found, don't look for him, Charley. He may have reasons."

"I have reasons, too."

"In that case." He opened the door for her. "Good luck, anyway."

"Thank you, Vern."

Downstairs in the lobby the old Negro was still mopping the tiled floor, humming to himself as he worked.

"Good night, Tom."

"Floor's wet, you walk easy."

"Yes, I will."

"A fine clear evening, ma'am."

She stepped out into the dusty street.

The wind went everywhere, like an inquisitive ghost, through keyholes, down chimneys, under the cracks of doors; and everything left gritty to the touch.

The beach was littered with the broken shafts of palm trees. In the little café near the breakwater the tables were layered with fine sand that blew in when the door was opened and gradually settled over everything. Sam, the proprietor, went around muttering to himself and making futile swipes with a dish towel.

Charlotte sat at the counter and ordered a cup of coffee. The phone was where she remembered it, at the end of the counter beside the cash register. The hope grew in her mind that it was the phone Lewis had used yesterday morning to call Vern. She and Lewis had often come here for a late supper. The food was terrible and the dishes never quite clean, but it was the sort of place where neither of them would be likely to meet people they knew. Besides, in the rear booth where they usually sat, there was a tiny window like a square porthole, with a view of the breakers crawling up the beach. *Our view,* Lewis called it, with a kind of sadness in his voice, as if he meant that it was the only view they would have together, from the small murky window.

Sam brought the coffee. He was a Greek from Brooklyn, a fat, curious-eyed man with spindly legs and narrow, delicate feet that could hardly support his weight. He talked a lot, always in a whisper out of the side of his mouth like a movie spy.

"How come you're sitting up here? The back booth's empty."

"I'm alone tonight."

"Mother of pearl, aren't we all," Sam said gloomily. "I'm thinking myself of maybe getting married again. I have the type of lady in mind, a nice widow with a little something in the bank and a little insurance. But they're hard to find and in this business the dice are loaded against you. Take a nice widow coming in here for instance—sees me in this lousy apron and don't see no further than the apron. Get what I mean? Sure ya do." He leaned his elbows on the counter to ease the weight off his feet. "That your steady boy friend you come in here with?"

"Yes. In fact, I'm looking for him now."

"Anything the matter?"

"No, I just—well, yes. We had a quarrel. I want to find him to apologize."

"He hasn't been in today. Say, he's got class, you know? I guess it's the clothes, nifty tweeds instead of a lousy apron like..."

"What about yesterday?"

"Oh yesterday, sure. He came in early for breakfast. Ate a couple of eggs, drank some coffee and asked if he could use the phone. I said sure, go ahead.. Though I'm telling *you*, confidentially, that I don't encourage people to use the phone. How do I know they aren't going to call their Aunt Daisy in Jersey City?"

He paused long enough to turn over a couple of hamburgers that were cooking on the gas grill.

"Well, he made the call, and then he bought a loaf of bread and a quart of milk and some cigarettes. He wasn't looking himself. He had on a pair of dungarees and an old mackinaw. I said, kidding-like, 'Going on a fishing trip?' He didn't answer. Paid his check and walked out. I was kind of curious, so I went to the window and watched where he went. He was heading hell for leather down the breakwater where all those dinghies are tied up. Well, then this girl in pink shorts happened to walk past with a rod and reel, and well, you know how it is. My eye kind of wandered. I'm very interested in rods and reels." He chuckled at his own joke, supporting his heaving stomach with the palms of his hands.

Charlotte didn't hear him. She knew now where Lewis was.

TWENTY-TWO

The breakwater was dark but there was a light in the harbor master's little office and the door was open. A young man was sitting on top of the desk examining the sole of one of his canvas shoes. He was about seventeen, clad in skin-tight levis and crew shirt, with a yachting cap pushed back on his head. He was full-grown but his face was beardless, and his manner had the uncertainty of adolescence.

When he saw Charlotte in the doorway he jumped down from the desk with an embarrassed grin.

"I'm looking for the harbor master," Charlotte said.

"He went home, ma'am."

"Are you in charge?"

"Well, kind of. I mean, he's my uncle and I'm just kind of hanging around for the summer vacation."

"There's a boat anchored here called the Mirabelle."

The boy's uncertainty vanished. "Oh sure, that's Mr. Johnson's cruising sloop. He let me go aboard her tonight when I asked him if I could."

"Tonight?" If Vern had been on the boat tonight it meant that her whole theory was wrong, that Lewis wasn't hiding there after all. She felt defeated, exhausted, like an animal that had been trying for hours to find its way out of a maze of closed traps and blind alleys.

He was looking at her curiously, his brown eyes as round and alert as a spaniel's. It was apparent that he wasn't used to well-dressed women coming alone to the breakwater at nearly eleven o'clock at night. "You want to go out to the Mirabelle, ma'am?"

"Yes. I—Mr. Johnson's a friend of mine."

"Oh, he is?"

"A very good friend. You can verify that if you like."

She couldn't understand the sudden blush that stained his cheeks and the lobes of his ears. "I guess you can take one of the skiffs that's down there on the float, ma'am, if you bring it back in the morning."

"I'll have it back in half an hour."

He didn't say anything, he seemed too embarrassed to speak.

"Look," Charlotte said. "If you're in any doubt, you can phone Mr. Johnson. I believe he's still at his office."

"Mr. Johnson's on board."

"On board?"

"Yes ma'am."

"I saw him at his office half an hour ago."

"No ma'am," the boy said stubbornly. "He's aboard. He said he was going to s-sleep there."

She went down the gangplank to the float, thinking, Vern can't have reached here ahead of me. But if he did, why? Did he suspect all the time that Lewis was hiding on the boat? Did he come to warn him? No, that's absurd. Vern doesn't even know what kind of trouble Lewis is in.

The heavy float was rolling gently in the ebbing tide. Half a dozen skiffs were drawn up on it, bottoms up. The boy eased one into the water and walked back up to the top of the gangplank silhouetted against the light of the tiny office.

The Mirabelle was anchored a hundred yards off shore, its sails furled, its cabin portholes dark. She tied the skiff up at the stern and climbed awkwardly up the ladder.

"Vern?"

She crossed the deck and opened the door of the cabin. Her eyes had adjusted to the darkness and she could make out the figure of a man lying on the lower bunk, face down.

She descended the five narrow steps, slowly, as if her legs were numb. "Vern?"

He stirred, moaned; one of his hands came up to his head as if to ward off a blow that he saw coming in a nightmare. She found the light and turned it on.

It wasn't Vern. It was Lewis.

He was sleeping, but still moving, moving his head back and forth, and shielding his face with his arms. The dream stopped as suddenly as it began, his hands dropped, the fight was over.

She knelt down and touched his cheek gently. "Lewis, it's me, Charley. Wake up, Lewis."

He opened his eyes. They were pink and swollen, as if from tears. In the dream he had fought and won—or fought and lost—and the fight, the effort, was real; his forehead was drenched with sweat.

"Lewis..."

He turned his face to the bulkhead. The back of his neck looked very young and vulnerable. "I have nothing to say, Charley."

"You can't go on hiding like this. They'll find you just as I did."

"I don't care."

"You must care. Things will be so much harder for you if they have to come and get you, harder for—for all of us."

He got up off the bunk without answering. There wasn't enough headroom in the cabin for him to stand upright. The portholes were closed and the air was suffocating and heavy with the odor of Bourbon. He seemed not drunk, but stunned, as if he had used the Bourbon not as a method of escape, but as a weapon against himself, had hit himself over the head with it in self-punishment.

"I must talk to you, Lewis. Come up on deck."

"It's too late for talk."

"No, no, it isn't." But her voice held no conviction, she knew it was too late. Easter had given her three hours and two of them were gone.

She went up on deck and he followed her. The shore looked far away, and the lights of the city as remote as stars.

While the little harbor waves slapped and sucked at the stern of the boat, she told him everything that Easter had said. Her voice was quiet and calm. It had no relation to the things she was saying or to the fear and pain and pity in her heart. *Evidence,* she repeated, *evidence,* and it seemed to her a word as final as death, more terrifying than murder.

When she had finished Lewis was silent for a long time, his head buried in his hands so that she couldn't see his face, find on it the expressions any innocent man would be wearing—shock, denial, protest.

When he finally looked up at her, there was no expression on his face at all. He spoke flatly, "On advice of counsel, I have nothing to say."

"You must say something, you must!"

"I'm sorry, Charley."

"Sorry. *Sorry.*" She felt hysteria rising in her throat like bile. She swallowed, fighting it down, but the harsh bitterness of its taste remained. She knew that he would say nothing to incriminate himself, not even if it meant saving her. She remembered the words Easter had spoken a few hours ago: "*He loves himself, too, and that's the big passion. You're running a poor second, Charlotte.*"

"If I could only understand," she said painfully. "If I knew why, *why...*"

He took her hand and pressed it against his hot dry cheek. "Perhaps some day you'll know all the answers... Don't draw away, don't be afraid."

But she was afraid. She looked down into the black water and thought of Violet.

"Tell me you loved me, Charley."

"I—I did love you."

"And now?"

"I don't know... You lied to me about Violet. You said you'd never even heard of her."

"It wasn't a lie then. I didn't know it was the same girl until I saw her picture the next morning. I—God, she was just a kid. I'd been drinking quite a bit. She kept hanging around me, I couldn't get rid of her, I... But it's too late now for excuses, explanations. No, you mustn't cry, Charley, please don't." She hid her face against the sleeve of his coat. He stroked her hair, awkwardly. "Tell me, Charley, do you believe in another life, a second chance?"

"I—I try to, but I can't."

"I can't, either. This is all there is, there isn't any more. No second chances." His eyes were fixed blindly on the dark horizon. "It's a funny ending to a dream, isn't it? Stop now. Stop crying, Charley. You'll come out all right, I promise you."

She wept for a long time, like a child, her fists jammed into her eyes. When she had stopped he wiped her face with his handkerchief and raised her to her feet. "You'd better leave now, Charley. Perhaps we'd both better leave."

"Where will you go?"

"I'll go home."

"Home?"

"Yes. You can tell Easter I'll be there waiting for him."

TWENTY-THREE

The cypresses that lined the walk fought the wind, bent and convulsed in fury like mad boneless dancers.

The veranda lights were lit, as if Lewis had deliberately turned them on like a good host, to welcome the guest he expected, Easter. Bold shafts of light struck the garden, and Charlotte could see that it was no longer Gwen's garden, formal and precise. The lawn was a clutter of broken flowers, and palm fronds and dry prickly oak leaves and little mauve dots, like confetti, that had once been part of jacaranda clusters. The wind had beaten the flowers. The stocks and dahlias cringed, half naked, on the ground; the foxgloves had toppled like poles and their pink bells rolled silently across the lawn.

The collies, herded together at the fence gate, made nervous little noises, as if they would have liked to bark but didn't dare, knowing that Gwen would appear with a folded newspaper in her hand and tap the wire fence with it warningly. They feared the newspaper and Gwen's displeasure more than they feared the lunatic wind, the unquiet night.

They went up the front steps in silence—Charlotte holding her coat collar over her face to shield it from the grinding dust, and Easter with his hands in his pockets, unaware of wind or dust.

The drapes of the living room had been pulled back all the way. Charlotte wondered whether this, like the veranda lights, was a gesture of welcome, an invitation to stop, to look in. On her first visit tonight the drapes had been closed, the house blacked out, and Gwen upstairs in her room with a bruised throat.

The bruise was hidden now in a froth of blue lace; and the woman who had received it, and the fear and pain it had caused, they were all hidden as rocks are hidden under a high tide.

Through the window Charlotte could see them both clearly, Gwen and Lewis. Gwen sat knitting, her feet resting on the little petit-point footstool, a silver tea service on the table beside her. The three collies huddled together on the davenport, uncomfortable and restless, but refusing to give up this special privilege. Lewis was standing by the fireplace, with an unopened magazine in his hand, as if he had picked it up and meant to read it when Gwen had finished talking.

The fire was lit. Its flames danced in the silver teapot and in the copper bowl filled with scarlet berries. The room looked gay as Christmas, the people natural, the scene commonplace: *"More tea, dear?"* *"No thanks, it's getting late."* *"Why, so it is, nearly midnight, and you have to get up for work in the morning."*

In the morning, if there was a morning.

"Please," Charlotte said, "let me go in alone first."

"I can't. I didn't want you even to come along. It's too dangerous."

"Not for me."

"Especially for you." Easter pressed the door chime.

A scurry of dogs in the hall inside, a single sharp bark, then Gwen's quick footsteps, the click of her heels on the parquet floor.

The door opened and Gwen stood on the threshold, bracing herself against the wind.

"Why, it's Dr. Keating—Charlotte!" she said with an excited little laugh. "My goodness, how nice to see you. Come out and see who's here, Lewis."

Lewis appeared in the doorway of the sitting room. He had changed his clothes and shaved. His face was as blank as a shuttered window. Only his eyes showed pain; they looked across the hall at Charlotte as if across an immense and unbridgeable canyon.

Gwen was flushed and smiling, as delighted as a child at unexpected company. "And you've brought a friend with you, Charlotte. How nice. Oh, this is fun, I think. Having company at this hour—it makes me feel so pleasantly wicked. Come in, come in, *please do.*" She didn't recognize Easter until he took off his hat. "Why, I know you, of course. You're the policeman who was here this afternoon. Mr. Easter, isn't it?"

"Yes, Mrs. Ballard."

"Well, Lewis, look who's here, a real policeman. I hope you haven't done anything, darling!"

The two men didn't look at each other.

"Well, my goodness," Gwen cried. "Everyone's so quiet. I haven't said anything wrong, have I?" She sighed, and turned back to Easter. "I guess I have. I always do. Please give me your hat and come in and sit down. Lewis and I were just having a chat and a cup of tea before going to bed. I adore tea. Charlotte scolds me, but..." She smiled nervously at Easter as he gave her his hat. One of the collies came over and sniffed at the hat and then at the cuffs of Easter's trousers. She tapped the dog's nose with her forefinger. "Go and lie down, Laddie. I—well, this is fun, isn't it? Come into the parlor. That's what I used to call it when I was a little girl—my parlor. And I still think it's a prettier word than sitting room or drawing room, don't you?"

No one answered. No one had to. Gwen didn't seem to expect or want an answer.

The parlor was stifling. The heat had withered the berries in the copper bowl, and the dogs sprawled in the doorway in the hope of a draft, their tongues out.

"I feel quite gay," Gwen said, pouring Charlotte a cup of tea. "Unexpected company, and Lewis home again, it's wonderful. You both know that

Lewis has been very naughty. He stayed away for two whole days all because of a little quarrel we had. But now he's home for good, aren't you, darling?"

Lewis spoke for the first time. "Yes, Gwen."

"Where on earth did you stay, darling?"

"On Vern's boat."

"Now isn't that absurd, staying on a wobbly old boat when you had your own nice house to come back to!"

"Absurd. Yes, I guess it was."

"And Lewis, dear, you must remember your manners. Perhaps Mr. Easter doesn't want tea but something stronger."

"Nothing for me, thanks," Easter said.

"You make me feel like a very poor hostess. You won't even sit down. I—well, it's been a lovely summer so far, hasn't it? I do hope it keeps up."

The wind pressed against the windows and the walls, until the whole house seemed to shake, ready to tear loose from its foundations and blow across the lawn like the silent bells of the foxgloves. A blast came clown the chimney; the flames leaped and a log jumped nervously and fell against the side of the grate.

Gwen jumped too, at the noisy shower of sparks. "Oh. Oh, that scared me. The wind—I know it's silly, but I hate the wind. Charlotte, I bet you're sitting there thinking how neurotic I am."

Charlotte shook her head. "No, I'm not."

"I bet you are, really. I know Lewis thinks I'm neurotic. Every time I get an ache or a little spell of forgetfulness Lewis thinks it's my mind, which is—which—which..." She paused, blinking. "This isn't a very gay party, I must say. Back home in Louisville we used to have the gayest parties. Daddy was very strict, though; everyone had to leave at twelve like Cinderella. Lewis dear, you remember."

"I only went to one," he answered.

"Oh, you were awfully handsome in those days; you were handsome and I was pretty. Like a Dresden doll, people used to say. Like a—a Dresden doll. Oh, quite, *quite* different from you, Charlotte, quite different. I was very small and my bones were so delicate Daddy was always afraid of me falling and breaking one." Her hands fussed with her hair. Charlotte saw that they had a spastic trembling, and the unpainted nails were bluish at the tips. "I never thought in those days that the world could be so cruel, so ugly and cruel and—it was a great shock to me when I found out, a great shock—a hell, a terrible hell—a..."

"Gwen," Lewis said.

She turned and frowned at him. "You mustn't interrupt me all the time. It's not polite. One of the things Daddy taught me at home was *never* to interrupt. Oh, we used to have some sessions on manners, I can tell you!

We'd go over and over things until I'd learned everything perfectly. Daddy would pretend that he was somebody like the Duke of Gloucester, say, and then he'd knock on the parlor door, rap, rap, rap, and say: 'The Duke of Gloucester presents his compliments to Miss Gwendolyn Ann Marshall!'... Lewis dear, isn't that someone knocking at the front door?"

"It's only the wind," Lewis said.

"You're quite mistaken. You're always mistaken, Lewis. You don't realize it but you're always making..." She went to the front door and opened it, and came back smiling, shaking her head. "Just as I said, it's the wind. Lewis, you owe me an apology."

Lewis turned his face away. It was ghastly in the firelight, distorted, bloodless, like a wax mask found by a child and pinched and mauled beyond recognition.

"Lewis, dear."

"Yes."

"You really should apologize. You've made another of your mistakes."

"I apologize."

"Well, you aren't very gracious about it."

"I—for God's sake, Gwen."

"And swearing at me in front of guests, that's very vulgar." She looked appealingly at Easter. "That man swore at me too, that awful little man."

"Voss," Easter said.

"Voss, that's it, that's his name. I told him how vulgar it was to swear in front of a lady but he only laughed at me."

"Gwen," Lewis said again. "Be quiet."

"I won't be quiet."

"He's a policeman."

"Well, I know he's a policeman. I'm not stupid. I'm not afraid of him, anyway. I haven't done anything wrong, except drive without my license."

"When did you drive without your license, Mrs. Ballard?" Easter asked, quietly.

"Now, that's childish, trying to trap me like that. I won't tell you, so there."

The dog, Laddie, suddenly rose on his haunches. Without warning he pointed his nose in the air and began to howl, a terrifying, mournful sound that seemed to come, not from the dog's throat but from the very origins of time. Twice he stopped to draw a new breath, and begin again; and when he had finished he slunk back into the hall as if in shame, his tail between his legs.

The smile had vanished from Gwen's face. "Someone has just died." She sipped the cold, bitter syrup left in the bottom of her cup. "I'm glad it's not me."

Charlotte glanced uneasily at Easter. He hadn't moved, hadn't even shifted his weight from one foot to another. He seemed satisfied to let Gwen continue talking while he picked out a fact here, a fact there, from her uneven flow of words.

Charlotte went over to Easter and said in a hurried whisper, "She's confused, irrational. Anything she says is. . ."

"Let me handle this."

"I heard that, Charlotte," Gwen cried. "I heard what you said."

"I was only..."

"You said something about me. Well, I've got something to say about you, too." She crossed the room towards Charlotte, with a slow graceful glide, as if she had suddenly remembered the times at home when she had walked with a book balanced on her head to improve her carriage.

"You want to hear it?"

"Yes."

"Trollop," she said. "Trollop."

Lewis called her back. "Gwen. Please, Gwen."

"Please, Gwen. You keep out of this, lecher. A trollop and a lecher. A fine pair, aren't they, Mr. Easter? And so clever at fooling poor old Gwen, so terribly clever that I've known all about the two of them for months and months. But I've had my revenges, little ones and big ones. Oh, when I think of the times Charlotte came here to attend me and I'd tell her how honest she was, how trustworthy, then I'd tell her all about Lewis. Her face—oh dear, it was really quite funny!"

Charlotte had backed away quietly, leaving the two of them facing each other, Gwen, like a doll suddenly endowed with a voice and blurting out anything and everything that had been stored up in its stuffed head during the years of silence; and Easter, a giant by contrast, cunning, dispassionate.

"And the big revenge?" he said.

"Gwen," Lewis said. "I warn you, anything you say now will be used..."

"I..." She tossed her head contemptuously: "I don't take advice from a lecher. The big revenge, well, don't you think it was a big revenge, Mr. Easter?"

"I'm not sure yet what it was, or how you managed it."

"You can't be very clever."

"I'm not."

"You could at least try to guess. You'll never get ahead in your work if you don't *try."*

"I'll try."

"Well, I should *think* so. Go on."

"My guess is that Violet came here last Monday afternoon to see your husband. She saw you instead."

"That's right. You remember Violet, don't you, Lewis?"

Lewis didn't look at her. "I—yes."

"Well, you should. She was carrying your baby, wasn't she?"

"Yes ."

"Isn't it funny, you gave *her* a baby but not me, not me, and *I'm* the one who wanted it!"

"I'm sorry."

"There isn't any baby now, is there, Lewis?"

"No—no!"

"And no Violet either. You and Charlotte killed her."

"No!"

"Well, morally you did. I was only the instrument. You and Charlotte are the real murderers."

"Leave Charlotte out of it."

"Why should I? I put her in. I sent the girl to her. You hear that, Lewis? I *sent* her! I thought what a wonderful thing it would be to bring your two trollops together."

The room was cooling as the fire died.

"Such a good idea, I thought. But it didn't work out as I planned. I wanted Charlotte to find out what kind of man Lewis really was. And I wanted, too, for her to get rid of Violet's baby, to spare me the disgrace and scandal of her bringing suit against Lewis, dragging my good name through the courts and the newspapers. But Charlotte refused. And that night after dinner Violet came back to me again. I was in the garden... Have you seen my garden, Mr. Easter?"

"Yes."

"It's beautiful, isn't it?"

"Very beautiful." Flowers beaten to the ground, wind-stripped trees, broken cypress. "Was she alone when she came the second time?"

"Two men drove her here in a car. The little one brought her across the lawn to where I was sitting on the swing. He said he was Violet's uncle and he thought Violet and I should talk about terms while we were waiting for Lewis. That was the word he used—terms. He left her there with me. She began to cry. Tears don't affect me any more—I've cried too much myself—but I was kind to her. I was brought up to be kind to everyone, especially my inferiors."

"Did she mention money?"

"No, I did. I asked her how much she'd take to leave town and never come back. She got hysterical then. She kept saying over and over again that Voss was trying to force her to take money but she didn't want any money. All she wanted was to get rid of the baby, to be 'ordinary' again, she called it. She talked as if the baby was a terrible disease."

Charlotte remembered the scene Violet had made in her office, the way she'd struck her thighs with her fists and cried: "I'll kill myself!... I don't even want money. I only want to be the way I was before, with nothing growing inside me."

Gwen's hands were fidgeting with the lace around her throat. "She asked to see Lewis, and when I said he wasn't here she accused me of lying, of trying to protect him. I told her I wasn't lying, that Lewis had gone on a fishing trip. She misunderstood what kind of fishing trip it was, and she threatened to go down to the wharf and wait for him. I said, 'All right, I'll go with you.' "

"And you did," Easter said.

"I did? Yes, I must have. I don't know how, though. Do you think we walked?"

"It's not far."

"Yes, I guess we walked. I'm not a very good driver. It was cold and foggy down there and there was a bad smell. 'I can't stand it,' she kept saying, 'I'll kill myself.' And she did. She did kill herself."

"No."

"She must have. I can't remember."

"Try."

"I won't try. I don't want to remember. Lewis, Lewis, help me! Don't let him make me remember! Lewis—Daddy!"

"It's all right." Easter said. "You don't have to remember if you don't want to."

"I don't?"

"No. Forget Violet."

"Yes. Yes, I think I'll forget all about her. She was an ignorant girl with no manners."

"You don't mind remembering about Voss though, do you? You don't like Voss. He swore at you."

"Yes, he did. He swore at me."

"You saw him again later that night?"

"I think so. I think it was that night. He came to call for Violet, and I told him she was on her way home." She rubbed her eyes. "I'm—I'm getting confused. I shouldn't be telling you all this, should I? Lewis is looking at me funny. Stop, Lewis, stop looking at me like that."

"I—all right, Gwen," Lewis said. "All right."

"You're mad at me for borrowing your gun."

"No, I'm not, Gwen. You couldn't help it."

"That's right, I really couldn't. There wasn't any other gun and I had to have one to protect myself."

"Mrs. Ballard," Easter said. "On Monday night when Voss came to get Violet, did he believe you when you told him she was on her way home?"

"No. He said he'd been here earlier and when no one answered the door he drove around a little while, and then he—he saw me walking with Violet down towards the wharf. He said he waited and watched, and I came back alone. He accused me—he said bad things..."

"That's when you gave him money?"

"I had to. All the money I had, the housekeeping money and the six hundred dollars I'd gotten on Saturday for the pair of blue merles I sold, and two rings and a necklace. He promised he'd keep quiet and go away and not come back."

"But he came back," Easter said.

"Yes, early this morning. Very early. It was still almost dark. Lewis hadn't phoned or anything. I was worried and couldn't sleep. I heard the car and looked out the window and saw them, Voss and the other man, walking across the driveway. I put on my shoes and coat, and then I went into Lewis' study and got one of the guns and hid it in the pocket of my coat.

"I went downstairs and opened the front door. I said, 'what do you want?' And Voss said something new had come up, that he and Eddie needed more money so they could get out of the country for good. 'We can't talk here,' I said, 'Lewis is upstairs in bed, he'll hear us.'"

Charlotte looked across the room at Lewis, and she knew from the tragic regret in his eyes that his thoughts were like her own: he should have been upstairs in bed that early morning and he should have been at home when Violet first came. If he had been, all four of them would still be alive, still have a future, Eddie and Violet and Voss, and Gwen herself. For Gwen the road ahead was dark and twisted, with here and there a patch of light and an arrow pointing back, back, back to the gay parties, to Daddy and the teddy bear and the smiling French doll, back to the kinder years, further back, and further, until the end of the road was the beginning.

"We went out to the car," Gwen said. "Voss got in the front seat and the other one, Eddie, got in the back with me, and he drove out past the cemetery. Eddie laughed as we went past and said, 'People are just dying to get in there.' I laughed too, and then I shot him, I shot him two or three times. Voss stopped the car. I told him I was going to shoot him, too. He asked me not to, but I did, anyway."

One of the dogs began to dream; tail twitched, paws moved in pursuit.

"He was a little man, not much bigger than I am, but he was heavy. I put my hands under his armpits and pulled him over into the back on top of Eddie. Then I got behind the wheel and started the car. I thought of driving it over a cliff, but I didn't want to kill myself because then who would look after the dogs? You understand?"

Easter nodded. "Of course."

"Well, then I remembered that Charlotte was away, and I thought, what a clever idea to drive the car into her garage and leave it there. I thought how surprised she'd be when she came back. And you *were* surprised, weren't you. Charlotte?"

"Yes," Charlotte said gravely. "Very surprised."

"I wish I'd been there to see your face. I've never liked your face anyway. Liar's face. Trollop's face. I'd like to split it open with a knife. I'd like to…"

"Gwen," Lewis said.

She turned to him. Her expression changed suddenly and completely. "Yes, Daddy?"

"Remember your manners."

"I'll try to, Daddy. Do forgive me for telling you the truth, Charlotte, trollop, please have another cup of tea, it's quite fresh, refreshing and—I have a headache. I'm nervous. Lewis, I'm so nervous."

"I know," he said.

"People oughtn't to make me nervous, ought they?"

"No Gwen."

"But they do. You must stop them."

"I will." He went over to her and put his hands on her trembling shoulders.

"You love me, Lewis?"

"Yes."

"You always have?"

"Yes."

"And you hate *her*; don't you? You despise her. You hate her face. You'd like to split it open with a knife, wouldn't you?"

"Gwen—oh God."

"Say it."

"No

"*Say it.*"

"I—hate her."

"And her face, what would you like to do with it?"

"Split—it open—with a knife."

"There. You see, Charlotte? Two against one. We just hate you, Lewis and I. Isn't that right, Mr. Easter? Why, where's Mr. Easter?"

"He's using the telephone," Lewis said. "He had a call to make."

She held one of his hands against her cheek. "We don't care, do we?"

"No, Gwen."

"Why, it's like old times. Carry me upstairs the way you used to."

"Not yet."

"Yes, now. I'm tired. I've danced all night."

He picked her up gently and carried her out into the hall. The tears that fell from his eyes lost themselves in her fading yellow curls. He went slowly up the stairs. She was tired—she had danced all night—and she fell asleep in his arms.

The wind had vanished, as if a great hole had opened in the sky and all the winds in the world had been sucked up into the hole.

Easter opened the wooden gate. The police had come and gone, the car had been driven away, and the glow of morning was in the East.

"Good-bye, Charlotte."

"Good-bye.

"Get some rest."

"No. I don't want any. I'm not tired." *I haven't danced all night.*

He touched her hand. "I'm sorry things didn't work out for you."

"It's my own fault. I asked for it." *Split it open with a knife.*

"I'm sorry about Ballard, too. I did him an injustice; he's a better man than I thought he was. He'll stick by her, and perhaps some day she'll be cured."

"Perhaps. Yes, perhaps."

"This isn't the time or place to tell you that I love you but I'm telling you, anyway. There are tough days ahead. Perhaps my love might be a comfort to you."

"Thank you," she whispered.

"Will it be?"

"Yes. A—great comfort." Tears pressed behind her eyes like cruel thumbs, until her eyeballs seemed ready to burst.

"Cry if you want to," he said.

"I never—I *never* cry."

"Cry now, long and hard. It will make things easier for you."

"I can't."

"You will, though." He bent down and kissed both of her tearless eyes. "Good-bye, Charlotte."

"Good-bye."

The gate closed, softly, like the leaf of a book falling into place.

She went back into her house and sat for a long time in Lewis' chair by the window, watching the brightening sky. She wasn't sure at what moment the city lights went out and morning came.

THE END